MISSION STATEMENT

Created more than twenty years ago by James Colby, the Colby Agency is now owned and operated by his wife, Victoria. Though relatively small, the agency has garnered a reputation second to none in the business of private investigations and personal security. Victoria Colby is highly respected by law enforcement and is well connected in government agencies where *discretion* is the operative word.

The Colby Agency employs the very finest in all aspects of investigation and protection. Each of the men and women who represents the agency must possess the qualities that James Colby himself personified: honor, loyalty and courage.

The Colby Agency is the place where clients go when only the absolute best will do.

Dear Reader,

The editors at Harlequin and Silhouette are thrilled to be able to bring you a brand-new featured author program for 2005! Signature Select aims to single out outstanding stories, contemporary themes and oft-requested classics by some of your favorite series authors and present them to you in a variety of formats bound by truly striking covers.

We want to provide several different types of reading experiences in the new Signature Select program. The Spotlight books offer a single "big read" by a talented series author, the Collections present three novellas on a selected theme in one volume, the Sagas contain sprawling, sometimes multi-generational family tales (often related to a favorite family first introduced in series) and the Miniseries feature requested previously published books, with two or, occasionally, three complete stories in one volume. The Signature Select program offers one book in each of these categories per month, and fans of limited continuity series will also find these continuing stories under the Signature Select umbrella.

In addition, these volumes bring you bonus features...different in every single book! You may learn more about the author in an extended interview, more about the setting or inspiration for the book, more about subjects related to the theme and, often, a bonus short read will be included. Authors and editors have been outdoing themselves in originating creative material for our bonus features—we're sure you'll be surprised and pleased with the results!

The Signature Select program strives to bring you a variety of reading experiences by authors you've come to love, as well as by rising stars you'll be glad you've discovered. Watch for new stories from Janelle Denison, Donna Kauffman, Leslie Kelly, Marie Ferrarella, Suzanne Forster, Stephanie Bond, Christine Rimmer and scores more of the brightest talents in romance fiction!

The excitement continues!

Warm wishes for happy reading,

Marsha Zinberg

Marsha Zinberg
Executive Editor
The Signature Select Program

MINISERIES

DEBRA·WEBB

FILES FROM THE
COLBY AGENCY

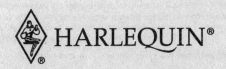

HARLEQUIN®

TORONTO • NEW YORK • LONDON
AMSTERDAM • PARIS • SYDNEY • HAMBURG
STOCKHOLM • ATHENS • TOKYO • MILAN • MADRID
PRAGUE • WARSAW • BUDAPEST • AUCKLAND

ISBN 0-373-21764-1

FILES FROM THE COLBY AGENCY

CONTENTS

Dear Reader,

Thank you so much for picking up this two-in-one volume of Colby Agency stories. I hope you'll enjoy reading these stories as much as I enjoyed writing them.

Nick Foster, Laura Proctor, Ian Michaels and Nicole Reed are among my very favorite characters. Proctor was my mother's maiden name and when I wrote *The Bodyguard's Baby* I considered Laura a member of my family. Ian Michaels of *Protective Custody* is one of my sexiest characters. Ian's sex appeal comes as easily as breathing. I think he's every woman's fantasy man.

Two of the things I look forward to most when starting a new story are the adventure barometer and the fear factor. I contemplate how much I can torture these characters and still have them survive with their hearts and souls intact.

Again, enjoy and I hope you'll watch for a brand-new Colby Agency story—*Colby Conspiracy* coming from Signature Select in October 2005!

Happy reading,

Debra Webb

THE BODYGUARD'S BABY

This book is dedicated to some of the people I love most—
my family. Erica, Melissa, Tanya, Johnny, Chad.
Chris and Robby, you mean the world to me.

A special thanks to Robby
for being the adorable inspiration for Laura's child.

Prologue

Victoria Colby studied Nick Foster's handsome profile for a long moment as he stared out the wall of glass that made up one side of her office. Nick kept his dark hair trimmed at precisely the perfect style and length, fashionably short, to accentuate his classic features. His attire received the same attention to detail. He dressed well and in a manner that drew one's eye to the breadth of his shoulders and the leanness of his waist. He looked more model than investigator.

The man was a perfectionist, personally and professionally. In this line of work those traits could be a definite plus. Victoria had worked hard to make the Colby Agency the best in the business. And carrying on the dream that had driven James, her beloved late husband, was all that mattered to Victoria now.

The Colby Agency was much more than just another private investigations firm; it had a staff second to none. All personnel recruited and employed were on the cutting edge of their field. And Victoria made it a point to see that they stayed at their best, physically and mentally.

Victoria cleared her throat, unnecessarily announcing her presence, and crossed the thick, beige Berber that carpeted her spacious office. Nick was probably aware of her the moment she stepped off the elevator. He missed nothing. "Good afternoon, Nick," she said, smiling pleasantly as she settled into the chair behind her desk.

"Victoria," he returned warily before taking the two steps necessary to reach the overstuffed wing chair in front of her desk. "You wanted to see me?" He grimaced slightly as he lowered his tall frame into the chair, but quickly masked the pain of the old injury and relaxed fully into the supple leather upholstery.

"Yes," she confirmed. Victoria had dreaded this meeting all day, but there was no putting it off any longer. She had noted the deepening lines around his mouth, the darkening circles beneath his eyes. The man was on a full-speed-ahead trip toward crash and burn. Firming her resolve, Victoria began, "Nick, we've worked together for five years, and I know you too well to pretend any longer that nothing is wrong. I've watched the change in you over the past two years. You haven't been the same since—"

"I do my job," he interrupted sharply, his assessing green eyes growing more wary.

"Yes," Victoria agreed. "You're a valuable asset to this agency. You do your job *and more.*" She understood all too well what Nick was attempting to do. She had been there. After losing James she'd buried herself in work, too. "And I'm sure you'll understand that what I'm doing now is *my* job." She paused a beat, allowing Nick to prepare himself for her next words. "As of today, you're on mandatory R & R. You will not set foot back in this building, nor will you conduct any business even remotely related to this agency for a period of fourteen days."

Instantly his gaze hardened, as did the usually pleasant lines of his angular face. "That's not necessary, Victoria. I'm ready for—"

"No," she cut him off, her tone final. "I've always trusted

your judgment, Nick." She shook her head. "But not this time. I'd hoped that your need to assuage your conscience would fade with time, but it hasn't. You're still struggling with demons you can't possibly hope to conquer by driving yourself into the ground." Victoria raised a hand to stay his protests. He snapped his mouth shut, but his tension escalated, manifesting itself in his posture and the grim set of his jaw.

Regret weighed heavily on Victoria's shoulders at having to call her top investigator, her second in charge actually, on the carpet like this. "You can't run forever, Nick. You'll either burn out or get yourself killed trying to prove whatever it is you feel the need to prove. When Sloan left I wasn't sure I would ever be able to work so closely with anyone else, but I was wrong. I don't want to lose you, Nick, but I won't allow you to self-destruct on my time either. Go home, spend some time with your brother, or find yourself a hobby." Victoria raised a speculative brow. "Or maybe a woman. Lord knows you could use one…or both."

Nick's gaze narrowed. "I don't recall seeing a category marked 'personal life' on my performance evaluation."

Necessity and irritation overrode Victoria's regret. "You see this desk?" With one manicured nail she tapped the polished oak surface of the desk that had once belonged to her husband. "The buck stops here, mister. When you go home at night you can thank God in heaven for whatever blessings you may have received that day. But here, in this building, I am the highest power. And, despite your long standing at this agency, whatever I say is the final word. You, Mr. Foster, are on vacation. Is that understood?"

He didn't flinch. "Absolutely."

"Good."

Nick got to his feet. The only indication that the move cost him was the tic in his jaw muscle and the thin line into which his lips compressed.

"Two weeks, Nick," Victoria reiterated as he strode slowly toward the door, his trademark limp a bit more pronounced than usual. "Get a life, and when you return to work I want to see a new attitude."

He paused at the door and shifted to face her. The other trademark gesture for which Nick Foster was known spread across his handsome face. Victoria imagined that the intensity and appeal of that smile had made many a heart flutter wildly.

"Yes ma'am," he drawled, then walked out the door.

*T*WO WEEKS.

What the hell was he supposed to do for two weeks? Nick slammed his final report into the outbox on his desk. Victoria just didn't get it. He had a life—*here.* Nick surveyed his upscale, corner office. Work was his life. He didn't care what the shrinks said—Nick Foster didn't need anything else.

Especially not a woman.

Ire twisted inside him when he considered Victoria's words again. Yeah, he always did a hell of a job on his assignments. Especially this last one. Victoria could always count on him. No one else at the agency would have gone so far out on a limb for a client, but unlike the rest, it didn't bother Nick.

He had nothing to lose.

If he had gotten himself killed, who the hell would have missed him?

Nick shrugged off the answer to that question. He stood, gritting his teeth at the pain that radiated through his right knee and up his thigh. Nothing like a needling reminder from the past, he mused, to keep a guy in touch with reality.

Reality had royally screwed him three years ago when he'd gotten this bum knee while protecting a client. Bad knee or no, he still did the best job possible. In fact, in all his years of service to the Colby Agency he had never failed—except once. He brutally squashed the memories that accompanied that line of thinking. That would never happen again. You couldn't lose if you weren't looking for anything to gain.

Nick jerked on his suit coat and grabbed his briefcase. What the hell? He hadn't been camping or fishing in a while. Maybe he would hone his survival skills with a couple of weeks in the wilderness. And maybe he would call Chad and make it a family venture—considering the two of them were all that was left of the Foster clan. Nick's right knee protested painfully when he skirted his desk too quickly.

He muttered a colorful expletive and then forced his attention away from the burning throb. He had ignored a hell of a lot worse.

The ergonomically modulated buzz from the telephone halted his thoughts as well as his indignant exit. Nick stared at the flickering red light with a mixture of annoyance and curiosity. Everyone else at the agency, including Victoria, had no doubt already left for the day. No one ever stayed this late but him. Why should he bother answering the phone? Hadn't Victoria ordered him to take a vacation starting immediately?

Just when he thought he could walk out the door without answering the damned thing, he snatched up the receiver and barked his usual greeting, "Foster."

"Nick, it's Ray Ingle."

Nick froze, his tension rocketed to a new level. "Ray," he echoed, certain that he must have heard wrong. Maybe his mind was playing tricks on him. Maybe he should have listened to the shrinks after all.

"It's been too long, buddy." Ray's chastisement was subtle.

"Yeah, it has," Nick said slowly as he leaned one hip against the edge of his desk, taking the weight off his bum leg.

He dropped his briefcase to the floor and raked his fingers through his hair as he waited for Ray to make the next move.

"I haven't called in a while." *Since we gave up on finding her,* he didn't have to add. "You haven't returned any of my calls in so long, I guess I didn't see the point anymore."

"I've been really busy, man," Nick offered by way of explanation, but the truth of the matter was he just hadn't wanted to make time. He and Ray, a Natchez police detective, had worked closely for months on that one case. And to no avail. Guilt congealed in Nick's gut.

"Sure, I know," Ray acknowledged quietly.

Nick straightened. "Look, I was just on my way out the door, is everything okay?" He hated himself for trying to cut the call short, but just hearing Ray's voice evoked more memories than Nick was prepared to deal with right now. He didn't know if he'd ever be able to deal with those memories.

"I saw *her.*"

The hair on the back of Nick's neck stood on end as adrenaline flowed swiftly through his rigid body. "Laura?" he murmured in disbelief, the sound of her name sending an old ache through his soul. If Ray had seen her...she couldn't be dead. Nick had known it all along.

"If it wasn't her, it was her frigging twin."

Nick moistened his suddenly dry lips. "Where?"

"I was following up on a possible homicide witness down in Bay Break and—"

"You're sure it was her?" Nick prodded, suddenly impatient with the need to know.

"I'm pretty sure, Nick. Hell, we turned a good portion of the good old South upside down looking for that girl. And there she was, plain as day." Ray sighed. "I don't know how and I don't know why, but it had to be her. I haven't told anyone else yet. I hate to upset our Governor on the eve of an election." He paused. "And, I figured you'd want to know first. I can give you a few hours head start, but then I'll have to inform him."

Emotion squeezed Nick's chest; he swallowed tightly. "I'm on my way."

Chapter One

She was being followed.

Oh God, *no*.

Panic shot through Laura Proctor, the surge of adrenaline urging her forward. The November wind whipped her hair across her face as she turned toward the town's square and scanned the sidewalk for the closest shop entrance. The last of autumn's leaves ripped from the trees at the wind's insistence, swirling and tumbling across the empty street. Someone bumped Laura's shoulder as they walked by, making her aware that she had suddenly stopped when she should be running.

Running for her life.

Instinctively her feet carried her along with the handful of passing pedestrians. She hadn't taken the time to disguise herself as she should have. The desire to avoid the possibility of being recognized was no longer a priority. The only thing that mattered now was finding a place to hide.

Any place.

She had to get away.

To get back to her baby. She couldn't be caught now.

Not now.

The knot of people crowding into the eastern entrance of the courthouse drew Laura's frenzied attention.

Election day. Thank God.

Laura rushed deep into the chattering throng. Once up the exterior steps, she allowed herself to be carried by the crowd into the huge marbled lobby. Weaving between the exuberant voters, she made her way to the stairwell. Almost stumbling in her haste, Laura flew down the stairs leading to the basement level.

If she could just make it to the west end, up the stairs and onto the street on the opposite side of the square, she would be home free. She had to make it, she determined as she licked her dry lips. The alternative was unthinkable.

Don't dwell on the negative. *Think, Laura, think!*

Okay, okay, she told herself as she glanced over her shoulder one last time before starting down the dimly lit, deserted corridor. If she cut through the alley next to Patterson's Mercantile, then circled around behind the assortment of shops until she reached Vine Street, she would have a straight shot to the house.

Mrs. Leeton's house.

And her son. God, she had to get to Robby.

Laura skidded to a halt at the foot of the west stairs. "No," she muttered, shaking her head. The door to the stairwell was draped with yellow tape. A handwritten sign read, Closed—Wet Paint. Laura grasped the knob and twisted, denial jetting through her.

She was trapped.

Laura blinked and forced herself to think harder.

Slow, deliberate footsteps echoed in the otherwise complete silence. She swung around toward the sound. He was coming down the stairs. In mere seconds he would cross the landing and descend the final steps leading to the basement...

To her.

Oh God. She had to hide. Now! Laura ran to a door, but it was locked. As was the next, and the next. Why were all the offices locked?

Election day.

Only the office serving as the voting polls remained open today. Fear tightened its mighty grip, shattering all rational thought. Laura bolted for the next possibility. Blessedly, the ladies' room door gave way, pushing inward with her weight. Moving silently past each unoccupied stall, Laura slipped inside the last one and closed the rickety old door behind her. She traced the flimsy lock with icy, trembling fingers only to find it broken. Climbing onto the toilet, she placed one foot on either side of the seat and hunkered into a crouch. Knowing her pursuer to be only seconds behind her, Laura uttered one more silent prayer.

Trembling with the effort to remain perfectly still, she swallowed the metallic taste of fear and concentrated on slowing and quieting her breathing. The heart that had stilled in her chest, now slammed mercilessly against her rib cage. Laura refused to consider how he could have found her. She had been so careful since returning to Bay Break. She fought back a wave of tears as she briefly wondered just how much her brother was willing to pay the men he sent after his only sister.

How could this keep happening?

Why didn't he just leave her alone?

How did they keep finding her?

And, God, what would happen to Robby if she were killed in the next three minutes as she fully expected to be if discovered? Anguish tore at her throat as she thought of her sweet, sweet baby. She wanted to scream…to cry…to run!

Stupid! Stupid! How could she have been so careless? She should never have left the house without taking precautions to conceal her identity. But Mrs. Leeton had insisted that Doc needed her at the clinic—that it was urgent. After all Doc had done for her son, how could Laura have refused to go? She closed her eyes and banished the tears that would not help the situation.

The slow groan of the bathroom door opening temporarily halted Laura's galloping heart. Everything inside her stilled as her too-short life flashed before her eyes.

She had failed.

Failed herself.

Failed to protect the only man she had ever loved.

And, most important, failed to make the proper arrangements for her son's safety in the event of this very moment.

Now she would die.

What would become of Robby? Who would care for him? Love him, as she loved him?

No one.

The answer twisted inside her like a mass of tangled barbed wire, shredding all hope. She had no one to turn to…no one to count on. A single tear rolled past her lashes and slid slowly down her cheek only to halt in a salty puddle at the corner of her mouth.

Something deep and primal inside Laura snapped.

By God, she wouldn't go down without a fight.

Laura's heart pounded back to warp speed. She swallowed the bitter bile that had risen in her throat as she heard the whoosh of the door closing and the solid thunk of boot heels against the tile floor. Each harsh, seemingly deafening sound brought death one step closer.

The first stall door banged against its enclosure as the hunter shoved the door inward looking for his prey. Then the second door, and the next and the next. Hinges whined and metal whacked against metal as he came ever closer to Laura's hiding place.

To her.

Her heart climbed higher in her throat. Her breath vaporized in her lungs. Tears burned in her eyes. She focused inward to her last image of Robby, all big toothy smiles, toddling across the floor, arms outstretched.

Blood roared in Laura's ears as her killer took the final step then paused before the gray, graffiti-covered metal door that stood between them. Did he know that she was there? Could he smell her fear? Could he hear her heart pounding?

Bracing her hands against the cold metal walls, Laura gritted her teeth and kicked the door outward as hard as she could. The answering grunt told her she had connected with her target—his face hopefully. Laura quickly scrambled to the floor, beneath the enclosure and into the next stall. Hot oaths and the scraping of boot heels echoed around her. Her body shaking, her breath coming in ragged spurts, Laura crawled from one stall to the next to retain cover. She had to get out of here. Had to run!

To get to Robby!

The door of the stall she had just wriggled into suddenly swung open. "Don't move," an angry male voice ordered.

Laura frowned. There was something vaguely familiar about that low, masculine drawl. As if in slow motion, her gaze traveled from the polished black boots, up the long jean-clad legs to the business end of the handgun trained on her. She blinked, feeling strangely disconnected from her body. Then her gaze shifted upward to look into the face of death.

Nick.

It was Nick.

"DON'T MAKE ME SORRY I put my weapon away," Nick growled close to her ear. Awareness punched him square in the gut when he inhaled the gentle fragrance that was Laura's alone. No store-bought perfume could ever match that natural sweetness. He clenched his jaw and simultaneously tightened his grip on her arm as they moved toward his rental car.

Hell, the Beretta had been overkill, he knew. Laura hadn't even been carrying a purse, much less a weapon of any sort. But Nick wasn't taking any chances this time. She hadn't had a weapon the last time either.

His right leg throbbed insistently, but he gritted his teeth and ignored the pulsing burn. He had found Laura, alive and well, and that's all he cared about right now.

Lucky for him Bay Break streets were deserted as far as he could see. He supposed that most of the residents out and about this morning were huddled in and around voting booths inside the courthouse, or sitting around a table in the local diner discussing how the election would turn out. Nick didn't keep up with Mississippi politics, but James Ed Proctor III's sensational reputation was hard to miss in the media. And, from what Nick had heard, whomever the man supported for Congress or the Senate was a sure winner.

The cold wind slapped at Nick's unshaven face. After a late night flight, a long drive and an even longer surveillance of the little town's streets before Laura made her midmorning appearance, Nick welcomed the unseasonably cold temperature to help keep him alert.

He had fully expected Bay Break to be a good deal warmer than Chicago, but he'd gotten fooled. According to the old-timers hanging around the general store, all the signs warned of an early snow. Nick didn't plan to hang around long enough to see if their predictions panned out. Between twelve hours of mainlining caffeine and the unanticipated cold, Nick felt more alert than one would expect after virtually no sleep in the last thirty hours. But by the time he drove to Jackson and did what he had to do, he would be in desperate need of some serious shut-eye. And, of course, there was that R & R Victoria had ordered. Yeah, right, Nick thought sarcastically.

Laura struggled in his grasp, yanking his attention back to

the here and now. Nick frowned when he considered the woman he was all but dragging down the sidewalk. There was something different about her, but he couldn't quite put his finger on it. She seemed softer somehow. He scowled at the path his thoughts wanted to take. He knew just how soft and delicate Laura Proctor was in all the places that made a man want a woman—except one. It took a woman with a cold, hard heart to walk away from a man who lay bleeding to death.

"You can't do this," Laura muttered heatedly. She scanned the sidewalks and streets. Looking for someone to call out to for help, Nick surmised.

"Who the hell do you think you are? You're not a cop," she added vehemently. "And I have rights!"

Anger kicked aside his foolish awareness of her as a woman and resurrected more bitter memories. Nick paused, then jerked her closer, his brutal hold eliciting a muffled yelp of pain, or maybe fear, at the moment he didn't really care which. "When somebody put a bullet into my chest and *you* left me to die, you lost your rights as far as I'm concerned."

Seconds ticked by as Laura tried her best to stare him down, her sky blue gaze watery behind thick lashes. She could cry a river of tears and he would still feel no sympathy for her. Nick mercilessly ignored the vulnerability peeking past that drop-dead stare, and turned the intimidation up a couple of notches. Laura's defiant expression wilted.

His point made, Nick escorted her the last few steps to the car. After unlocking the driver's side door, he pulled it open and ushered Laura inside. Her long blond hair trailed over his hand, momentarily distracting him and making his groin tighten. He squeezed his hand into a fist and forced away the unwanted desire. He had come here to take her back, not take up where they had left off. Laura Proctor would never make a fool of him again. And this time, he would be the one walking away.

As he had anticipated, once in the car she bolted for the passenger's side. With a smug smile, Nick slid behind the wheel and started the engine, almost drowning out her surprised gasp when she couldn't open the door.

"You bastard," she snarled, her eyes unnaturally dark with anger. Her breasts rose and fell with her every frustrated breath. "This is kidnapping!"

Nick's smile widened into a grin of pure satisfaction. "Consider it a citizen's arrest," he offered. Before he could back out of the parking slot Laura flew at him, a clawing, kicking tangle of arms and legs.

Nick shoved the gearshift back into Park. After several seconds of heated battle he subdued her, but not without a slash across his throat from her nails. He shook her, none too gently. "Look," he ground out. "I'm trying *not* to hurt you."

"Sure," she hissed. "You don't want to hurt me, you just want to get me killed."

For one fleeting instant Nick allowed himself to feel her fear. There had supposedly been a couple of attempts on her life two years ago. Could she still be in danger? Even now, after all she had put him through, Nick's gut clenched at the thought. Hell, he couldn't say for sure that there had ever been any real danger in the first place. According to the reports he had been privy to, Laura had possessed a wild streak, not to mention an overactive imagination. Her older brother, Mississippi's esteemed Governor, was always getting her out of one scrape or another. Who was to say that the whole thing was anything more than her vivid imagination? And the guy she had been romantically linked to back then was over the edge in Nick's opinion. He doubted her poor taste in associates had changed since.

Nick swallowed hard at the thought of Laura with another man.

Did he care?

No, he told himself. The lie, unspoken, soured in his throat.

"You don't have to worry, Laura. I'm taking you back home, to your brother. I'm—"

"My brother?" She quickly retreated to the passenger's side of the car, as far away from Nick as possible. "I can't go back home! Don't you understand? It's not safe."

Nick leveled a ruthless gaze on her panicked one. Her lower lip quivered beneath his visual assault, he suppressed the emotion that instantly clutched at his chest. How could she look so innocent? So truly frightened for her life? And, damn him, how could he still care? "You don't have an option. In fact, if you'll remember correctly, the last time *you* were supposedly in danger *I'm* the one who almost bought the farm."

Something in her eyes changed, softened with what looked like regret. But it was too late for that now. Way too late.

Their gazes still locked, Nick shifted to Reverse. "Buckle up, baby, we're out of here," he ground out, then glanced over his shoulder before backing into the street.

Laura Proctor was going back to face her brother and the law. Nick had every intention of uncovering the real story about what happened their last day together at her brother's cabin as well. Protecting Laura and seeing her safely returned to the new Governor after the election two years ago had been Nick's assignment. But things had gone wrong fast, and Laura was hiding at least part of the answers.

Including the part where she recognized the man who almost killed Nick. The one she had obviously disappeared with that same day. Ironic, Nick thought wryly, that he had found her and would be delivering her to her brother right after an election—just two years later than planned.

LAURA HAD TO DO something. Nick, the arrogant bastard, was going to get her killed. She glared at his perfect profile and winced inwardly. God, the man was breathtaking. It hurt to look at him and know what she knew. He had haunted her dreams every night for the past two years. He'd ruined her for anyone else. A dozen snippets of memory flashed before her eyes. The way it felt to be held by Nick. The way he made love to her. Her heart squeezed with remembered pain. He had been fully prepared to give his life to protect hers. Yet she could never trust him with her secret, and she sure couldn't go back to Jackson with him.

The small sense of relief Laura had felt when she had realized the man holding the gun on her was Nick instead of some hired killer died a sure and swift death when he announced why he had tracked her down.

He still wanted to finish the job he had been assigned two years ago, to return her safely to her brother. And that was exactly the reason Laura had not been able to go to Nick for help. He was too honorable a man to ignore his responsibility to James Ed. No way would Nick have done things Laura's way. He took his job way too seriously.

She had always known that Nick could have found her eventually if he had really wanted to—but he hadn't. He had apparently stopped trying. Unlike James Ed's men, whom she gave the slip without much difficulty, Nick wouldn't be so easy. He was too damned good, the best. If anyone could have caught Laura during the past two years, he could have. Why now, she wondered, after all this time? But the answer to that question didn't really matter at the moment. Right now Laura desperately needed to think of something fast. Something that would give her an opportunity to escape. She glared at the space where the unlock button used to be, and then at the useless door handle he had somehow disabled. Nick Foster was just a little too smart for his own good.

And hers.

Well, Laura decided, she hadn't eluded her brother this long without being pretty smart herself. She would find a way. Going back to James Ed was suicide. And she could never allow anyone—especially Nick—to discover her secret. She had to protect Robby at all costs. Even if after getting Robby settled some place safe it meant going back to her brother, Laura would do it to lead any threat away from her child.

She would never let anyone harm her son.

Never.

But how would Doc know what had happened to her? Would Mrs. Leeton be able to take care of Robby if Laura never returned? Unsettled by the thought, Laura snapped from her disturbing contemplation, and realized that they were already headed out of town.

To Jackson.

Desperation crowded her throat.

She needed to go back to Mrs. Leeton's house first.

To her son. She couldn't leave without making some sort of arrangements.

There was no other option at the moment.

"We have to go back," she said quickly.

"Forget it." Nick's focus remained steady on the road. A muscle flexed in his square jaw, the only visible indication of his own tension.

Laura frantically groped for some reasonable explanation he would find acceptable for turning around. Nothing came. A new kind of fear mushroomed inside her. She had to think of something.

Now!

"My baby!" she blurted when the Please Come Again sign loomed closer. "I have to get my baby."

Nick threw a suspicious glance in her direction. "What baby?" he asked, sarcasm dripping from his tone.

"My…I have…a son," she admitted, defeat sucking the heart from her chest. How would she ever protect her baby?

Nick's expression shifted from suspicious to incredulous. "I'm not falling for any of your tricks, Laura."

Trembling with the crazy mixture of emotions flooding her body, Laura swiped at the tears she had only just noticed were slipping down her cheeks. Dammit, why did she have to cry? She was supposed to be tough—had to be tough. "Please take me back, Nick. I have to get my son," she pleaded, any hope of appearing even remotely tough dashed.

Something, some emotion, flitted across his handsome face so fast Laura couldn't quite read it. She fought to ignore what looked entirely too much like hurt that remained. She knew just how much Nick had suffered because of her. He had almost died. She winced inwardly at the memory. But she couldn't permit herself to feel any sympathy for him. He certainly harbored none for her. She had to stay focused on keeping her son safe. Robby was all that really mattered. And she could never allow Nick to suspect the truth about her child.

Laura didn't even want to imagine what Nick would do if he found out he had a son.

A child she had kept from him for almost two years.

NICK PARKED the rented sedan on the street in front of the small white frame house Laura identified as belonging to a Mrs. Leeton. Emotions churned in his gut. What was it to him if Laura Proctor had gotten herself pregnant since he had last seen her? Or, hell, maybe even shortly before he had met her.

Nothing.

Less than nothing, he reiterated for good measure.

She had simply been an assignment back then, and Nick's

sole motivation for taking her back to her brother now was to clear up his record. Laura Proctor represented a black mark on his otherwise perfect record, and he was about to wipe it clean. If he had kept his head on straight back then he wouldn't have screwed up the assignment in the first place. And he sure as hell wouldn't have allowed himself to believe the woman almost virginal. What a joke.

On him.

Nick reached for the door handle, but Laura grabbed his arm. He stared for a long moment at the small, pale hand clutching at him before he met her fearful gaze. "What?" he growled.

"Please don't do this, Nick," she begged. "Please just walk away. Pretend you never saw me." She moistened her full, lush lips and blinked back the tears shining in her eyes. "Please, just let us go."

"Save your breath, Laura." A muscle jumped in his jaw, keeping time with the pounding in his skull. Don't even think about feeling sorry for her, man, he reminded himself. You let your guard down once and it almost cost you your life. "Nothing you can say will change my mind," he added, the recall of Laura's betrayal making his tone harsh.

Her desperate grip tightened on the sleeve of his jacket. "You don't understand. He'll kill me, and maybe even my son." She squeezed her eyes shut, her breath hitched as it slipped past her pink lips. "Oh, God, what am I going to do?"

Nick tamped down the surge of protectiveness that surfaced where Laura was concerned. His chest tightened with an emotion he refused to label. He focused his attention on the street and dredged up the memory of waking up alone and barely alive in the hospital. "Who will kill you, Laura? The guy you watched put a bullet in me before you ran away?" He turned back to her then, the look of pain in her eyes giving him perverse pleasure. "Just how far were you willing to go to cause your brother trouble? Was it all just some kind of game to you?"

Her eyes closed again, fresh tears trickled down those soft cheeks. She was good. She looked the picture of innocence and sweetness. He almost laughed at that. Obviously the hotshot she had been involved with two years ago, or someone since had left her with an unexpected gift. Maybe it had been the guy who had put the bullet in Nick. Laura Proctor would have a hell of a time promoting that innocent act with an illegitimate baby on her hip. Well, that wasn't his problem, even if the thought did make some prehistoric territorial male gene rage inside him.

"Are we going in, or do we head straight for Jackson?" he demanded impatiently, drumming his fingers on the steering wheel for effect.

Laura brushed her cheek with the back of her hand. "I want to get my son first," she murmured, defeat sagging her slim shoulders.

"Well, let's do it then," he shot back, trying his level best not to think about Laura having sex with another man, much less having the man's child. Damn, he shouldn't care.

But, somehow, he still did.

Nick called himself every kind of fool as he emerged from the car, years of training overriding his distraction as he surveyed their surroundings. Vine was a short, dead-end street dotted with half a dozen small frame houses. A dog barked at one of the houses on the far end of the quiet street. Two driveways had vehicles parked in them, indicating someone could be home. Either Mrs. Leeton didn't own a car or she wasn't home, he noted after another scan of the house before them. Nick reached beneath his jacket and adjusted the weapon at the small of his back. There was no way of knowing what to expect next out of Laura or the people with whom she associated.

Laura scrambled out of the car and into the vee created by his body and the open car door. It took Nick a full five seconds to check his body's reaction at her nearness. Laura's gaze collided with his, the startled expression in her eyes giving away her own physical reaction. Nick breathed a crude, four-letter word. Laura shrank from him as if he had slapped her. He didn't want to feel any of this, he only wanted to do what had to be done. But his male equipment obviously had other ideas.

"I know you'll never believe me, but it didn't happen the way you think," Laura said softly, defeatedly. She looked so vulnerable in that worn denim jacket that was at least two sizes too big, the overlong sleeves rolled up so that her small hands just barely peeked out. But the faded denim encasing her tiny waist and slender hips was breath-stealingly snug, as was the dirt-streaked T-shirt that snuggled against her breasts.

Nick swallowed hard and lifted his gaze to the face he had never wanted to see again, yet prayed with all his heart he would find just around the next corner. For months after her disappearance his heart rate had accelerated at the sight of any woman on the street with hair the color of spun gold and whose walk or build reminded him of Laura. Each time, hoping he had found her, his disappointment had proven devastating. And now she stood right before him, alive and every bit as beautiful as the day he had first laid eyes on her. Could he have found her long ago had he truly wanted to? Or was believing the possibility that she was dead or, at the very least, lost to him forever simply easier?

Victoria had ordered him to stop looking for Laura. Her own brother had believed her dead. But Nick had never fully believed it. Yet he had stopped looking all the same. If she was alive and she didn't want to contact him, he wasn't going after her. Then Ray had called and the need for revenge had blotted out all else.

A wisp of hair fluttered against her soft, creamy cheek and Nick resisted the urge to touch her there. To wrap those golden strands around his fingers and then allow his thumb to slide over her full, lush lips.

"Please don't make me go back, Nick," she said, shattering the trance he had slipped into.

Briefly he wondered if she still felt it too, then chastised himself for even allowing the thought to materialize. Laura Proctor had no warm, fuzzy feelings for him. Actions speak louder than words, Nick reminded the part of him that stupidly clung to hope, and her actions had been crystal clear two years ago. She had left him to die.

"If you want to pick up your kid, I would suggest that you do it before I lose patience," he snapped, using his anger to fight the other crazy, mixed-up emotions roiling inside him.

"Yes," she murmured. "I want to pick up my son." She looked away, then reached up to sweep the tendrils of hair from her face.

The ugly slash on the inside of her wrist caught Nick's eye. He captured that hand in his and forced her to allow him to inspect it. He clenched his jaw at the memory that she had allegedly tried to commit suicide only a few weeks before they had met. But the woman he had known for such a short time in that quiet cabin by the river would never have done anything like that. She had been too full of life and anticipation of what came next. She wouldn't have walked away leaving him to die, either—but Laura had.

And that was the bottom line: she couldn't be trusted.

His hold on her hand bordering brutal, Nick led Laura up the walk and across the porch of the silent house. The whole damned street looked and felt deserted. He glanced down at the woman at his side. If this turned out to be a ploy of some sort, she would definitely regret it. He nodded at her questioning look, and she rapped against the door.

Laura held her breath as she waited for Mrs. Leeton, a retired nurse, to answer the door. The woman was old and riddled with arthritis, so Laura waited as patiently as she could
for the key to turn in the lock. Until three years ago, Mrs. Leeton had worked with Doc for what seemed like forever. When
Laura showed up a week ago needing Doc's help, he had
asked Mrs. Leeton to take Laura and Robby in. The elderly
woman had readily agreed. Laura hadn't really liked the idea
of leaving Robby alone with Mrs. Leeton this morning, but
what else could she do? Mrs. Leeton had insisted that Doc
needed Laura right away.

When the door's lock finally turned, anxiety tightened
Laura's chest and that breath she had been holding seeped out
of its own accord. Would Nick recognize his own child?
Would he demand that she turn his son over to him? Nick
wasn't the same man she had known two years ago. He was
harder now, *colder.*

Would he take Robby to get back at her? Or would he simply take him out of fear for his son's well-being? Just another
reason she could never have turned to Nick for help no matter how bad things got. James Ed had convinced Nick and
everyone else that she was mentally unstable. Nick would
never in a million years have allowed a woman considered
mentally unstable to raise his son. He would have taken
Robby, Laura knew it with all her heart.

Oh, God, was she doing the wrong thing by even coming
back here? Why didn't she just let Nick take her back to Jackson without mentioning Robby? Doc would have taken care
of her baby until Laura could figure out a way to escape…*if*
she figured out a way.

The door creaked open a bit and old Mrs. Leeton peered
through the narrow gap. Laura frowned at the look of distrust
and caution in the woman's eyes. Did she not recognize

Laura? That was impossible. Laura and Robby had been living here for a week. The idea was ludicrous. Hysteria was obviously affecting Laura's judgment.

"Mrs. Leeton, I've had a change in plans. I have to leave
right away," Laura told her as calmly as she could. "Please let
Doc know for me. I just—" she glanced at the brooding man
at her side "—need to get Robby and we'll be on our way."

"Who are you and what do you want?"

Alarm rushed through Laura's veins at the unexpected
question. "Mrs. Leeton, it's me, Laura. I've come back to get
Robby. Please let me in." Nick shifted beside her, but Laura
didn't take her eyes off the old woman. Something was wrong.
Very wrong.

"I don't know who you are or what you want, but if you
don't leave I'm going to call the police," Mrs. Leeton said
crossly.

Outright panic slammed into Laura then. "I need to get my
son." Ignoring her protests, Laura pushed past the woman and
into her living room. Nick apparently followed. Laura was
vaguely aware of his soothing tone as he tried to placate the
shrieking old woman.

"Robby!" Laura rushed from room to room, her heart
pounding harder and harder. Oh God, oh God, oh God. *He's
not here.* The cold, hard reality raced through her veins. Laura
shook her head as if to deny the words that formed in her head.
No, that can't be! She had left him here less than an hour ago.
It can't be!

Laura turned around in the middle of the living room,
slowly surveying the floor and furniture for any evidence of
her son.

Nothing.

Not one single toy or diaper. Not the first item that would
indicate that her son had ever even been there.

He was gone.

She could feel the emptiness.

Frantic, Laura pressed her fist to her lips, then looked from Nick, who was staring at her with a peculiar expression, to the old woman who glared at her accusingly. Laura clasped her hands in front of her as she drew in a long, shaky breath. "Mrs. Leeton, please, where is my baby?"

The old woman's gaze narrowed, something distinctly evil flashed in her eyes. "Like I said before, I don't know you, and there is no baby here. There has never been a baby here."

Chapter Two

"There's no need to call the police, Mrs. Leeton," Nick assured the agitated old woman. He shot a pointed look at Laura. "We've obviously made a mistake."

Laura jerked out of his grasp. "I'm not leaving without my son!" She grabbed the old woman's shoulders, forcing Mrs. Leeton to look directly at her. "Mrs. Leeton, why are you doing this? Where's Robby? Who took him?"

"Get out! Get out!" the old woman screeched. "Or I'll call the police!"

"We're leaving right now." Nick carefully, but firmly, pulled Laura away from the protesting old woman. "Now," he repeated when she resisted.

"I can't go without my baby." The haunted look on Laura's face tore at Nick's already scarred heart. "She's lying. She knows where he is!" Laura insisted. Her eyes, huge and round with panic, overflowed with the emotion ripping at her own heart. How could he not believe her?

But he had trusted her once before....

Nick forced his gaze from Laura to the old woman. "I apologize for the confusion, Mrs. Leeton." He tightened his grip on Laura when she fought his hold. "We won't bother you again." This time Nick snaked his left arm around Laura's waist and pulled her against him. His gaze connected with hers and he warned her with his eyes that she had better listen up. "We're leaving—*now*," he ground out for emphasis. Laura sagged against him, emotion shaking her petite frame.

"If that crazy girl sets foot back on my property I'm calling the police!" Mrs. Leeton shouted behind them.

Nick didn't respond to her threat. He had no intention of returning to the woman's house. If Laura had a son, he wasn't here, that much was clear.

Laura clung helplessly to Nick as he strode back to the rental car, her violent sobs rattling him like nothing else in the past two years had. He automatically tuned out the intensifying pain radiating from his knee upward. He didn't have time for that now. He glanced down at the woman at his side. Whether she had a child and where that child might be was not his concern. He ignored the instant protest that tightened his chest. Taking her back to James Ed was all he came to do, Nick reminded himself. Laura had a brother, an influential brother, who could help her with whatever personal problems—real or imagined—she might have.

Nick opened the car door, intent on ushering Laura inside. Hell, it was too damned cold to stand outside and debate anything. He could calm Laura down once they were in the car. As if suddenly realizing that they were actually leaving, she twisted around to face him.

"I have to find Robby," she said, her voice breaking on a harsh sob. "You have to believe me, Nick. I left him with Mrs. Leeton not more than an hour ago." Another shudder wracked her body.

Nick pulled her close again, his own body automatically seeking to comfort hers. He forced himself to think rationally, ruthlessly suppressing the urge to take her sweet face in his hands and promise her anything. "Show me some proof that you have a son, Laura. Convince me."

For the space of two foolish heartbeats Laura stared into his eyes, the blue of hers growing almost translucent with some emotion Nick couldn't quite identify. Her upturned face too close for comfort.

"He's real," she whispered, her breath feathering across his lips, making him yearn to taste her, to hold her tighter.

"Prove it," he demanded instead. "Show me pictures, a birth certificate, a favorite toy, clothing, any evidence that you have a child."

She shifted, her body brushing against his and sending a jolt of desire through him. "My purse…" Laura frowned, then looked toward Mrs. Leeton's house. "I left my purse and what few clothes we brought with us in there."

Nick followed her gaze and studied the small white frame house for a moment. "We definitely aren't going back," he said flatly, then returned his attention to the woman putting his defenses through an emotional wringer. "I don't want the local police involved."

Instantly, Laura recoiled from him. Anger and bitterness etched themselves across the tender landscape of her face. Her eyes were still red-rimmed from her tears, but sparks of rage flew from their watery blue depths. "Of course not," she spat the words with heated contempt. "We wouldn't want to do anything that would bring the wrong kind of attention to the almighty Governor of Mississippi, now would we?"

"Get in the car, Laura." Irritation stiffened Nick's spine. He had no intention of making the Proctors' domestic difficulties personal this go-around. "Now," he added when she didn't immediately move.

Her eyes still shooting daggers at him, Laura turned to obey, but suddenly whipped back around. "Doc," she said. "Doc will back me up. He'll tell you about Robby."

Tired of beating a dead horse, Nick blew out a loud, impatient breath. "Who's Doc?"

"My doctor," Laura explained. "Robby was really sick. Doc's the reason I came back here, I knew I could trust him," she added quickly as she slid behind the wheel, then scooted to the passenger's side of the car. "Let's go!"

Nick braced his forearm on the roof of the car and leaned down to look her in the eye. He held her gaze for a long moment, some warped inner compulsion urging him to believe her. He straightened, taking a moment to scan the quiet neighborhood, then Mrs. Leeton's house once more. Something about this whole situation just didn't feel right. Maybe there was some truth to Laura's story. Nick had always trusted his instincts. And they had never let him down...except once.

"Hurry, Nick, we're wasting time!"

Still warring with himself, Nick dropped behind the wheel and started the engine. He turned to his passenger and leveled his most intimidating gaze on hers. "If you're yanking me around, Laura, you're going to regret it."

LAURA STARED at the scrawled writing on the crudely crafted sign hanging in the window of Doc's clinic. The breath rushed past her lips, leaving a cloud of white in the cold air as she read the words that obliterated the last of her hope. "Gone out of town, be back as soon as possible." This couldn't be. She shook her head as denial surged through her.

It just could not be.

Her pulse pounded in her ears. Her heart threatened to burst from her chest. Laura squeezed her burning eyes shut. *Robby, where are you? Please, God,* she prayed, *don't let them hurt my baby. Please, don't let them hurt my baby.*

"That's rather convenient," Nick remarked dryly from somewhere behind her.

Laura clamped one hand over her mouth to hold back the agonizing scream that burgeoned in her throat. How could she make Nick believe her now? Mrs. Leeton was lying or crazy, or maybe both. Doc had disappeared. Doc's new nurse would be where? Laura wondered. The woman worked part-time with another doctor in some nearby small town. Where? Laura racked her brain, mentally ticking off the closest ones. She couldn't remember what Doc had told her. His longtime secretary had retired and moved to Florida months ago. He hadn't hired anyone else, preferring to do the paperwork himself now. Who could Laura call? She couldn't think. She closed her eyes again and stifled a sob that threatened to break loose. She had to keep her head on straight. She had to think clearly.

Who could have taken Robby?

Why?

Realization struck like lightning on a sultry summer night, acknowledging pain hot on its heels like answering thunder.

James Ed.

It had to be him, or one of his henchmen. They had found out about Robby and taken him to get to Laura. That would be the one surefire way to bring her home. She had realized that day two years ago at the cabin that her dear brother intended to kill her. She just hadn't known why. But that epiphany had come to her eventually. *The money.* He wanted Laura's trust fund. He was willing to kill her to get it. And now Robby was caught in the middle.

What about Doc? Could he be in on it? Was his sudden disappearance planned? Laura shook her head emphatically. No way. Doc loved her. And she trusted him. He wouldn't do that. Laura read the sign in the window again. But where could he be? He had asked her to come to the clinic. He'd told Mrs. Leeton it was urgent. Had he somehow heard that someone was in town looking for her? Maybe he wanted to warn her. Could he have taken Robby somewhere to safety?

Laura prayed that was the case. But how could she be sure? Could she leave town without knowing that her son was safe? She swallowed tightly.

No. She had to find him.

"I know Doc's here," she said aloud, as if that would make it so. "He has to be."

"Let's go, Laura. I'm tired of playing games with you."

Laura turned around slowly and faced the man who seemed to have set all this in motion. The man she still loved deep in her heart. The man who had given her the child that she could not bear to lose. But she could never tell him the truth.

Never.

Nick's green eyes were accusing, and full of bitterness. Defeat weighed heavily on Laura's shoulders as she met that unsympathetic gaze. Pain riddled her insides. She had lost her son and no one on earth cared or wanted to help her. She was alone, just as she had been alone since the day her parents had died when she was ten years old. Nothing but a burden to her much older brother, Laura had known from day one that he couldn't wait to be rid of her. As soon as she had come home from college, James Ed had tried to push her into marrying the son of one of his business associates, but Laura had refused. Then the attempts on her life had begun.

She supposed that it was poetic justice of sorts. James Ed had considered her a nuisance her entire life, but being the responsible, upstanding man he wanted everyone to believe he was, he had offered Laura an out—marry Rafe Manning. Rafe was young, reasonably handsome and rich. What more should she want? Why couldn't she be the good, obedient sister James Ed wanted her to be?

If only James Ed had known. Rafe's wild stunts had made

Laura's little exploits look like adolescent mishaps. Between the alcohol and the cocaine, Rafe was anything but marriage material. Not to mention the apparently insignificant fact that Laura had no desire to marry Rafe or anyone else at the time. She had been too mixed up herself, too young.

So Laura had thumbed her nose at her big brother's offer, and he had chosen an alternative method of ridding himself of his apparently troublesome sister. Maybe Rafe had been in on it, as well. How much would James Ed have paid him to see that his new bride had a fatal accident? James Ed always preferred the easy way out. Hiring someone to do his dirty work for him was a way of life.

Perversely, Laura wondered if her showing up now would be an inconvenience considering James Ed had no doubt already taken control of her trust fund. Only weeks from her twenty-fifth birthday, Laura would be entitled to the money herself. Then again, that might be the whole point to this little reunion. James Ed would make sure that she didn't show up to claim her trust fund. What would a man, brother or not, do to maintain control of that much money?

Nick stepped closer and Laura jerked back to the here and now. Robby was gone. Doc was gone. What did anything else matter? Panic skittering up her spine once more, she backed away when Nick reached for her. She had to find Robby and Doc. Laura rushed to the door of the house that served as both clinic and home to Doc Holland. She banged on the old oak-and-glass door and called out his name. He had to be here. He simply would not just disappear. She twisted the knob and shook the door. It was locked up tight.

Doc never locked the door to his clinic.

"This isn't right," she muttered. Laura moved to the parlor window. She cupped her hands around her eyes and peered through the ancient, slightly wavy, translucent glass. Everything looked to be in order. But it couldn't be.

"He wouldn't just leave like this," she reminded herself aloud. Bounding off the porch, Laura rushed to the next window at the side of the house. The kitchen appeared neat and tidy, the way Doc always kept it.

But something was wrong. Laura could feel it all the way to her bones. Something very bad had happened to Doc. Her heart thudded painfully. She knew Doc too well. He would never just disappear with Robby without leaving her some sort of word. "They've gotten to him, too," she whispered, the words lost to the biting wind. Forcing herself to act rather than react, Laura ran to the next window, then the next one after that.

That same sense of emptiness she had felt at Mrs. Leeton's echoed inside her.

"No one's here, Laura."

She struggled against the fresh onslaught of tears, then turned on Nick. "He has to be here," she snapped. Her heart couldn't bear the possibility that her child was in the hands of strangers who might want to harm him. Or that something bad had happened to Doc. "Don't you understand? Without him…" Anguish constricted her throat; she couldn't say the rest out loud.

Nick lifted one brow and glared at her unsympathetically. "We're leaving *now*. No more chasing our tails." He snagged her right arm before she could retreat. "Don't make this any more difficult than it already is," he warned.

Difficult? Laura could only stare at him, vaguely aware that he was now leading her back to the car. Did he truly think her situation was merely difficult? Could he not see that someone had cut her heart right out of her chest? Her child was missing! And she had to find him. Somehow…no matter what it cost her.

Another thought suddenly occurred to Laura—Doc's fishing cabin. Maybe he had gone to the cabin to hide Robby. Hope bloomed in Laura's chest. It wasn't totally outside the realm of possibility, she assured herself. She paused before getting into the car and closed her eyes for a moment to allow that hope to warm her. Please, God, she prayed once more, let me find my baby.

Now, all she had to do was convince Nick to take her there. She opened her eyes and her gaze immediately collided with his intense green one. Despite everything, desire sparked inside her. How she wanted to tell Nick the truth—to make him believe in her again. But she couldn't. And when they arrived at the cabin, if her son was not there, Laura would do whatever she had to in order to escape. She would go to James Ed all right. But she would go alone and on her own terms. Somehow Laura would devise a fail-safe plan to get her son back.

Whatever it took, she would do it.

NICK KEPT a firm hold on Laura as they emerged from the car outside Dr. Holland's rustic fishing cabin. The place was in the middle of nowhere, surrounded by woods on three sides and the unpredictable Mississippi River on the fourth. The cabin sat so close to the water's edge, Nick felt sure it flooded regularly. But from the looks of things, there appeared to be no amenities like electricity. It served only as modest shelter for the hard-core fisherman or hunter. So what did a little water hurt now and then? he mused. Most likely nothing.

Now that he had gotten a good look at the place, Nick was surprised there had been a road accessible by car at all. Once again, quiet surrounded them. Only the occasional lapping of the water against a primitive old dock broke the utter silence. The sun had peaked and was now making its trek westward. Nick would give Laura five minutes to look around and then they were heading to Jackson. They had already wasted entirely too much time.

She hadn't spoken other than to give him directions since they left the clinic. Nick glanced at her solemn face now and wondered what was going on in that head of hers. His gut told him he didn't want to know. And his gut was seldom wrong.

At the steps to the dilapidated porch, Laura pulled free of his loosening grip and raced to the door. Nick followed more slowly, allowing her some space to discover what he already knew: there was no one here. Considering nothing about the cabin's environment appeared disturbed in any way, and the lack of tracks, human or otherwise, there hadn't been anyone here in quite a while. Nick swore softly at the pain that knifed through his knee when he took the final step up onto the porch.

Damn his knee injury, and damn this place. He plowed his fingers through his hair and shifted his weight to his left side.

The wind rustled through the treetops, momentarily interrupting the rhythmic sound of the lapping water. Nick scanned the dense woods and then the murky river, a definite sense of unease pricked at him. Maybe it was because the remote location reminded him of the place he and Laura had shared two years ago, or maybe it was just restlessness—the need to get on with this. Whatever the case, Nick's tension escalated to a higher state of alert. If he still smoked, he'd sure as hell light up now. But he'd quit long ago. He had even stopped carrying matches.

"Doc's not here. No one's here."

Nick met Laura's fearful gaze. Drawing in a halting breath, she rubbed at the renewed tears with the back of her hand. She looked so vulnerable, so fragile. He wanted to hold her and assure her that everything would be all right as soon as she was back home. But what if he was wrong? What if someone still intended to harm her?

And what if he were the biggest fool that ever put one foot in front of the other? Don't swallow the bait, Foster. You've seen this song and dance before. "Let's get on the road then," he suggested, self-disgust making his tone more curt than he had intended.

She blinked those long, thick lashes and backed away a step. "I can't go with you, Nick." Laura shook her head slowly from side to side. "I have to find Robby. I…I can't leave without him. If you won't help me, I'll just have to do it alone."

Keeping his gaze leveled on hers, Nick cautiously closed the distance between them. "Don't do anything stupid, Laura," he warned. "If you say you have a kid, I'm sure it's true. And if you do, I can't imagine why anyone would want to take him, can you? What about the boy's father?"

The cornered-animal look that stole across her face gave her away about two seconds before she darted back inside the cabin. She had almost made it across the solitary room and to the back door when Nick caught, then trapped her between his body and a makeshift kitchen cabinet. Anger and pain battled for immediate attention, but at the moment jealousy of a man he had never even met had him by the throat. He leaned in close, pressing her against the rough wood counter, forcing her to acknowledge his superior physical strength.

"Does Rafe know about his son? Or is there some other unlucky fellow still wondering whatever happened to his sweet little Laura?" Nick snarled like the wounded animal he was.

In a self-protective gesture, Laura braced her hands against his chest, unknowingly wreaking havoc with his senses. How could she still affect him this way? Her scent tantalized him, made him want to touch her, taste her, in all the ways he had that one night. Every muscle in his body hardened at the imagined sensation of touching Laura again. When she turned that sweet face up to his, her eyes wide with worry and pleading for his understanding, his resolve cracked….

"He doesn't know about Robby." She licked those full pink lips and a single tear slid slowly down one porcelain cheek. "I'm afraid I won't find him, Nick. Please help me."

…his resolve crumbled. Nick allowed himself to touch her. His fingertips glided over smooth, perfect skin, tracing the path of that lone tear. The sensation of touching Laura like he had dreamed of doing for so very long short-circuited all rational thought.

Slowly, regret nipping at his heels already, Nick lowered his head. He saw her lips tremble just before he took them with his own. Her soft, yielding sigh sent a ripple of sensual pleasure through him. She tasted just like he remembered, sweet and innocent and so very delicate. Like a cherished rose trustingly opening to the sun's warmth, Laura opened for him. And when he thrust his tongue inside her sweet, inviting mouth the past slipped away. Only the moment remained…touching Laura, tasting her and holding her close, then closer still.

Nick threaded his fingers into her long blond hair, reveling in the silky texture as he cradled the back of her head. "Laura," he murmured against her mouth, and she responded, knotting her fists in his shirt and pulling him closer. His body melded with hers, her softness molding to his every hard contour as he deepened the already mind-blowing kiss.

Lust pounded through him with every beat of his heart. Nick traced the outline of Laura's soft body, his palms lingering over the rise of her breasts, then moved lower to cup her bottom and pull her more firmly into him. She slid one tentative hand down his chest, then between their grinding bodies. Laura caressed him intimately. Nick groaned loudly into her mouth as she rubbed his erection again and again through his jeans.

Her tongue dueled with his, taking control of the kiss, just as her body now controlled his. Her firm breasts pressed into his chest, her nipples pebbled peaks beneath the thin cotton of her T-shirt. The urge to make love to Laura—here, now—overwhelmed all else as she propelled him ever closer toward climax with nothing more than her hand, and in spite of the layers of clothing still separating them.

The unexpected blow to the side of his head sent Nick's equilibrium reeling. He staggered back a couple of steps and Laura took off like a shot. He stared at the thick ceramic mug shattered on the primitive wooden floor. He hadn't even noticed it on the counter. Nick shook his head to clear it and took several halting steps in the general direction of the door. When he got his hands on Laura he intended to wring her neck. At the moment he had to focus on reversing the flow of blood from below his belt to above his neck.

She was already at the car when he stumbled across the porch, his body still reeling from her touch. He rubbed the throbbing place just behind his temple then checked his fingertips for any sign of blood. No blood, just a hell of a lump rising. A half-dozen or so four-letter words tumbled from his mouth as he lurched toward the car, his knee throbbing with each unsteady step. Pure, unadulterated rage flashed through him like a wild fire. She would regret this, he promised himself.

Nick knew by Laura's horrified expression that she had just discovered that the keys weren't in the ignition. Did she think he was stupid as well as gullible? In a last-ditch effort to save herself, she locked the doors.

Grinning like the idiot he now recognized himself to be, Nick reached into his pocket and retrieved the keys, then proceeded to dangle them at her. "Going somewhere?" He inserted the key into the door's lock and glared at her. "I don't think so." He jerked the door open and leaned inside.

Laura tried to climb over the seat and into the back but Nick caught her by the waist.

"Let me go!" she screamed, slapping, scratching and kicking with all her might. "I have to find my son!"

Once Nick had restrained her against the passenger's side door, he glowered at Laura for three long beats before he spoke. "You have two choices," he growled. "You can sit here quietly while I drive to Jackson, or I can tie you up and put you in the trunk. It's your call, Laura, what's it going to be?"

Chapter Three

Laura sat absolutely still as Nick parked the car at the rear of James Ed's private estate per security's instructions. She forced away the thoughts and emotions that tugged at her senses. Nick's touch, his kiss, the feel of his arms around her once more. She still wanted him, no matter that her whole world was spinning out of control. Commanding her attention back to the newest level of her nightmare, Laura lifted her gaze to the stately residence before her. The place was every bit as ostentatious as she had expected. Nothing but the best for James Ed, she thought with disgust.

In a few hours every available space out front would be filled with Mercedes, Cadillacs and limousines as the official victory party got under way. According to Nick's telephone conversation with James Ed, of which Laura had only overheard Nick's end, a celebration was planned for the Governor's cohorts who had won big in today's election. Laura was to be taken in through the back. That way there would be no chance that a guest arriving early or some of the hired help might see her. James Ed was still protecting his good name.

But Laura didn't care. A kind of numbness had settled over her at this point. The knowledge that she might never see

Robby again, and that she was going to die had drained her of all energy. She felt spent, useless.

She surveyed again the well-lit mansion and considered what appeared to make her brother happy. Money and power. Those were the things that mattered to him. He could keep Laura's trust fund. She didn't care. She only wanted her son back. But James Ed wouldn't care what Laura wanted. He had never cared about her. Otherwise he would have left her alone after she disappeared rather than hunting her down like an animal. She had barely escaped his hired gunmen on two other occasions. And now Laura would answer doubly to James Ed for all the trouble she had caused him.

But he couldn't hurt her anymore, that was a fact. He had already taken away the only thing in this world that mattered to Laura.

Laura looked up to find Nick reaching back inside the car to unbuckle her seat belt. His lips were moving, so she knew he was speaking to her, but his words didn't register. On autopilot, Laura scooted across the seat and pushed out into the cold night air to stand next to Nick. She looked up at him, the light from a nearby lamppost casting his handsome face in shadows and angles. She knew Nick was a good man, but he had been blinded by her brother's charisma just like everyone else. None of this was Nick's fault, not really. He was only doing what he thought was right. His job.

Would Robby look like him when he grew up? she suddenly wondered. Even at fifteen months, he already had those devilish green eyes and that thick black hair.

Yes, Laura decided, her son would grow up to be every bit as handsome as his father. She frowned and her mouth went unbearably dry. The father he would never know…and the mother he wouldn't remember. She blinked—too late. Hot tears leaked past her lashes.

"They're waiting for us inside," Nick said, drawing her back to the present.

Laura swallowed but it didn't help. She brushed the moisture from her cheeks with the backs of her hands and took a deep, fortifying breath. She might as well get this over with. No point in dragging it out.

"I'm ready," she managed.

"Good."

Nick smiled then and Laura's heart fluttered beneath her breast. It was the first time today she had seen him smile, and just like she remembered, it was breathtaking. Robby would have a heart-stopping smile like that, too.

"This way, Mr. Foster."

Startled, Laura turned toward the unfamiliar male voice. The order came from a man in a black suit. A member of her brother's security staff, Laura realized upon closer inspection. She noted the wire that extended from his starched white collar to the small earpiece he wore. The lack of inflection in his tone as well as his deadpan gaze confirmed Laura's assumption.

Nick took Laura by the arm and ushered her forward as he followed the security guy. No one spoke as they moved across the verandah and toward the French doors at the back of the house. Laura instinctively absorbed every detail of the house's exterior. Her brother had spared no expense on exterior lighting. Of course that could be a hindrance if she somehow managed to escape. The darkness proved an ally at times. Not that her chance of escaping was likely. Laura eyed the man in black's tall frame with diminishing hope. Still, she needed to pay attention to the details. As long as she was still breathing, there was hope. *Focus, Laura,* she commanded her foggy brain.

A wide balcony spanned the rear of the house, supported by massive, ornate white columns. Three sets of French doors lined the first as well as the second floor. At least there were sev-

eral avenues of escape, Laura noted, allowing that small measure of hope to seed inside her hollow heart. Maybe, just maybe,
she would live long enough to at least attempt a getaway.

They crossed a very deserted, very elegant dining room and
entered an enormous kitchen. Gleaming cabinetry and stain-
less steel monopolized the decorating scheme. The delicious
scents of exquisite entrées and baked goods hung in the warm,
moist air. Laura remembered then that she hadn't eaten today,
but her stomach felt queasy rather than empty. Besides, she
had no desire to share her last meal with her brother, or to eat
it in his house. She would starve first.

Several pots with lids steamed on the stovetop. Security
had apparently temporarily vacated the staff upon hearing of
her arrival. As soon as the all clear signal was given the
kitchen would quickly refill with the staff required to pull off
this late night gala.

James Ed always rode the side of caution. And he never
passed up an occasion to celebrate, to show off his many assets.

Laura's stomach knotted with the knowledge that her own
brother hated her this much—or maybe it had nothing to do
with her. Maybe it was simply the money.

Maybe…

Maybe Robby was here. A new kind of expectation shot
through Laura. James Ed could have brought Robby here to
use him as leverage to get what he wanted.

Nick firmed his grip on her right arm as if somehow sensing that her emotions had shifted. She had to get away from
him. He read her entirely too well. Escape scenarios flashed
through her mind as they mounted the service stairs. Laura's
heart pounded harder with each step she took. She felt hot and
cold at the same time. She rubbed the clammy palm of her
free hand against her hip, then squeezed her eyes shut for just
a second against the dizziness that threatened. She could do

this. Laura would do whatever it took to find her son and escape. James Ed would not win.

"Governor Proctor asked that you wait in here."

Nick thanked the man, then led Laura into what appeared to be James Ed's private study. Flames crackled in the fireplace, the warmth suffusing with the rich, dark paneling of the room. A wide mahogany desk with accompanying leather-tufted chair occupied one side of the room. Behind the desk, shelves filled with law books lined the wall from floor to ceiling. Leather wing chairs were stationed strategically before the massive desk. An ornate sideboard displayed fine crystal and exquisite decanters of expensive liquors. No one could accuse James Ed of lacking good taste; it was loyalty that escaped him.

Anxiety tightened Laura's chest, making it difficult to breathe. She had to concentrate. If she somehow freed herself from Nick's grasp and found Robby, could she make it off the grounds without being caught? Nick narrowed his gaze at her as if he had again read her thoughts. The man was entirely too perceptive.

"Take it easy, Laura, your brother will take good care of you," he said almost gently.

Laura shook her head, a pitiful outward display of her inner turmoil. "You just don't get it." She moistened her painfully dry lips and manufactured Nick a weak smile, hoping her words would penetrate that thick skull of his. "It would have been simpler if you'd just killed me yourself."

Laura knew she would not soon forget the expression that stole across Nick's features at that moment. The combination of emotions that danced across his face were as clear as writing on the wall. He cared for her, but he was confused. He trusted James Ed, just like everyone else, and he didn't quite trust Laura. Because she had hurt him badly. Left him to die—he thought. But she hadn't. And now he would never know what really happened, and, what was worse, he would never know his son.

"Laura, I'm sure—"

"Laura?"

A bone-deep chill settled over Laura at the sound of James Ed's distinctive voice. Nick turned immediately to greet the Governor. James Ed, tall, still thin and handsome, hadn't changed much, except for the sprinkling of gray at his sandy temples, and that was likely store-bought to give him a more distinguished appearance. Laura couldn't read the strange mixture of emotions on his face as he approached her. Fear sent her stumbling back several steps when he came too close, but his huge desk halted her.

"Laura, sweet Jesus, I didn't think I would ever see you again. I thought…I thought—dear God, you really are *alive*."

Feeling as trapped as a deer in the headlights of oncoming traffic, Laura froze when her brother threw his arms around her and hugged her tight. He murmured over and over how glad he was to see her. Resisting the urge to retch, Laura closed her eyes and prayed for a miracle. At this point, deep in her heart, she knew it would take nothing short of a miracle to escape and find her child.

James Ed's uncharacteristic actions dumbfounded Laura, adding confusion to the anxiety already tearing at her heart. He had never been the touchy-feely type. Then realization hit her. It was a show for Nick's benefit. James Ed wanted Nick to believe that he truly was thankful to have his baby sister home. When her brother drew back, tears clung to his salon-tanned face, further evidence of his feigned sincerity. The man was a master at misrepresentation and deceit. A true politician, heart and soul.

Laura slumped against the desk when he finally released

her. She felt boneless with an exhaustion that went too deep. Nick had no way of knowing that he had just delivered her like the sacrificial lamb for slaughter. It was his job, she reminded herself. Nick worked for James Ed. She had known he would do this if he ever found her, just as she had known he would take her son away if he discovered his existence. And suddenly Laura understood what she had wanted to deny all day. It was over, and she had lost.

Robby was lost.

Laura's eyes closed against the pain that accompanied that thought, and the memory of her baby's smile haunted her soul.

"Nick, thank you so much for bringing her back to us. I don't know how to repay you."

Nick accepted the hand James Ed offered. "I was only doing what I was assigned to do two years ago." Nick wondered why it suddenly felt all wrong.

"You're a man of your word." James Ed gave Nick's hand another hearty shake. "I like that. If there's ever anything I can do for you, don't hesitate to ask."

Nick studied the Governor's sincere expression. He considered himself a good judge of character, and Laura's fears just didn't ring true when Nick looked her brother square in the eye. He read no deceit or hatred in the man's gaze. But his gut reaction told him that Laura truly believed in the threat.

"There is one thing," Nick began, hesitant to offend the man, but certain he couldn't leave without clearing the air.

"*Laura!*" Sandra, James Ed's wife, flew across the room and pulled Laura into her arms. "Honey, I am so glad to have you back home. You don't know how your brother and I have prayed that somehow you really were alive and would come back to us."

Nick couldn't reconcile what Laura had described with the reunion happening right in front of him, and still something didn't feel right about the whole situation. Something elemental that he couldn't quite put his finger on.

"You were saying, Nick," James Ed prompted, the relieved smile on his face further evidence that Laura had to be wrong.

Nick studied the Governor for another long moment before he began once more. He knew that what he was about to say would definitely put a damper on this seemingly happy event. A few feet away he could hear Sandra fussing over a near catatonic Laura. What the hell, Nick had always been a straightforward kind of guy. Why stop now?

"Laura is convinced that you're the one behind the threat to her life, two years ago and now," Nick stated flatly.

You could have heard the proverbial pin drop for the next ten seconds. The look of profound disbelief on James Ed's face morphed into horror right before Nick's eyes. Nick would have staked his life on the man's innocence right then and there. James Ed couldn't possibly be guilty of what Laura had accused him. Slowly, James Ed turned to face his sister, whose defeated, lifeless expression had not changed.

"Laura, you can't really believe that. My God, I'm your brother."

"Honey, James Ed has been beside himself since the day you disappeared. How could you think that he had anything to do with trying to harm you?" Sandra stroked Laura's long, blond hair as a mother would a beloved daughter. But Laura made no response. In spite of everything she had done, Nick ached to give Laura that kind of comfort himself—to see if she would respond to him as she had that one night.

Suddenly, Laura straightened, dodging Sandra's touch and pushing away from the desk that had likely kept her vertical. She took several shaky steps until she was face-to-face with her brother. She stared up at him. Nick tensed, remembering the hefty mug she had used to bash him upside the head.

Luckily for James Ed there was nothing in her reach at the moment.

"If you really mean what you say, big brother, then do me one favor," Laura challenged, her voice strangely emotionless, but much stronger than Nick would have believed her capable of at the moment.

Nick readied himself to tackle her if she started swinging at James Ed. The lump on the side of his head undeniable proof that Laura could be a wildcat when the urge struck her.

"Laura." She flinched when James Ed took her by the shoulders, but she didn't back off. "I will do anything within my power for you. Anything," he repeated passionately. "Just name it, honey."

"Give me back my son," she demanded, her voice cracking with the emotion she could no longer conceal. Laura's whole body trembled then, her upright position in serious jeopardy.

Nick moved to her side, pulled her from a stunned James Ed's grasp and into his own arms. "Shh, Laura, it's okay," he murmured against her soft hair as he held her tight. Her sobs would be contained no longer, she shook with the force of them.

"Nick, I don't know what she's talking about." James Ed threw up his hands, his exasperation clear.

"What on earth can she mean?" Sandra reiterated as she hurried to her husband's side. She looked every bit as confused and genuinely concerned as James Ed.

"Please make him tell you, Nick, please," Laura begged, her fists clenched in the lapels of his jacket. "I don't care what he does to me, but don't let him hurt my baby." The look of pure fear and absolute pain on her sweet face wrenched his gut.

Confusion reigned. For the first time in his entire life, Nick didn't know what to do. As much as he knew he shouldn't, he wanted desperately to believe Laura. To take her away from here and keep her safe from any and all harm.

"Tell me, *please*," James Ed urged. "What is this about a child?"

In abbreviated form, Nick recited the events that had taken place in Bay Break, all the while holding Laura close, giving her the only comfort he could. "Laura insists that she has a son," he concluded. "I didn't find any evidence to corroborate her story, but—" he shrugged "—she stands by it."

Laura pounded her fists against his chest, demanding Nick's full attention. "I do have a son! His name is Robby and he's—"

"Laura," James Ed broke in, his tone calm and soothing despite the unnerving story Nick had just related to him.

Laura whirled in Nick's arms, but he held her back when she would have flung herself at James Ed. "You stole my son! Don't try to tell me you didn't!"

"Laura, please!" Sandra scolded gently. "You aren't making sense. What child?"

Laura turned to her. "Sandra, make him tell me!"

Nick tightened his hold on Laura, his protective instincts kicking into high gear. He still felt connected to her; he couldn't pretend that he didn't. "So you don't have her son?" he asked the Governor pointedly.

James Ed closed his eyes and pinched the bridge of his nose. Several long seconds passed before he released a heavy breath, opened his eyes and then spoke, "It's worse than I thought."

"What's that supposed to mean?" Laura challenged, her voice strained.

James Ed settled a sympathetic gaze on his sister. "Laura, there can't possibly be any baby." He held up his hands to stay her protests, a look of pained defeat revealing itself on his face. "Just hear me out."

Laura sagged against Nick then, the fight going out of her.

Nick wasn't sure how much more she would be able to stand before collapsing completely.

"Laura," James Ed began hesitantly. "Until the day before yesterday, when you escaped, you had spent the last eighteen months in a mental institution in New Orleans."

Nick felt Laura's gasp of disbelief. "That's a lie," she cried.

James Ed massaged his right temple as if an ache had begun there. "Apparently when you ran away two years ago, you wound up in New Orleans. You were found in an alley a few months later and hospitalized." He paused to stare at the floor. "The diagnosis was trauma-induced amnesia, and schizophrenia. The doctor says you haven't responded well to the drug therapy, but there's still hope."

Laura shook her head. "That's a lie. I've never been to New Orleans."

"Laura, honey, please listen to your brother," Sandra coaxed.

"You had no ID, no money. They assumed you were homeless and really didn't attempt to find out where you'd come from. And that's where you've been ever since. If you hadn't escaped, we might never have known you were even alive." His gaze softened with sadness. "You were considered a threat to yourself…as well as others." A beat of sickening silence passed. "Detective Ingle spotted you yesterday." James Ed looked to Nick then. "Ray told me you would be bringing Laura home. He received a copy of the New Orleans APB on the Jane Doe escapee just a few hours ago. It didn't take long to put two and two together. We've already contacted the hospital. The treating physician there faxed me a copy of his report."

Laura turned back to face Nick. "He's lying, Nick. You have to believe me!"

Nick searched her eyes, trying to look past the panic and fear for the truth. "Laura, why would he lie?" All the cards were stacked against her; James Ed had no motivation that

Nick could see for wanting to harm her. And Laura had no proof of any of her accusations, or that she had a child.

"Honey, I would never lie to you." James Ed moved closer. "I am so sorry that this has happened. If we had known how sick you were two years ago, maybe we could have prevented this total breakdown—"

"Why are you doing this?" Laura cried. "I'm not crazy. I just want my son back!"

"I think it's time to call Dr. Beckman in," Sandra suggested quietly.

"Who?" Laura demanded. Her body shook so badly now that Nick's arms were all that kept her upright. Nick's own concern mounted swiftly.

"Wait," James Ed told Sandra, then turned to Laura. He studied her for a time before continuing. "All right, Laura, tell us where you've been if not in New Orleans."

"Darling, don't put yourself and Laura through this now," Sandra pleaded softly.

James Ed shook his head. "I want to hear Laura's side. I won't be guilty of failing to listen again." He gave Sandra a pointed look. "I want to know where *she* believes she has been."

"You know where I've been," Laura snapped. "You've had someone tracking me like an animal."

"Please, Laura, you can't believe that." James Ed reached for her, but she shunned his touch.

"Stay away from me!"

"Surely we can sort all this out in the morning after Laura's had a good night's rest," Sandra offered quickly. "We're all upset. Let's not make things worse by pushing Laura when she's obviously exhausted." Sandra placed a comforting hand on James Ed's arm. "And we do have guests arriving shortly, unless you'd like me to cancel…."

"You're right, of course, dear," James Ed relented with a

heavy sigh. "Laura needs to rest. Canceling dinner is probably wise, too. I should have realized that earlier. We've all had a shock."

"I'll get the doctor." Sandra hurried toward the door.

Laura stiffened. "I don't need a doctor."

"Honey, this is for your own good," James Ed assured her. "We've had Dr. Beckman, a close friend, standing by since we found out…what happened. He has spoken with the doctor in New Orleans and understands the specifics of your case. He'll give you something to calm you down, and we can work all this out in the morning."

"No!" Laura struggled in Nick's arms. "Don't do this, James Ed, please!"

Nick didn't like the way this was going. Before he could protest, Sandra rushed back into the room followed by a short, older man carrying a small black case.

"Nick, please don't let them do this to me."

Nick looked from Laura to the doctor who had just taken a hypodermic needle from his bag. Nick's uncertain gaze shifted to the Governor. "I don't know about this, James Ed," Nick said slowly.

"It's okay, Nick, he's only going to give her a sedative," James Ed explained tiredly. "It's for her own good. Considering the state she's in she might hurt herself."

The image of the scars on Laura's wrists flashed through Nick's mind. Maybe James Ed knew what he was doing. She was his sister. If there was no child, then Laura was seriously delusional. But—

"Don't!" Laura shouted when the doctor came closer. "Help me, Nick! You have to help me!"

"Nick, you're going to have to help *us*," James Ed pressed as he reached for Laura. "You must see that she desperately needs a sedative."

Nick pulled Laura closer, the look he shot James Ed stopped him cold. "This doesn't feel right."

"It's perfectly safe, Mr. Foster," the doctor assured Nick. "She needs rest right now. Her present condition isn't conducive to her own welfare."

Nick felt confused. His head ached from the blow Laura had dealt him. The image of her scarred wrists kept flitting through his mind. He wasn't sure how to proceed. His heart said one thing, but his brain another. He stared down at the trembling woman in his arms. What was the best thing for her? The dark circles beneath her wide blue eyes and the even paler cast to her complexion gave him his answer. She needed to rest. She needed the kind of help Nick couldn't give her. But *this* just didn't feel right.

Sandra reached for Laura this time. "No," Nick said harshly. "I don't think—"

"Your job is over now, Nick," Sandra interrupted calmly, patiently. "You should let us do ours."

"It's for the best, Nick," James Ed said with defeat.

"Mr. Foster, I'll have to ask you to leave now."

Nick's gaze shot over his shoulder toward the man who had just spoken. A suit from James Ed's private security staff stood directly behind Nick. His jaw hardened at the realization that he had been so caught up in Laura's plight that he hadn't heard him approach.

"Get lost," Nick warned.

"Let's not make this anymore unpleasant than necessary, sir," the man in black suggested pointedly.

Nick held his challenging stare for several tense seconds, then reluctantly released Laura. He wouldn't do anything to make bad matters worse…at least not right now.

When Sandra and Dr. Beckman closed in on Laura, the look of betrayal in her eyes ripped the heart right out of Nick's chest. "Please don't let them hurt my baby," she murmured, then winced when the needle penetrated the soft skin of her delicate shoulder.

Nick turned to James Ed, a white-hot rage suddenly detonating inside him. "If you're holding anything back—"

The Governor shook his head in solemn defeat. "Trust me, Nick."

Chapter Four

"She isn't well," Sandra said softly.

"I know."

"What are you going to do?"

"I don't know," James Ed answered hesitantly. His pause before continuing seemed an eternity. "But I have to do something. I can't allow her to continue this way."

"What do you mean?" Caution and the barest hint of uncertainty tinged Sandra's words. "Laura is your sister," she reminded softly. "Now that she's back, there are changes…"

James Ed breathed a heavy sigh. "Do you think I could forget that significant detail?"

"I'm sorry. Of course not."

Laura struggled to maintain her focus on the quiet conversation going on above her. Blackness hovered very near, threatening to drag her back into the abyss of unconsciousness. Her entire body felt leaden, lifeless. She wasn't sure she could move if she tried. She could open her eyes. Laura had managed to lift her heavy lids once or twice before Sandra and James Ed entered the room.

How long had she been here? she wondered. Long enough that the sedative the doctor had administered had begun to wear off. Though still groggy, Laura's mind was slowly clearing. But she couldn't have been here too long. Twenty-four hours, maybe? Though Laura had no way of knowing the precise drug she had been given, she recognized the aftereffects. Whatever it was, it was strong and long lasting. She'd had it before....

Before she had escaped her brother's clutches. Before she fell in love with Nick and had Robby.

A soul-deep ache wrenched through her. Laura moaned in spite of herself. Where was Robby? Was he safe? Oh God, she had to find her baby. But if she opened her eyes now they would know she was listening. Why hadn't Nick helped her? Because he was one of them, Laura reminded herself. He had always been on their side. No one believed her. No one would help her.

"She's waking up," James Ed warned, something that sounded vaguely like fear in his tone. "Where is the medication Dr. Beckman left?"

"You go ahead and get ready for bed," Sandra suggested. "You didn't get much sleep last night with Laura's arrival. I'll see to her, and then I'll join you."

James Ed released a long breath. "All right."

Laura heard the door close as James Ed left the room. Her heart thudded against her rib cage. She had to do something. Maybe Sandra would believe her. She opened her eyes and struggled to focus on her sister-in-law's image. A golden glow from the lamp on the bedside table defined Sandra's dark, slender features. Smiling, she sat down on the edge of the mattress at Laura's side. Laura's lethargic fingers fisted in the cool sheet and dragged it up around her neck, as if the thin linen would somehow protect her. She had to get away from here. Somehow.

"Help me," Laura whispered.

"Oh, now, don't you worry, everything is going to be fine." Sandra smoothed a soothing hand over Laura's hair. "You shouldn't be frightened. James Ed and I only want the best for you, dear. Don't you see that?"

Her lids drooping with the overwhelming need to surrender, Laura mentally fought the sedative. She would not go back to sleep. She concentrated on staying awake. Don't go to sleep, she told herself. You have to do this for Robby. Robby…oh God, would she ever see her baby again? And Nick? Nick was lost to her, too.

Sandra retrieved something from the night table. Laura's drowsy gaze followed her movements. A prescription bottle. Sandra slipped off the top and tapped two small pills into her palm. Laura frowned, trying to focus…to see more clearly. More medicine! She didn't want more.

"Here." Sandra placed the medication against Laura's lips. "Take these and rest, Laura. We want you to get well as soon as possible. Dr. Beckman said these would help."

Laura pressed her lips together and turned her head. She would not take anything else. She had to wake up. Tears burned her eyes and her body trembled with the effort required to resist.

Sandra shook her head sympathetically. "Honey, if you don't take the medication, James Ed will only make me call Dr. Beckman again. You don't want that, do you?"

A sob constricted Laura's throat. Slowly, her lips trembling with the effort, she opened her mouth. Tears blurred her vision as Sandra pushed the pills past Laura's lips. Laura took a small sip of the water Sandra offered next.

"That's a good girl," Sandra said softly. She fussed with the covers around Laura and then stood. "You rest, honey, I'll be right down the hall."

Laura watched as Sandra closed the door behind her. Laura quickly spat the two pills into her hand. She shuddered at the bitter aftertaste they left in her mouth. Her fingers curled into

a fist around the dissolving medication. She cursed her
brother, cursed God for allowing this to happen, then cursed
herself for being a fool. Gritting her teeth with the effort,
Laura forced her sluggish body to a sitting position. With the
back of her hand she wiped at the bitter taste on her tongue.
She shuddered again, barely restraining the urge to gag.

Laura took a deep breath and surveyed the dimly lit room.
She had to get out of here. But how would she get out? She
would most likely be caught the moment she stepped into the
hallway. Security was probably lurking out there somewhere.
French doors and several windows lined one wall. The balcony, she remembered. The balcony at the back of the house.
Maybe she could get out that way. A single door, probably to
a bathroom or a closet, Laura surmised, stood partially open
on the other side of the room. Still wearing the clothes she
had arrived in, Laura pushed to her feet, then staggered across
the room to what she hoped was a bathroom. Her legs were
rubbery, and her head felt as if it might just roll off her shoulders like a runaway bowling ball.

Cool tile suddenly took the place of the plush carpeting beneath her feet. Laura breathed a sigh of relief that the door
did, in fact, lead to a bathroom. She lurched to the vanity and
lowered her head to the faucet. Water. She moaned her relief
at the feel of the refreshing liquid against her lips, on her
tongue, and then as it slid down her parched throat. Laura
rinsed the bitter taste from her mouth, then washed the gritty
pill residue from her hand. She shivered as her foggy brain
reacted to the sound of the running water, making her keenly
aware of the need to relieve herself in another way.

After taking care of that necessity, Laura caught sight of
her reflection as she paused to wash her hands. The dim glow
from the other room ·offered little illumination, but Laura
could see that her eyes were swollen and red, and her face

looked pale and puffy. She splashed cold water onto her face several times to help her wake up, then finger-combed her tousled hair. All she had to do was pull herself together enough to find a way to climb down from the balcony. Laura frowned when the coldness of the tile floor again invaded her senses. She needed her shoes. Where were her shoes?

Laura lurched back into the bedroom. She searched the room, the closet, under the bed, everywhere she knew to look and to no avail. Her shoes were not to be found. Exhausted, Laura plopped onto the edge of the bed. She had to have shoes. It was too damned cold to make a run for it barefoot. She would have to head for some sort of cover—the woods, maybe. How could she run without her shoes?

Think, Laura, she ordered her fuzzy brain. They must have removed her shoes when they took her jacket. She stared down at the stained T-shirt she wore. She had to remember. What room was she in when they took her jacket? The study or in this bedroom? Robby was depending on her. She had to get out of here. But somehow she needed to search the house first. Robby could be here. Her heart bumped into overdrive at the thought of how long it had been since she had seen her son. She let go a halting breath. He had been missing over twenty-four hours now, if her calculations were correct. She scanned the room for a clock, but didn't see one. Laura squeezed her eyes shut then.

Please God, keep my baby safe. I don't care if I die tonight, she beseeched, *just don't let anything happen to my baby.*

Her body weak and trembling, Laura dropped to her hands and knees on the floor. For one long moment she wanted to curl into the fetal position and cry. Laura shook off the urge to close her eyes and allow the drug to drag her back into oblivion. She had to find those damned shoes. Slowly, carefully, she crawled around the large room and searched every square foot again. Still nothing. Too weary now to even crawl back to the bed. Laura leaned her head against the wall and allowed her eyes to close. She was so tired. She could rest for just one minute. She scrubbed a hand over her face…she could not go back to sleep…she had to find her shoes.

To find Robby.

All she needed was one more moment of rest….

The blackness embraced Laura as she surrendered to the inevitable.

LAURA WASN'T SURE how much time had passed when she awoke. Hours probably, her muscles cramped from the position in which she had fallen asleep. It was still night she knew since only the dimmest glow of light filtered through her closed, immensely heavy lids. Groaning, she sat up straighter and stretched her shoulders, first one side, then the other. She frowned, trying to remember what she was supposed to do. Her shoes. That's right. She needed to find her shoes and get out of here. Laura shoved the hair back from her face and licked her dry lips.

"Okay," she mumbled. Shoes, she needed her shoes. She had to get up first. Laura forced her reluctant lids open and blinked to focus in the near darkness. Eerie pink eyes behind a black ski mask met her bleary gaze. Laura opened her mouth to scream, but a gloved hand clamped over her lips.

"So, Sleeping Beauty is awake," a male voice rasped.

Laura drew back from the threat; the wall halted her retreat. His hand pressed down more brutally over her mouth. She shook her head and tried to beg for her life, but her words were stifled by black leather.

"You," he said disgustedly. "Have caused me a great deal of extra trouble." Something sharp pricked her neck. Laura's heart slammed mercilessly against her rib cage. He had a knife. A cry twisted in her throat.

He jerked Laura to her feet. The remaining fog in her brain cleared instantly. This man had come to kill her. She was going to die.

No! her mind screamed. She had to find Robby.

Laura stiffened against him. He was strong, but not very large. If she struggled hard enough—

"Don't move," he growled next to her ear. The tip of the knife pierced the skin at the base of her throat again.

Laura suppressed the violent tremble that threatened to rack her body. Blood trickled down and over her collarbone. Hysteria threatened her flimsy hold on calm. She had to think! Her frantic gaze latched on to the open French doors. He had probably entered her room from the balcony. If he could come in that way, she could escape by the same route. All she had to do was get away from him…from the knife.

His arm tightened around her as if she had uttered her thoughts aloud. "Time to die, princess," he murmured, then licked her cheek. The foul stench of his breath sent nausea rising into her throat.

Laura swallowed convulsively. She squeezed her eyes shut and focused on a mental picture of her son to escape the reality of what was happening. Her sweet, sweet child. The tip of the knife trailed over one breast.

"Too bad you didn't stay gone." He twisted her face up to his. Those icy eyes flashed with rage.

The air vaporized in Laura's lungs. He was going to kill her and there was no one to help her. No one. Nick didn't believe her. And her own brother had probably hired this man.

"Now you have to die." He eased his hand from her lips only to press his mouth over hers. The feel of wool from his ski mask chafed her cheeks. Laura struggled. The knife blade quickly came up to her throat again.

Laura wilted when he forced his tongue into her mouth.

Tears seeped past her tightly closed lids. Her entire body convulsed at the sickening invasion. Rage like she had never experienced before surged through her next. Laura's eyes opened wide and she clamped down hard with her teeth on the bastard's tongue. The sting of the knife blade slid down her chest when he snapped his head back. Laura jerked out of his momentarily slack hold. She flung herself toward the balcony. She had to escape.

"Come back here, you bitch," he growled, his words slightly slurred.

Laura slammed the French doors shut behind her. He pushed hard against them. Laura fought with all her body weight to prevent the doors from opening. Her feet slipped on the slick painted surface of the balcony. One door opened slightly before she could regain her footing. He reached a hand between the doors and grabbed her by the hair. Laura screamed. The sound echoed in the darkness around her. She slammed against the door with every ounce of force she had. The man swore, released her and jerked his arm back inside.

Too weak to stand any longer, Laura dropped to her knees. She held on to the door handles with all her might. The handles shook in her hold. She leaned harder against the doors. Surely someone would come into her room at any moment. James Ed had around-the-clock security, Laura was certain. If they would come, then she would have proof that she had been telling the truth all along. Seconds clicked by. Someone had to come, didn't they? A sob twisted inside her chest. She was so tired. And no one was coming. No one cared.

Laura screamed when the door shoved hard against her, hard enough to dislodge her weight. She scrambled away from the threat. Panic had obliterated all reason. She had to get away. To find her child.

"Laura!"

Laura stilled. Was that Nick's voice? Hope welled in her chest. He was coming back for her.

"Laura." James Ed crouched next to her. "What happened?"

Laura lifted her gaze to his, disappointment shuddered through her. It wasn't Nick. She must have imagined his voice. "Please help me," she pleaded with her brother.

"Sweet Jesus!" James Ed stared at her chest. "Laura, are you hurt?"

She stared down at herself. Blood. Her T-shirt was red with blood. Her blood. The blackness threatened again. Laura struggled to remain conscious. She was bleeding. The knife. Her gaze flew to her brother's. "He tried to kill me," she murmured.

James Ed shook his head, his face lined with worry. "Who tried to kill you, Laura? There's no one here."

Laura looked past James Ed to the bedroom she had barely escaped with her life. The overhead lights were on now. A man in a black suit stood in the middle of the room. Security. Laura remembered him from when she had first arrived. She frowned. Security had to have seen the intruder. Surely he couldn't have gotten past a professional security team. Could he be hiding somewhere in the house? Why weren't they looking for him?

Sandra was next to her now. "Let's get you back inside and see exactly what you've done to yourself."

"No," Laura denied. "There was a man. He tried to kill me. He had a knife."

"Come on, Laura." James Ed helped Laura to her feet. "Don't make this any worse than it already is."

"I found this, sir."

The man held a large kitchen knife gingerly between his thumb and forefinger. Light glistened from the wide blade. Blood—her blood, Laura realized—stained the otherwise shiny edge.

Sandra scrutinized the knife. "It's from *our* kitchen," she said slowly, her gaze shifting quickly to James Ed.

"Dear God," he breathed.

Despite the lingering effects of the sedative, Laura realized the implications. "No," she protested. "There was someone here. He—"

"That's enough, Laura," James Ed commanded harshly. She glared up at him. "We've had more than enough excitement for one night," he added a bit more calmly. "Now, let's get you back in bed and attend to your injuries."

Shaking her head, Laura jerked from his grasp. "You can't keep me here." Laura backed away from him. "I have to find my son."

James Ed only stared at her, something akin to sympathy glimmered in his blue eyes. For one fleeting instant Laura wondered if she could be wrong about her brother. Probably not.

"Miss Proctor, I have to insist that you cooperate with the Governor."

Laura turned slowly to face the man who had spoken. The security guy from the night before. She didn't know his name. Laura met his cold, dark gaze. He extended his hand, and Laura dragged her gaze down to stare at the offered assistance. She looked back to her brother, then to Sandra. Laura swallowed the rush of fear that crowded into her throat. How could she fight all of them?

She shifted her gaze back to the man offering his hand. "They're going to kill me, you know," she said wearily. Laura blinked as tears burned her eyes.

"Laura, please don't say things like that," Sandra insisted gently. "Please lie down and let me take care of you. You've hurt yourself."

Laura shook her head. "It doesn't matter." She brushed past the guy in the black suit and walked to the bed. Laura climbed amid the tangled covers and squeezed her eyes shut. "Just go away," she murmured. "Just…go away."

A long moment of silence passed before anyone responded to her request.

"Lock it this time," James Ed ordered, his voice coming from near the door. "And I want someone stationed outside her room. I don't want her hurting herself again."

"Should we call Dr. Beckman?" Sandra suggested quietly.

"I think it's too late for that," James Ed returned just as quietly. "This has gone way beyond Beckman."

"Excuse me, sir," a new male voice interrupted. "There is a gentleman downstairs to see you."

"At this hour?" James Ed demanded. "Who is it?"

Silence.

"I think you had better come and see for yourself, Governor."

NICK STOOD in the middle of Governor Proctor's private study. He was mad as hell. He had no idea what the hell had gone on here tonight, but he had clearly seen Laura on that balcony. Fear and fury in equal measures twisted inside him. If tonight was any indication of James Ed's ability to take care of his sister, it stunk. And Nick had no intention of leaving her welfare to chance.

Maybe Victoria was right, maybe he had lost his perspective. Victoria had wanted to assign Ian Michaels to Laura's case when Nick called and informed her of his plan to hang around. She had stood by her assertion that Nick needed a vacation. But Nick had managed to convince her otherwise—against her better judgment. Nick blew out a disgusted breath. What the hell was wrong with him? He should have flown back to Chicago last night instead of skulking outside James Ed's house watching for trouble. If security had caught him, how would he have explained his uninvited presence? Nick had just about convinced himself to leave after more than twenty-four hours of surveillance, when Laura had flown out onto that balcony screaming bloody murder. Now, Nick didn't care what James Ed thought.

Nick closed his eyes and shook his head. Here he was allowing history to repeat itself—at his expense. Laura Proctor had almost gotten him killed once. And now he was back in her life as though nothing had ever happened between them. Nick swore softly, cursing his own stupidity.

But he just couldn't leave her like this.

"Nick, sorry you had to wait." Governor Proctor breezed in, a suit flanking him. "I thought you had to get back to Chicago? What's going on?"

"I was about to ask you the same question." Nick met him halfway across the room and accepted the hand he extended. "I saw Laura on the balcony." Nick had called out to her, but she hadn't heard him.

James Ed shook his hand firmly, then sighed mightily. Worry marred his face. "I'm not sure I know what happened."

"Where's Laura?" Nick felt a muscle tic in his tense jaw.

James Ed dropped his gaze and slowly shook his head. "She's in her room, heavily sedated." He lifted his gaze back to Nick's and shrugged listlessly. "Tonight's episode was intensely frightening. I was afraid she would—" he swallowed "—fall off the balcony."

Renewed fear slammed into Nick like a sucker punch to the gut. "Is she all right?"

"Physically she'll be okay," he explained. "But she's convinced that someone is trying to kill her."

"And you don't believe that?" Nick noted the lines of fatigue around the Governor's eyes and mouth before he looked away. "You're certain she's all right. I heard her scream and the next thing I knew she was struggling against the French doors as if someone were trying to get to her."

"That was me," James Ed explained. "I'll take you up in a moment and you can see for yourself." He shook his head wearily. "But honestly, Nick, I don't know what I believe." He gestured to the chair in front of his desk. "Please, have a seat. I have to do something. But first I have to think this through." He skirted the desk and settled heavily into the high-back leather chair behind it.

Nick didn't have to look to know that the Governor's bodyguard remained by the door. Slowly, Nick moved to stand behind one of the wing chairs near the desk. He wasn't ready to sit just yet. He watched James Ed's reaction closely as Nick asked his next question. "I don't know what's happening here, James Ed. Your actions indicate to me that you don't believe Laura, yet you believed her two years ago. That's why you hired me in the first place."

"Did I?" He met Nick's analyzing gaze. "Or was I simply desperate for someone else to take responsibility for my out-of-control sister?"

"And the man who shot me?" Nick lifted one brow in skepticism. "Was he another figment of her imagination as well?"

James Ed closed his eyes and let go a weary breath. "I don't know," he said quietly. "I only know that Laura is alive and she needs help." He opened his eyes, the same translucent blue as Laura's, and met Nick's gaze. "The kind of help I can't give her. I'm afraid for her life."

The image of Laura's scarred wrists loomed large in Nick's mind. He tensed. Maybe James Ed had a right to be scared of what Laura might do to herself. Nick couldn't be sure. Too much of what was going on still baffled him. Something had been nagging at him since he left her here last night. And he hadn't been able to leave because of it. Nick couldn't put his finger on it just yet, but something wasn't as it should be. Maybe he just needed to get Laura out of his system. Whatever it was, he had to do this. He needed closure with Laura and both their demons.

"Tomorrow I'm calling a private hospital that Dr. Beckman has recommended to me." James Ed lifted his gaze to Nick. "I don't know what else to do. Every waking moment she rants on about her child, then tonight she claims someone tried to kill her. I'm at a complete loss."

"And what if she's telling the truth," Nick offered.

James Ed searched his desk for a moment, then picked up a piece of paper and handed it to Nick. "There's the report from the hospital in Louisiana. See for yourself."

Nick scanned the report that had been faxed to Beckman. The conclusions it indicated were very incriminating. If half of this turned out to be true, Laura was a very sick lady. He leaned forward and passed the report back to James Ed. "I'm still not convinced."

James Ed stroked his forehead as if a headache had begun there. "What is it that you would suggest then, Nick? I only want to keep her from hurting herself and to find a way to help her." He straightened abruptly and banged his fist against the polished desk. "Damn it! I love my sister. I want her to be well. If these doctors can help her, what choice do I have?"

Silence screamed between them for one long beat. "Give me a chance to see if I can get through to her." Nick shrugged. "Let me look into the allegations she has made."

James Ed's weary expression grew guarded. "I'm listening."

"Two weeks. I choose the place," Nick went on. "And there will be absolutely no interference from you or anyone else."

James Ed frowned. "What do you mean interference?"

"You won't see Laura until I bring her back to you."

"What kind of request is that?" James Ed demanded crossly. "She's my sister!"

"What do you have to lose?" Nick said flatly. He couldn't get to the bottom of what was going on with Laura unless he had her all to himself. There could be no distractions or interference.

The Governor pushed to his feet, irritation lining his distinguished features. "Fine." He glowered at Nick. "I'm only doing this because I'm desperate and I trust you. I hope you know that, Foster. Now, where are you planning to take her?"

"I'd like to take her to your country house near Bay Break. It's quiet and out of the way," Nick explained. "And Laura mentioned that her childhood there was happy."

James Ed blinked, then looked away. "Laura did love it there as a child." He closed his eyes for a moment before he continued. "And that would protect Laura from the paparazzi that follows me."

Nick considered the Governor's last words for a bit. Was his concern for his sister or for his image? Maybe Laura's accusations were making Nick paranoid. One thing was certain, before he left Laura this time, Nick would know exactly what and who was behind Laura's problems—even if it turned out to be Laura herself. That possibility went against Nick's instincts, but time would tell.

"When would you like to begin?" James Ed asked.

Nick couldn't be sure, but he thought he saw something resembling hope in James Ed's gaze. "We'll leave right away," Nick suggested.

"I'll call Rutherford and have him prepare the house." James Ed surveyed his desk as if looking for something he had just remembered. "Sandra will put some things together in a bag for Laura."

"Good." Nick turned to leave.

"Nick."

He shifted to face James Ed once more. "Yes."

"Take good care of her, would you?"

Nick dipped his head in silent acknowledgment.

NICK STOOD at the foot of Laura's bed and watched her sleep for several minutes. He closed his eyes and willed away the need to hold her. She looked so small and vulnerable. And Nick wanted more than anything to protect her. He opened his eyes and stared at the soft blond hair spread across her pillow. He wanted to hold her to him and protect her forever. That's what he really wanted. But could he do that? He had seen the report with his own eyes. He swallowed. Laura could be very ill.

That reality didn't stop him from wanting her. Laura's problems had almost cost him his life once before. Apparently that didn't carry much weight with Nick either, because it sure as hell hadn't kept him from hanging around when his assignment was technically over. Giving himself credit, there was more to his being here than simply bone-deep need and desire.

Something wasn't right with this whole picture. James Ed appeared every bit the loving, concerned brother. By the same token Laura seemed as sane as anyone else Nick knew. He lifted one brow sardonically. That didn't say much for Nick's selected associates.

Nick's thoughts turned somber once more. Laura was convinced that she had a child. He frowned. According to James Ed and the hospital report, that was impossible. Nick massaged his forehead. Well, he had two weeks to decide what the real truth was. And the only way he would ever be able to do that was if he kept his head screwed on straight. He couldn't allow her to get to him again. One way or another he would get to the truth. He owed it to himself...and he owed it to Laura. The image of her stricken face when he had left her haunted his every waking moment. Nick swallowed hard. He simply couldn't walk away without looking back. No matter what had happened in the past. He just couldn't do it.

Nick stepped quietly to the side of the bed. He sat down next to Laura and watched her breathe for a time. She was so beautiful. Nick cursed himself. He wasn't supposed to dwell on that undeniable fact. He lifted his hand to sweep the hair from her face, but hesitated before touching her. He swallowed hard as he allowed his fingertips to graze her soft cheek. That simple touch sent desire hurdling through his veins.

"Laura," he whispered tautly. "Wake up, Laura."

Her lids fluttered open to reveal those big, beautiful blue eyes. It took her a moment to focus on his face. Drugs, he realized grimly. James Ed had said she was heavily sedated.

"Nick?" She frowned, clearly confused.

"It's okay, Laura," he assured her.

She struggled to a sitting position. Nick's gaze riveted to her bloodstained T-shirt. The same T-shirt she had been wearing when he brought her here.

"What the hell happened?" he demanded softly. Before Nick could determine where the blood had come from, Laura flung her arms around him and buried her face in his neck.

"I prayed you'd come back for me," she murmured, her words catching on a tiny sob.

Hesitantly, Nick put his arms around her and pulled her close. "It's okay. I'm here now, and this time I'm not leaving without you." The feel of her fragile, trembling body in his arms made him want to scream at the injustice of it all. How could life be so unfair to her…and to him?

Laura drew back from him, her eyes were glassy, her movements sluggish. "Nick, I just need you to do one thing for me."

"What's that?" he asked, visually searching her upper body for signs of injury. The idea that someone had hurt Laura seared in his brain.

"Please, Nick," she murmured, "find my baby."

Chapter Five

"This child doesn't look neglected to me." Elsa touched the small dark head of the sleeping child. "Where was he found?"

"It's not our job to ask questions."

"I'm only saying that he looks perfectly healthy and well cared for in my opinion," Elsa argued irritably. The child slept like the dead. He rarely cried and ate like a horse. And when he was awake, he played with hardly any fuss. This was no neglected and abandoned child.

"Who's asking for your opinion?"

"I'm entitled to my opinion."

"That you are. You'd do well to remember your place and to keep your opinions to yourself."

"Don't you wonder where he came from?" Elsa wondered how her longtime friend could simply pretend not to notice the obvious inconsistencies.

"No. And if you know what's good for you, you'll put those silly notions out of your head and be about your work. There are some things we're better off not knowing."

Elsa's gaze again wandered to the sleeping child. He really was none of her concern—not in that way anyhow. And asking questions and jumping to conclusions weren't included in her duties.

Perhaps her friend was right.

NICK STARED at a framed photograph of Laura as a child while he waited for his call to be transferred to Ian's office. Perched in the saddle atop a sandy-colored pony, Laura beamed at the camera, her smile wide and bright. Nick decided the moment had been captured when she was about five. All that angel blond hair hung around her slim shoulders like a cape of silk. Her big brother, James Ed, who would have been about twenty-one, sported an Ole Miss letter sweater and gripped the lead line to the pony's bridal. His own smile appeared every bit as bright as his sister's.

A frown furrowed Nick's brow. What happened, he wondered, between then and now to change their lives so drastically? With a heavy sigh, he placed the picture in its original position on the oak mantel. Nick stared at the frozen frame in time for a second or two more. Had James Ed been a doting brother then? Did he really care about Laura the way he claimed to now? Laura certainly didn't think so.

Ian Michaels's accented voice sounded in Nick's ear, drawing his attention back to the cellular telephone and the call he had made. "Hey, Ian, it's Nick. I need you to check on a few things for me." Nick paused for Ian to grab a pen. "Review the file on Laura Proctor again and see if you can dig up anything new." Nick scrubbed a hand over his unshaven face, then frowned at the realization that he hadn't taken time to shave. After getting Laura settled in the Proctor country home, he had stayed up what was left of the night—early morning actually—watching over her.

"I didn't find anything when I ran that background check on her brother a couple of years ago." Another frown creased Nick's forehead. He'd been pretty distraught at the time; maybe he missed something. "I want you to look again. See if I overlooked anything at all. Something just isn't kosher down here. I can feel it," Nick added thoughtfully. He listened as Ian mentioned several areas that might turn up something new if he dug deeply enough.

"Sounds good," Nick agreed. "And, listen, check out that hospital in Louisiana that claims to have provided care for Laura for the past eighteen months. I want to know the kind of treatment she received, the medication she took—hell, I want to know what she ate for the last year and a half." Nick smiled at Ian's suggested means of collecting the requested and highly sensitive information. "Just don't get caught," Nick said. "Call me as soon as you have anything."

Nick flipped the mouthpiece closed and deposited the phone into his jacket pocket. He massaged his chin and considered his next move. There really wasn't much he could do until he heard from Ian. He let go a heavy breath. Except for keeping Laura out of trouble and, of course, getting the truth out of her. He should probably check on her now, he realized.

The Proctor country home was a ranch-style house of about three thousand square feet that was more mansion than home. Polished oak floors and rich, dark wainscoting and stark white walls represented the mainstay of the decor. The furnishings were an eclectic blend of antiques and contemporary, complemented by oriental wool rugs. The place was well maintained. The caretaker, Mr. Rutherford, appeared to stay on top of things. Upon James Ed's instructions, Rutherford had dropped by and adjusted the thermostat to a more comfortable setting, even stocked the refrigerator before Nick and Laura arrived. The old man had gone to a lot of trouble in the middle of the night. He also left a note with his telephone number in case they needed anything. Nick wasn't sure the guy could be of any real assistance to him unless the central heating unit died or the water heater went out, but he appreciated the gesture.

From the foyer Nick took the west hall and headed in the direction of Laura's bedroom. There were two bedrooms and two bathrooms at each end of the house. Laura's was the far-thest from the main part of the house. Nick's was directly across the hall from hers. Nick opened the door and walked quietly across the plush carpeting to her bedside. She hadn't moved since the last time he checked on her. That bothered him. Laura hadn't shown any true violent tendencies in his opinion. A faint smile tilted his lips. Well, except for the way she crowned him with that coffee mug. Nick touched the still tender place at his temple. But that had been in self-defense, at least from Laura's standpoint. Yet they had kept her drugged as if she were a serious threat.

Nick considered the shallow knife wound on her chest and the tiny prick at the base of her throat. The injuries weren't consistent with anything self-inflicted in his opinion. Anger kindled inside him when he considered that no one had tended the injuries. He had done that himself, and then replaced the bloodstained T-shirt with a clean one Sandra had provided. Oh, Sandra had been apologetic enough. She had tried, she insisted, to take care of the wounds, but Laura had fought her touch. Nick wasn't sure he fully believed the woman, but that really didn't matter now.

Laura was safe for the moment. And one damned way or another he intended to see that she stayed that way. When she was up to it, he would get the answers he wanted. But first he had to unravel the mystery of where Laura had been and what she had been doing for the past two years. His gut told him that the answers he wanted about the man who shot him were somehow tangled in those missing months.

The pills Sandra had given him for Laura right before they left Jackson caught his eye. Nick sat down on the edge of the bed and picked up the prescription bottle to review the label. Take one or two every twelve hours. The pharmacist he had called this morning for information regarding the drug had said that the dosage was the strongest available. He had seemed surprised at the instructions to administer the medication more than once in a twenty-four hour period. Nick sighed and set the bottle back on the night table. The medication was strong enough that Laura hadn't moved a muscle.

Nick watched her breathe for a long while, just as he had done for hours last night. He closed his eyes and resisted the urge to touch her. Touching her would be a serious mistake. He had to stay in control of the situation this time. Nick pushed to his feet. Whenever she roused from the drug-induced slumber, she would likely be hungry. Nick left the room without looking back. A quick inventory of what the kitchen had to offer would keep him occupied for a while. If any supplies were needed he would just call Mr. Rutherford and put in an order.

When Nick reached the spacious kitchen a light knock sounded from the back door. A quick look through a nearby window revealed an older man, in his sixties maybe, waiting on the back stoop. Mr. Rutherford, Nick presumed from the overalls and the work boots.

"Howdie, young fella," the old man announced as soon as Nick opened the door. "I'm Carl Rutherford. Came by to see if you had everything you needed."

"Good morning, Mr. Rutherford. I'm Nick Foster." Nick pushed a smile into place and extended his hand.

"A pleasure to meet you, Mr. Foster." Rutherford clasped Nick's hand and shook it firmly

"Please, call me Nick. And thank you, you've taken care of everything here quite nicely."

Mr. Rutherford beamed with pride. "I've been seeing after this place for nearly thirty years." His expression grew suddenly somber. "How's Miss Laura this morning?"

Nick hesitated only a moment before stepping back.

"Come in, Mr. Rutherford. I was about to have another cup of coffee."

"You can call me Carl," he insisted as he stepped inside.

Nick gestured for him to have a seat, then closed and locked the door. "How do you take it, Carl? Black?"

Carl settled himself into a chair at the breakfast table. "No sir, I like a little cream in mine if that's not too much trouble."

Nick shot him an amused look. "No trouble at all. You asked about Laura." Nick withdrew two cups from the cabinet near the sink and placed them on the counter. He had already gone through one pot. "She's sleeping right now." Nick frowned as he poured the dark liquid into the cups. "I'm not sure I can answer your question about her well-being with any real accuracy."

Carl huffed an indignant breath. "Was never a thing wrong with that little girl as long as she lived here."

Nick eyed the old man curiously as he stirred the cream into his coffee. "Tell me about Laura…before," he suggested cautiously. "Maybe that will give me some insight to what's going on now," he added at the older man's suspicious look.

Carl folded his arms over his chest and leaned back in his chair, lifting the two front legs off the floor. "She was a mighty sweet little thing growing up. Everybody loved her. Like an angel she was."

Nick had made that same connection several times himself. There was just something angelic and seemingly vulnerable about Laura's features. "She never got into trouble in school?" Nick placed both cups on the table and sat down across from his talkative visitor.

Carl shook his head adamantly. "No sir." He waved off the obvious conclusions. "Oh, the tale was that she got a little wild right before she went off to college." He made a scoffing sound in his throat. "That's why James Ed rushed her off to that fancy college up north."

"And you don't think that was the case?" Nick watched the older man's swiftly changing expressions.

"Land sakes no!" The chair legs plopped back to the floor. "Wasn't a thing wrong with that little girl except she had a mind of her own. She didn't fall into step like James Ed demanded." He harrumphed. "Why she was just like her daddy, that's all."

"Like her father how?" Nick's interest was piqued now. He sipped his coffee and listened patiently.

"You see, I worked for James Ed's granddaddy, James Senior, when I first moved to this county," Carl explained. "Right before James Ed's daddy, James Junior, went off to college he got a little wild."

Nick eyed him skeptically. "What do you mean wild?"

The old man shrugged. "Oh, you know, running with the wrong crowd. Even got himself involved with a girl from the wrong side of the tracks."

"Rebellious, like Laura?"

Carl nodded. "So the tale goes."

"What happened?"

"Well, James Junior got himself hustled off to one of them Ivy League law schools." The old man frowned in concentration. "Harvard, I believe it was. There was a bit of a stir about it. All the big shots hereabouts have always gone to Ole Miss. James Senior went to Ole Miss."

"But not James Ed's father?"

"Nope." Carl took a hefty swallow of his coffee. "When James Junior got back, he joined his daddy's law practice and married a girl of the right standing, if you know what I mean."

Nick considered his words for a time before he spoke. "What happened to the other girl?"

"Can't rightly say."

"So you think James Ed ushered Laura off to school in Boston in order to keep her out of trouble here."

"Yep." He leveled a pointed look at Nick. "But I think it amounted to nothing more than James Ed being too busy taking care of business and building his political career to deal with a hard-to-handle teenager." Red staining his cheeks as if realizing too late he had said too much, Carl scooted his chair back and got to his feet. "Thank you for the coffee, Nick. I'd better get going. Lots to do, you know." He turned before going out the door and met Nick's gaze one last time. "Give Laura my best, will you?"

Nick assured him that he would do just that. After the old man left Nick paced restlessly. He slid off his jacket and hung it on the back of a chair. For the next half hour he played the conversation over and over in his head, looking for any kind of connection. Each time he came up blank. Not taking any chances, he put in another quick call to Ian and added James Ed's daddy to the list of pasts to be looked into.

Maybe if he looked long and hard enough he would find at least some answers.

LAURA LICKED her dry lips and tried to swallow. Her throat felt like a dusty road. With a great deal of effort she opened her eyes. Focus came slowly. Where was she? Pink walls. Shelves lined with stuffed animals and a collection of dolls brought a smile to her parched lips.

Home.

She was home.

And Nick was here.

The events of the past few days came crashing into her consciousness. Laura wilted with reaction. *Her baby.* Oh, God, where was her baby? Clenching her jaw, she forced the overwhelming grief away. She had to get up. She couldn't find her baby like this.

Her arms trembling, Laura pushed to a sitting position. Her muscles were sore and one leg was asleep. Grimacing at the foul taste in her mouth and the bitter knots in her stomach, Laura stumbled out of bed. She made her way to the bathroom and took care of necessary business, including brushing her teeth. Using her hand, she thirstily drank from the faucet, then splashed some of the cool water on her face. Laura felt like she had been on a three-day drinking binge. She supposed she should be thankful for the dulling effects of the drugs, for if she were to have to face this nightmare with full command of her senses—

Laura couldn't complete the thought. Focus on something else, she ordered herself. Clumsily she fumbled through drawers until she found a hairbrush. Straightening out the mess her hair was in took some time and focused effort. Though still groggy, she felt at least a little human then.

Dressed in nothing but an oversized T-shirt and panties from the bag Sandra had sent along, Laura went in search of Nick. She needed to know if he had made any headway in the search for her son.

Laura's heart squeezed at the thought of her baby. A wave of dizziness washed over her. She sagged against the wall for a few seconds to allow the weakness to pass. *Please, God,* she prayed, *don't let anyone hurt my baby.* She closed her eyes tightly to hold back the burn of tears. Crying would accomplish nothing.

Robby, where are you? she wanted to scream.

Laura forced her eyes open and pushed away from the wall. She had to be strong. Her son was depending on her. If no one would believe her, she would have to find a way to escape. Somehow she would find Robby herself.

Somehow…somehow.

A touch of warmth welled inside her when she considered that Nick had rescued her. Maybe he believed her just a little. That shred of hope meant more to her than he would ever know.

Laura passed through the foyer and checked both the den and the living room. No Nick. She frowned and for the first time noticed it was dark outside. Had she slept through another day? God, how long had her baby been missing now? She repressed the thought. One thing at a time. She had to find Nick first.

The scent of food suddenly hit her nostrils. Laura staggered with reaction. How long had it been since she had eaten? She shook her head. She had no idea. Following the mouthwatering aroma, Laura found Nick in the kitchen hovering over the stove. She opened her mouth to call his name, but caught herself. She propped against the doorjamb instead and took some time to admire the father of her child.

Nick wore his thick black hair shorter than she remembered, Laura realized for the first time. But it looked good on him, she admitted. Nick was one of those guys who had a perpetual tan, the kind you couldn't buy and you couldn't get on the beach. His skin was flawless. And those lips. Full and sensual, almost feminine. Laura took a long, deep breath to slow the rush of desire flowing through her. From the beginning she had been fiercely attracted to the man. Laura had only made love with one other man, and that one time had proven more experimental than passionate.

There was just something about Nick. Laura closed her eyes and relived the night they had spent making love. A storm had raged outside, roaring like a wild beast with its thunder. Flash after flash of lightning had lit the room, silhouetting their entwined bodies in shadows on the wall. His kiss, his touch, the feel of his bare skin against hers….

"Laura?"

Laura's lids fluttered open, her attention drifted back from the sweet memory of making love with Nick, of making their baby. Those assessing green eyes, the color of polished jade met hers.

"Feeling better?"

A trembling smile curled her lips. Her heart wanted so to trust this man. Every fiber of her being cried out with need in his presence. "A little," she replied. Laura shoved a handful of hair behind her ear and trudged slowly across the room. Damn, she hated this zombie-status feeling. She leaned against the counter and peered into the steaming pot. Soup. She closed her eyes and inhaled deeply of the heavenly scent.

"Hungry? You slept through lunch."

The sound of his deep voice rasped through her soul. That knowing gaze remained on hers, analyzing. "Yes," she murmured. With Nick wearing jeans and a tight-fitting polo shirt, Laura had an amazing view of all that muscled terrain she remembered with unerring accuracy.

Nick reached for a bowl. "Have a seat," he suggested.

Laura frowned when she noted the gun tucked into his waistband, but the image of those strange pink eyes made her glad Nick was armed.

"Sit down, Laura."

She snapped her gaze to his. Food. Oh yeah. He wanted her to eat. Though food would never fill the emptiness inside her, she knew she had to eat. But only the feel of her baby in her arms would ever make her whole again.

"Have you learned anything about my son?" she asked abruptly.

Nick shifted his intense gaze to the steaming soup. "I have a man working on it." After thoroughly stirring it, he met her gaze once more. "But to answer your question, no. We don't have any more details other than those you gave me."

Which were sketchy at best, he didn't add. Laura could hear the subtle censoring in his tone. Anxiety twisted in her chest. "I've got to find him, Nick." She sucked in a harsh breath. "Please, don't keep me here like a prisoner when my son is out there somewhere." She shook her head slowly. "I have to find him."

Nick clicked the stove off and turned his full attention to her. "You're not a prisoner, Laura. I didn't wake you this afternoon and give you the scheduled dose of medicine for that very reason. I want your head clear. I want to help you."

Hope bloomed in Laura's chest. "You believe me?" she whispered, weak with relief. Laura blinked back the moisture pooling in her eyes.

He studied her for a long moment before he answered. "Let's just say, I'm willing to go with that theory until I have reason *not* to." He cocked his head speculatively. "Can you live with that?"

Laura gave a jerky nod. "As long as we find my baby I can live with anything."

Warning flashed in those green depths. "If you make a run for it, or give me one second of grief—"

"I won't," Laura put in quickly. "I swear, Nick. I'll do whatever you say."

Tension throbbed in the silence that followed. "All right," he finally said, then gestured to the table. "Have a seat and I'll be your server for the evening." A smile slid across those full lips.

Laura nodded and made herself comfortable at the table. Nick might still have reservations, but at least he planned to give her the benefit of the doubt. That's all she could ask at this point. And he had effectively stalled James Ed's plans to send her away.

Her eyes drinking in his masculine beauty, and comparing

each physical trait to that of her small son, Laura watched Nick prepare her dinner and set it before her. Robby looked so much like his father. Laura longed to share that secret with Nick.

But she couldn't.

Not until she proved her case—her sanity. She frowned. She had to find her son, and then prove herself a fit mother to the man who possessed the power to legally take her child from her. Laura's heart ached at the possibility that Nick would likely never forgive her for keeping his son from him. He would probably hate her. She shook off that particular dread. She had enough to worry about right now. Some things would have to wait their turn to add another scar to her heart.

"Water or milk?" he asked.

"Water is fine," she replied with a small smile. "I'm still feeling a little queasy." His answering smile as he sat down across the table from her took her breath away.

Laura squeezed her eyes shut and tried to clear the lingering haze that continued to make coherent thought a difficult task. Not to mention she couldn't keep drooling over Nick. Maybe once she got some food into her empty stomach she could think more rationally. Uncertain as to how her queasy stomach would react, Laura took a small taste of the soup. Swallowing proved the hardest step in the process. Finally, she managed.

"I hope that look on your face has nothing to do with the palatability of the cuisine."

With a wavering smile, Laura swallowed again, then shook her head. "It's wonderful. I'm just not as hungry as I first thought." Her stomach roiled in protest of that tiny taste.

Nick's concerned expression tugged at her raw emotions. "You need to eat, Laura."

She sipped her water, trying her level best not to rush from the table and purge her body of that single sip. "I know." How could she eat when she didn't know if her child had been fed? Laura froze, the glass of water halfway to her mouth. The glass plunked back to the table, her hand no longer able to support its weight. She couldn't.

Nick was suddenly at her side asking her if she was all right. Laura turned to him and stared into those green eyes that looked so much like Robby's. Don't lose it, Laura. She drew in an agitated breath. If you lose it he'll believe James Ed and the hospital report, and then you'll never find Robby. Laura blinked at the flash of fear she saw in Nick's eyes. He still cared, but would that be enough?

"I'm okay," Laura said stiffly. She clenched her hands into tight fists beneath the table. "I'm just not hungry that's all." She manufactured a dim smile for his benefit. "I'm sure it's just the medicine affecting my appetite."

Nick moved back to his own chair then. "You'll probably wake up in the middle of the night starved," he suggested warmly.

Laura nodded, struggling to keep her smile in place. He had gone to all this trouble for her, the least she could do was try to force down a few bites.

Nick folded his napkin carefully and laid it aside before meeting her gaze again. Laura moistened her lips in anxious anticipation of what was coming next. Did he know something that he hadn't wanted to tell her? Her heart butted against her rib cage. Something about Robby?

"We need to talk, Laura," he said quietly.

Laura's heart stilled in her chest. Adrenaline surged then, urging her heart back into a panicked rhythm.

That penetrating gaze bored into hers. "I need you to start at the beginning and tell me everything." He pressed her with that intense gaze. "And I mean everything. I can't help you if you hold anything back."

This wasn't about Robby. Relief so profound shook her that Laura trembled in its aftermath. "You're right, Nick," she said wearily. "There's a lot we need to talk about." She shrugged halfheartedly. "But I'm still not thinking clearly. Is it all right if we wait until morning when my head is a bit clearer?" Please let him say yes! Her emotions were far too raw right now, and she still felt groggy. She had to be in better control of herself before answering any questions. She might make a mistake. Laura couldn't risk saying the wrong thing while under the lingering influence of the medication.

"Tomorrow then," Nick relented.

Laura stood, intent on getting back to her room before he changed his mind. "I think I'll have a bath and crawl back into bed." She turned and headed for the door, concentrating on putting one foot in front of the other without swaying.

"Laura."

She paused. Laura closed her eyes and took a fortifying breath before she turned back to him. "Yes."

Nick sipped his water, then licked his lips. She shivered. "Don't lock the door in case I need to check on you," he told her.

Irritation roared through Laura's veins at his blatant reminder that he didn't completely trust her. "Sure," she said tightly.

Her movements still spasmodic and somewhat sluggish, Laura stormed back to her room. She jerked off her clothes and threw them on the unmade bed. Once in the bathroom, she not only slammed the door, but locked it for spite. She was an adult. She could certainly bathe herself without incident, she fumed, as she adjusted the faucet to a temperature as hot as her body would tolerate. The warm water would relax her aching muscles. Laura grabbed a towel and tossed it onto the chair next to the tub. Her reflection in the mirror suddenly caught her attention. The shallow half-moon slash on her upper chest zoomed into vivid focus.

The memory of the intruder who tried to kill her shattered all other thought. Image after image flooded her mind. Glittering pinkish eyes. The oddest color she had ever seen. The black ski mask. The glint of light on the wide blade of the knife. Her blood. *Time to die, princess.* Laura grasped the cool porcelain of the sink basin. She clenched her teeth to prevent the scream that twisted in her throat.

You're okay, you're okay, she told herself over and over. *You're safe. Nick is here now. He'll keep you safe.* Laura drew in a long, harsh breath. She had to stay calm. *You can't find Robby if you're hysterical all the time.*

The sound of the water filling the expansive garden tub behind her finally invaded Laura's consciousness. She relaxed her white-knuckled grip on the basin and turned slowly toward the brimming bath. Cool night air caressed her heated skin. Laura closed her eyes and savored the coolness. Nick must have opened a window. She inhaled deeply of the fresh air. She would feel better tomorrow, be more clearheaded. And maybe tomorrow would bring news of Robby. Hope shimmered through Laura as she stepped into the tub. The sooner she took her bath and got into bed, the sooner she would go to sleep and tomorrow would come.

Please, God, please let me find my baby.

Laura turned off the water and settled into its warm depths. She closed her eyes and allowed the heat to do its work. Absolute quiet surrounded her, except for the occasional drip of the faucet. Each tiny droplet echoed as it splashed into the steaming water, the sound magnified by the utter silence. Laura softly moaned her surrender as complete calm overtook her. Tension and pain slipped away. Fear and anxiety evaporated as the warmth lulled her toward a tranquil state just this side of sleep. She was so very tired. So sleepy…

She was under the water.

Laura struggled upward, but powerful hands held her down. Strong fingers gouged into her shoulders. She opened her eyes to see but inky blackness greeted her. Who turned out the lights? Her lungs burned with the need for oxygen. She wanted to scream. Laura flailed her arms, reaching, searching, grasping at thin air. Mental darkness threatened. *Don't pass out! Fight!* Her nails made contact with bare skin. She dug in deep. The grip on her loosened. She plunged upward. Blessed air filled her lungs.

Laura screamed long and loud before her head was forced beneath the water once more.

Chapter Six

Nick loaded the soiled dinnerware and utensils into the dishwasher and closed the door. He braced his hands on the counter and stared into the darkness beyond the kitchen window. Tomorrow he would have to make sure Laura ate something. She wouldn't regain her strength without food, and she would need all her energy to get through the next few days.

She was going to have to make a believer out of Nick. Laura would have to prove to him that someone had tried to kill her and that a child did exist…somewhere.

Laura's child.

Nick frowned at that thought. The idea had niggled at him for a while now. He and Laura had only made love once. If she did have a child, and if…he were the father—an unfamiliar emotion stirred inside him—that would make the baby…about fifteen months old. He would simply ask her the child's age. He shook his head in denial. That wasn't possible. If Laura had been pregnant with his child, surely she would have come to him for help rather than…

Nick cut off that line of thinking. There was no point in running scenarios when he still didn't know exactly what had happened two years ago. Nor did he know the real story about the events that led up to Laura's disappearance. As soon as

Laura was up to it, he intended to find out every detail. He would give her the benefit of the doubt on the kid. If she said she had a son, maybe she did. He couldn't imagine what purpose that particular lie served.

Unless, he considered reluctantly, she was suffering from the mental condition listed in the report from the hospital. Nick rubbed at the ache starting right between his eyes. And if she were in the hospital all that time, did that negate the possibility that there was a child? No point in working that angle until he had some word from Ian. In the meantime, Nick would just have to concentrate on getting some answers from Laura. He wasn't going to bring up the medication either—unless she asked for it. He had an uneasy feeling about those damned pills. Besides, he needed her head clear if he planned to ascertain any reliable answers.

Just another job, he told himself for the hundredth time. Nothing else. Laura Proctor was his assignment, and he damned sure intended to get the job done right this time. Getting to the bottom of this tangled mystery once and for all was the only thing that kept Nick here. That and his damned sense of justice. If there was any chance Laura was right and James Ed had set all this up…

Who was he kidding? Nick had spent more than twenty-four hours monitoring James Ed's house because he couldn't bear to leave Laura under those circumstances. Fool that he was, he still wanted to protect her. Poised to push the dishwasher's cycle button, a muffled sound made Nick hesitate. He quickly analyzed the auditory sensation. A scream? Dread pooled in his gut.

Laura.

Nick bolted from the kitchen, shouting her name. Dodging family heirlooms as he flew down the hall, Nick ticked off a mental checklist of items in a bathroom with which one could hurt oneself. Razor topped the accounting. Nick cursed himself for not checking the room first. Why the hell had he allowed her even this much free rein? His heart pounded with the fear mushrooming inside him.

He skidded to a stop outside the closed door and twisted the knob. Locked. "Laura!" he banged hard on the door. "Laura, answer me, dammit!"

Water sloshed and something clattered to the floor. He could hear Laura's frantic gasps for air between coughing jags. "Laura!" Nick clenched his jaw and slammed his shoulder into the door, once, twice. The lock gave way and he shoved into the dark, humid room. He flipped on the overhead light.

Naked and dripping wet, Laura was on her hands and knees next to the tub. She struggled to catch her breath, water pooled on the tiled floor around her. An assortment of scented candles and a silver tray were scattered about near the end of the tub. No blood anywhere that he could see. Relief rushed through Nick. He grabbed the towel draped across a chair and, ignoring the pain roaring in his knee, knelt next to Laura. Gently, he wrapped the towel around her trembling body and drew her into his arms.

Nick sat down on the edge of the tub and pulled Laura onto his lap. "It's okay," he murmured against her damp hair. "I've got you." Nick swiped back the wet strands clinging to her face. "What happened, honey, did you fall asleep in the water?" Nick called himself every kind of fool for not considering that the drugs still in her system might make her drowsy again. His gut clenched at the idea of what could have happened.

Still gulping in uneven breaths, Laura lifted her face to his. "He…he tried to drown me. I…" She sucked in another shaky breath. "I screamed…" Her eyes were huge with fear. "The window." Laura lifted one trembling hand and pointed to the window. "He went out the window."

Frowning, Nick followed her gesture. He stared at the half-open window and the curtain shifting in the cold night air. "Why did you open the window? It's freezing outside."

Laura drew back and searched his gaze, confusion cluttering her sweet face. "I didn't," she said slowly. "I thought you did." She frowned. "He must have come—"

"Now why the hell would I do something as stupid as leaving the window open?" he demanded, disbelief coloring his tone.

One blond brow arched, accenting the irritation that captured her features. "But you thought I did *something that stupid?*"

Nick shook his head. "I didn't mean it like that," he defended.

"Sure you did." Laura struggled out of his grasp, jerked to her feet and promptly slipped on the wet tile.

He steadied her, his grasp firm on her damp arms. Nick stood then, and glared down at her. He refused to acknowledge all the naked flesh available for admiration. He couldn't think about that right now. "I only meant," he ground out impatiently, "that *someone* opened the window and it wasn't me."

She smiled saccharinely. "So, of course, it was me."

"Well, there doesn't seem to be anyone else around," he said hotly. A muscle jumped in his tightly clenched jaw, adding another degree of tension to the annoyance already building inside him.

Laura shrugged out of his grasp. "No joke, Sherlock." She adjusted the towel so that it covered more of her upper chest, including the healing injuries from her last encounter with...who or whatever.

Nick forced away the unreasonable fear that accompanied that memory. There was no evidence that anyone else was in the damned room but Laura that time either. The image of her naked body slammed into his brain, reminding him of what he had seen with his own eyes. Nick had memorized every perfect inch of her two years ago; tonight's refresher had only made bad matters worse. She was still as beautiful, as vulnerable as she had been then.

Focusing on the task to counter his other emotions, Nick stepped to the window, closed and locked it before turning back to a fuming Laura. "I'll have to check the security system to find out why the alarm didn't go off when the window was opened. In the meantime, why don't you tell me exactly what happened," he suggested as calmly as possible.

"We're wasting time," she snapped. "Whoever tried to hold my head under the water—" she shuddered visibly, then stiffened "—is getting away." Laura fanned back a drying tendril of blond silk. "You're the one with the gun. Are you going to help me or what?"

Nick released a disgusted breath. "Laura, there is no one else here."

"Fine." She pivoted and stamped determinedly toward the door, slipping again in her haste.

Nick reached for her but she quickly regained her balance and stormed out the door. His arm dropped back to his side. Now this, he mused, was the Laura he remembered. Sassy and determined. Grimacing with each step, Nick stalked into the bedroom after her. He snapped to attention at the sight of Laura shimmying into her jeans, the tight denim catching on the damp skin of her shapely backside. Apparently deciding time was of the essence, she had foregone panties.

"What—" Nick cleared his throat. "What the hell do you think you're doing?"

Laura yanked an oversized T-shirt over her head and turned to face him just as the soft cotton fell over her breasts. "I'm going after him."

Nick choked out a sound of disbelief. He braced his hands at his waist and shook his head. "No you're not."

Laura stepped into her sneakers, plopped down onto the end of the bed and tied first one and then the other, her fiercely determined gaze never leaving his. If this was a war of wills, she need not waste her time. Nick could outwait Job himself when he set his mind to it.

"Just try and stop me," she challenged as she shot back to her feet. Laura flipped her still-damp hair over her shoulders. "I'm tired of being treated like I'm a few bricks shy of a load. And I'm sick of no one believing anything I say." She walked right up to him. "Someone took my son. The same someone that's trying to kill me." She glowered at Nick, her eyes glittering with the rage mounting inside her. "You can either help me or get out of my way."

One second turned to five as Nick met her glower with lead in his own. When it was clear she had no intention of backing down, Nick's mouth slid into a slow smile. What the hell? He could use a walk in the cold air after this little encounter. The image of her naked, shapely rear flashed through his mind and sent a jolt of desire straight to his groin. "All right. We do it your way." Hope flashed in her eyes. "This time," he added firmly. Nick stepped aside and Laura darted past him.

"We need a flashlight," he called out as she disappeared around a corner.

"It's in the kitchen. I'll get it!" she shouted determinedly.

Nick moved his head slowly from side to side. He had to be crazier than she was supposed to be to do this. It was late. Laura should be in bed. His knee hurt like hell, and he could damned sure use a little shut-eye. He had hardly slept at all the last three nights. But he couldn't bring himself to deny her this. She was so sure…a part of him wanted to believe her. That same part that had fallen for a sassy, innocently seductive Laura two years ago.

"Got it." Laura almost hit him head-on when she barreled through the kitchen doorway.

"Good," he muttered. Nick followed Laura to the den but stopped her when she would have thrown the patio door open and burst out into the November darkness. "Hold on there, hotshot." She cast him a withering look. "I'm the one with the gun, remember?"

Laura blinked. "Right." She stepped back, yielding to Nick's lead.

More for her benefit than anything else, Nick drew his weapon from its position at the small of his back. "Stay behind me," he instructed. She bobbed her head up and down in adamant agreement. "And don't turn the flashlight on unless I tell you."

Nick flipped the latch and slid the door open. Instantly, the cold air slapped him in the face, escalating his senses to a higher state of alert. He surveyed the backyard for a full thirty seconds before stepping onto the patio. Slowly, with as much stealth as possible with Laura right behind him, he made his way down the back of the house until he reached the window outside the bathroom that connected to Laura's bedroom.

"Give me the light." Nick took the yellow plastic instrument and slid the switch to the on position. As thoroughly as possible with nothing but a small circle of illumination, Nick examined the area around the window. The window itself, the ledge, the portion of brick wall from the ledge to the ground, then the ground. Nothing. The window showed no signs of forced entry. With the ground frozen, there wouldn't be any tracks, and the nearby shrubbery appeared undisturbed. Nick crouched down and examined the dormant-for-the-winter grass a little closer just to be sure. He saw absolutely no indication that anyone had been there, but with the current weather conditions that determination would not be conclusive.

"Did you find anything?" Laura chafed her bare arms with her hands for warmth.

"Let's go back inside," Nick urged. "It's freezing out here."

Laura dug in her heels when he would have ushered her toward the patio. She lifted her chin defiantly. "You still don't believe me."

"Look." Nick tucked his weapon back into his waistband. "It's not a matter of whether or not I believe you." His grip tightened on the smooth plastic of the flashlight, its beam lighting the ground around their feet. "The fact of the matter is there's nothing to go on—either way."

Nick caught her by one arm when she would have walked away. "*If* anyone was here, there's no one here now and—"

"Go to hell, Foster," she said from between clenched teeth.

His fingers tightened around her smooth flesh. "And," he repeated, "there is no indication that anyone climbed in or out this window."

"He was here," she insisted, her voice low and fierce with anger. "He tried to drown me. And you know what?" She jerked with emotion. "I think he's going to keep trying to kill me until he succeeds. Will you believe me then, Nick?"

This time Nick released her. He watched until she disappeared through the patio door. He closed his eyes and fought the need to run after her. To assure her that he would never let that happen. What was he supposed to believe? All the facts pointed to Laura as being mentally unstable, suicidal even. Nick flinched at the idea. Not one single shred of evidence existed to support her claims, except the knife wounds James Ed wanted him to believe were self-inflicted. James Ed didn't appear to have any reason to lie. Nick opened his eyes and shook his head. Then why the hell did he want—need—to believe her so badly?

Disgusted with himself as well as the situation, Nick strode slowly toward the still-open door. Maybe he was the wrong man for this job. Apparently he couldn't maintain a proper perspective in Laura's presence. "Big surprise," he muttered.

Nick's gut suddenly clenched. The hair on the back of his neck stood on end. He stopped stock-still. Someone was watching. He felt it as strongly as he felt his own heart beating in his chest. Nick turned around ever so slowly and surveyed the yard once more. Taking his time, he studied each dark corner, watching, waiting for any movement whatsoever.

Nothing.

Nick scrubbed a hand over his beard-roughened face and considered the possibility that maybe he couldn't trust his own instincts anymore. Maybe paranoia was like hysteria, contagious.

One thing was certain, time would tell the tale. In Nick's experience, given time all things became clear.

Nick just hoped that time would be on their side.

"HARDHEADED JERK," Laura muttered as she flung another dresser drawer open. She rifled through the contents, then slammed it shut. She needed a change of clothes. Her own clothes. Surely there would be something here she could wear.

Laura paused in her search and tried to remember the last time she had been here and what she had brought with her. Two years ago. The final barbecue bash of the summer. She remembered. James Ed had insisted she come along. He had invited Rafe. It was Labor Day weekend. Only two months before…

Closing her eyes, Laura fought the memories that tugged at her ability to stay focused. Two months before she met Nick, fell in love with his self-assurance and intensity. Ten years older than her, he seemed to know everything, to be able to do anything. He was so strong, yet so tender. The way he had made love to her changed something deep inside her forever. And he had given her Robby. Tears threatened her flimsy composure. Laura clutched the edge of the dresser when emotion kicked her hard in the stomach. How was she supposed to go on when she didn't know if her baby was safe or not. Had he eaten? Was someone bathing him and keeping his diapers changed? Pain slashed through her, making her knees weak.

No! Laura straightened with a jerk. No. Robby was fine and she was going to find him. She refused to believe anything else. Somehow she would get away and find him. Somehow…

Laura jerked the next drawer open and forced herself to continue her search. The next drawer contained some under-clothes and socks, the one after that an old pink sweater. Laura exhaled a puff of relief. At least it was a start. All she had to do was get away from Nick, then she would go back to Doc's clinic and look for clues—

"Laura."

Startled from her plans, she met his gaze in the mirror above the dresser. He stood in the doorway, looking too con-cerned and too damned good. Laura willed away her heart's reaction to the father of her child. She didn't want to feel this way about Nick. She didn't want to love him. He would never believe her. Never help her the way she needed him to. Laura clenched her teeth and blinked away the emotion shining in her eyes. She didn't need Nick. She could take care of her-self and her son…

…if she could just find him.

"What are you doing?" His gaze strayed to the items she had stacked on top of the dresser.

To lie was her first thought, but Nick was too smart for that. He would see through her in about two seconds. "I'm pack-ing myself a bag." Laura turned to face him. She gripped the edge of the dresser's polished wood surface for extra support. "Because the first chance I get I'm out of here."

Nick took two steps in her direction. He paused then and slowly looked the room over as if seeing her childhood sum-

mer sanctuary for the first time, and wanting to commit what
he saw to memory. Finally, his gaze moved back to hers, dark,
intense. Laura shivered with awareness. Heat stirred inside
her. She wanted to touch him, to have him touch her. She
swallowed.

"And you think I'm going to allow you to do that."

It wasn't a question, she knew. She leveled her gaze on his,
and poured every ounce of determination she possessed into
that unsettling eye contact. "You have to sleep sometime."

Two more steps disappeared behind him. "Is that a threat?"

"Yes." Laura's heart rate accelerated. "It is."

"Just for the moment, let's say you were successful in your
plan." He paused, cocked his handsome head and assessed her
thoroughly. Laura stiffened to prevent her body's need to
tremble beneath his blatant act of intimidation. Did he have
any idea how he still affected her? "What will you do?"

She held her spine rigid when her body wanted to sag with
despair as her harsh reality momentarily pushed aside all else.
"I'll find my baby," she told him.

He moved closer. The smooth movement of denim-en-
cased muscle dragged her attention to those long legs and the
limp that had first endeared him to her. Nick had gotten that
limp by taking a bullet intended for a client he had been assigned to protect the year before Laura met him. He had taken
a bullet for her, too. Because that's the kind of man he was.
And despite his distrust of her, he had still come back to get
her. To protect her. Laura's breathing grew shallow and irreg-
ular as renewed need twisted inside her. Giving herself a mental shake, Laura jerked her gaze back to his intense, analyzing
one. She had to focus. But she was exhausted, mentally and
physically. She needed so much for Nick to hold her right
now. But at the same time, Laura needed to escape his watch.

"And the man who's trying to kill you?"

Laura's lips trembled then tightened with the blast of outrage that raced through her at his words. He didn't fully believe her. Why the hell was he asking? "I've been outmaneuvering him for two years. I can do it again."

"Until recently you mean," he suggested quietly. Another half yard of carpet disappeared between them.

"He would never have caught up with me and my son if it hadn't been for you," she told him tautly. Bottom line, Nick was one of the bad guys now. Why didn't he just leave her alone? Why had he come back for her? A tiny seed of hope sprouted in her heart despite her efforts to resist that very emotion.

"So you consider this to be my fault?"

"That's right." Laura pressed back against the dresser as he came closer still. "I hope you can live with it," she added bitterly.

He stopped two steps away. "Oh, I can live with it," he said with complete certainty. "If you can live with this."

Before Laura could fathom what he intended, Nick jerked his shirt from his waistband and pulled it over his head in one fluid motion. Laura's heart slammed mercilessly against her sternum. Her gaze riveted to his bare chest. Broad, tanned, muscled and sprinkled with dark hair. The memory of touching him, making love with him, swirled inside her. Then she saw it. The single jagged scar that marred that amazing terrain just beneath his heart. Laura's own heart dropped to her stomach then. A little higher and Nick would certainly have died.

"But I almost didn't live with it," he said, his voice dangerously low. A muscle flexed in that square jaw of his. "So while we're on the subject of blame, why don't you tell me about the guy you watched put this bullet hole in me. The one you disappeared with while I was bleeding to death." His fingers moved gently over the scar, but there was nothing gentle about his voice or his expression.

Fear, regret, pain churned inside her, but Laura fought to maintain her composure. She had to do this, had to say what needed to be said—for the good it would do. How could he think she had willingly left him to die? "It was my fault that you got shot," she said in a rush. Surprise flickered in Nick's gaze. "Not one day has gone by since that I haven't wished I could go back and somehow prevent what happened. But I swear to you, Nick, I didn't go anywhere with him. He tried to kill me, too."

Wariness slipped into his expression. "But you recognized him, Laura. I saw it in your eyes."

Laura raked her fingers through her wet hair. Her hands trembled so she clenched them into tight fists. God, how could she ever explain everything? "Look," she began wearily. "I admit that I got into some trouble in college." She met Nick's guarded gaze. "Just like James Ed said. But I know now that I was just desperate for his attention." Laura closed her eyes and forced away the bitter memories twisting inside her brain. "I needed him and he was never there for me. He just wanted me away from him." She stared at the floor for a while before she continued. "When I came home after graduation, he tried to marry me off to Rafe Manning." Laura didn't miss Nick's reaction to Rafe's name. She tamped down the renewed burst of hope that maybe he did feel something for her.

"But you refused," he prompted.

Laura nodded. "James Ed wasn't very happy. And I pretty much made a fool of myself about it," she admitted. "But the car accident and all that other stuff was not my fault." She leveled her gaze on Nick's, hoping to convey the depth of her sincerity. "I tried to tell James Ed that the brakes failed, but he wouldn't listen to anything I had to say."

Nick snagged her hand. His thumb glided across the scar marking her wrist. "And this?"

Laura lifted her free hand and stared at the white slash of a scar. "All I know is that I came home from a party one night." She licked her dry lips. "James Ed and I had argued before I left. So I had a little too much to drink I guess. I came home and crashed on the bed. I woke up the next day in a hospital under suicide watch."

"You don't know for sure what happened then," Nick clarified.

She sucked in a weary breath. "I know I didn't do it. I was passed out. Besides, I had no reason to want to die."

Nick considered her words for a moment, then said, "Now, tell me about the man who shot me."

Laura tried without success to read Nick's closed expression. Did he believe anything she said? Would he believe what she was about to tell him now? Well, it was the truth. That's all she could do was give him the truth. "I saw him in James Ed's private office at the house a couple of times."

Nick's hands fisted at his sides, something fierce flashed in his eyes. "So you do know him?"

"I don't know him. I only saw him—"

"Be careful what you say next, Laura." There was no mistaking the emotion in his voice or his gaze then. Rage. Vengeance. "I know more than you think."

Laura shook her head in confused denial. "Why would you believe that? I did not know him. I still don't."

"I heard everything," Nick ground out.

"Everything?" She shook her head. "I don't understand what you mean." Laura had no idea what Nick was talking about.

Nick smiled, it was far from pleasant. "Oh you're good, Laura. Too good."

"What the hell are you talking about?"

"Before I blacked out completely, he told you that you didn't need me anymore, that it was just you and him now,"

Nick said coldly. "I heard him say it. You didn't deny it then, don't even think about denying it now."

Laura frowned, trying to remember. She allowed the painful memory to play out in her mind. She had screamed something like "why did you hurt him?" at the man after he shot Nick. Then he had said—oh God, she remembered. Laura met Nick's accusing glare. "He didn't mean it the way you think," she explained. "He meant that he had me where he wanted me—without protection."

"You expect me to believe that?"

Laura nodded. "I swear, Nick, it's the truth. I had never seen the man before in my life except the times I saw him in James Ed's office. That's what this is all about," she argued vehemently. "My brother wants me dead!"

"So you didn't leave willingly with the shooter?"

Astonishment struck her hard. Why wouldn't he believe her? "How could you think I left with him? That I left you hurt? He dragged me out to the riverbank and tried to kill me. He wanted it to look like a murder-suicide." Laura shook her head at Nick's still wary expression. How could she make him believe her? "The storm was still going strong. He lost his balance, and we both went over the edge. He hit his head on a rock on the way down. He never resurfaced, then I got swept away. I woke up the next day several miles down river. I was lost. It took me two days to find my way out of the woods."

"But you never came back, never let anyone know you were alive," Nick reminded her bitterly.

Laura slumped in defeat. "I thought you were dead. I knew my brother was trying to kill me. I didn't think coming back would be too bright."

"What about after you found out I was alive. Why not then? You could have come to me for help."

Uncertainty seized her. She had to tread carefully here.

Laura couldn't risk allowing him to discover the truth about
Robby. "You worked for James Ed. I knew you would take
me back to him. And that's just exactly what you did," she reminded him curtly.

Nick hesitated, his green eyes bored relentlessly into hers.
Something she couldn't read flickered in that fierce gaze.
"Even after what we had shared, you didn't trust me?"

"Did you trust me? Our whole relationship stemmed from
proximity and your desire to protect me. I…" Laura swallowed tightly. "I needed you so desperately. But how could I
know that it was safe to trust you completely?"

The seconds turned to minutes before Nick responded.
"You couldn't have," he offered flatly. "It's late. You should
get some rest," he said, effectively changing the subject. "I'll
check all the doors and windows, then I'll reset the alarm.
Somehow it failed," he added. He picked up his shirt and
started for the door.

Laura wasn't sure whether to be relieved or disappointed
that he had left their discussion at a standoff of sorts. He had
admitted what she knew as well. Two years ago everything
had happened so fast there was no time to learn each other.
What happened then hadn't been their fault. Just like now. Circumstances had brought them together, then torn them apart.
She closed her eyes and took a slow, deep breath. She was
tired. Sleep would come easily. Laura shivered. What if someone came into the house again? Maybe sleep wouldn't come
so easily, she decided. The alarm system was obviously no de-
terrent. And Nick couldn't be everywhere at once.

At the door Nick turned back to her. "One more question,"
he said offhandedly.

Laura's gaze connected with his. "What's that?"

"How old is your baby?"

Laura's breath fled from her lungs. "Why do you ask?" she

managed, her voice devoid of all inflection, her body paralyzed by uncertainty.

"Is there anything I should know about your child?"

She knew exactly what he meant. *Is the child mine?* Laura swallowed the words that wanted to spill out of her. "No," she said instead. Something in his expression changed. "There's nothing you need to know." She blinked back the tears that burned behind her eyes. "Except that I have to find him." She clamped down on her lower lip for a moment to hold her emotions at bay. "I'll die if anything happens to him."

He looked away. "Sleep. We'll talk more in the morning."

Laura watched him leave. Oh God. Why didn't she just tell him the truth?

Because she couldn't live without her son. And if Nick knew the truth, he would take Robby away. After all, Laura was considered unstable. And she couldn't prove any differently. Hadn't tonight's little episode added fuel to the fire? Laura shuddered at the memory of how those strong hands had held her beneath the water.

How would she ever be able to close her eyes now? Knowing her killer was near?

Panic slithering up her spine, Laura ran to first one window, then the next to make sure they were locked. She crawled into the bed and hugged her pillow to her chest.

No way would she be able to let her guard down tonight, even though Nick would be right next door.

All she had to do was stay awake….

Chapter Seven

Elsa smiled as she spooned another taste of strained carrots into the little boy's mouth. He was such a good child. How could anyone believe that this child had been neglected in any way? Elsa frowned. And the only way a mother would abandon a baby this healthy and sweet would be if she were dead.

She stalled, the spoon halfway to the baby's open mouth. If the mother and father were dead, why the abandonment story? The baby gurgled and swung his little fists about in protest. Elsa scolded herself for allowing her mind to drift.

"Okay, little one, be patient." She popped the next bite into his waiting mouth. "I'm just an old woman, and too slow for the lively likes of you," she cooed. The little boy loudly chanted his agreement in baby talk.

Elsa frowned again. This wasn't right. She had worked here for a very long time and nothing like this had ever happened before. Maybe she should slip in and take a look at the child's file. There would be a perfect opportunity day after tomorrow with the director away.

Elsa nodded resolutely. Yes, she would see what she could find out. Not that it would really do any good, but it would put her mind at ease.

LAURA JERKED AWAKE. Sunlight streamed in through the partially opened blinds. She rubbed her eyes and tried to gather her thoughts. She had finally given in and fallen asleep a few hours ago. Laura stilled. She had been dreaming. The image of Robby smiling and playing with his food filled her mind's eye. Laura closed her eyes and allowed the dream to warm her. She prayed that it was a good sign. Robby had to be all right.

Two loud raps echoed from the door. "Laura, are you up in there? In about three seconds I'm coming in," he warned.

So that's what woke her. Laura bounded off the bed and hurried to the door. Today she would find a way to prove to Nick that Robby was real. Then maybe he would put some serious effort into helping her. If not, she would set out on her own. She reached the door just as Nick opened it.

The grim expression on his face loudly proclaimed his thoughts without his having to open his mouth. For at least a moment he must have thought she had made good on her threat to make a run for it. The realization that he had even considered her capable of giving him the slip lightened Laura's mood considerably.

"Good morning," she said with exaggerated cheer. God, why did he have to look so good? Her pulse reacted the moment her eyes lit on him.

He took stock of the room and then settled his searching gaze on hers. "Really, what's good about it?"

Laura studied his chiseled features as she shoved her unbrushed hair back from her face. She cringed inwardly when she considered how she must look. Her hair a mess, her clothes slept in, no makeup. But not Nick. He always looked picture-perfect. Never a hair out of place. He looked as if he had taken great pains with every aspect of his appearance. But Laura knew that wasn't the case. Perfection came naturally to Nick. It was the same with his lovemaking. Slow, thorough. Laura's mouth went unbearably dry.

"We're alive," she offered in answer to his question, and directing her mind away from his expertise between the sheets. "That's definitely good. And maybe today I'll find my son."

"There's coffee in the kitchen," he said impassively. He ignored her comment about Robby. "We should finish last night's discussion."

"Okay," Laura replied just as impassively. "Give me five minutes to change." Today was his last chance, she reminded that part of her that wanted so to believe in him. If he didn't help her today…

Nick's gaze traveled down the length of her and back. She didn't miss the glint of male appreciation, but his gaze was hard when he met hers once more. "Five minutes. I've got a lot of questions that need answers." Without another word, he turned and walked away.

Laura shoved the door closed behind him. She blew out a breath of annoyance. *Men.* She would never understand them. She was the victim here! Laura railed silently. Why did he make her feel like the villain? Someone tried to kill her last night. *Again.* Why wouldn't Nick believe her?

James Ed. Laura crossed her arms over her chest and considered her loving brother. He had done this to her. Taken her life away, taken her child and the man she loved. And for what? Laura shook her head in aversion. Money. It was all about the money.

To hell with the money.

Maybe it was time Laura got down on his level. James Ed wasn't the only one who could play dirty. Laura clenched her teeth until her jaws hurt. Whatever it takes, she promised herself. One way or another she would get her son back.

SEVEN MINUTES LATER, Nick noted impatiently, Laura breezed into the kitchen looking for all the world like a little girl. Jeans hugged her shapely legs while an oversized pink sweater engulfed the rest of her. Her hair was pulled back high on her head in a ponytail. Her sweet face was freshly scrubbed and bright with hope. Nick's chest constricted. He swallowed that damned burning need to take her in his arms and just hold her. He couldn't do that. It would jeopardize his perspective even further. He had a job to do. He shifted in his chair. Damn. Three seconds in her presence and his body was already reacting.

Things between them had always been like this—fast and furious. But neither was to blame. Their circumstances were equally fast and furious. Despite that fact, something drew Nick to her, made him want to believe her. To trust her. Whether Laura was telling the complete truth or not, something was wrong here. His instincts warned him that Laura was in real danger. Evidence or no, things just didn't add up.

Laura popped a slice of bread into the toaster. Nick sipped his coffee and watched her graceful, confident movements. The drug had worn off completely now, he decided. Good. That would make things a lot easier, unless, of course, she became overwrought. Nick set his cup on the table and started to speak but speech eluded him when Laura bent over and poked around in the fridge.

He averted his gaze from her heart-shaped rear and passed a hand over his face. "I'm glad to see your appetite is back."

"I just realized I was starving." Milk in one hand, jam in the other, Laura shoved the fridge door closed with one slender hip. "I have no idea when I ate last." She smiled as if knowing some secret he wasn't privy to. Nick almost groaned at the angelic gesture. "But I'm about to make up for at least part of it."

"The man," Nick began, drawing her attention from spreading strawberry jam on her toast to him. "Did he actually tell you that James Ed hired him to kill you?" Nick had replayed their conversation a dozen times during the night. He kept coming up with the same questions. Questions he needed answered. And only Laura could answer them. Half the night had been spent running scenarios, the other half fighting the need to go to her bed. Nick tensed. That couldn't happen—even if she were to invite him, which was highly unlikely. This go-around Nick had to remain as personally detached as possible. It was the only way to really protect Laura, and to get to the bottom of whatever was going on.

Laura placed the butter knife on the counter. She frowned thoughtfully. "No, not in so many words. But when I asked him why he was doing this, he said 'for the money, of course.'" Laura shrugged. "Who would stand to gain from my death?" She met Nick's gaze then, hers certain in her conclusion. "James Ed."

"I checked his financial standing forward and backward. His assets were a bit shaky prior to the election two years ago, but he recovered. Most politicians barely skate through the election process without financial crisis. James Ed didn't seem to need your trust badly enough to kill for it, in my opinion." Nick pushed his now cold coffee aside. "He appeared to have enough money already."

Laura deposited her skimpy breakfast on the table and dropped into a chair. "Then why would that man have wanted to kill me if he weren't working for my brother?"

Nick lifted one shoulder in a semblance of a shrug. "It could have been a kidnap-ransom plot gone awry," he suggested. That had been the police's theory two years ago.

Laura shook her head. "No. He intended to kill me, then and there. What good's a ransom if the sacrificial lamb is already dead?"

She definitely had a point there. If only Nick had remembered more details about the man's physical features, maybe they could have nailed down his intent and his associates two years ago. But Nick had barely survived the gunshot and ensuing surgery. The entire event was forever a blur in his mind—except for the snatch of conversation he had heard. Nick would never forget that. The guy was dead according to Laura. Whatever had motivated him, he had gotten his in the end.

Nick took a deep breath and forced the old rage to retreat. "Maybe he was just a nutcase who wanted to get back at James Ed," he suggested.

Laura laughed humorlessly. "You just don't want to believe that James Ed is behind this little soap opera." She leveled her determined gaze on Nick's. "He tried to marry me off, then he tried to prove me mentally unstable. And when all that failed, he got desperate and hired someone to kill me. Think about it," she urged fiercely. "Ten million dollars is a lot of motivation. If I married, was pronounced mentally incompetent or dead before my twenty-fifth birthday, big brother gained control of the money. No matter what your investigation turned up, he wanted that money." Laura leaned back in her chair. "He still does." Laura blinked. "If he hasn't gotten it already."

Nick shook his head, still denying her assertion. "But why? He had enough of his own."

"Is there ever enough?"

Nick just couldn't reconcile the picture Laura painted with the man he knew. James Ed had truly grieved after Laura's disappearance. His happiness at having her back home was so clear a blind man could have seen it. "It just doesn't feel right," he countered.

Laura sighed. "I don't know anything to say that will convince you, but I know I'm right. And somehow he found out about my son and took him to get at me. He knows I won't go far as long as there's any chance my child is here somewhere." Her gaze grew distant. "How can I run from James Ed when he holds my heart in his hands?"

Laura's words touched Nick so deeply that he couldn't speak for a time. If Laura had a child, he would definitely help her find him. And if he discovered that James Ed was behind the threat to Laura, the man would not live to regret it. Finally, Nick looked from her untouched toast to her. "You should eat," he said quietly. No one was going to hurt Laura again. *But what about the hospital report?* his more logical side argued.

She shook her head. "No. You have something else to say." She pressed him with her gaze, reading him like an open book. "Say it."

"All right. How do you explain the hospital report? I read it myself." *Give me an answer I can live with,* Nick urged silently.

Laura pressed her lips together and blinked rapidly to fight the fresh tears shining in her eyes. "You know I've even considered that maybe I am crazy. Maybe I imagined the last two years." She shrugged one thin shoulder. "Maybe Robby isn't real." Laura flattened her palms on the table and slowly shook her head from side to side. "But I can't even imagine that. He is real, Nick. As real as you and me. And I have to find him, no matter what it takes." She drew in a bolstering breath. "There's no way I can live without him. He's all I have in this world. Can you understand that?"

Long minutes passed with nothing but silence and a kind of tension that only old lovers could feel between them. Emotions he knew he shouldn't feel battled with his need to stick with the facts. "Prove it," he demanded softly. "I need hard evidence, Laura."

"Okay." Laura licked her trembling lips. "Take me to the

clinic where he was born. They have records. Would that be proof enough?" she asked sarcastically.

"Absolutely," he said gently.

"Fine." Laura stood. "We should get started then. The clinic is a good half-day drive from here."

"First," Nick ordered, "you'll eat. Then we'll go." Nick held her gaze with his until she relented and settled back into her chair. A single tear trekked down one soft cheek. Every cell that made him who he was reacted to her pain, ached to reach out to her. The strength and determination radiating beneath all that vulnerability played havoc with his defenses. "You show me one slip of evidence and I swear I'll move heaven and earth to find your child," he vowed.

WELCOME TO PLEASANT RIDGE the sign read.

Laura's heart rate accelerated. She suppressed the excitement bubbling inside her at finally reaching the small Alabama town where Robby was born. In just a few short minutes she would have the proof she needed. Then Nick would help her find her baby. Laura brushed back the tears of relief. *Hold on, girl,* she told herself. *You'll find him. Nick won't let you down. He promised.*

Laura glanced at the strong profile of the man behind the wheel. He was so good-looking. She had fallen hard and fast for him two years ago, and had loved him ever since. A tiny smile tugged at Laura's lips. Confusion had reigned supreme in her life back then with the insanity revolving around the election and James Ed's strange behavior. Laura's smile dipped into a frown. And the attempts on her life. Nick had charged in and taken control of everything, including her heart. She had rebelled at first. Just another man trying to tell her what to do, and who would believe nothing she said, Laura had assumed. But Nick proved her wrong on that score. He reached out to her, made her want to trust him.

But nothing had prepared her for the way he made love to her. Only her second sexual experience, Laura's unskilled enthusiasm couldn't hold a candle to Nick's complete mastery of the art. She trembled inside at the memory of how easily he had coaxed the woman in her to bloom with just his touch, his kiss. Then when he had been inside her, all else had ceased to exist. There was only Nick and the way he loved her.

Hours had melted away as they had loved each other that one night. Then that murderous thief had barged in unimpeded and stolen the life she could have had with Nick. Laura clutched the car door's armrest and closed her eyes as the painful pictures flashed through her mind. Her heart pounded harder and harder with each passing frame of memory. Nick had pushed her behind him to protect her. Unarmed, he had looked death square in the eye without hesitation.

The sound of the gun firing echoed in Laura's ears. Nick had fallen at her feet, but the other man had grabbed her before she could help Nick. He had forced the small handgun into her hand, closed her fingers around it, then pitched it to the floor a few feet away from where Nick lay bleeding to death. Laura hadn't understood then that he was setting her up as Nick's killer.

Laura shivered and forced the memories away. Nick was alive. Somehow he had managed to find his cell phone in the tangled sheet on the floor. The call to 9-1-1 before he had lost consciousness was all that had saved him. Laura had read the story in the newspaper. She had been listed as missing, possibly dead. She swallowed, but not dead enough to suit her brother. If the world thought she was dead, why hadn't James Ed left it at that? She was out of his hair. He could have the money. Why had he hunted her down and dragged her back home?

Maybe, Laura thought with a frown, he hadn't been able to access the trust fund without producing a body. Or maybe he was afraid she would show up when she turned twenty-five and demand *her* money. She considered her brother's obvious determination. He wanted her dead, whatever the reason. Laura turned her attention back to the driver. Unless she could convince Nick that she was right very soon, she was as good as dead. Eventually he would have to turn her over to James Ed.

And where would that leave Robby?

"Is this the place?"

Laura jerked from her disturbing reverie. Nick had parked and was watching her closely, too closely. Laura quickly surveyed the one-story building in front of them. She nodded. "Yeah, this is it." Pleasant Ridge Medical Clinic was lettered on the plate glass window. Not much had changed as far as Laura could see. Thankfully the clinic still opened on Saturdays. There were several other cars in the parking lot, but that was the norm. People came from all over the county for low-cost and, in some cases, free medical care. The cost was based on income, but the service was as good as anyplace else. Laura had been extremely pleased with her care, as well as Robby's, here.

"What name did you use?"

Laura turned to Nick, but hesitated. Would he find her choice of aliases suspicious? There was no other way. She needed those records. "Forester," she said quickly before she lost her nerve. "Rhonda Forester for me, Robert—" Laura's heart skidded to a halt in her chest. Her son's full name was Robert Nicholas Forester. Oh God. "I named my son Robert."

"Just follow my lead," Nick told her as he opened the car door. "Don't say anything unless I ask you a question."

Laura nodded and scooted out after him. She followed Nick toward the entrance. She clenched and unclenched her hands, then smoothed the damp palms over the fuzzy material of her bulky sweater. There was no other alternative. She had to do this. Laura would deal with Nick's suspicions later. Right now she had to do what she had to do. Proving Robby existed was her primary goal. Without proof Nick wouldn't help her. Laura shivered and hugged herself. She had forgotten her jacket in her rush this morning.

Nick pulled the door open and waited for Laura to enter first. She met his gaze one last time before going inside. Okay, Laura, you can do this. Laura forced a smile for the numerous patients who glanced her way as she crossed the waiting room. Nick followed close behind her. She stopped in front of the receptionist's window and waited for the young blond woman to look up from her work.

"May I help you?"

She was new, Laura noted. The receptionist before was blond as well, but a little older.

"I certainly hope so," Nick said with a charming smile. The receptionist warmed to him immediately.

"What can I do for you, sir?"

Laura looked away. She didn't need to see this interaction, and she sure didn't need to feel what she was feeling as a result. Women probably responded to Nick this way all the time.

Nick displayed his Colby Agency ID. "My name is Foster. I'm a private investigator from Chicago."

The woman was impressed, Laura noticed when she allowed herself a peek in her direction.

"I'm working on a child abduction case."

"Oh my," the receptionist named Jill, according to her name tag, said on a little gasp. "How can I help you?"

"The child, a boy, was born here last…" Nick looked to Laura.

"August sixth," she finished, praying that Nick wouldn't do the math. Jill looked doubtfully from Laura to Nick.

"Records you might have to corroborate that birth would be of tremendous assistance," he added.

"Well, our records are private," Jill said slowly, caution finally outweighing Nick's charm.

Nick smiled reassuringly at her. "I don't need to see your records. I just need you to verify the birth, and that the child was a boy and left this clinic alive and well. His name was Robert Forester, the mother was Rhonda."

Jill looked uncertain. "I don't see any harm in that."

"It's perfectly legal for you to answer that question," Nick offered placatingly. "I'm sure you would much rather answer that simple question than to be subpoenaed to court."

Jill's eyes widened. "It'll take just a minute to locate the file."

"Take your time."

Nick openly studied Laura then. What was he thinking? she wondered anxiously. Was he doing the mental calculations to determine Robby's date of conception? Laura swallowed hard and forced her attention to Jill's search at the file cabinets. Now Nick would know that Robby was real. That Laura had a child. That James Ed was lying. That the hospital report from Louisiana was a fake.

Frowning, Jill glanced back in their direction. "You're sure of the name?"

Nick looked to Laura for confirmation. She nodded stiffly. Ice filled her veins. No. The records had to be here.

Jill shook her head and stepped back to the window. "I'm sorry, but we have no record of a Forester, Robert or Rhonda. Are you certain that's the right name?"

"That can't be," Laura argued, a mixture of anger and fear gripping her heart. "Dr. Nader was the doctor on call. The records have to be here."

"I'm sorry. I looked twice. There is no Forester."

Laura leveled her gaze on the other woman's. "Where can I find Dr. Nader then?" she demanded.

Jill looked to Nick then back to Laura. "I've only worked here for six months. Dr. Nader left before I came. I think he moved somewhere out west."

Laura shook her head in denial. "That can't be. The records have to be here," she repeated.

"Ma'am, I'm sorry. I can't give you something I don't have," the receptionist offered apologetically. "All births are registered at the state office. You could check there."

"But—"

"Let's go, Laura." Nick was next to her now, ushering her away from the window. "Thank you," he said glancing back at the receptionist.

"No, Nick." Laura pulled out of his grasp. "She has to be wrong." Confusion added to the emotions already knotting inside her.

Nick leveled his steady gaze on hers. "Let's go."

Trembling with reaction to the multitude of emotions clutching at her, Laura surrendered to Nick's orders. What choice did she have? She sagged with defeat. How would she ever prove her case now?

"Wait!"

Nick turned back to the receptionist, pulling Laura around with him. "Yes."

How could he be so damned calm? Laura wanted to scream. She wanted to run hard and fast—somewhere, anywhere.

"I almost forgot," Jill explained. "Right after I came to work here there was a break-in. Some files were stolen."

"Some?" Nick pressed.

"I can't say for sure what files." Jill frowned. "It was the strangest thing. The files were stolen and our computer's database was wiped clean. But nothing else."

"No drugs were taken?"

Jill shook her head. "Not a one."

NICK SWORE silently as he watched Laura storm across the parking lot. He followed more slowly, taking the time to study her. He wasn't at all sure how much more she could take. The cool wind shifted all that long blond hair around her shoulders as she slumped against the locked car door. His instincts told him that whatever happened at this clinic it definitely wasn't a coincidence. The robbery was a blatant cover-up. If Laura had a child why would anyone want to conceal that fact? If James Ed was somehow involved in all this as Laura thought, what difference would the kid make? But something was all wrong.

He hoped like hell that Ian would call soon. Nick needed a break in this case. He needed something—anything—to go on. There was no way he could cover Laura and do the kind of research required to solve this enigma. But Ian Michaels was as good as they came at ferreting out the truth.

And right now, Nick needed the truth desperately. He couldn't help Laura until he knew what was fact and what was fiction. One thing was certain, someone was trying to push Laura over the edge. Nick had no intention of allowing that to happen. He paused in front of her. "We should be getting back," he suggested quietly.

"He did this. I don't know how, but he did." Laura lifted her chin defiantly, but her eyes gave her away.

Nick couldn't bear to see that much hurt in her eyes. He tried to take a breath, but his chest was too heavy. How could he watch this happen and do nothing? But what could he do? He had no proof.

"Laura, we'll get to the bottom of this," he told her with as much assurance as he could impart.

She shook her head and blinked back her tears. "He's won," she admitted on a sob. "Look." She swallowed convulsively and swiped at her damp cheeks. "I've made a decision, I want you to take me back to Jackson…to my brother. Maybe if he gets what he wants he won't hurt Robby." She searched Nick's eyes for a time before she continued. "I just need you to promise me one thing." She trembled with the effort of maintaining her flimsy hold on composure.

Nick waited silently for her to finish, but his entire being screamed in agony. The need to touch her, to hold her was overwhelming.

"No matter how the chips fall, no matter what anyone tells you, find my son and take care of him for me, would you?"

His resolve crumbled. Nick took her in his arms and pulled her close. There were no words he could say because he didn't have any answers, the only thing he could do was hold her. Laura's arms went around his neck. Nick closed his eyes and savored the feel of her, the scent of her. He would gladly give his life right now to make her happy again.

"Nick."

Nick opened his eyes and drew back to find her looking up at him. That sweet face so filled with sadness.

"Promise me," she whispered. "Promise me you'll find him."

His gaze riveted to those full, pink lips. So soft, so sad and so very close. Nick shook his head slowly, in answer to her question or in denial of what he wanted more than anything to do, he couldn't be sure. "I'm not taking you back until I know it's safe." His voice was rough with emotion. Emotions he could no longer hold at bay.

Challenge rose in her eyes. "You're going to let them put me in that hospital, aren't you?"

He had to touch her. He lifted one hand to her cheek and allowed his fingers to trace the hot, salty path of her tears. He swallowed hard. "No one is going to touch you until I have some answers."

She searched his gaze, something besides the sorrow flickered in her own. "You're touching me," she murmured.

His fingers stilled at the base of her throat. "Do you want me to stop?" It was his turn to do the searching this time. He wanted to see the same desire that was wreaking havoc with his senses mirrored in her eyes.

She moistened her lips and gifted him with a shaky smile. "No, I don't want you to stop."

Nick lowered his head when he saw that answering spark of desire in her blue eyes. Slowly, as if an eternity yawned between them, his lips descended to hers. How could he have survived the past two years without her? She tasted of that same sweet heat that had burned in his memory every waking moment of every day for those two long years. His body hardened at the rush of bittersweet need that saturated his being. Nick threaded his fingers into her silky hair, loosening it from its constraints, and deepened the kiss. Her lips opened slightly and Nick delved inside. The traffic on the nearby street, the cold November wind, all ceased to exist.

Laura tiptoed to press her soft body more firmly against him. Nick groaned his approval. His left arm tightened around her waist, pulling her into his arousal. Laura whimpered her own response. The need to make love to her was staggering in its intensity.

He had to stop. To get back in control. Nick pulled back. His breath ragged, his loins screaming for release. Laura's lids fluttered open. Her swollen lips beckoned his.

He clenched his jaw and stepped away from her. "We should get back."

Laura nodded, the sadness rushing back into those big blue eyes.

Nick reached to insert the key into the lock but she stayed his hand. "Wait," she said breathlessly.

His gaze collided with hers. "What?"

"There's one more possibility," she said quickly, hope filling her gaze once more. "I can't believe I didn't think of her already."

"Laura, you're not making sense." Reality had just crashed in on Nick. He had allowed himself to fall into that same old trap. Dammit. How had he let that happen again? Yes, he had reason to believe her now. But he wasn't supposed to allow himself to cross the line this time. Hadn't he learned his lesson two years ago? Obviously not or he wouldn't have kissed her.

Laura snagged the keys and hurriedly unlocked her door. She pitched them back to him then. "Come on!"

He was a Class-A fool. Nick cursed himself repeatedly as he rounded the hood and unlocked his own door. He slid behind the wheel and shot his passenger, the bane of his pathetic existence, a heated glower. "Where are we going?"

She smiled, a wide, genuine smile and pointed to his left. "That direction. I'll explain on the way."

Chapter Eight

Laura stared in disbelief at the vacant house. The For Sale sign creaked as the wind shifted it, the sound heralding yet another failure. Jane Mallory had been Laura's last hope. Defeat weighed heavily on her shoulders. Laura closed her eyes and fought the sting of tears. It was as if destiny had determined her fate already. Now there was no one she could turn to. She and Robby had moved so often and stayed so much to themselves that few people would be able to verify Laura's story. And Jane Mallory had been the last one on the list.

"Do you mind telling me why we're standing on the front walk of an empty house?" Nick inquired in that nonchalant tone Laura hated.

She turned on him, a bolt of anger sending a burst of adrenaline through her. Even the memory of his kiss couldn't assuage her anger. Laura admitted to herself then and there that she was falling in love with the man all over again, but did he have to be so damned logical? *Because he's an honorable man, you idiot,* she scolded herself. Nick was only trying to be objective. To do what's right. Laura took a deep breath and summoned her patience.

"This is where Jane Mallory lived. She was the attending nurse at my son's delivery." Laura shot him an irritated look.

"Robby and I stayed with her for a couple of weeks while I recovered."

Nick looked from Laura to the empty house. He tucked his hands into his pockets. "Looks like another dead end."

"You know, Foster, your perceptiveness amazes me."

Irritation flickered in his green eyes. "What do you want from me, Laura?" He raked the fingers of one hand through his hair. "I'm following up on every lead you toss my way. I've got one of the Agency's finest investigating your brother, your sister-in-law and anybody else that has anything to gain by offing you. What else do you expect me to do?"

Laura leveled her gaze on his. "I want you to tell me that you believe me." Laura stepped closer to him. "Tell me that all these dead ends don't mean that all is lost." Laura stabbed his chest with her index finger as anger banished all else. "Tell me that my son is safe and that I'm going to find him—if not today, for sure tomorrow." A sob twisted in her throat, challenging her newfound bravado. "That's what I want from you, Nick."

The cold wind whipped around them, adding another layer of agony to her suffocating misery. How would she live without her son? She couldn't.

"Answer me, dammit," she demanded. Laura wilted when she saw the truth in his eyes. He couldn't make those kind of promises.

"I can't give you what you want, Laura. Not today, maybe not even tomorrow. But I will keep trying to find the answers you need until I've exhausted every possibility."

Laura looked up at the darkening sky. Why was this happening to her? What had she done to deserve this? She hugged herself to fight the chill coming more from the inside than the outside. What could she do now? *She needed a gun.* Nick's gun, she decided grimly. She would make James Ed tell her where her son was. Laura blinked at the irrational thought.

With sudden clarity, she realized that she was now beyond simply desperate, and extreme measures might be the only way.

Next door an elderly woman shuffled onto her porch and retrieved the evening paper. She pulled her sweater more tightly around her as she surveyed the deserted street. She smiled when her gaze lit on Laura. Her movements slow with age, she turned and started back across the porch.

Nick was saying something but Laura ignored him. This was a small town. Neighbors kept up with neighbors in a place like this. Hope rushed through Laura, urging her to act. She put one foot in front of the other even before her brain made the decision to move. This woman would know where Mrs. Mallory had moved.

"Ma'am," Laura shouted before the old woman could disappear inside her house. "Ma'am!" She took the porch steps two at a time.

A welcoming smile greeted Laura. "Hello. Is there something I can help you with?" The woman shook her gray head. "I don't know a thing about what the real estate agent is asking for the house, but I can tell you it's a fine old place."

Laura returned her smile. "Hi, my name is Laura Proctor. Mrs. Mallory is a friend of mine. I was wondering where she had moved to."

The woman frowned. "Oh my." She clutched her newspaper to her chest. "I thought everyone knew."

A chunk of ice formed in Laura's stomach. "Knew what?" she asked faintly. Laura felt Nick's gaze heavy on her from his position on the steps.

"I'm sorry, dear, Jane passed away a few months back."

Laura's knees buckled but Nick was at her side now, supporting her. "But I was here, with her, in August of last year. She was fine," Laura insisted.

The old woman nodded. "It was very sudden. A heart attack." She pointed to the neighboring yard. "She was always in that yard since she retired this spring, weeding and planting. Just got herself too hot, I reckon. It was a real shame. We had been neighbors for more than forty years."

Laura clamped her hand over her mouth for a moment to hold back the sob that wanted to break loose. When she had composed herself, she struggled with her next words, "Thank you for telling me." Laura closed her eyes and shook her head, exhaustion and anxiety sucking her toward panic. "I didn't know."

The old woman smiled kindly. "If you're not from around here, how could you have known? Jane never did marry and she didn't have any folks except one estranged brother." The woman shook her head. "A real shame that was. He didn't even come to her funeral. Course I'm not sure he even knew." She frowned. "Come to think of it, he probably didn't. At least his son hadn't known. Did you know Jane had a brother?"

Laura moistened her painfully dry lips. "No, I'm sorry I didn't know any of her family."

"Far as I knew that's all there was, but about four months ago, not long after Jane died, a fella showed up asking about her. A long-lost nephew it seems. Odd sort if you ask me."

A chill raced up Laura's spine. "Odd? What do you mean?"

The old woman rocked back on her heels. "Well I hate to speak poorly of Jane's folks, but he didn't look a thing like her or her brother. I'd never seen the brother, mind you, but I had seen his picture. Jane was a big woman, brawny even. So was that brother of hers. But this nephew, he was kinda short and stubby like. I suppose he took after his mama's side of the family. Strange fella," she added thoughtfully. "Wore long sleeves even in the July heat."

"What color were his eyes?" The question came out of nowhere, but the image of those eerie pink-colored eyes flickered in Laura's mind.

"Can't rightly say. He wore them dark glasses. And gloves." She chuckled a rusty sound. "I thought that was mighty strange myself." She tapped her chin with one finger. "Maybe it was because he had such pale skin. Like a corpse." She frowned as if working hard to conjure the stranger's image. "And the whitest hair I've ever seen on a young man."

Nick's grip tightened on Laura's waist. Only then did she realize that she was leaning fully against him. Her legs had gone boneless. White hair, pink eyes, pale skin. *Albino.*

Laura turned in Nick's arms. "It's him," she murmured. "He's the one who broke into my room at James Ed's." Oh God. Laura closed her eyes and tried to slow the spinning inside her head. *The files were stolen and our computer's database was wiped clean. Jane passed away a few months back.*

The next thing Laura knew she was on the porch swing. She could hear Nick's deep voice as he questioned the woman about the strange nephew, but the words didn't quite register. *Time to die, princess.* Laura jerked at the memory. Why was this man trying to kill her? Why was he erasing all traces of Robby's existence? She swallowed. Laura didn't want to consider the reasons.

A wave of nausea washed over her. What did her sweet, innocent child have to do with any of this? *Nothing.* Laura trembled with the rage rising swiftly inside her.

Her child had nothing to do with any of this. And if James Ed harmed one hair on her son's head, he was a dead man. Laura's breath raged in and out of her lungs. For the first time in her life the thought of someone's death brought a sense of comfort to her. Death would not be a harsh enough punishment for him if her child was hurt. Not nearly bad enough.

Laura's gaze moved to Nick. She had to get away from him. He would only hold her back. He would never allow her to do what she wanted to do. Nick was too honorable and straightforward to resort to what Laura had in mind. James Ed held all the answers.

And Laura intended to get them out of him one way or another.

"HE USED THE NAME Dirk Mallory." Nick paused while Ian made a note of the alias the albino guy had used. "He may or may not be connected to James Ed or the man who shot me, but it's worth checking into." Nick knew Laura was convinced that this was the man. He had no more to go on now in the way of hard evidence than he'd had three days ago, but his instincts told him to trust Laura on this one. Too many strange little coincidences and events added up to just one thing—a cover-up. "What do you have for me?"

"Governor Proctor has performed some pretty amazing financial acrobatics the past two years," Ian told him. "And he has definitely accessed Laura's trust fund. That would hardly be considered illegal since he had every right to do so with her sudden disappearance, and the assumption that she was dead. "

Nick swore under his breath. Maybe Laura was right. But, like Ian said, James Ed's use of the trust fund the last couple of years was strictly on the up-and-up. It still didn't prove that he tried to kill his own sister to get it.

"I also uncovered some rather strange details in Sandra's background."

Nick's attention jerked back to the conversation. "Good, anything is better than nothing."

"You already knew that she was adopted at the age of thirteen after spending one year in a state-run orphanage in Louisiana," Ian suggested.

Nick frowned in concentration. "Yeah, I remember that. The little wife was as clean as a whistle though. I remember that, too."

"Maybe, maybe not," Ian countered. "Her biological mother was one Sharon Spencer from a rural community just outside Bay Break."

"And?"

"And," Ian continued, "Sharon was involved with James Ed's father before he went off to college. There was a pretty big scandal before the Proctors enforced a gag order of sorts, and then sent their straying heir off to Harvard."

Rutherford's words echoed in Nick's head. "Damn," he breathed. The old man knew something, that's why he had innocently dropped that ancient gossip.

"Anything on what became of her?" Nick inquired hopefully.

"According to my source, she married the town drunk who died two years after Sandra's birth. Ten years after that, Sharon went off the deep end and the county took the child."

Nick passed a hand over his face. "So Sandra grew up, until the age of twelve at least, in a household where the Proctor name was mud. And her mother was a fruitcake."

"That would be my analysis," Ian agreed.

"I want to know everything you can find on Sandra Proctor, her first steps, her first kiss—everything."

"No problem," Ian assured him. "I should be able to get back to you later tomorrow on that. I have an excellent source."

Nick blew out a breath and plowed his fingers through his hair. "What about the report from the psychiatric hospital, Serenity Sanitarium?"

"That one's a bit more tricky."

"I need to know if that report's legit," Nick insisted. "That's the biggest fly in the ointment. I have to know if there's any chance Laura was really a patient there."

"Would you care to hazard a guess as to who one of the long-term residents of that facility is?" Ian inquired in a cocky tone.

Nick considered the question, then smiled with satisfaction. "One Sharon Spencer."

"Bingo."

"Excellent work, Ian," Nick praised. That gave Sandra a connection to the hospital. Maybe she or James Ed knew someone employed there who was willing to forge reports.

"Actually, it wasn't that difficult. I found a great source right up front."

Nick raised a speculative brow. "Who is your source?"

"Carl Rutherford."

"Son of a bitch," Nick hissed. "Why didn't that old geezer tell me all this?"

"He was afraid you were one of James Ed's bought-and-paid-for strong arms. He said more than he intended on the day the two of you met."

Nick didn't miss the amusement in Ian's tone. "Well, I guess you can't blame a guy for being cautious."

"That's it for now," Ian said. "I'll check in with you again within twenty-four hours."

"One more thing," Nick added before Ian could hang up. "Find out if the birth of a baby named Robert Forester was registered in the state of Alabama sometime in August last year."

"No problem," Ian assured him.

"Thanks, Ian." Nick ended the call. He stood for a long moment and allowed the information to absorb more fully into his consciousness. He had no proof that Laura had a child or where she had actually been for the past two years. Despite Laura's claims, James Ed still surfaced from all this smelling pretty much like a rose in Nick's opinion. But then, there was this new light on Sandra. Nick massaged his chin as he considered the kind and demure first lady of Mississippi.

Sandra appeared as elated as anyone to have Laura back home. Sandra's school and college records indicated a disciplined, well-adjusted student. As first lady she was involved with numerous charities and a devoted churchgoer. The perfect wife to James Ed and surrogate mother to her young sister-in-law. No children of her own though. She and James Ed couldn't have children, Nick remembered. He wasn't sure of the reason, but he had found no indication that the problem was an issue. Sandra seemed to accept Laura as a substitute for a child of her own.

But how was that possible considering this new information? Sandra had grown up dirt-poor in a home with a drunk for a father and a mother who was mentally unstable. And where the Proctors represented everything she didn't have.

Uneasiness stole over Nick. That combination spelled trouble with a capital *T*. Nick exhaled heavily and passed a hand over his face. But why would Sandra go to such lengths to get Laura's money when James Ed would be in control of the trust fund, not her. Or did she have that much power over her husband? Nick wondered briefly. It just didn't ring true. James Ed was doing well on his own merit. *Is there ever enough?* Laura's words filtered through his mind. Why would Sandra kidnap Laura's child if James Ed already had access to the trust fund? Maybe it was simply a matter of not wanting to have to pay it back. Even with Laura considered unstable, her child would be heir to her trust fund unless the will specified otherwise. That could be a distinct possibility, Nick decided.

The missing files, the knife wounds on Laura's throat and chest. The events in the cabin when he was shot. Laura's explanation of how the man had tried to kill her on that riverbank two years ago. Nick suppressed a shudder. He had lost his heart that night, and very nearly his life. That one incident might not have anything to do with the rest. The police labeled the case as a kidnapping gone sour. According to Laura, the man who shot Nick and tried to kill her died in the river that night. And she had seen him in James Ed's office more than once.

Anyone or thing that could provide hard evidence that Laura had a child had conveniently disappeared. Nick wondered again about the strange nephew who had shown up at Jane Mallory's neighbor's house. Nick supposed he could have been the real thing. And what about the hospital report? How convenient that Sandra's mother was a long-term resident of the very facility which provided the only hard evidence that existed as to Laura's whereabouts during the past months.

None of it actually added up to anything conclusive. And he doubted it would until he knew more facts. The only thing Nick knew for certain was that he had to protect Laura. He thought again about the way kissing her had made him feel, and the realization that he still cared deeply for her hit him hard. A weary breath slipped past Nick's lips. It was late. He couldn't deal with any of this right now. He glanced at the clock on the mantel above the fireplace. Midnight. He should check on Laura and get some sleep. Maybe Ian would come up with something more on Sandra tomorrow.

Rain pattered quietly on the roof. A storm had been threatening the entire drive home. Nick was glad the wet stuff had held off until they got back to Bay Break. The door to Laura's room was open. Nick slipped in soundlessly. The light from the bedside table cast a golden glow on her sweet face and silky hair. Laura had been so exhausted and overwhelmed, she had hardly spoken a word during the return trip. She had gone straight to bed as soon as they got home.

She was tired. Nick moved to her bedside and crouched down next to her. Tired or not, Laura was beautiful. Her bare shoulders made Nick wonder if she was naked beneath that sheet and thin cotton blanket. His mouth parched instantly at the thought. His eyes feasted on the perfection of the satiny skin revealed before him. Rage stirred inside him when his gaze traced the small slash mark, then flitted back to the tiny puncture wounds on her throat. Forcing the anger away, Nick shifted his slow perusal to her sweet face. All emotion melted, leaving him weak with want. Her lashes, a few shades darker than her blond hair, shadowed her soft cheeks. Those full, pink lips were parted slightly as if she were waiting for his kiss.

Cursing himself as a glutton for punishment, Nick allowed his gaze to trace her tempting jawline, then down the curve of her delicate throat to the pulse beating rhythmically there. He licked his lips hungrily and resisted the urge to touch her slender shoulder, to feel the warm smoothness of her skin. His body turned rock hard with desire.

Something snagged his attention. He frowned. Nick jerked his gaze back to her shoulder, near her neck. He moved closer to get a better look. The bottom fell out of Nick's stomach when his brain assimilated what his eyes found there.

Bruises. Small, oblong, barely visible marks that discolored her otherwise perfect, creamy skin.

He…he tried to drown me.

No way could Laura have made those bruises on herself. The position and size of which could only be labeled as finger marks. A churning mixture of rage and fear rising inside him, Nick eased down onto the side of the bed next to her. This, Nick seethed, was hard evidence.

"Laura." He shook her gently. "Laura, honey, wake up. We need to talk."

She moaned a protest and hugged her pillow. Nick's body ached with the need to hold her that way. "Laura." He shook her again. "We have to talk."

Laura sat up with a start. The sheet fell, exposing one high, firm breast briefly before she covered herself. "What?" she demanded irritably.

Nick leveled his determined gaze on her bleary one. "I want you to start at the beginning and tell me everything. Again."

LAURA WATCHED Nick pace back and forth across the room. She stood in the middle of the room, the sheet hugged close around her. She wished he had given her time to put some clothes on before he started this inquisition. After her long cry in the shower where Nick wouldn't hear or see her, she hadn't had the energy or the desire to dig up anything to sleep in. She had wanted to escape into sleep. She didn't want to think about the missing files or Mrs. Mallory's death.

Or the nephew.

Laura shivered. She blocked the memory of the man with the strange eyes who had tried to kill her twice already. The bathroom had been dark and she hadn't actually seen his eyes that time. But she knew. Deep in her heart, Laura knew it was him. And with that instinct came the realization that he had probably been the one to take her son. James Ed would never have bothered himself with that part. Her heart shuddered at that thought.

"Does that about sum it up?"

Nick's question jerked Laura to attention. "What?" she asked as she forced herself to focus on him once more.

"Dammit, Laura," he growled. He jammed his hands at his waist and moved in her direction. "I need your full attention here."

"I'm sorry." She pushed the hair back from her face. "You're going to have to start over."

Nick swore under his breath. Those green eyes flashed with barely checked fury. What had him all worked up? Laura wondered, her own irritation kindling. Certainly nothing they had learned today. Though she knew with a measure of certainty that the nephew was the man after her, she couldn't prove that to Nick. She had proven *nothing* today.

The emptiness of that one word echoed around her. The only glimmer of hope in all this was that Nick was beginning to believe her.

"You came home that summer from college, and things were tense you said."

Laura nodded. "At first I thought it was because I hadn't put as much into school as James Ed had. He wanted me to be the perfect student, the perfect sister." She frowned, remembering her brother's disappointment. "But it didn't take long for me to figure out that it had nothing to do with me. It was the campaign for the Governor's office."

"And then Rafe Manning came on the scene."

Again Laura noted that change in Nick's eyes, in his posture, when he spoke of Rafe. "Right," she replied. "I dated him a few times because I was bored, but we didn't hit it off. James Ed tried to push the issue. Apparently he and Rafe's father were tight." Laura shrugged. "You know the rest."

Nick folded his arms over his chest and massaged his chin with his thumb and forefinger. The movement drew Laura's eyes to that sexy cleft in his chin. Emotion stirred inside her. Robby had a cleft just like that.

. "Not once during all of this did you ever suspect Sandra of being involved?"

Taken aback by his question, Laura stared at him in amazement. "Sandra?" Laura shook her head slowly from side to side. "That's ridiculous. Sandra has never been anything but kind to me."

"What would you say if I told you that Sandra might not be who you think she is," Nick offered, his gaze intent on hers, watching, analyzing.

Laura frowned. "What does that mean?"

"Sandra's mother was involved with your father."

"That's not possible. Sandra's mother is dead."

"Did Sandra tell you that?"

Laura nodded, feeling as if another rug was about to be snatched from under her feet.

"Sandra's mother is on a permanent ward at Serenity Sanitarium."

Laura stilled as her brain absorbed the impact of his words. That was the hospital James Ed claimed she had been committed to for the past eighteen months. Sandra's mother was alive? And a patient there? "Why would Sandra lie?" The question echoed in the room; only then did Laura realize she had said it aloud.

Nick placed a reassuring hand on her arm, his fingers caressed her bare skin. That simple touch sent heat spearing through her. "I don't know, but we're damned sure going to find out."

Laura's gaze connected with his. "Why the sudden change of heart, Nick?" Laura examined his now impassive gaze closely. "Are you trying to tell me that you really do believe me now?"

He lifted those long fingers to her throat and touched her gingerly. He swallowed hard, the play of muscle beneath tanned skin made Laura ache to touch him there, the same way he was touching her.

"Believing you wasn't the problem, Laura. Let's just say I finally got that hard evidence." His gaze followed the movements of his fingers.

Laura stumbled away from him. She pivoted and hurried to the dresser, then stared at her reflection in the mirror. Several long, thin bruises marked her skin where strong fingers had held her beneath the water's surface.

Nick came up behind her, watching her in the mirror. "Laura, I'm sorry I let this happen. I should have believed you sooner." He touched her elbow. Laura flinched. "I won't let anyone hurt you again. I swear," he added softly.

Laura shunned his touch. "It took this," she gestured to the bruises, "to make you believe that someone was trying to kill me." Fury rose in Laura then. "What about my child? Do you believe in him yet?"

Nick's gaze wavered. "Of course I believe you, but we have to have proof."

"You bastard. You still don't really believe me."

Nick let go a heavy breath. "That's not true," he argued.

"Then look me in the eye and tell me that you believe I have a son. That his name is Robby and he's the most important thing in my life," she ground out, a sob knotting her chest.

Nick's concerned gaze collided with hers.

"Say it, damn you!" Laura trembled with the intensity of her fury. "Say it," she demanded when his response didn't come quickly enough.

Nick blinked. "It's not a matter of making me believe you—we have to be able to prove it to James Ed." He added quickly, "And the police."

She shoved at his chest with one hand and held the sheet to her breast with the other. "Get away from me! I don't give a damn about your proof!"

"Laura." Nick dodged her next attempt at doing him bodily harm. He grabbed her by both arms and held her still. "Laura, listen to me."

"I don't want to hear anything you have to say." Laura trembled, his long fingers splayed on her flesh and urged her closer.

"Laura." He breathed her name, the feel of his warm breath soft on her face. "I have to operate on facts, not assumptions. I can't go back to Jackson and demand to know where your son is when I have no physical proof that he exists."

Laura knew he was right. Deep in her heart, she knew. But that didn't stop the ache tearing at her insides. She needed to find her son more than she needed to take her next breath.

"I have to find him," she murmured. How many days had it been now? Laura squeezed her eyes shut. God, she didn't want to think about that.

"Please trust me, Laura," Nick pleaded. He angled his head down to look into her eyes when she opened them. "I won't let you down if you'll just trust me."

Laura met that intense green gaze and found herself drowning in the emotions reflected there. Desire, need… The same emotions she felt detonating inside her. She did trust Nick. He would never do anything to hurt her. She knew that. And she needed him so much. To hold her, to make her forget for just a little while. She needed him to love her the way he had before. She needed to reaffirm this thing between them, to feel his strong arms around her. Nick would help her, she knew he would. His strength was all that kept her sane right now.

"Hold me, Nick." Laura went into his arms. She slid her own arms around his lean waist and held him tightly. His scent, something spicy and male, enveloped her. And then his strong arms were around her, holding her, protecting her.

Nick pressed a tender kiss to her hair. "I just need you to trust me, honey, that's all." His lips found her temple and brushed another of those gentle kisses there. "Please trust me."

Laura closed her eyes and allowed instinct to take over. She needed Nick to take her away from this painful reality. To hold her and promise her that everything would be all right. Her hands moved over his strong back, feeling, caressing. She could feel the muscled landscape of his broad chest pressing against her breasts. Her nipples pebbled at the thought of how his warm skin would feel against hers.

His fingers threaded into her hair and pulled her face up to his. "You should get some rest," he said thickly, his gaze never left her mouth. "I won't be far away."

Laura shook her head, drawing his gaze to hers. "Don't leave me," she said in the barest of whispers. Laura tiptoed and quickly kissed his full lips. Nick sucked in a sharp breath. "I want you, Nick. I want you now."

He drew back slightly. "You're not thinking clearly, Laura." He searched her gaze, her face, then licked his lips, yearning clear in his eyes. "I don't want you to regret anything."

Determined to show him just how badly she wanted him, Laura stepped back and allowed the sheet to fall to the floor. "I do want," she told him. "I want you."

Nick's gaze moved slowly over her body. Laura felt its caress as surely as if he were touching her with those skilled hands.

"I want you, too," he admitted quietly. "But you're vulnerable right now and I don't want to take advantage of that." His eyes contradicted his words. He did want to do just that. He wanted it as badly as she did.

"The decision isn't yours," Laura concluded. "It's mine." She recovered the step she had retreated. Her eyes steady on his, Laura reached up and slowly began to unbutton his shirt. His gaze dropped to her hands and he watched as she bared his chest. The knowledge that he was watching her and responding sent a surge of power pulsing through her veins, heating her already too warm body.

Laura held out her hand. "Your weapon, sir."

Nick looked from her hand to her. Laura saw the flicker of hesitation in his eyes. She stepped back and opened the drawer to the night table. "I'm only going to put it away," she explained.

He nodded, then reached behind his back and retrieved the

weapon. Nick's gaze held hers as he placed the ominous looking weapon in Laura's open palm.

She smiled, her lips trembling with the effort. "Thank you."
Nick would never know how much that gesture meant to her.
He could have put the gun away himself, but he hadn't. He
trusted her at least a little.

Laura closed the drawer and turned to find him right behind her, she looked up into those sea green eyes and melted
at what she saw. Savage need, overwhelming desire. Nick took
her hand in his and pressed a kiss against her palm, then
placed it over his heart. Laura felt weak with emotion. Knotting her hands in his shirt, she pulled it from his jeans, then
pushed it off his broad shoulders until it dropped to the floor.

For a time Laura simply admired the exquisite terrain of
his muscled chest. She touched the scar and electricity
charged through her. Leaning forward, she kissed that place
and thanked God once more that Nick was alive. Laura flattened her hands against his hair-roughened chest and allowed
her palms to mold to the contours of that awesome torso. She
closed her eyes and committed each ripple and ridge to memory. Desire sizzled inside her, making her bold, making her
need. Her fingers slipped into the waistband of his jeans and
circled his lean waist.

Nick groaned low in his throat. "Laura," he rasped. "How
long do you plan to torture me this way?"

She released the button to his fly, then slowly lowered the
zipper, the sound echoing around them. "As long as it takes,"
she assured him, her voice low and husky.

Laura knelt in front of him. The immense pleasure in his
eyes added to her own. She pulled one boot off, then the
other. The socks were rolled off next. Slowly, she tugged his
jeans down those long, muscled legs. Each inch of flesh she
revealed made breathing that much more difficult. When his

jeans had been disposed of, Laura sat back on her heels and admired his amazing body. Wide, wide shoulders that narrowed into a lean waist and hips, then long, muscled legs. She studied the scarred right knee momentarily, remembering the life he had saved by taking a bullet. Laura closed her eyes and forced away the possibility that he might get caught in the crossfire of all this madness again. She couldn't bear the thought of Nick being hurt again. The realization that his getting hurt or worse was a very distinct possibility hit her hard. She had to make sure that didn't happen. Everyone around her that she cared about was being hurt or worse.

Suppressing the thought, Laura's gaze moved back up those long, powerful legs. Black briefs concealed the part of him that made her wet and achy. Nick had taught her what it was to be a woman in the purest, most primitive sense of the word. Not one day had gone by in the past two years that her body had not yearned for his. Now, at last, she would know that pleasure once more.

One last time.

With painstaking slowness, Laura slid his briefs down and off. Nick groaned loudly when she pressed a kiss to one lean hip. His arousal nudged her shoulder sending a shard of desire slicing through her. She wanted him inside her. Now.

Laura stood, braced her hands against his chest and tiptoed to kiss his firm lips. His eyes opened and the savage fire burning there seared her from the inside out.

"No more," he growled. Nick lifted her into his arms as if she weighed nothing at all. Three steps later and they were on the bed.

"My turn now," he warned.

Laura bit down on her lower lip to hold back her cry of need as he kissed his way down her body. He paused to love her breasts. Taking his time, he laved and suckled each until

Laura thought she would die of it. He gave the same attention to her belly button, licking, sucking, arousing.

Nick suddenly stilled. His fingers traced her side. "What's this?" he murmured.

Trying to make sense of his question through her haze of lust, Laura stared down at where his fingers touched her. *Stretch marks.* Few and faint, but there just the same. Why hadn't she thought of that before?

"Stretch marks," she answered. "From my pregnancy. Everyone gets them."

Nick traced the pale marks hesitantly.

"Your evidence," Laura added when he remained silent.

Nick smiled at her then. "Absolutely," he concurred. A predatory gleam brightened his beautiful green eyes. "And my pleasure as well." His tongue followed the same path his fingers had taken.

Laura moaned her approval.

His fingers trailed down her skin until they found that part of her which throbbed for his touch. Laura arched upward when one long finger slipped inside her. His thumb made tiny circles around her most intimate place of desire.

"Nick," she murmured. Instinctively her hips moved against his hand. A second finger slipped inside and Laura cried out.

His mouth captured hers. Slowly, thoroughly he kissed her, his tongue mimicking the rhythm of his fingers. The feel of his lips, soft, yet firm and commanding, commanding her with devastating precision. His tongue touched all the sensitive places in her mouth, a sweet torture to which she gladly surrendered. Laura writhed with the tension coiling tighter and tighter inside her. She gasped for air when his mouth finally lifted from hers. His ragged breath fanned her lips, igniting another fire in her soul. Nick moved between her thighs.

Those magic fingers, hot and moist from her body, slid over her hip and beneath her to lift her toward him. Release crashed down on Laura the moment he entered her, stretching, filling, completing.

Nick covered her mouth with his and took her scream just as she took him inside her. His fingers entwined with hers, pulling her hands above her head. Slowly, drawing out the exquisite pleasure, Nick thrust fully inside her again and again. Her tension building even faster than the first time, Laura met his thrusts, urging him to hurry. Her heart pounding, her breath trapped in her lungs, Laura spiraled toward release once more. One last thrust and Nick followed her to that special place of pure sensation.

His breathing as jagged and labored as hers, Nick pressed his forehead to Laura's. "Are you all right?"

Laura nodded once, unable to speak.

"Rest now. We'll talk later," he told her as he rolled over and pulled her into his protective embrace.

Laura closed her eyes against the tears. How she loved this man. But they would never be able to be a family. No matter how he felt about her at this moment, when he discovered the truth, he would despise her for keeping his son from him for so long.

Laura had to find a way to get away from Nick. He had been hurt by her too much already. Nick had taken a bullet and almost died for her. She had kept his son from him all this time. He deserved better. She could not risk him being hurt by James Ed's men again. If something happened to her Robby would need his father. Nick only had to take one look at Robby to know that the child belonged to him. And she knew in her heart that Nick would not stop looking for him now no matter what happened. He had urged James Ed to give him this time with Laura. Nick had stuck his neck out for her too many times already. Decision behind her, Laura considered her best course of action. Too much time had been wasted already. Doc's office might hold some clue to where he had gone. And maybe even some proof of her child's existence. Something she could take to the police.

Laura had to find her baby. But she had to make sure Nick stayed out of the line of fire this time.

This was between her and James Ed.

Chapter Nine

The scent of an angel tantalized him. Nick snuggled more deeply into his pillow. *Laura.* He smiled and opened his eyes to the bright morning light spilling into the room. He reached for the woman who had turned his world upside down once more.

"Good morning," she murmured.

Nick kissed the tip of her nose. "Morning," he rasped. "Did you know that you look like an angel when you wake up?"

Laura giggled. God, how good it felt to hear that. But Nick wanted more than a glimpse of the woman he had fallen in love with. He wanted her to laugh out loud. To drive him crazy like she did two years ago. While he watched, sadness filled her gaze once more, and Nick knew she had remembered that her son was still missing.

"Hungry?" he inquired, trying to keep the mood light. "I could eat a horse."

She smiled. "You're always hungry." Laura searched his gaze for what seemed like forever, as if she were afraid it might be the last time she could look at him this way. "You go take care of breakfast. I want a long, hot bath," she said suggestively. "Maybe you can even join me."

"Maybe I'm not as hungry as I thought." Nick nuzzled her neck, then nipped the lobe of her ear.

Laura gasped and pulled away from his exploring mouth. "For once I am," she murmured.

Nick bowed his head. "Your wish is my command, madam."

Laura giggled again as she scurried from the room. Nick watched her departure in rapt appreciation. He loved every square inch of her petite little body.

"Don't lock the door," he called out after her. "I'll be there in fifteen minutes."

"I'll be waiting," she called from the bathroom. The sound of water rushing into the tub obliterated any possibility of further conversation.

Nick threw back the sheet and got out of bed. He stretched, feeling better than he had in a very long time. He pulled on his jeans, tucked his weapon into his waistband and started toward the kitchen. This was the way it should be, the two of them together making love, sharing moments like this morning.

But there was Laura's child. Nick slowed in his progress toward the kitchen. He scrubbed a hand over his stomach. The notion of a child would take some getting used to. Nick certainly wanted children of his own. He paused at the kitchen doorway. Did it matter to him that this child belonged to another man? A slow smile claimed Nick's mouth. Hell no. Nick would love Laura's child just like his own.

Feeling like a tremendous weight had been lifted from his shoulders, Nick set to the task of making breakfast. He whistled as he worked. Nothing like great sex with the woman you love to make a man happy, he decided. All he had to do now was sort all this insanity out.

Twenty minutes later and Nick was ready to join Laura. At this point he might only get to dry her back. He grinned. But that was fine with him. Nick sauntered down the hall, anticipation pounding through his veins. He could make love to

Laura for the rest of his life and never stop wanting more of her. He tapped on the closed bathroom door.

"Ready or not here I come," he teased. Nick turned the knob and pushed the door open. Steam billowed out to engulf him. Nick frowned. What the hell? He stepped into the bathroom and water pooled around his feet. His heart rate blasted into overdrive, pumping fear and adrenaline through his tense body. He fanned his arms to part the steam. Water was pouring over the side of the tub. Where was Laura? Fear hurdled through Nick's veins. He peered down at the tub. No Laura. Thank God. He swallowed hard as he leaned down and turned the swiftly flowing water off, then opened the drain.

Nick straightened and took a breath. His next thought sent anger rushing through him, neutralizing the fear he had felt. He crossed the wet floor to the window, parted the curtain and cleared a spot of fog from the glass. Peering out, his suspicion was confirmed. His rental car was gone.

Nick swore hotly.

Laura was gone.

His fury burning off the last of the fear lingering in his chest, Nick stamped into Laura's bedroom. Pain roared up his leg, and his knee almost buckled in protest. He closed his eyes and gritted his teeth until the pain subsided to a more tolerable level. Taking a bit more care, he tugged on his shirt and socks and stepped into his boots.

How the hell had he let last night happen? Nick cursed himself again. It was two years ago all over again, only this time he wasn't bleeding. At least not on the outside, he amended. With all that had happened, how could he still feel this way about Laura?

He was a fool, that's why.

He had sworn that he wouldn't get sucked into the Proctor family saga this time. He headed to the door, pulling his jacket on and automatically checking the weapon at the small of his back as he went. Damn it, damn it. Here he was, heart deep in tangled emotions and deadly deceptions.

He had really screwed up this time. He should have known Laura was up to something. She had given in to his plan of action last night all too easily. She was desperate to find her son. And desperate people did desperate things. Nick knew that all too well. He should have reassured her rather than pushing for answers about her pregnancy. She had ended up unwilling to discuss the issue. Nick cursed himself again. Making love to Laura again had only served to reinforce the feeling that she was his and his alone. The thought that she had been with another man, even once, still tore at his heart. He shouldn't have pressured her about the child's father. He should have insisted they do things his way and his way only. He should have realized that something was up this morning.

Damn it, he was a complete idiot.

Nick followed the driveway until it intersected the highway. He glanced left. That direction would take her to Jackson. He didn't think Laura would head that way, not alone and unarmed. His gaze shifted right. It was only five miles to town. That was the direction he needed to take. His knee complained sharply at the thought. Nick shifted his weight to the other leg. Why would Laura go into town?

Nick swore when he considered that she may have gone back to the old woman's house. That's all he needed was for the old hag to call the police and get Laura thrown into jail. James Ed would…

He didn't want to consider that his instincts had gone that far south where James Ed was concerned. Protecting James Ed's interests, including Laura, was the job Nick had signed on to do. But solving the puzzle that was Laura Proctor's predicament was Nick's ultimate goal. Nick's gut instinct just wouldn't permit him to believe that James Ed was the villain here.

And neither was Laura. She had definitely been attacked. There was no question in his mind about that. And she had obviously been pregnant. The stretch marks were there and Nick had noticed other subtle changes to her body. Her breasts were fuller. However, making love to her had proven the same—mind-blowing. The scent of her still clung to his skin, the memory of her tight, hot body was tattooed across his brain, easily arousing him even now.

Nick shook himself from the memory. He didn't have time for that right now. He had to find Laura. His attention jerked to the road when an old truck slowed as it approached him. He squinted to identify the driver.

Rutherford.

Headed in the direction of Jackson, the old man passed slowly, did a precarious U-turn, then stopped on the edge of the road right in front of Nick.

"Need a ride young fella?"

Nick braced his hands on the door and leaned into the open window. "I suppose that depends upon where you're headed, old man," Nick said tersely. He was still annoyed that Rutherford had spilled his guts to Ian and not him. Maybe Nick had gotten too close to all this. Whatever the case, he didn't like being jerked around or bypassed.

The old man eyed him suspiciously for one long minute, then one side of his mouth hitched up in a smile. He pushed his John Deere cap up and scratched his forehead. "I'm headed to the same place you're headed, I reckon," he replied cryptically.

Nick eyed him with mounting skepticism. "Is that a fact?"

Rutherford settled his cap back into place and adopted a knowing look. "It is if it's an angel you're looking for."

"You know where Laura is?"

The old man grinned widely. "I sure do. I was out to the barn for a ladder." He nodded toward the large barn right off the pages of a New England calendar that sat behind and to one side of the Proctor house. "Planned on cleaning out the gutters today. That rain last night pretty much cleared the rest of the leaves from the trees."

"You saw her leave," Nick prodded impatiently.

"She come running outta that house like the devil himself was on her heels." Rutherford cocked a bushy gray brow. "But you never did come out."

Nick tamped down the response that immediately came to mind. "Which way did she go?" he said instead.

"She jumped into that car of yours and took off toward town." He frowned. "I figured something was up so I followed her. She drove straight to Doc Holland's office. Didn't appear to be nobody there though, but she went on around back like she knowed what she was about. Then I got to thinking that maybe I should come back and get you. Seeing as you're supposed to be keeping an eye on her and all."

Nick jerked the door open and climbed in. "Thanks," he snapped. The fact that the man was right didn't help Nick's disposition.

Rutherford pulled back out onto the highway. He cast Nick a conspiratorial wink. "You have to watch those angels, young fella, they got themselves wings. They can fly away before you know they're gone."

Nick manufactured a caustic smile. "Thanks, I'll remember that." When he caught up with Laura, he fully intended to clip those wings.

In no time at all Mr. Rutherford chugged into the driveway leading to Doc Holland's place. Nick's black rental car was parked at an odd angle next to the porch. He opened his door before Rutherford braked to a full stop. Nick slid out and closed the door behind him.

"Thanks for the ride," he said, taking another look at the old man behind the wheel. "And thanks for your help with Laura's situation," he added contritely. Hell, the man had done him a favor. Nick should be considerably more grateful.

Carl Rutherford's expression turned serious. "You just make sure that little girl don't do no permanent disappearing act."

Nick nodded and backed up a step as the old truck lurched forward. When Mr. Rutherford had exited the other end of the horseshoe-shaped drive, Nick turned his attention to the house-cum-clinic before him. What the hell was she doing here? Nick shook his head. Looking for more evidence to support her case, he felt sure. Or for the Doc, whichever she could find. Nick frowned. The place was awfully quiet for there to be anyone home—he glanced around the property—and no other vehicles besides his rental car were in the vicinity. Nick trudged slowly toward the house, the wet leaves made little sound beneath his feet as he crossed the tree-lined yard.

Not taking any chances on the possibility of anyone else having followed her, Nick withdrew his weapon. If "Pinkie" showed his ghostly mug, Nick would give him something to remember him by. The thought that the bastard had hurt Laura again and maybe taken her son burned in Nick's gut.

Nick moved cautiously across the porch to the front door. It was locked. The sign officially proclaiming the doctor's absence still hung in a nearby window. He obviously hadn't returned. Surveying the quiet street, Nick moved down the side of the house. A couple of blocks off the small town square and lined by trees and shrubbery, the place was fairly secluded. The back of the house looked much like the front with a wide porch spanning the length of it. The back door stood open. Good. Nick preferred an avenue of access that didn't require breaking a window. An open door was invitation enough to skirt the boundaries of breaking and entering.

Not that a minor technicality would have kept him from going in, Nick mused. Upon reaching the door, he saw that Laura had beat him to it anyway. One glass pane in the door had been shattered. A handy rock lay on the painted porch floor. Nick swore under his breath. What the hell was she thinking? The police surely patrolled the area. Nick eased inside, scanning left to right as his eyes adjusted to the natural early morning interior light. The large old-fashioned kitchen looked homey and quite empty. Silently, Nick weaved between the massive oak furnishings and made his way to the dimly lit hall.

A sound reached him. He frowned in concentration. *Crying*. Laura! Hard as it proved, Nick remained absolutely still until he got a fix on the direction of the heart rending weeping. Farther down the hall and to the right. Nick moved soundlessly toward the door he had estimated would lead him to Laura. The soft sound of her tears echoed in the silent house. If anyone had hurt her…

Rage twisting inside him, Nick paused next to the open doorway and listened for any other sound coming from the room. Nothing. Taking a deep breath and firming his grip on his weapon, Nick swung into position in front of the door. He scanned what appeared to be an office for any threat. The place had been tossed. It looked as if a tornado had ripped through it. Maintaining his fire-ready stance, Nick dropped his gaze to the floor where Laura huddled…

…over what was obviously a very dead man.

BLOOD.

Laura stared at her hands. The warm, sticky red stuff oozed between her fingers. She had tried to help Doc but it was too late.

Too late.

Dizziness washed over her, making her want to give in to the darkness that threatened her consciousness. Who would do this to Doc? Laura's gaze riveted once more to the large kitchen knife protruding from his chest. She swallowed back the bitter bile rising in her throat.

She had done this. Laura moaned a sob. She had come back to Bay Break and brought nothing but pain, loss and death to those she loved most.

Robby...

Doc...

And Nick.

Laura closed her eyes and surrendered to the flood of emotion pressing against the back of her throat. She was responsible for this senseless violence.

"Oh, God," she murmured as she rocked back and forth. "I killed him. I killed him," she chanted.

"Laura."

Slowly, Laura looked up into the stony features of Nick's grim face. "Doc's dead," she told him weakly.

Nick knelt next to her then and checked Doc's pulse.

"It's too late," she whispered. "He's gone. Robby's gone, too." A heart-wrenching sob tore from her lips. Laura slumped in defeat. *Too late. Too late. Too late,* her mind screamed.

"Come on, Laura, we have to get you out of here."

Nick was moving her. She could feel his strong arms around her as he lifted her. Laura's head dropped onto his shoulder.

Doc was dead.

Robby was lost.

And it was all her fault.

Laura's stomach churned violently. The room spun wildly when Nick settled her back onto her feet near the kitchen sink.

Laura moaned a protest when he began washing the blood from her hands. *No, no, no,* her mind chanted.

"Oh, God." Laura dropped her head into the sink and vomited violently. The image of Doc's blood pooling around his dead body was forever imprinted in her memory. The sound of Robby's cries for mommy rang in her ears.

"It's okay, baby, it's okay," Nick murmured softly as he held her hair back from her face. He turned on the tap to wash away the pungent bile.

When the urge to heave passed, Laura cupped her hand and cooled her mouth and throat with as much water as she dared drink with her stomach still quivering inside her. She splashed the liquid relief on her face, then swiped the excess moisture away with her hand. *Doc was dead.*

Nick lifted her onto the counter and inspected her closely, a mixture of fear and concern etched on his face. "You're not hurt?" He brushed the damp hair back from her face.

Laura shook her head. Nausea threatened at even that simple movement. *Doc was dead.*

She squeezed her eyes shut to block the horrifying images. "This is my fault. I shouldn't have come here."

"You have to tell me what happened," Nick urged gently. "Why did you run away from me?"

She swallowed, then shuddered, more from grief than the bitter taste still clinging to the back of her throat. "I didn't run away," she told him. "I thought if I could find my file, that maybe Doc had made some sort of notations regarding Robby. Then James Ed couldn't pretend my son doesn't exist." Laura closed her eyes and suppressed the mental replay of the scene she had found. She opened her eyes to him then. "I want to do this alone, Nick. I don't want you to help me anymore. It's not safe. I won't risk you getting hurt again."

"There was no one else here when you arrived?" Nick seemed to ignore all that she had just said.

Laura shook her head. "Just…just…" She gestured vaguely toward the hall. "Doc," she finished weakly.

"Laura, I need you to think very carefully. Was the door open when you arrived?"

"I…I broke the glass and unlocked the door," she told him. Laura allowed her frantic gaze to meet his now unreadable one. Those piercing green eyes bored into hers, searching, analyzing.

"Did you touch anything besides the door?"

"What?"

"Did you touch anything at all, Laura, anything besides the door?" he demanded impatiently.

She thought hard. What did she touch? Nothing…everything, maybe. "I can't remember." What was he thinking?

His fingers, like steel bands, curled around her arms; he gave her a little shake. "Listen to me," he ground out. "The blood hasn't congealed yet. Do you know what that means?"

Laura's stomach roiled at the mental picture Nick's words evoked. "I don't want to hear this…." She tried to escape his firm hold. "Just let me go, Nick."

"Dammit, Laura," he growled. "Whoever killed Doc hasn't been gone long. Doc was out of town, remember? He probably arrived back in town and surprised someone in his office. Think! Think about what you saw first when you came inside. What did you hear?"

Laura concentrated hard. She heard…silence. Her gaze connected to Nick's. "Nothing. There was silence." She swallowed. "But I could smell the blood." A sob snatched at Laura's flimsy hold on composure. "The moment I walked in I could smell it."

Nick swore under his breath. "You're sure," he repeated slowly, "that you didn't touch anything."

"I don't think so." Laura let go a shaky breath. "But I can't be sure. I was…I was hysterical." A kind of numbness had set in now, Laura realized. She didn't really feel anything at all, just tired. So very tired.

"Don't move," Nick instructed harshly.

Laura nodded. She clamped her hand over her mouth and fought the urge to scream. She felt her eyes go round with remembered horror. Doc was dead. Robby was lost. Oh, God. Oh, God. She had to do something.

But what?

Minutes or hours passed before Nick came back. Laura couldn't be sure which. He swiped the faucet and the area around the sink with a hand towel. Laura frowned. What was he doing?

"Can you stand?" he asked, his expression closed.

"Yes," she murmured.

Nick lifted her off the counter and settled Laura on her feet. "Don't move, don't touch anything," he ordered.

Laura blinked, confused. Nick swiped the counter, then ushered her toward the back door. Once they were on the porch, he gave the doorknob, the door and its surrounding casing the same treatment. Still too dazed to marshal the strength to question his actions, Laura watched as he threw the rock she had used to break the glass deep into the woods at the back of the yard. She tried to think what all this meant, but her mind kept going back to the image of Doc lying dead on the floor. Laura shuddered and forced the images away.

Nick took her hand and led her back to the car. He pitched the towel he had used into the back seat. As if she were as fragile as glass, he settled Laura into the passenger's seat and buckled her seat belt. Laura watched him move to the other side of the car and slide behind the wheel. Memories of their lovemaking suddenly filled her, warmed her. Laura closed her eyes and savored the remembered heat of Nick's skin against hers. His lips on her body, his kiss. The last time they had made love Robby had been conceived.

And now he was lost. Laura's heart shuddered in her chest. Her baby. She had to find her baby.

"Nick, we have to find my baby," she urged. Laura shifted in the seat. "Don't you see. They're erasing every trace of my baby's existence." She shook her head. "It's as if he has disappeared into thin air. Never existed."

Nick cast her an understanding look as he pulled the car out onto the street. "I'm calling Ian when we get back to the house." He glanced back at her then. "I'm making arrangements to take you someplace safe. Too much I don't understand is going on around here. I'm not taking any chances."

Fear rolled over Laura in suffocating waves. "No! I can't leave without Robby."

"The point is not negotiable."

Laura caught a glimpse of Vine Street as Nick crossed town. Desperation like she had never known before slammed into Laura. She had left Robby with Mrs. Leeton. She had to know where he was. She wasn't the fragile old woman she pretended to be. She knew. She had to know.

"Take me to Mrs. Leeton's house." The quiet force in those few words surprised even Laura. She had to go back.

Nick cast a glance in her direction. "All right," he agreed without hesitation and to her complete surprise.

Laura closed her eyes and prayed that Mrs. Leeton would tell the truth…and that it wouldn't be too late.

NICK BANGED on the door again, louder this time. The old woman would have to be deaf not to hear him. Laura stood next to him, impatiently shifting her weight from one foot to the other.

"She's not going to answer because she knows you're on to her now," Laura insisted.

He glanced at his watch. "Give her a minute. It's early and she's old. Maybe she's still in bed."

Laura huffed a breath and crossed her arms over her chest.

Nick released a long, slow breath of his own. *I killed him. I killed him,* kept echoing in his brain. He passed a weary hand over his face. She couldn't have, of course. But someone had intended to make it look as though she had. Her file had been lying right next to the Doc's body, the contents missing.

Nick shook his head at his own stupidity. In his irrational desire to protect Laura, he had tampered with evidence by wiping down the place, including any prints the real killer might have left behind. He was a bigger fool than even he had imagined.

"She isn't coming to the door," Laura prodded.

Nick cut her a look. He reached into his pocket and retrieved his all-purpose key. Laura watched in silent amazement as he quickly and efficiently "unlocked" the door.

Laura rushed past him before he could step aside. Nick surveyed the quiet parlor while Laura rushed from one room to the next calling the old woman's name.

Mrs. Leeton was history.

Nick scanned the parlor.

She had either gotten out of Dodge or she was pushing up daisies somewhere like the Doc. Laura rushed back into the room.

"She's not here," she said wearily.

Nick picked up a picture frame and studied the smiling couple inside. "She's gone."

"But her things are still here," Laura argued. "Her clothes, her pictures." She gestured to the frame in his hand.

Nick turned the silver frame so that Laura could see it. "Lovely couple," he noted. "But they came with the frame."

Laura frowned, then quickly scanned the two frames hanging on the far wall. "Why would she take the pictures and leave the frames hanging?"

Nick placed the frame back on the table. "She doesn't want anyone to know she's gone." He crossed the room, stared out the window at nothing in particular, then looked back to Laura. "Can you tell if any of her clothes are gone?"

Laura shrugged. "It's hard to tell. There are clothes in the closets and in the dresser drawers, but I can't be sure if they're all there."

"I'll bet they're not," he assured her. "Where's the kitchen?"

Laura led him to the small immaculate kitchen. The woman was definitely obsessive-compulsive about housecleaning, he noted. He glanced at the shiny tile floors and sparkling white countertops. Nick walked to the refrigerator and opened the door. He leaned down and peered inside for a moment or two.

"She's been gone at least three days," he said when he had straightened and closed the door.

"How do you know that?"

"The milk expired day before yesterday," he explained. Nick nodded toward the calendar hanging from a magnet on the appliance door.

Laura stepped closer to see what had caught Nick's eyes. Mrs. Leeton had meticulously marked off each day until day before yesterday. "Oh, God," she murmured.

Laura swayed. Nick caught her. "Come on, Laura, there's nothing else we can do here."

Nick locked the door and led Laura to the car. He watched her for signs of shock or panic. She had seen too much today. He didn't see how she could tolerate much more defeat. It was a miracle she hadn't fallen completely apart.

Once they were back at the house, Nick would insist that

Laura lie down. Then he would call Ian and set up a new location to take Laura. Things were definitely getting too hot around here. One way or another, he intended to get to the bottom of this mess. But first he had to make sure Laura was safe. It wouldn't be long before Dr. Holland's body was discovered. Time was running out for Laura's freedom. If James Ed suspected Laura was in any way involved with Doc's murder, he would insist that she be sent away now.

Maybe, Nick decided, he would tilt the odds in their favor. A quick call to his old friend Ray would set things in motion.

NICK PULLED the afghan over Laura. He hoped she would sleep for a while. She had been so despondent over the Doc's death that Nick had been worried out of his mind. Shortly after finally lying down, she had fallen asleep on the couch and Nick was immensely thankful. He didn't think he could bear one more moment of her self-deprecation. She blamed herself for Doc's death. If she hadn't come back here, she kept saying. But her baby had been sick. With no insurance and no money, she hadn't known who else to turn to. Now Doc was dead.

Nick blew out a breath. He wished he could find one single shred of real proof that Laura did, in fact, have a child. The stretch marks indicated a pregnancy, but proved nothing as to her having had a live birth. He had to have solid evidence.

Shaking his head in disgust, Nick walked to the kitchen and numbly went through the motions of brewing coffee. Hell, he hadn't even had a cup of coffee today. He glanced at the clock on the wall; two o'clock. He had a feeling that this was going to be one hell of a long day. He had busied himself earlier with cleaning up the water in the bathroom, but now he felt that old restless feeling. They were getting closer to the truth now. He could feel it.

With a cup of strong coffee in his hand, Nick sat down at the table and pulled out his cellular phone. He hadn't wanted to make this call until he was certain Laura wouldn't hear. He punched in the number for information, then requested Ray's home number. Less than two minutes later he was holding for his old friend, Detective Ray Ingle.

"Hey buddyro, what's up?" Ray quipped, sounding a great deal more relaxed than the last time Nick had spoken to him.

"The easier question would be what's not," Nick told him with humor in his tone though he felt none at all.

"I hear you're hanging out in Mississippi for a week or two."

"Yeah, I just can't seem to learn my lesson right the first time." Nick compressed his lips into a thin line. Beating around the bush wasn't going to make telling Ray what he had to tell him any easier.

"Hell." Ray laughed. "If you hang around down here long enough, maybe we'll make a real Southern gentleman out of you yet."

Nick smiled in spite of himself. "Thanks, but I think I'll stick with what I know best."

Silence waited between them for several long seconds.

"What's really up, man?" Ray ventured solemnly.

Nick stretched his neck in an effort to chase away the tension building there. "There's been a murder here in Bay Break."

"I see," Ray answered much more calmly than Nick had anticipated.

"Dr. Holland. Sometime this morning I think. His office has been trashed."

"Do the locals know yet?"

"Not yet."

"Is there anything else I should know?" Ray asked pointedly. "I won't even ask how you know all this."

"You may find Laura's prints in there," Nick admitted. "Hell, you'll probably find mine, too."

"Anything else?"

Nick hesitated only a second. "No."

Another long beat of silence passed.

"What is it you want me to do?" Ray asked finally.

"I know the locals will request a detective from your office to conduct the investigation." Nick moistened his lips. "I need you to make sure we're clean on this one."

"Are you?"

"I wouldn't ask if we weren't."

"Does the Governor know about this?"

"No," Nick said quickly. "And I'd appreciate it if you didn't tell him."

"What's going on, Nick?"

Nick heard the tension in Ray's voice. "I just need some more time to figure this out. I don't want Laura connected to anything that might muddy the waters."

"All right," Ray agreed. "I'll take care of it."

"Thanks, man," Nick said. "You know if you ever need anything at all, I'll be there for you."

"Don't think I'll forget it, slick," Ray said frankly.

"Let me know if you come up with any suspects," Nick added before he could hang up.

"Hey," Ray blurted before the connection was cut.

Nick pressed the phone back to his ear. "Yeah, Ray, I'm still here."

"What's the deal with the kid?"

Nick froze. Had James Ed told Ray about Laura's claims of having a child. Maybe James Ed had Ray looking into the possibility. Nick shook his head. No way. Ray would have told him right up front.

"What kid?" Nick asked slowly, reserving reaction.

Ray made a sound of disbelief. "Hell man, the kid Laura had with her when I spotted her down there. What kid did you think I meant?"

Nick's chest constricted. "Laura had a child with her when you saw her?"

"Yeah," Ray said, confusion coloring his tone. "A baby, maybe a year or so old. You couldn't miss him, he—"

"Her child is missing," Nick interrupted.

"Missing? What do—"

"Thanks, Ray," Nick said quickly, cutting him off. "Gotta go. I'll explain later." Nick closed the phone and tossed it onto the table.

He stood, the chair scraping across the floor in protest of his abrupt move. James Ed had definitely lied about Laura being in the hospital for the past eighteen months. She had been telling the truth all along. There really was a child.

Laura's child.

And now Nick had the evidence he needed to prove it.

Chapter Ten

Laura woke with a start. It was dark outside. She had slept the afternoon away again. She licked her dry lips and swallowed, the effort required to do so seeming monumental. How could she have slept so long? The medication was no longer in her system. Exhaustion, she supposed. Sleep had brought blessed relief. She had been able to leave reality behind. To escape…

Doc was dead.

The memory hit like a tidal wave. Laura squeezed her eyes shut and resisted the urge to cry. She refused to cry. Crying would accomplish nothing. She had to do something.

Doc was dead.

The files were missing.

Mrs. Mallory was gone.

Mrs. Leeton had disappeared.

Anyone who knew anything about Robby's birth was no longer available to help Laura. There was no one. Desperation crashed in on her all over again.

She would just have to help herself.

She could do it.

Nick would help her, but she wasn't going to allow him to take that risk. Doc had tried to help her and he was dead.

Laura clenched her teeth and forced her weary, grief-stricken mind to concentrate on forming a plan. If she could get her hands on a gun...

Nick would need his gun to protect himself.

Doc had a gun. She remembered seeing it on her first visit with Doc when she returned to Bay Break with Robby. Doc had shown her that he kept it loaded and in the drawer by his bed. If anyone showed up to cause trouble for Laura he knew how to use it, too, he had said. Doc loved her. When this nightmare started she had hoped that maybe he had Robby with him, hiding out somewhere.

Another wave of fierce grief tore at Laura's heart. But he was dead. Gone forever. The albino had killed him. James Ed's henchman. Laura knew it as surely as she knew her own name. He would kill Nick, too, if he got in James Ed's way. Laura would not permit that to happen.

A sense of calm settled over Laura with the decision. It would be simple. All she had to do was take the car like she did this morning, drop by the clinic to get the gun and head to Jackson. She would get the truth out of James Ed one way or another. Nick would never suspect that she would go back to her brother's house. At least not until it was too late. But first, she had to escape Nick's watchful eye. He would be monitoring her even more closely now.

Throwing back the afghan, Laura sat up and pushed the hair from her face. She looked around the den. No Nick. Maybe he had decided to take a shower. She listened. Nothing. She didn't smell food cooking either, so he probably wasn't in the kitchen. But he wouldn't be far away that was for sure.

Laura pushed to her feet. She closed her eyes and waited for the dizziness to pass. She needed to eat, but couldn't bring herself to even think of food. Her body was so weak. Laura took slow, deep breaths. When the walls had stopped spinning around her, she moved toward the kitchen. Though she rarely drank it, coffee would be good now. Laura shuffled into the hall and bumped straight into Nick. It was as if he had some sort of sixth sense about her. She smiled a secret smile. Except for this morning. She had definitely thrown him off balance then. Or maybe it was the lovemaking the night before. Warmth flowed instantly through Laura at the thought of making love with Nick.

"Laura." He smiled and brushed her cheek with gentle fingers. "I've been waiting for you to wake up. We need to talk, sweetheart."

The desire to tell Nick the truth about his son almost overwhelmed all else. She looked into those caring green eyes and remembered every detail of the way he had made love to her. The tenderness, the heat. The same as two years ago when she had fallen in love with this special man in the first place. Nick was the most caring, giving person she had ever met. He was the only person since her parents had died who believed in her at all. He was nothing like her brother. He was unlike any man she had ever met. And she had to protect Nick. He would willingly die for her if it came down to it. Laura had to make sure that didn't happen.

Laura shook off the lingering doubts regarding what she was about to do. She had to do it for Nick. "What did you want to talk about," she asked casually. Talking would give her time to devise a plan. She stilled. As long as he didn't start pressuring her again about her baby's father. God, if he suspected the truth for one minute...

"Let's go back into the den and get comfortable," he suggested.

For two long beats Laura could only stare into those caring jade depths. She loved this man so. The truth was going to forever change how he felt about her. Could she bear that?

Finally, she nodded. "Okay." She allowed Nick to usher her back into the den and to the sofa. She sat down obediently and sent up a silent prayer that he hadn't figured things out yet. Laura knew she had to tell him eventually. Just not now. She couldn't deal with anything else right now.

Nick paced in a kind of circle for a moment as if he couldn't decide how to begin. Laura swallowed hard. Surely he didn't have bad news that he feared passing on to her. Laura closed her eyes for a second to calm herself. No, she couldn't take more bad news at the moment. The image of Doc lying life-less on the floor of his office flashed before her eyes.

"I spoke with Detective Ingle this afternoon," Nick began, jerking her splintered attention back to him.

"Robby?" Terror snaked around Laura's heart and she in-stantly slammed a mental door shut on her fears. She had to be strong. Otherwise she wouldn't be able to find Robby or to lead the albino away from Nick.

Nick paused a few feet away, his back turned to her he bowed his head. "I'm sorry, Laura, I should—"

Shattering glass interrupted Nick's words. Laura's startled gaze darted to the window across the room. A gust of wind blew the curtains outward, they fluttered briefly then fell back into place. Fragments of glass littered the carpet. Laura frowned. She stood—

Nick's arms went around her and they hurtled to the floor, overturning the sofa table in the process. The telephone and lamp crashed to the floor. The dial tone buzzed from the dis-lodged receiver.

Stunned, Laura lay against the carpet for a several seconds before she could think. Nick's body covered her own, protect-ing her. "Nick, what's going on?" she whispered hoarsely. The answer to her question struck her like a jolt of electricity. Her breath thinned in her lungs. Someone had shot through the window. Ice formed in Laura's stomach. *He* was out there. He was shooting at them.

"Nick!" Laura twisted her neck to an awkward angle to try and see his face. His eyes were closed, blood dripped down his forehead. She realized then that his full body weight was bearing down on her. Terror ignited within Laura. She pushed with all her might to roll herself and Nick over. She scrambled onto all fours and lowered her cheek to his face. He was breathing. Thank God. She quickly studied the injury that started an inch or so above his right eyebrow and disappeared into his hairline.

Please don't let him be hurt badly, she prayed.

Laura's hands shook as she traced the path the bullet had made with her fingers. Her lips trembled and she clamped down on her lower one to hold back the sobs twisting in her throat. Nick's warm blood stained her fingers. The vision of Doc lying in a pool of blood reeled past her eyes. Laura forced away the vivid memory. She had to help Nick. She frowned at the large bump rising on the left side of his forehead, near that temple. Laura glanced at the overturned table and broken lamp. He must have hit his head on the way down. The bullet appeared to have only grazed his head. She prayed she was right about that. He was still breathing but out cold. Could there be internal damage? Renewed terror zipped through her.

Laura shook him gently. "Nick. Nick, please wake up."

Laura's chest tightened with a rush of panic. She had to get help. She crawled to the other side of the table and snatched up the receiver and uprighted the telephone's base. Something cold and hard pressed to the back of her head.

"Hang it up," a coarse voice ordered.

It was him. She knew that voice. In her panic to help Nick, Laura had completely forgotten that he was somewhere outside. Now, he was here.

"Now," he commanded harshly. "Or I'll put another bullet in your boyfriend and finish him off."

Laura dropped the receiver onto its base and quickly stood. "He needs help," Laura pleaded. "Just let me call for help and then I'll do anything you want."

His weapon trained on her heart, the albino circled around her then glanced down at Nick. Laura gasped when he kicked Nick in the side.

"Stop!" she shrieked.

The albino grinned. "He'll live." He cocked one pale brow. "But he might not if you don't do exactly as I say."

Laura grabbed control of herself. She nodded adamantly. "What do you want me to do?"

He gestured toward the hall. "Outside, princess."

Laura led the way to the front door. She said one more silent prayer that Nick would be all right. Once outside, she turned to the man and asked, "What now?" Whatever it took to appease him and keep him away from Nick.

He glanced around the dark yard as if trying to decide. "The barn," he suggested. "Lots of imaginative possibilities in a barn."

Laura shuddered, but quickly composed herself. She needed calm. She needed to think. She had to think of a way to defend herself. If he killed her now, he might go back inside the house and kill Nick as well.

"Let's make this easy on the both of us," the man murmured next to her ear as he ushered her in the direction of the barn. "I'm going to kill you, and you're going to let me. Got that?"

Laura's eyes widened in fear, but she squashed the paralyzing emotion. She racked her brain to remember what might be in the barn that could help her.

"Got that?" he demanded, the gun boring into her skull.

Laura nodded jerkily.

"Good," he acknowledged.

The scent of hay and stored fuels filled Laura's lungs as they entered the big double doors of the barn which stood partially open. No one ever bothered to close them, she remembered as if it mattered now. The albino made a halfhearted attempt at closing them. That effort would be to no avail Laura knew, the doors would only drift open again. They always did. But who would notice tonight?

Nick. Tears streamed down Laura's cheeks. She suddenly found herself praying that he didn't wake up and come to her rescue. Maybe if he stayed in the house, this bastard would just leave after he did what James Ed had paid him to do. Laura trembled. She didn't want to die. She wanted to be with her son, and she wanted to be with Nick.

But her life meant nothing if either of them was hurt by this. Laura closed her eyes against the painful possibility. Her captor flipped a switch and a long fluorescent light blinked to life overhead. Laura blinked quickly, her frantic gaze searched for anything that might aid her escape. The light's dim glow lit the center of the spacious barn, but the stalls remained in shadow. At one time, when she was a child, she remembered abruptly, there had been horses in this barn. But not anymore. Not in a long time. James Ed had gotten rid of what he had called an unnecessary nuisance.

The albino shoved her to the floor. "Don't move," he warned as he surveyed their surroundings. A smile lifted one side of his grim mouth when his gaze lit on something in particular. Laura shifted to see what it was that had captured his attention.

"Perfect," he muttered. Keeping the rifle aimed at her chest and his gaze trained on Laura, he walked to the row of hooks lining one wall and took down a sturdy-looking rope coiled there. Rope in hand, he moved back to tower over her. Laura committed every detail of his appearance to memory. Ghostly white hair and skin, and those eerie pink eyes. He wasn't very tall, but was solidly built. And strong, Laura remembered well. If she got away this time, she fully intended to be able to describe him to Nick.

"One peep out of you and I'll kill you now," he warned as he fiddled with the rope. "Then I'll kill lover boy just for the hell of it."

Not allowing his threat to frighten her further, Laura concentrated on his actions. Was he going to tie her up? She ordered the hysteria rising inside her to retreat, and her mind to focus. She had to escape. He was going to kill her this time, that was certain. The finality of that realization was oddly calming. Laura scanned her immediate surroundings for a weapon of some sort. A pitchfork stood on the wall farthest from her. She chewed her lip as she considered the distance. She would never be able to reach it before he shot her.

This was hopeless. There was nothing she could do.

Laura felt weak with regret. The thought that she would never see Nick or Robby again was a bone-deep ache.

No! she told herself. She had to do something. She couldn't just let him do this. She needed to get the albino talking. She had to stall him. At least it was some sort of plan. Maybe if she distracted him he would screw up somehow.

"Why did you have to kill Doc?" she demanded, her voice harsher than she had intended.

He cut his evil gaze to her and grinned. It was then that Laura noted the one thing about him that wasn't white—his teeth. They were a hideous yellow. She shivered.

"The old man was lucky once," he informed her haughtily. "When I came for him, he had left town. He had himself a sudden personal emergency." He laughed as if relishing Doc's troubles. "His only living relative, a sister out in Arkansas, had herself a heart attack and died."

"How do you know that?" Laura asked sharply, annoyed that he derived pleasure from Doc's loss.

"I was there at the clinic. One of the patients leaving that morning told me," he retorted. "If he hadn't left so quickly I would have taken care of him then and there." He shook his head with feigned regret. "But then he showed up this morning. Bad timing, too. I was taking your file." He frowned; his hands stilled on the rope. "Pissed me off that I couldn't get it the day he disappeared, but there were too many witnesses who saw me in his yard. I couldn't risk doing anything suspicious. So I left." That sick smile lifted his lips again. "People aren't likely to forget how I look."

Laura shivered. That was the truth if she had ever heard it. "You killed Doc just because he helped me?"

"I killed Doc because he knew too much."

Same difference, Laura thought with growing disgust.

"What about Mrs. Leeton, did you kill her, too, or was she working with you?" Laura clenched her teeth at the thought that the woman had betrayed her. Had helped someone steal her son. Laura's lips quivered with as much anger as fear.

"Not yet," he said casually. "The old bag disappeared. But I'll find her."

"Where's my son?" Laura held her breath. She feared the answer, but she had to know. Please, God, she prayed, don't let him have hurt my baby.

"You're not going to be needing him," he suggested as he tightened the strange knot in the rope. "Unless you want him buried with you."

Laura jumped to her feet, fury shot through her. "If you've hurt my son," she threatened.

"Don't worry, princess, he's worth too much alive." The albino recoiled the rope. "But you," he allowed that evil gaze to travel over her, "you're worth a whole lot more dead. And I'm tired of playing with you now. It's time to get down to business."

NICK ROUSED slowly to a piercing pain that knifed right through his skull. He touched his forehead and blood darkened his fingertips.

"What the hell happened?" he muttered.

He sat up, groaning with the pain pounding inside his head. He pushed to his feet and the room spun around him. Nick closed his eyes and fought the vertigo threatening his vertical position. He took a step and something crushed under his boot. Wiping the blood from his face, Nick stared down at the broken lamp and overturned table. The events that had taken place slammed into him with such force that he staggered.

"Laura." Nick scanned the room, then rushed into the hall. The front door stood open. The cold November wind had blown leaves into the hall. They skittered this way and that across the shiny hardwood like lost souls.

Nick hurried out onto the porch, his step still unsteady. The rental car was in the driveway where he had left it. He looked from left to right. Which way would the son of a bitch have taken her?

A shriek cut through the dark fabric of the night. Nick whirled in the direction of the sound. The barn. The barest glow of light filtered past the half-open doors. Nick ran like hell. He clenched his jaw against the resulting pain twisting in his knee and then shooting up his right thigh. He ignored the fierce throb still hammering inside his head. He had to get to her. Nick pushed harder despite the grinding pain and the vertigo still pulling at him. He stumbled, barely catching himself before he hit the ground. Nick swore and propelled himself toward the barn. He skidded to a stop near one wide door. Commanding his respiration to slow, he inched toward the crack where the door hinged to the doorway. He leaned forward and peered through the narrow opening.

Nick jerked back at what he saw. Laura was standing on a small stepladder. A length of rope had been strung over a rafter, its noose snug around her neck. Nick swallowed the terror that climbed into his throat. He carefully stepped back up to the narrow slit and forced himself to look again. The albino stood near her, talking to her, the barrel of his weapon jabbed into her stomach. Absolute fear held Laura's every feature captive. She clutched frantically at the rope as if it were too tight already.

A crimson rage engulfed Nick. The son of a bitch was a dead man. Nick remembered to breathe, breathe deeply and slowly. He needed to focus. He couldn't risk Laura getting hurt. But the albino was *dead*.

Nick moved soundlessly toward the open doorway. He needed to get as close as possible without being detected. Taking one last deep breath, Nick stepped into the reaching fingers of light and began the slow, careful journey toward his target. He moved to the far right, toward the shadows near the stalls. If he could circle around and come up directly behind the bastard, Nick would hopefully prevent any sudden or unexpected moves when he took him down.

"Go ahead," the albino sneered. "Don't be a wimp. Scream all you want. Nobody's going to hear you. Lover boy is out cold." He moved closer to Laura. "Sound effects always add to the pleasure."

"Just tell me where my son is," Laura demanded hoarsely.

"Now this isn't going to be so bad." The albino gestured toward her precarious position with the barrel of his high-powered rifle. "It'll take about four minutes, depending on how long you can hold your breath, for you to pass out, and then it'll all be over. And everyone will live happily ever after. They'll all say, poor Laura, we did everything we could for her but she still committed suicide in the end."

"Swear to me that my son is safe," Laura spat vehemently.

Nick blocked the emotion that crowded his thinking at the sound of her desperation. She wasn't afraid to die, she was only afraid for her child. His throat constricted. The child no one had believed in, including him at first. Nick's lips compressed into a thin line, he barely restrained the roar of rage filling him now.

"Don't you worry about that baby boy of yours," the albino taunted. "He's going to make someone very happy. Happy enough to pay me all the money I'll ever need," he added in a sickeningly cocky voice.

Laura stiffened, the old, rickety stepladder rocked precariously beneath her.

"Don't move, princess," he warned. "I wouldn't want you to actually kill yourself." He stepped closer to her. "I want the pleasure of giving you that final little push myself. Then I'm going in the house and finish off your friend."

"You promised if I did what you said that you would leave Nick alone," she challenged.

The albino made a sound of approval in his throat. "I love it when you talk back."

Laura turned her face away from him. Nick stopped dead in his tracks when her terrified gaze flickered back to him. He shook his head but it was too late. Recognition and relief flared in her expression. Seeing the change, the albino whirled toward Nick. Nick took a bead right between his pink eyes.

"Drop it," Nick ordered.

The albino smiled. "Well, what do you know. That head of yours must be harder than I thought."

"Cut her down," Nick growled savagely. "Or you die where you stand."

The bastard stroked his cheek with his free hand, his weapon trained on Laura's face now. Nick tightened his grip on his Beretta in anticipation of the right opportunity to take this son of a bitch down.

"See here, wise guy," he smirked, "this is my little party and you weren't invited. Don't you know that two's company and three's a crowd?"

"Cut her down," Nick repeated coldly, the thought of killing the man making him feel decidedly calm. "And I'll let you live."

"What's to keep me from shooting her first?"

Nick heard the uncertainty in the albino's voice then. "Just one thing," Nick paused for effect, "the closed-casket funeral required since I'm about to take the top of your head off." Nick snugged his finger on the trigger.

"Wouldn't want that, now would we?" the albino relented.

His gaze locked with Nick's, the albino slowly began to lower his weapon. Nick took a step forward. And then everything lapsed into slow motion. The albino kicked his right foot outward. The stepladder clattered to the floor. A startled scream shattered the still air. Nick's horrified gaze riveted to Laura. Her arms stretched over her head, she struggled to grasp the rope and keep her weight from pulling her downward. Her legs dangled in thin air. Her face contorted with fear and desperation.

The albino kept his weapon trained on Laura as he backed toward the door. Uncertainty flashed again in those strange eyes. "Are you going to waste precious seconds trying to decide if you can put a bullet in me before she asphyxiates? How long do you think she can hold her breath?" he added with a twisted smile.

Instantly, Nick found himself beneath Laura, supporting

her weight to keep life-giving air flowing in and out of her lungs. His heart slammed mercilessly against his rib cage.

"Can you get the noose off?" he asked hoarsely. Nick felt himself tremble with delayed reaction. The vision of Laura dangling from the end of that damned rope swept through his brain.

Gasping for breath between sobs, Laura didn't answer for a while. "I think so," she rasped, then coughed.

Nick's gaze shot to the barn doors. The albino was gone.

But Laura was alive. Nick closed his eyes and held her lower body more tightly in his arms.

At the moment, nothing else mattered.

Chapter Eleven

"My baby's alive," Laura whispered. "He told me my baby was alive. I…" She shuddered. "You're still bleeding. I have to get you to a hospital."

"Shh," Nick soothed. "I'm fine. The bullet didn't do as much damage as that damned table."

Laura caressed his cheek with trembling fingers, her worried gaze examining him closely. "But there's so much blood."

"I'm fine." He pressed a kiss to her forehead, then pulled her close against his chest. "Just let me hold you a minute." Nick sat on the cold dirt floor and held Laura in his arms. She trembled and he held her closer. He'd almost lost her tonight. He should have anticipated that the bastard would make a move after killing Doc. He was growing impatient.

Laura had been through so much already. Her missing child. Her son. Ray's words echoed inside Nick's head, *"A baby, maybe a year or so old."*

Laura's child.

Ray had seen her with the child. Ian would no doubt confirm tomorrow that the clinic Nick and Laura had visited had, indeed, registered the birth of a Robert Forester with the registrar's office in Montgomery. That would be more hard evidence. Laura had a child, and by noon tomorrow Nick would be able to prove it.

James Ed had lied. Nick couldn't believe he had been that wrong about the man. He had seemed genuinely overjoyed to have Laura back home. To know that she was alive and unharmed.

And Sandra. She might not even know her mother was alive. Her adoptive parents may have told her that the woman died years ago. What would Sandra stand to gain from Laura's death? Nothing, as far as Nick could see. It wasn't as if she and James Ed had needed the money that desperately. Of course, once it was available, they had apparently taken advantage of it. But Sandra wasn't in control of the money, James Ed was. All evidence pointed to James Ed.

Just like Laura said.

Nick frowned. Still, something about that scenario didn't quite fit. Didn't sit right with him. He blew out a disgusted breath. Nick closed his eyes and cursed himself for not believing her in the first place. He should have followed his instincts instead of allowing the past and his pride to get in the way. His eyes burned with regret. It shouldn't have taken him so long to come around.

He was a fool twice over.

Nick placed a soft kiss against Laura's hair. "Let me get you inside," he murmured. "We'll talk then."

"Okay," she said weakly. She stared into his eyes, her own bright with tears. "But first I want to get that wound cleaned up."

Nick nodded and they stood together. His grasp on her arms tightened to steady her when she swayed. She glanced around the dimly lit barn, her eyes wide with fear. Her body tensed as he slid his right arm around her waist.

"It's all right, honey, he's gone. I don't think he'll be back,"

Nick assured her. He couldn't bear the fear in her eyes. If the bastard did come back he was a dead man.

Taking his time so as not to rush her, Nick ushered Laura in the direction of the house. Her skin felt as cold as ice. He had to get her inside and warmed up. He shuddered inwardly again at the thought of how close he had come to losing her tonight. Shock was a definite threat at the moment. A warm bath and hot coffee or cocoa would do the trick. He would call Ian and then Nick and Laura would talk. He wasn't sure she could tolerate any more surprises, good or bad right now. When she was up to it, he would tell Laura that she didn't have to worry anymore.

One way or another Nick would find her child. If he had to beat the truth out of James Ed with his bare hands.

Half an hour later Laura had cleaned and bandaged the wound on his forehead where the bullet had grazed him. Nick had a hell of a lump where the table had gotten in his way, but there was nothing to be done about that. Nick had settled Laura in the wide garden tub and then he'd put in a call to Ian while warming some milk for cocoa. Tracking down the identity of the albino probably wouldn't be difficult, Nick considered as he carried the steaming cocoa to the bathroom.

He paused inside the bathroom door just to look at Laura. Mounds of frothy bubbles enveloped her, hiding that exquisite feminine body. She had bundled all that silky blond hair atop her head in the sexiest heap Nick had ever seen. He loved every sweet, perfect thing about her. A fierce stab of desire sliced through him, making his groin tighten. How he wanted to touch her. But not tonight, he reminded the hungry beast inside him. Laura needed to rest tonight.

Relaxed within the warm depths, her eyes closed, Nick couldn't read what Laura's emotional state was now that the day's events had had time to be absorbed fully. His throat con-

stricted at the thought of just how much she had endured over
the past two years. Running for her life, and with a baby. How
had he ever doubted her? If James Ed were behind all this—
Nick shook his head slowly, resolutely—he would pay. He
forced a deep, calming breath. Going off half-cocked wouldn't
help, but there would definitely be a day of reckoning.

Nick's errant gaze moved back to Laura's face, then traveled down one soft cheek, past her delicate jaw and over the
fragile column of her throat. Anger unfurled inside him when
his gaze traced the offensive marks caused by the rope. The
abrasions, already shadowed with a purplish tinge, were stark
against her creamy skin. The albino had better hope Nick
didn't find him.

Adopting a calm he didn't feel, Nick crossed the quiet
room and sat down on the edge of the luxurious tub. Laura's
lids slowly fluttered open revealing those soft blue eyes. Nick
smiled, then placed her cocoa near the elaborate gold faucet.

"It's warm," he told her. "You should drink it before it
cools."

Laura moistened those full, pink lips. "I suppose it's safe
to say that you believe me about James Ed now," she suggested with just a hint of bitterness.

Nick nodded. He deserved a good swift kick in the ass. "It
would be safe to say that, yes. All the evidence seems to point
to him."

Her expression solemn, those sweet lips trembled. "We
have enough evidence to prove my son exists, too?"

Nick's gaze remained locked with hers for a long moment
as he considered whether to tell her about the call to Ray. No,
he decided, she'd had enough for one night. She needed to
relax, not get all worked up again. "Yes. We can prove your
child is real." He didn't want to think about another man
touching Laura. She belonged to him….

Laura blinked away the moisture shining in those huge blue orbs. "You'll make James Ed tell the truth?"

Nick smiled then. It didn't matter who the father was. Nick would find Laura's child. "Absolutely."

"He said that someone is going to pay him a lot of money for my baby." She swallowed, then pulled her lower lip between her teeth as she composed herself. "I can't believe my own brother would sell my baby."

"We'll get him back, Laura."

Her arms folded over her breasts, Laura sat bolt upright. "I want you to take me to James Ed. I want you to take me right now, Nick," she demanded. "I don't want to waste any more time."

For a moment Nick couldn't speak. Suds slipped over her satiny shoulders and down her slender arms. Laura was a wonderful mother. The kind any child would want, he realized suddenly. The kind of mother he wanted for his own children. She was sweet and beautiful and kind. And all that sass buried beneath her worry for her child pulled at him like nothing else ever had. She was everything he wanted.

"First thing in the morning," he countered finally, a restless feeling stirring deep inside him. "We'll head for Jackson then."

She pressed Nick with her solemn gaze. "And you'll do whatever it takes to get the truth out of my brother?"

"You can count on it." He would have the truth out of James Ed...or else.

"Swear it, Nick," she insisted. "Swear to me that you'll do whatever it takes."

"I swear," he replied softly.

Laura nodded her satisfaction. Several tendrils of that golden silk fell around her face, and clung to that soft neck. "That's all I can ask of you." A frown wrinkled her pretty forehead. "Does your head hurt much?"

"Not much," he whispered. The need to touch her over-whelmed all else. Slowly, while maintaining that intense eye contact, Nick allowed his fingertips to glide over one smooth cheek. Want gripped him with such ferocity that for a long moment he couldn't breathe. "You can ask anything you want of me," he murmured.

Laura took his hand in hers and pressed a soft kiss to his palm, her gaze never leaving his. "And would you give me anything I ask, Nick?" she whispered. A hot flash of desire kindled in her eyes.

He nodded, no longer capable of articulation.

"You're sure you're up to it?" she teased, a smile playing about the corners of her full mouth.

Nick hoped the grunt he uttered was sufficient response.

When Laura slid his hand down to her breast he knew it was. He squeezed. Her head lolled back and her eyes closed in sweet ecstasy. Nick watched as Laura guided his hand to all the places she wanted him to touch. Her other breast, then lower to her flat stomach, then lower still.

Nick groaned when she parted her thighs and opened for him. He slipped his middle finger inside her hot, moist body. A shudder wracked him as an instant climax threatened. Nick clenched his jaw and grabbed back control. Laura was the only woman who ever made him want to come with nothing more than a touch. Nick gripped the edge of the tub with his free hand as he moved that small part of himself rhythmically in-side her. Her moans of pleasure urged him on. Her lips parted slightly as her breathing became labored. Nick used the pad of his thumb to massage her tiny nub of desire until it swelled beneath his touch. She reared back, thrusting her firm white breasts upward, as if begging for his attention. Determined to watch, Nick resisted the urge to taste her. Water and bubbles slipped over her smooth breasts. Her dusky nipples tightened and budded right before his eyes. Nick licked his lips. His arousal throbbed insistently, and he jerked with restraint.

Laura's fingers splayed on the sides of the tub, providing leverage as she arched against his hand. Nick growled with need when he felt the first tremors of her release. He moved more quickly, propelling her toward that peak. Laura cried out as her inner muscles tightened around Nick's finger. His own need for release roared inside him. Nick leaned forward and covered Laura's mouth with his own. She took him hungrily, sucking his tongue into her mouth. Nick groaned. His arms plunged into the water and around her. He pulled her to him savagely, his body needing to feel hers against him.

"I need to be inside you," he breathed against her lips.

"Now, Nick," she murmured greedily. "Hurry."

Holding her firmly against him, Nick lifted Laura from the tub. Water sloshed over the side. Wet heat and suds from her damp skin soaked into his shirtfront. Laura's legs wrapped instinctively around his waist. Nick stumbled toward the door, his mouth still plundering hers. Hot and sweet. She tasted so good. He had to get her to the bed. He couldn't hold out much longer. Nick backed into a wall, cursed—the word lost in the kiss—and groped for the door with one hand.

"No," Laura protested between kisses. "Here," she demanded.

Nick pivoted and pressed her back against the wall. His hips ground into her softness. Nick groaned deep in his throat. Squeezing Laura's thigh with one hand, he wrenched his jeans open.

Laura arched against him, her fingers dug into his shoulders. "Hurry, Nick," she moaned. "Hurry." Her breath came in fierce little spurts. She needed him as much as he needed her. The thought sent another jolt of desire raging through him, almost snapping his control.

Laura screamed at the first nudge of his arousal. Nick

grunted, intent on plunging deep inside her. Breathtaking, gut-wrenching sensations washed over him when he finally pushed fully into Laura's hot, tight body. He sagged against her for the space of one beat as the powerful tide of pleasure almost took him over the edge. His heart pounded hard in time with Laura's. He gulped a much-needed breath.

Her arms tightened around his neck and she pulled him closer. "Nick," she murmured as her eyes closed in an expression of pleasure-pain. "Oh, Nick."

Capturing her sweet lips with his own, Nick began the slow, shallow thrusting that would bring Laura to the brink of release once more. He clenched his jaw and resisted the urge to swiftly drive into his own release. Her thighs tightened on his waist, urging him into a faster rhythm. The air raged in and out of Nick's lungs as he pushed ever closer to climax. The case and all its ugliness faded into insignificance, leaving only Laura behind. Her taste, her scent filled him, mind and body. The final, tense seconds before climax brought complete clarity to Nick's tortured soul.

And he knew in that crystal clear moment that his life would never be the same. He loved her. He had always loved her. She was part of him. She completed him.

The rocking explosion that followed left him weak-kneed and feeling totally helpless in her arms. Nick's gaze moved to hers, she smiled, and something near his heart shifted.

NICK'S NAKED FLESH felt hot against hers, Laura snuggled closer, then smiled. She wanted to feel all of him. To hold him closer still.

For as long as it lasted.

Laura's smile melted. She swallowed back the fear that crowded into her throat. The bandage on his forehead served as a reminder of just how close she had come to losing him tonight. Laura couldn't protect Nick anymore than she had protected Robby. Hurt twisted inside her.

And, dear God, what would Nick do when he discovered the truth? There would be no denying Robby's parentage when they found him. He looked so much like Nick. And Nick had promised her that they would definitely find her baby.

Blinking back the uncertainty, Laura redirected her focus to Nick's long, lean body pressed so intimately to hers. He had said they would talk. But he seemed content for the moment to simply lie next to her without words or questions of any sort. The cool sheets draped their heated skin. She glanced at the clock on the bedside table: 9:00 p.m. What was Robby doing now? she wondered. Her heart squeezed painfully. Was he sleeping soundly in a bed somewhere safe? If someone intended to pay a great deal of money for him, surely they were treating him well. Laura shivered at the thought of someone else cuddling and loving her sweet baby. The idea that he might call someone else mommy tore at her heart. She had to find him.

"You cold?" Nick asked, the words rumbling from his chest.

"I'm fine," Laura said quickly. She immediately regretted the shortness of her response.

Nick shifted onto one elbow and peered down at her. He frowned. The white bandage stark against his dark coloring. "We'll find him, Laura," he assured her. "Don't doubt that."

She essayed a faint smile. "I know." Nick was the kindest, most honorable man she knew. He deserved so much more than she had to give him.

Nick's frown deepened and he fell silent for a few moments. Laura's heart skipped into an erratic staccato. She recognized the precise instant that realization dawned. The air evacuated her lungs.

"You told the receptionist at the clinic that Robby was born on August sixth," he said slowly, thoughtfully.

Laura licked her lips. Ice rushed through her veins. "That's right."

Three seconds later the mental calculations were complete. Nick's gaze landed fully onto hers. "Forester. You used the name Forester."

Laura nodded. Speech wasn't an option.

Suspicion crept into his wary green eyes. "Robert?"

"Robert," she managed to agree.

"Robert what?" His tone held no inflection; his eyes were openly accusing now.

Laura drew in a deep breath. She met that accusing gaze. "Robert Nicholas Forester."

There was no way to describe the expression that claimed Nick's features then. Something between rage and wonder battled for control, but, in the end, the rage proved victorious.

Nick sat up, putting distance between them. "He's my son."

Laura knew it wasn't a question. She also knew with complete certainty that Nick would never forgive her for keeping his son from him.

"Yes," she said finally. Had it not been for the fierceness of his piercing gaze, uttering that solitary word would almost have been a relief. But there was no way to garner any good feelings from what she saw in Nick's eyes.

Nick shot out of bed. His back turned to her, he pulled on his jeans. Laura sat up. She hugged the sheet to her chest and willed the emotions threatening to consume her to retreat.

He shifted back to face her, then raked those long, tanned fingers through his uncharacteristically mussed hair. A muscle flexed rhythmically in his tense jaw. "Why didn't you tell me?" His hands fisted at his sides. "Why didn't you come to me as soon as you knew you were pregnant?"

"You were one of them," she said quietly, defeatedly.

Slowly, but surely every nuance of emotion disappeared

from Nick's eyes and expression. That cold, hard, unfeeling mask slipped firmly into place like the slamming of a door. His broad, muscled chest heaved with the rage no doubt building inside him.

"I was never one of them," he said coldly.

Tears stung her eyes, but Laura refused to cry. "You worked for James Ed. I couldn't be sure that I could trust you." She met his gaze with hope in hers. "When you first found me this time you didn't believe anything I told you. Then, later, I was going to tell you but so much happened."

"Believing you and trusting you are two entirely different things," he snapped. "Don't mistake the two."

Laura struggled to her feet, dragging the tangled sheet with her. They were back to the trust issue. "I couldn't tell you," she told him with as much force as she could summon. "I was afraid for my life, Nick! Don't you get it? James Ed was trying to kill me."

"What did that have to do with trusting me?" he demanded, his tone low and lethal.

Laura shook her head at his inability to see the obvious. "James Ed hired you. Your loyalty was to him."

"We made love, Laura," he ground out. "That didn't spell anything out for you?"

"I was afraid," she said wearily.

"You kept my son from me all this time and all you've got to say is that you were afraid?" Contempt edged his voice.

"I had to protect my child," Laura argued. The starch seeped out of her spine and standing proved difficult.

"Well you did a hell of a job, didn't you?"

The tears would not be contained then. The humiliating liquid emotion slipped down her cheeks. "I did the best I could considering the circumstances."

Nick stepped closer, his body rigid with fury. "But that

wasn't good enough, was it? And it never once occurred to you to call on me for help?"

Anger surged, steeling her resolve. "Forget all that. The important thing now is finding him," Laura countered, her tone as lethal as his.

"I will find him," Nick promised. "And when I do, I'll make sure nothing like this ever happens to him again."

Stunned, Laura could only stare into those cold, emotionless eyes. This was her worst nightmare come true. Not only had she lost her son, but if she did find him he would still be lost even then. Nick's cell phone splintered the ensuing silence. His gaze still riveted to hers, he snatched the phone from the bedside table and snapped his greeting.

Blocking out all other thought, Nick listened carefully as Ian relayed his latest findings.

"The albino is a Rodney Canton, a dirty P.I. with a most impressive rap sheet. Kidnapping, assault with a deadly weapon and worse."

Nick shifted his weight from his throbbing right knee. "Is there any connection between him and the Proctors?"

"No, not directly. But he worked with a Brock Redmond who owned and operated a P.I. office in Natchez for years. Funny thing is," Ian continued, "this Redmond fellow disappeared suddenly about two years ago. No one has seen him since."

Nick frowned. "Do you have a physical description?"

"Oh yes. He fits perfectly the description Laura provided of the man who shot you."

Anticipation nudged at Nick. "Any connection to James Ed?"

Ian laughed. "A long and productive connection. James Ed hired Redmond on several occasions to provide the lowdown on potential staff members."

"Do you have anything that will stand up in a court of law to back that up?"

"I'm looking at the man's files."

Nick shook his head. "I'm not sure I want to know how you managed that."

"It would seem that Redmond stiffed his secretary out of two months' pay when he disappeared." Amusement colored Ian's tone. "So she confiscated his files. She has been most helpful."

"Nothing else on Sandra?"

"The jury is still out on the first lady," Ian told him. "But the evidence against James Ed is undeniable. If Redmond is the man who shot you, and he appears to be, then James Ed is in this up to his politically incorrect neck."

"Good work, Ian. I'll touch base with you tomorrow."

Ian hesitated. "You sound a little strange, Nick. Is there anything you're not telling me?"

"I'll fill you in tomorrow." Nick flipped the phone closed before Ian could say anything else.

Nick had a son.

And James Ed Proctor was about to discover that Nick was more than just a man of his word. He was a man of action. Only Nick wasn't sure James Ed was going to like the action Nick had in mind. He intended to find his son if he had to wring the child's location one syllable at a time out of James Ed's scrawny neck. Nick would not stop until he found his son.

Nick shot Laura a withering look. "Get dressed. We're going to Jackson.

A NARROW SLIT of moonlight sliced through the darkness of the room from the gap between the heavily lined drapes. Propelled by her dreams, Elsa tossed restlessly beneath the thick covers. A cold sweat dampened her skin, making her nightgown stick to her in all the uncomfortable places.

It was wrong, it was wrong, her mind chanted.

Elsa sat up with a start. She blinked, then pushed her disheveled hair from her sweat-dampened face. She looked at the clock. Almost midnight. It seemed so much later. Elsa blew out a breath of weariness. The dreams. Oh, the dreams were so disturbing. She shook herself. But they were only dreams.

Soon it would be a new day.

The day.

Today the little boy's new family would come to take him away to their home. Elsa passed a hand over her face and tried to reconcile herself to that fact. She shook her head. It wasn't right. Deep inside, past all the indifference and looking the other way, she knew it wasn't right.

She swallowed. She had to do something.

Yes. A sense of calmness settled over her.

She had to do something.

Chapter Twelve

Uneasiness crawled up Nick's spine the moment he parked behind the Governor's home. The second floor of the house stood in darkness, a few lights glowed downstairs. Nick found it particularly odd that security had not already approached the car. He knew from experience how difficult it was to out-maneuver those guys.

"What are we waiting for?"

Nick shifted his attention to the woman seated next to him. It was the first time she had spoken since they left Bay Break. Renewed anger flooded Nick when he met her hesitant gaze. She had lied to him. Kept his son from him. Nick's fingers tightened on the steering wheel. No matter what her reasons, and no matter what that more foolish part of him wanted to feel, Nick wasn't sure he could ever forgive her for that.

"Something isn't right," Nick told her, emotion making his voice harsh in the hushed darkness that shrouded them.

"I don't care," Laura said with a shake of her head. "I have to find Robby."

Nick snagged her left arm. "You'll do exactly as I say, Laura," he ground out. "I'm going in and you're staying right here."

"No way," she argued. "I'm going in, too. You can't stop me." The warning in her voice was that of a desperate mother's.

He blew out an impatient breath. "All right, but stay right behind me. No wandering off on your own."

Laura nodded her understanding.

Nick emerged from the car. He scanned the dark yard as he repositioned the Beretta beneath his jacket at the small of his back. Every instinct warned Nick that trouble awaited them inside. Finding his son and keeping Laura safe, no matter what she had done, were top priority. Laura climbed out behind him. They walked straight up to the back of the house without encountering anyone.

Where the hell was security? Nick wondered grimly. James Ed was too cautious a man to be caught with his pants down like this. Nick reached out and grasped Laura's arm as they stepped up to the verandah. No sense risking her making any sudden moves. Laura stalled at the French door leading to the rear entry hall.

"Promise me you won't let him talk his way out of this, Nick," she urged. "No matter what James Ed says, you have to believe me. He tried to kill me and he took away my son."

Nick met her fearful gaze in the darkness. "No one is talking their way out of anything," he said pointedly. Including you, he didn't add. Nick set his jaw hard and reached for the doorbell. He paused. Maybe he didn't want to announce their arrival.

He turned back to Laura. "Stay right behind me," he ordered tersely. When she nodded he reached for the brass handle on one French door and opened it. An eerie silence greeted them as they entered the dimly lit hall. Nick felt Laura move closer. He scanned the long, empty corridor with mounting tension. Something was definitely wrong. Very wrong.

The long hall extended the width of the house from backdoor to front, with two ninety-degree turns in between. Nick paused and surveyed each room they passed. No Governor. No First Lady. No staff or security.

Every nerve ending had gone on full-scale alert by the time they reached the parlor. To Nick's relief, James Ed sat on the sofa, his head bowed over what appeared to be a photo album. Other photo albums were scattered on the sofa table. Wearing a robe and pajamas, James Ed appeared deeply involved in the pictures.

"Governor," Nick said, announcing their presence.

James Ed looked up, then quickly removed his glasses. "Nick?" He frowned. Something that resembled regret stole across his features when his gaze landed on his sister. "Laura?" James Ed pushed to his feet. "You're here."

Ignoring his comment, Nick crossed the room. Laura remained near the door. "There are a few questions I need to ask you," Nick told him quietly.

James Ed's gaze lingered on Laura. "You look as if you're feeling much better, Laura," he remarked with a sad smile.

Again, Nick couldn't shake the feeling that James Ed was serious in his concern for his much younger sister.

"Where's my son?" Laura demanded.

James Ed's expression turned distant. "I don't understand all this," he said, his tone remote.

"Laura does have a child," Nick ground out. It took every ounce of willpower he possessed not to grab the Governor by the throat. "I'm about to give you one last opportunity to redeem yourself here, James Ed. Why did you hire someone to kill Laura and where is the baby?"

"I would never do anything to hurt you, Laura," James Ed insisted. "You must believe that." His sincere gaze turned to Nick's. "I love her too much."

"Tell me about your associate, Brock Redmond," Nick suggested coolly.

Denial flickered across the Governor's features. "I didn't hire him to do this."

"So you admit that you do know him," Nick pressed.

James Ed hesitated, his expression distracted now. "What?"

"It's over, James Ed. We know what you did."

James Ed shook his head slowly. "I…I don't want to talk now. I'm not feeling well. Please go away."

"Redmond is the man who shot me, and left me for dead. He," Nick added bitterly, "is the man who tried to kill Laura on the riverbank that same night. And you hired him."

"You're wrong," James Ed argued wearily. "Brock Redmond is—"

"Was," Nick cut in. "He's dead."

James Ed seemed to shrink right before Nick's eyes. "I didn't know," he murmured. "I didn't know…."

Laura couldn't stand idly by and do nothing a moment longer. She had to find Robby. While Nick and James Ed were caught up in their discussion, Laura used the moment to slip back into the hall. They had already checked the downstairs rooms. Laura glanced at the wide staircase that flowed up to the second floor. He had to be upstairs. She frowned at the thought that Sandra was probably watching him. Why would Sandra go along with James Ed? She had never mentioned to Laura that she even wanted a child. Being the perfect political wife had always appeared to be enough for her.

Pushing the disturbing question aside, Laura rushed up the seemingly endless stairs. Once on the second-story landing she paused to listen. Laura strained with the effort to hear even the slightest noise. Something, some indistinguishable sound touched her ears. She turned to her right and followed the soft sound to the far end of the corridor. The room was on the right and across the hall from James Ed and Sandra's bedroom.

The closer Laura came to the door the louder and clearer the sound became. Music, she realized.

A lullaby.

Laura stopped dead in her tracks. A chill raced up her spine and spread across her scalp.

"Robby," she murmured. Laura ran the last few feet and burst into the room. She smoothed her hand over the wall until she found a light switch. A soft golden glow filled the bedroom when she flipped it to the on position. Blue walls embellished with white clouds, gold stars and moons wrapped the space in warmth. Beautiful cherrywood furniture, including a large rocking chair, filled the room. A lavish crib, adorned with a coverlet bearing those same moons, stars and clouds stood near the open French doors. Blue, gauzy curtains fluttered in the cool night air. A windup mobile slowly turned, playing the familiar tune.

Her heart rising in her throat, Laura blindly walked the few steps that separated her from the crib. She braced her hands on the side rails and peered down at the fluffy coverlet and matching pillow and bumper pads.

The crib was empty save for linens.

No Robby.

Laura gasped, a pained, choking sort of half sob sound.

"I've been expecting you."

Tears streaming down her cheeks, Laura turned slowly to face the cold, emotionless voice.

Sandra.

"Why?" The word struggled past the lump constricting Laura's throat. How could Sandra do this? Laura had trusted Sandra, loved her even. Had thought that Sandra loved her. How could this be?

Sandra laughed. She waved the gun Laura had only just noticed in the air. "Why not?"

"Where is my son?" Laura demanded more sharply.

"I wasn't finished with the first question," Sandra snapped.

"In the beginning it was simply the money," she said boldly. She fixed Laura with an evil look. "It should have been mine anyway. If your meddling grandfather hadn't stepped in, my mother would have had the life she deserved. *I* would have had the life I deserved—your life."

Laura shook her head in confusion. "What are you talking about?"

Sandra smiled. "Oh, that's right you wouldn't know, would you?" She stepped closer to Laura, the gun pointed at her chest. "Your dear father was once in love with my mother. But she wasn't good enough for that blue blood that ran through his veins. So, your loving grandfather took care of the situation. He sent your father off to Harvard where he met your sweet, equally blue-blooded mother."

"What does this have to do with anything?" Laura didn't care about the past. The only thing she wanted was to find her son.

"Everything, my dear, everything." She used the barrel of the weapon to turn Laura's chin when she would have looked away. "You see, after your father deserted her, my mother married my sorry-excuse-for-a-father. He was a drunk and beat us both every chance he got."

Laura shook her head, fear and sympathy warred inside her. "I'm sorry, but what does that have to do with my son?" she murmured.

"I'm getting to that," Sandra snapped, her eyes sparkled with hatred. "Be patient. Not a day went by that my mother didn't remind me of what should have been ours." She poked Laura in the chest with the muzzle of the gun. "Money, position, power. Instead, we lived in poverty. Finally my mother had to be hospitalized and I was sent away."

Despite what Sandra had done, Laura's heart went out to the little girl who had suffered such injustices. Unlike James Ed, who was driven by greed, Sandra's evilness grew out of a horrible childhood. "But your adopted parents were good to you," Laura countered. "You told me so yourself."

"You can't make up for the past, Laura. What's done is done. And one way or another I intended to have what was mine." Another sinister smile spread across her face. "Of course I might never have been born had my mother not married the drunk who sired me. But, fate finally smiled on me. Your parents got themselves killed in that car accident and James Ed was all alone with a little sister to raise." Sandra drew in a pleased breath. "By then I was all grown-up, had a different name and lived with parents who were socially acceptable."

Laura searched her mind for some way to get away from Sandra. The woman was deranged. Laura had to get to Nick and tell him about this room—she surveyed the beautiful nursery—and Sandra's crazy story.

"You like my baby's nursery?"

Laura blinked. Her gaze collided with Sandra's once more. "But you can't have children," she said before she thought.

Sandra's expression grew fierce. "Yes, well, that crazy old lady Leeton saw to that."

"What?" This just kept getting more confusing, more bizarre. Laura gripped the side rail more tightly. What did Mrs. Leeton have to do with Sandra's past? Mrs. Leeton had been Doc's nurse in Bay Break for as long as Laura could remember.

"I wanted to make sure I had James Ed right where I wanted him, so I got pregnant to seal our fate. But he didn't want children," she added with disgust. "He claimed he needed to get his political career off the ground and get you raised before he had children of his own." She sneered at Laura. "So I had to take care of that before he found out." She frowned. "Something went wrong. The stupid old nurse kept telling me that it wasn't her fault, that she had done the best she could. But I knew better. I could have killed her," Sandra said coldly. "But I decided I might need her in the future." She laughed then. "Guess I was right."

"Where is Robby?" Laura demanded, her anger suddenly overriding any misplaced sympathy she had felt.

"Why do you keep asking me that?" Sandra said haughtily. "You've been in a hospital for the past eighteen months. You have no proof that Robby even exists. I've seen to that. Who would ever believe you?"

"Nick believes me," Laura bit out.

Sandra shrugged. "Big deal. I can take care of Nick." Her lips compressed into a grim line. "I thought I had him out of the way once before. But Redmond screwed up. Oh well," she added with amusement. "He got his, didn't he, princess?"

Ice formed in Laura's stomach. "*You* sent Redmond to kill me?"

"Well, of course," she retorted unapologetically. "You didn't think James Ed had the balls to do it, did you?"

Laura shook her head. "I didn't have anything to do with what happened to your mother. How could you hate me so much?"

"I already told you," she intoned. "You had my life. And now I intend to have it all. Everything that should have been mine all along. The name, the money, everything."

"Where's my son?" Laura stepped nearer, putting herself nose to nose with Sandra.

Sandra pressed the muzzle of her gun into Laura's stomach as a reminder of who was in charge. "I knew you didn't die in that river with Redmond." Her eyes narrowed. "I knew it. So I sent Redmond's partner to look for you. It took him almost a year, but he found you." Sandra's eyes lit with a glow that was not sane. "And lo and behold what did he discover? You'd had yourself a baby."

"Where's my son?" Laura demanded again.

"With my dark hair and hazel eyes, he was perfect," Sandra continued as if Laura had said nothing. "But, of course, with James Ed's career to consider, I had to make it all look legal. That wasn't so hard. Over the years I've gotten to know the hospital administrator at Serenity Sanitarium pretty well—" she smiled that evil smile again "—very well, in fact. So that part was easy. Canton, of course, was willing to do anything for enough money. Killing you and making it look like a suicide sounded like fun to him. All he had to do was find you." Sandra breathed a relieved sigh. "When you showed up in Bay Break, it was like a gift from God. Doc had no way of knowing that his former nurse owed me such a huge favor. She called me the instant you showed up at her house."

Rage rushed through Laura's veins. "You had Doc murdered."

"Unfortunately it was a necessary step in the process. He had a long and prosperous life, what's the big deal?"

"I want my son back," Laura said dangerously. At the moment she was prepared to kill Sandra with her bare hands if necessary.

"Enough," Sandra announced savagely. She gestured to the French doors. "Let's go onto the balcony. I wouldn't want to sully *my* son's new room."

She jabbed Laura with the gun when she hesitated. "I said move," she ordered.

Laura took one last look at the crib, then walked through the open doors. The barrel of the gun urging her forward, she walked straight across the wide balcony to the ornate railing. Laura stared into the darkness searching for some avenue of escape.

"Now jump."

Startled by her demand, Laura pivoted to face Sandra. "What?" She had expected the woman to simply shoot her.

Sandra stepped to the railing. "I said jump. I have to keep this on the up-and-up." She rolled her eyes. "Poor unstable

Laura, she threw herself off the balcony after killing her lover and trying to kill her own brother. Not to mention poor old Doc."

Nick. Oh God. Frantic to stall her, Laura asked, "What makes you think James Ed will go along with you killing Nick?"

"James Ed will do whatever I tell him to." Sandra's smile widened. "Or else he'll have an accident, too." Her smile disappeared just as quickly. "Now jump."

Remembering her lesson in the barn well, Laura flicked a glance toward the open doors as if she had heard or seen something. Sandra followed her gaze. In that moment of distraction, Laura knocked Sandra's arm upward. The gun fired, momentarily deafening Laura. Laura kicked her in the shin and drove her fist into Sandra's wrist with all her strength. The gun flew from her grasp and slid across the floor.

"Die, damn you," Sandra hissed as she grabbed Laura by the throat and slammed into her with her full body weight.

Laura stumbled back upon impact. She struggled to breathe and to pull Sandra's hands free of her throat. Laura pivoted, trying to shake Sandra loose, and lost her balance. Laura fell backwards. The rail cut into her back, breaking Laura's fall. Sandra leaned over her, her fingers cutting off the air to Laura's lungs. Determination contorted Sandra's features as she clamped down harder on Laura's throat.

"Die," Sandra shrieked.

Laura arched upward to throw her off. Sandra twisted, then went over the rail, pulling Laura with her.

THE LOUD REPORT of a weapon jerked Nick from the useless argument with James Ed. He turned to the door. Laura was gone. Damn. Nick ran into the hall.

"Laura!"

Nick took the stairs two at a time. He raced toward the one open door where light glowed. The room was empty. He frowned when his brain assimilated the visual assessment that it was a nursery. A shriek drew his gaze to the open balcony doors. Nick sprinted across the room and onto the balcony just in time to see Sandra and Laura go over the edge of the railing.

Outright panic slammed into him. Fear clawed at his chest as he rushed to the railing. Sandra lay on the concrete walk below. Laura was hanging on to one spindle. His heart hammering with fear, Nick leaned over the rail and reached for her.

"Give me your hand, Laura," he said quickly.

Straining with the effort to hang on, Laura reached one shaky hand toward his. The spindle she clung to snapped and Nick barely snagged her hand before she fell. Slowly, his hold on her slipping more than once, he pulled a trembling Laura over the rail and into his arms.

"Sandra stole my baby," Laura cried.

"It's okay," Nick assured her. "You're safe now."

"She sent security away, you know," James Ed remarked behind them as if nothing out of the ordinary had happened.

Nick turned to him, sensing a change in his tone. James Ed picked up the weapon on the floor, then stared at it a moment before lifting his gaze to Nick and Laura. His grip tightened around the weapon and Nick tensed for battle.

"I suppose it was for the best," he added.

"Put the gun down, James Ed," Nick told him calmly. He moved Laura behind him, but didn't reach for his own weapon. He didn't want to scare James Ed into doing something stupid. The man had just had his whole world turned upside down. He was obviously in shock.

"This is really all my fault," James Ed continued in a voice totally devoid of emotion. He shrugged halfheartedly. "I needed money to keep up appearances. I'm sure Sandra only thought she was helping me. She didn't mean to hurt anyone. I'm certain of that."

Nick felt Laura go rigid behind him.

James Ed shook his head in defeat. "I believed everything Sandra told me. I trusted her unconditionally."

Nick held Laura back when she would have rushed toward her brother. She wanted answers, now. Nick glanced over his shoulder and told her with his eyes to stay put. He took one cautious step toward James Ed. James Ed's gaze flickered to him.

"You do believe me, don't you?" James Ed looked past Nick and searched Laura's face as if looking for some sign of forgiveness. "I didn't know. You were so wild and unhappy it seemed. That's why I tried to marry you off to Rafe. I hoped that he could do a better job of making you happy. I had so many responsibilities already. I just couldn't give you what you needed."

Nick moved one more step closer. "So you didn't know about Sandra's scheme to kill Laura."

James Ed's expression filled with remorse. "I almost lost my mind when Laura disappeared." He waved the gun in frustration. "I had no idea that Sandra had hired Redmond behind my back," James Ed insisted. He shrugged wearily. "I truly thought Laura was unstable. Sandra had me convinced. Then Laura disappeared and I thought she was dead. Eventually I used the trust fund, but not until I felt sure Laura wasn't coming back," he added quickly. "I didn't want to but Sandra insisted that Laura would have wanted me to have the money."

"But Sandra wasn't convinced that Laura was gone for good," Nick suggested. "She kept looking." More space disappeared between them.

James Ed nodded. "Apparently. I didn't know until tonight what she had done." He pressed Nick with his gaze, searching for understanding, beseeching him to believe. "That other man, Redmond's partner, showed up a few hours ago and told Sandra what happened." James Ed dropped his head in defeat. "I couldn't believe she had done it." A sob cracked his voice. "I couldn't believe that I had been so blind. I thought Laura was imagining the episodes, that she truly was unstable." His shoulders sagged in defeat. "I loved Sandra. I trusted her."

"Give me the gun, James Ed," Nick told him again.

James Ed stared at the weapon for a long moment as if it held the answers to all his worries. "I don't deserve to live after what I've allowed to happen."

Nick grabbed James Ed's arm when he would have lifted the weapon. "That's not the issue right now," Nick argued. "Right now *we* have to find Laura's son."

James Ed relinquished the weapon. His gaze moved to Laura. "Can you ever forgive me, Laura? I'd give anything if this hadn't happened."

Laura was next to Nick then. She lifted her chin and glared at her brother with little or no sympathy. "Where is my son?" she demanded.

He shook his head slowly. "I'd give my life right now to be able to tell you. But, I swear, I don't know where your child is, Laura. We—" James Ed glanced at the room beyond the open doors, then at the balcony railing over which Sandra had disappeared. He winced. "—we were going to adopt a child. Sandra had made all the necessary arrangements. We were supposed to bring him home tomorrow."

"Him?" Nick echoed.

James Ed nodded. "A little boy just over a year old."

"Where is he?" Laura pressed.

"At the orphanage in Louisiana." James Ed looked thoughtful for a moment. "Sandra was there for a while when she was a child, and someone rescued her. She thought it only fitting…" His voice trailed off.

Laura tugged at Nick's sleeve. "Let's go!"

Nick pulled his cell phone from his pocket. "We have to get the police out here first." He glanced at James Ed who had wandered to a nearby chair and dropped into it. "We can't leave him like this."

"I'm not waiting," she argued.

Nick grasped her arm when she would have rushed away. "You will wait."

"I have to find my son," she cried, desperation in her voice.

Nick saw the pain and worry in her eyes; he hardened his heart to what he wanted to feel. "He's my son, too."

Chapter Thirteen

Laura awoke with a start. Shops, sidewalks and pedestrians lined the street. It was daylight now. Eight o'clock, according to the digital clock on the dash. Traffic moved at a snail's pace, morning rush hour apparently. Laura rubbed the back of her hand over her jaw, then massaged her stiff neck as she sat up straighter in the car seat. She wondered if this place was Careytown. She glanced at the driver's grim profile. Nick's beard-shadowed face was chiseled in stone, the white bandage stark against his dark skin and hair. He hadn't spoken a word to her since they left her brother's house. It had been almost four o'clock in the morning before the police had allowed them to leave.

A banner announcing Careytown's fifth annual Thanksgiving Festival draped from crossing light to crossing light over the busy street. Laura's heart skittered into overdrive. She was almost there. Very soon, possibly in just a few short minutes, she would be able to hold her son in her arms once more.

Laura closed her eyes briefly and summoned the memory of Robby's sweet baby scent. Her arms ached to hold him. But what kind of court battle lay before her? Laura blinked. Her gaze darted back to Nick's granitelike features. He was never going to forgive her for keeping Robby a secret. In his opinion, she should have turned to him for help in the first place.

But she just couldn't take the chance that he wouldn't turn her over to James Ed.

James Ed.

Regret trickled through Laura. She had blamed James Ed for everything all this time, when it had been Sandra all along. Laura still couldn't believe that Sandra had harbored such ill will toward her all those years. Had wanted her dead. Had wanted to steal her son.

Laura shook off the disturbing thoughts. Sandra was dead. She would never be able to harm Robby or Laura again. Canton was still at large, but hopefully the police would find him soon. She and James Ed would work things out eventually, she supposed. After all, he was her brother. The only thing that mattered now, Laura resolved, was getting her son back. She glanced at Nick again. She would just have to deal with his demands when the time came. No judge in his right mind would take her son away from her. But Nick was a good man….

Joint custody.

The phrase tore at Laura's heart. How would she be able to survive days or weeks without her son? Even if she knew he was safe in Nick's care. And what if Nick married someone else? Fear and hurt gripped Laura with such intensity that she thought she might be sick at her stomach. There could even be someone in his life right now. Nick was a very good-looking man.

But he had made love to her just last night. Laura swallowed tightly. It wasn't uncommon for people to cling to each other during or after near-death encounters. It had happened two years ago. Last night was probably no different. The time she had spent in Nick's arms obviously hadn't affected him as it had her. She loved him with all her heart. She would give most anything if they could be a family. Laura closed her eyes and fought the tears brimming. She would not cry. She was about to be reunited with her child. If any tears were shed today, they would be tears of joy.

"This is it," Nick said quietly.

Laura jerked to attention. He guided the car into the parking lot of an old, but well-maintained two-story building. The parking lot wasn't large, but Laura could see a huge fenced-in play yard behind the building. Multicolored playground equipment and numerous trees, bare for the winter, claimed the play yard landscape. The exterior of the building wasn't particularly bright, but it was clean and neat. If the staff took such good care of the property, surely they cared equally well for the children.

Nick was out of the car and opening her door before Laura realized they had parked. She shook off the distraction and emerged into the cool November morning.

Just a few more moments, she told herself. The first genuine smile in too many days to recall lifted her lips. *Thank you, God,* she prayed. Laura folded her arms over her chest and ignored the biting wind. Her son was in there somewhere and she was about to find him.

"Are you all right?" Nick's voice was gentle, laced with concern.

Laura looked up at him and mentally acknowledged the mistake she had made. She should have told Nick. She should have gone to him for help long ago. He was the father of her child. He was a good man. She should have trusted him. But she hadn't. And now she would pay dearly for that mistake.

The cost would be Nick's trust. If he had ever even considered trusting her, he wouldn't now. And there was no way he would ever love her the way she loved him.

"I'm fine," she managed past the lump in her throat. It was a lie, she wanted to scream. She would never be fine again.

"Then let's go get our son."

Our son. The words echoed through her soul.

Nick's long fingers curled around Laura's elbow as he guided her up the long walk and through the double doors leading into the Careytown Home for Children. A wide, tiled corridor rolled out before them. Doors lined both walls. A sign proclaimed one as the main office.

A few moments later they entered the cheery office. A sunny yellow, the walls displayed hundreds of framed photographs. On closer inspection, Laura realized the pictures were of children of all ages. An older lady wearing a cartoon character T-shirt greeted them.

"May I help you?" She smiled kindly.

"I'm Nick Foster and this is Laura Proctor. I believe someone called to let you know we were coming."

The woman's smile immediately crumpled. "Yes. Our director received a call at home a couple of hours ago." She attempted another smile, which proved decidedly less enthusiastic than her previous one. She stood. "Follow me, please."

Uneasiness slid over Laura. Something was wrong. Her heart bumped into an erratic rhythm as a dozen possibilities flashed through her mind. They were too close now. Things just couldn't go wrong. Laura followed Nick and the receptionist into an inner office. Laura moistened her lips and squared her shoulders. Robby was safe. He was here and when Laura left, she would have her baby in her arms.

A woman of about forty waited for them inside the small office. Her hair was pulled back in a tight bun, revealing her attractive features. At present, those features were cluttered with what could only be labeled worry.

"Ms. Proctor. Mr. Foster." She shook first Laura's hand, then Nick's. "I'm Mary Flannigan, the director. Please have a seat," she offered nervously.

"I'm sure you can understand that we're in somewhat of a hurry," Nick told her candidly.

With obvious effort, she produced a smile. "Of course." Mrs. Flannigan retrieved a file from her desk. "Before we go any further, I'll need you to identify the child."

Laura moved closer to the woman's desk. "Identify?"

Mrs. Flannigan opened the file. "We photograph all our children for our records."

The woman opened the folder and Laura's gaze latched onto the pictures of Robby. He smiled at the camera, those mischievous green eyes bright with happiness. "It's him," Laura breathed the words. Her fingers went instinctively to the photographs to caress her son's image. Tears rolled down her cheeks. "That's my baby," she murmured, awe in her voice.

Nick touched one of the pictures, his fingers tracing the image of his son. Laura watched the myriad emotions move across his handsome face.

"He's beautiful, isn't he?" Laura said softly.

Nick nodded. Laura knew that he couldn't possibly speak right now. He had just gotten the first glimpse of his son. A son he couldn't have denied even if he had been so inclined. Robby looked so very much like him.

Laura released the breath she had been holding and shifted her attention to Mrs. Flannigan. Maybe the lady was simply nervous over the mistake. She had placed a stolen child into adoption proceedings, unknowingly, of course.

"I'd like you to bring my son to me now," Laura said as calmly as she could.

Mrs. Flannigan looked first at Laura, then at Nick. As if somehow sensing that Nick would take the news better than Laura, she directed her words to him. "I am so sorry that this has happened." She shook her head. "I've been the director at this home for ten years and nothing like this has ever happened. Our staff is thoroughly screened."

"Get to the point, Mrs. Flannigan. Where is Robby?" Nick insisted.

"I don't know."

Laura's heart dropped to her feet. Her muscles went limp and passing out seemed a distinct possibility. "What?"

"When I arrived this morning, the night nurse was in a panic. Your child—" she moistened her lips "—was missing. When the midnight rounds were made he was there, but at seven this morning he was gone."

"Gone?" Nick leaned forward slightly, his intimidating frame looming over the woman's desk. "Don't you have security here?"

Mrs. Flannigan nodded. "Excellent security. No one gets in or out without a key after hours. We believe that one of our staff members took your son."

"No." Laura shook her head in denial. This couldn't be. She had only just found this place. He couldn't be gone.

"I thought you said you screen your staff," Nick countered hotly.

"We do, Mr. Foster. Elsa Benning is an excellent employee. I can't imagine why she has done this. She has worked here for more than twenty years. It doesn't make sense."

"How do you know it was her?" Nick demanded.

Mrs. Flannigan smoothed a hand over her hair. "She hasn't reported for duty this morning. In twenty years she hasn't missed a day." The director blinked beneath Nick's ruthless gaze. "She is the only employee who holds a key and who is unaccounted for this morning."

"No." Laura backed away from the reality. "No, this can't be."

"I am so terribly sorry. The Louisiana State Police have issued an APB."

"Laura." Nick moved toward her.

"No." Laura shook her head adamantly. "He has to be here."

"Ms. Proctor." The director stepped to Nick's side. "If it's any consolation to you at all, Elsa is a good woman. I don't believe she would hurt your baby."

NICK SETTLED an almost catatonic Laura into the passenger's seat. He reached across her and buckled her seat belt. He had put a call into Ian to bring him up to speed. Nick closed the door and braced his hands on the top of the rented car. He squeezed his eyes shut and called the image of his son to mind. Dark hair, green eyes, chubby cheeks. Nick clenched his teeth to hold back the rage that wanted to burst from him.

Okay, he told himself. *Pull it together, man. You can't lose it now. Not here. Not in front of Laura.* His whole body ached at the look of pain and defeat sucking the life out of her. Nick straightened. By God he was going to find his son. One way or another. As much as Nick wanted his son, he wanted even more to reunite him with his mother. He couldn't bear to watch Laura suffer a minute longer. He skirted the hood and jerked his own door open. Nick dropped behind the wheel and snapped his seat belt into place. Laura had been through enough. Robby had been through enough.

And someone was going to pay.

Nick slammed his fist against the steering wheel again and again until the pain finally penetrated the layers of anger and frustration consuming him. Laura only looked at him, too grief stricken to react.

The cell phone in his jacket pocket rang insistently. Nick blew out a heavy breath. He reached inside his jacket and retrieved the damned thing. He couldn't ignore it, it might be Ian.

"Foster," he said tautly. He had to get back in control.

"Nick, it's Ray."

Nick frowned. Why would Ray be calling him? The murder investigation. Damn. Nick massaged his forehead. He didn't want to do this right now. "Yeah, Ray, what's up?"

"I called James Ed's house and a policeman told me to call this number."

Nick impatiently plowed his fingers through his hair. "What can I do for you?"

"I'm not sure. But you mentioned that Laura's baby was missing." Ray exhaled mightily. "Maybe it's nothing, but a woman showed up here first thing this morning with a baby that looks the right age and the hair color's right. I remember all that black hair. She says she thinks the kid was stolen or something. We're running a check on her now."

Adrenaline pumped through Nick's veins. "What's her name?"

"One Elsa Benning."

"We're on our way." Nick started the car, then frowned. "Ray," he said before disconnecting, "do me one favor."

"Sure, buddy, anything."

"Don't let that woman and child out of your sight."

TIRES SQUEALING, Nick turned the wheel sharply, guiding the car into the precinct parking lot. Laura jerked forward when he braked to an abrupt halt. They had made the trip to Natchez in record time. She was out of the car right behind Nick. Her son was in that police station.

Laura rushed up the walk and into the building, Nick right on her heels.

"Detective Ingle," Nick said to the first officer they met in the corridor.

"Down the hall, fifth door on the left."

Laura was on her way before Nick could thank the man. Her heart pounding, her skin stinging with adrenaline, she burst through the door the officer had indicated. A half dozen desks filled the large room. Laura scanned each one. Her gaze locked on the back of a gray-haired lady. She sat in a chair, facing a desk. A tall man stood behind it shuffling through files. Ignoring all else, Laura rushed to the woman. Her heart pounding so hard in her chest that she felt certain it would burst from her rib cage, Laura stepped around the woman's chair.

Robby sat in her lap, pulling at the large ornate buttons on her jacket. Relief so profound swamped her, that Laura thought she might die of it. She dropped to her knees at the stranger's side. Laura held out her arms. "How's mommy's baby?" she murmured softly.

Robby reacted instantly. He flung his chubby little arms and bounced in the woman's lap. The woman, Elsa, smiled down at Laura and shifted Robby into Laura's arms.

Laura held Robby close. She inhaled deeply of his sweet baby scent. "Oh, my baby," she whispered into his soft hair. Emotions flooded her being so quickly and with such force that Laura could not think clearly.

The old woman nodded knowingly, capturing Laura's overwhelmed attention. "I knew this was no abandoned baby. Today they were going to give him to the adoptive couple." She shook her head. "I knew it wasn't right. So I brought him back to the police station in the city where they said he had been found."

"Thank you," Laura choked out. Robby tugged at her hair and made baby sounds as if nothing had ever been amiss. "I know you took good care of him."

"I did at that," Elsa agreed. "That's my job."

Laura smiled at the woman, then struggled to her feet. She turned to Ray Ingle, Nick's detective friend. "Thank you, Detective Ingle."

His lopsided smile warmed her. "Just doing my job, ma'am."

Taking a deep breath for courage, Laura turned to Nick. She manufactured a watery smile. "This is your son, Robby."

Total and complete awe claimed Nick's features. He touched Robby's hand. Instinctively Robby curled chubby little fingers around Nick's finger. The smile on Nick's face made Laura weak in the knees. She wanted so to offer Nick the opportunity to hold his son, but she couldn't bring herself to let go of him just yet.

"Hey, man," Ray exclaimed. "You've been holding out on me."

Nick just grinned at Ray, his eyes barely leaving Robby for a second.

"Canton is still at large," Ray mentioned quietly.

Laura turned to him, then looked at Nick.

"That's not good. Laura and Robby aren't safe as long as he's on the street," Nick returned, his gaze still riveted on his son.

Laura's arms tightened around her baby. "What will we do?"

"Do you have some place you can lay low until he's caught?" Ray asked Laura.

She glanced at Nick, then back to Ray and shook her head. "I couldn't possibly go to my brother's house, or the house in Bay Break." Laura had no money she could access without lengthy legalities. For one fleeting second fear slipped back into her heart. She snuggled her baby's head. None of that mattered.

She had Robby now.

"Laura, you can stay—" Nick began.

She shook her head, cutting him off. "That's not a good idea right now."

"Ma'am," Ray interrupted. "You and your little boy are welcome to stay with me and my wife until you figure this thing out."

Laura kissed Robby's satiny forehead. "Oh, I couldn't impose like that. I'm sure we can find some place."

"Why you'd be doing us a favor." Ray smiled widely. "You see, we're about to have our first child. My wife was an only child and has never had to care for a little one. She could use the practice." Ray blushed to the roots of his hair. "That is if you wouldn't mind."

Relief bolstered Laura's sagging resolve. "Thank you, Detective, that would be wonderful."

"I'll call my wife," he suggested quickly.

"You take good care of that fine little boy," Elsa said quietly.

Laura's gaze connected with the dark brown eyes of the older woman who had brought Robby here. "Thank you. I'll do my best." Belatedly, Laura shifted her attention back to Detective Ingle. "Is she going to be in trouble?"

"Don't you worry none about me," Elsa argued.

Ray shot Elsa a smile then turned back to Laura. "Apparently since her instincts were on the money, no charges will be pressed. And she won't lose her job," he added quickly. "But she will be on probation with Mrs. Flannigan for a while."

Elsa poohed Ray's comment. "Mary Flannigan will consider herself lucky I'm back. She couldn't get along without me."

Laura smiled down at Elsa. "I'm sure she couldn't."

Knowing she couldn't avoid the inevitable any longer, Laura turned back to Nick. She steeled herself. It was impossible to read what he was thinking at the moment. "I've been on the run for a long time, Nick. So much has happened." She hugged Robby to her heart. "I need some time to pull myself together, before you take any legal steps to share custody." When he hesitated, Laura added quickly, "I'm not asking for forever, just a few weeks to figure out what happens next in my life."

Nick's gaze was intent on hers for several seconds before he answered. "All right. I can live with that as long as you keep me posted of exactly where you are and how—" his gaze moved to Robby "—and how my son is doing."

Laura stiffly nodded her agreement.

It was over.

She had gotten Robby back safe and sound.

She was safe.

But she had lost Nick.

Chapter Fourteen

Two weeks had passed. Nick had not tried to see Robby or take any legal action, giving selflessly the time Laura had requested. She knew it was difficult for him. He called every day. Each time he asked the same question, how was his son? And then, how was she? Did he really care? Laura wondered. The way she did about him. She couldn't blame him if he didn't. And she certainly couldn't expect him to put off being with his son much longer. She could hear the growing anticipation in his voice with each call. Laura gazed forlornly at the salad on her plate. Though she felt more rested than she had in years, she had no appetite. Laura looked at her baby seated happily in the Ingles' brand new high chair, where he played with his food. His smiles and excited baby words let her know that Robby, too, was happy and rested. Laura's gaze shifted to her very pregnant hostess. Joy Ingle watched every move that Robby made with glowing anticipation.

Ray had been right. This time with Robby had done his wife a world of good, and greatly boosted her caregiving confidence. Laura was glad she had come. If only she could find that kind of happiness in her own life.

The doorbell chimed.

Joy frowned. "Who can that be? It's too early for Ray to be home for lunch," she said, glancing at the clock on the wall.

"I'll get it." Laura pushed to her feet. "I'm through anyway."

Joy smiled. "Thank you. I'll just bask in your son's eating antics."

Laura returned her smile, then headed for the front door. She breathed a sigh of satisfaction as she moved through the Ingle home. Ray and Joy were so much in love. When their baby came, he would lack for nothing in that department. Laura lifted a skeptical brow. Or any other department for that matter. She only wished Robby were going to grow up in a home filled with love and both his mother and father. How on earth would they ever manage sharing him? And if Nick married someone else?

Laura pushed the disturbing thoughts aside and paused in front of the door. Still cautious, she peered through the viewfinder. She didn't recognize the man waiting outside the door. Tall and handsome, he had dark hair and wore an impeccable black business suit.

Laura opened the door a crack, leaving the security chain in place. "May I help you?"

"Laura Proctor?"

Laura studied his steady gray gaze. "Yes."

"My name is Ian Michaels. I'm an associate of Nick's at the Colby Agency." The European accent, coupled with his dark good looks reminded Laura of James Bond.

She shook off the silly notion. Laura remembered the name. Nick had called him frequently, but she had never met the man. "Do you have any ID?"

"Of course." With practiced grace, Mr. Michaels removed the case containing his picture ID and held it up for Laura's inspection. "I have some news regarding your case."

Laura frowned. "Why didn't Nick come?"

"He thought you would be more comfortable if I took care of the final details."

Laura moistened her lips instead of allowing the frown tugging at her mouth to surface. Nick didn't want to come. He didn't want to see her. She supposed she really couldn't blame him. Laura had done a lot of thinking in the past two weeks. She had made a serious error in judgment. She should have trusted Nick. It was wrong for her to keep his son from him. Now she would face the consequences.

She removed the chain and opened the door. "Come in, Mr. Michaels."

He smiled. "Call me Ian."

Laura nodded and closed the door. She led the way to the living room and sat down on the sofa. Ian settled into a chair facing her.

"Laura, is everything all right?"

Joy hovered near the door, her expression wary.

"Yes," Laura assured her. "This is Ian Michaels, a friend of Nick's."

Ian stood. "It's a pleasure to meet you, Mrs. Ingle."

Laura watched the wariness melt from Joy's expression, only to be replaced by pure feminine appreciation. James Bond, all right, Laura decided.

Joy backed away from the door. "I'll just get back to Robby." She smiled. "Nice to meet you, Mr. Michaels."

Ian nodded. After Joy had gone, he sat down again. He settled his gaze back on Laura. "Canton has been caught," he said quietly. "He's being held by the authorities in Georgia awaiting extradition to Mississippi to face murder charges related to Dr. Holland's death."

Relief rushed through Laura. "Good. I'll breathe a lot easier knowing he's behind bars." Canton represented the last hurdle to a normal life.

"Nick has taken the liberty of upgrading security at your family home near Bay Break. You may return there whenever you're ready. He also suggested that you acquire a dog. A large dog," Ian added with a slight smile.

Laura couldn't help the answering smile. "Robby would love a dog."

"Good," Ian said with obvious relief. "Because Nick has already taken that liberty as well. A Mr. Rutherford is caring for the animal until you return."

Laura's smile widened at the thought of Mr. Rutherford. She hadn't seen him in ages. The day he had stopped by and talked to Nick she had been sleeping. Maybe it was time to go home. She swallowed tightly. Of course, it would never be the same. Doc was gone. And she still wasn't sure if she could forgive James Ed. He had called twice to check on her through Ray. With all that had taken place, James Ed had resigned as governor. According to Ray, James Ed had decided to return to practicing law.

"Detective Ingle tells me that James Ed has been cleared of all suspicion."

"That's correct," Ian confirmed.

Laura nodded. "I guess we'll work things out someday." For the first time in her life, Laura felt truly alone. She forced the thought away. She had Robby. She didn't need anyone else. Nick's image sifted through her mind, making a liar out of her.

"Mrs. Leeton has also been located. She has confessed to her part in your son's kidnapping."

Laura blinked back the moisture. "That's good." How could people she had known and trusted all of her life be so evil?

"It appears that James Ed and Sandra did not go through your entire trust fund. There is some money left."

Laura frowned. "I assumed he used all the money."

"Most of it," Ian explained. "But he has insisted on putting back all that he could. In fact, he plans to sell his private estate to add to that amount."

"I'm glad that some of the money is still there," Laura said with relief. Though she had her education, the idea of leaving her son with anyone after all they had been through was unthinkable, though she knew mothers did so everyday. After losing him once, Laura wasn't sure she could take the chance of leaving him in anyone else's care. "But I'd rather he didn't sell his home for me. If you would see that he gets that message I would appreciate it."

"Certainly," Ian offered. He paused for a moment. "Laura, the situation between you and Nick is none of my business, but I think you're both making a serious mistake."

Laura lifted her chin and leveled her gaze on this handsome stranger who seemed to read her entirely too well. "I don't know what else I can do. Nick doesn't appear to be interested in working anything out. Whenever he calls to check on Robby he never asks if I would like to talk about my plans. I have no idea what he wants. And, frankly, I'm tired of worrying about it."

Ian considered her words for a time. "Nick is suffering, too. He wants to do the right thing for his son. He's convinced that there is no hope for a relationship between the two of you, but he doesn't want to hurt you by taking legal steps."

Laura sat very still. "Did he tell you that?"

"Not in so many words. But I know him. He won't risk hurting you. But each day that passes knowing he can't be with his son, destroys another small part of him."

Laura shot to her feet. "Thank you very much, Mr. Michaels, for making me the bad guy." Suddenly restless, she paced back and forth in front of him.

Ian stood. "That's not my intent. I only wanted you to know that Nick—"

"Look." Laura's hands went to her hips. "I know I made a mistake, okay? I admit that. But it's done. I can't undo it. If Nick can't get past this, then what am I supposed to do?"

"You could start by telling him what you just told me," Ian suggested. "Nick doesn't want to take a wrong step where you and Robby are concerned. He's waiting for you to make the first move. He cares a great deal for you."

Laura's gaze connected with his. "And if you're wrong?"

Ian smiled, a lethal combination of confidence and masculinity. "I'm rarely wrong."

And somehow Laura knew he was right.

Laura locked the door behind Ian when he left. She sagged against it and heaved a beleaguered sigh. The first move. A knowing smile tilted Laura's lips. She had learned her lesson about not going out on a limb to trust the people she cared about. She would make a move all right.

All Nick Foster had to do was react.

NICK SHOVED the completed files into the out basket on his desk. Hell, it was Friday. If Mildred came up with any more paperwork for him today, her long-standing position at the Colby Agency would be in serious jeopardy. Nick smiled. The surface gesture felt strange on his lips after so long with nothing to smile about. The agency wouldn't be able to function without Mildred. She kept everyone straight, including Victoria.

Nick closed his eyes and allowed the images that usually haunted him free rein. Hell, it was late, he was tired. Why not add insult to injury? The memory of making love to Laura always surfaced first. Nick's fists clenched in reaction. The feel of her soft body beneath his. Her taste, her sweet smell. How would he live the rest of his life without being with her that way again? How would he live without her?

But he had ruined any chance of that with his arrogant pride. Nick had slowly, but surely come to terms with Laura's actions. She had been protecting her baby. Fear had kept her from coming to him. It still stung that she hadn't trusted him. But Nick had to remember that Laura had only been twenty-two at the time. Too young to make all the right decisions. Hell, he was thirty-four and he still screwed up regularly. Case in point, his handling of the situation with Laura.

Robby's chubby cheeks loomed as big as life in Nick's mind. His son. It still humbled him to think that he had a son. A son that wouldn't even know him at this rate. Nick had to do something. But what?

Laura apparently had no intention of ever speaking to him regarding her personal plans. He had given her every opportunity by always asking how she was when he called to check on Robby. What was he supposed to do? If he took steps to gain visitation rights he would only be making bad matters worse. How could he take Robby from his mother and bring him all the way to Chicago for weeks at a time? Nick knew he couldn't do that to Laura. There had to be a solution.

There had to be one, he repeated, as if the answer would come to him from his sheer determination.

But he had probably blown it with his unforgiving attitude.

A soft knock sounded at Nick's door. He looked up to find the subject of his reverie standing in his doorway. Stunned, Nick pushed to his feet.

"Laura." His first thought was that something was wrong.

"Hello, Nick." She smiled, Nick's breath caught. "May we come in?" She shifted Robby to her other hip.

The little boy looked as if he had grown considerably in the past two weeks. How could Nick allow one more day to go by without having his son in his life? He was not above begging at this point. But he wouldn't hurt Laura. The decision to work something out had to be hers. Her entire life had been spent with people manipulating her and telling her what to do. Nick wouldn't do that. He couldn't, no matter what it cost him personally.

Nick jerked himself to attention. "Yes, please, come in." He moved around to the front of his desk, his gaze riveted to the squirming baby in Laura's arms. A colorful diaper bag hung over one shoulder. Between the bulky coat, the diaper bag, and the baby Laura was barely visible.

"Have a seat," Nick offered belatedly.

"No." Laura shook her head. "I need to say this right now before I lose my courage."

Nick's gaze connected with hers. Confusion formed a worry line between his brows. She had come all this way without calling first. "Is something wrong?"

Laura met his gaze head-on. "I've done a lot of thinking, Nick. And you're right. It was a mistake for me to keep Robby from you. I should have trusted you. I was wrong." She looked away for a moment. "But it's done and I can't take it back."

"Laura, I—"

She held up her free hand, halting his words. "Let me finish, please."

Nick relented with a nod. Anticipation stabbed at his chest. Could Laura possibly want to try again? Would she give him a second chance to prove that he loved her? And he did love her—with all his heart. He loved his son, too.

"I've decided that Robby needs to get to know his father. Enough time has been wasted already." Laura blinked, but not before Nick saw the uncertainty in her eyes.

She took the two steps that separated them and dropped the diaper bag at his feet. She thrust Robby at him. Surprised by her action, Nick put his arms around his son with the same uncertainty that he had seen in Laura's eyes. All else ceased to matter when Robby clung to Nick's chest. His little hands fisted in Nick's shirt. A foreign sensation seized Nick's heart. Nothing had ever felt like this before.

This was his child.

"So," Laura said, drawing Nick's awestruck attention back to her. "Here he is." She blinked again and backed toward the door a step. "Instructions are in the bag regarding what he likes to eat, and what he's allowed to drink. I'm at the Sheraton. Call me if you need anything, otherwise I'll pick Robby up on Monday." Moisture shining in her eyes, Laura whirled toward the door and started in that direction.

She was leaving.

Panic seized Nick. She couldn't do this—he didn't know the first thing about taking care of a baby. "Laura," Nick called to her swiftly retreating back. And, besides, he wanted her to stay. "Don't go," he added quietly. Robby bounced in Nick's arms, as if adding his agreement.

She paused at the door, then turned slowly to face him. Tears trekked down her cheeks. "Everything he needs is in the bag. You don't need me," she said, her voice quaking.

Nick swallowed with extreme difficulty. His arms tightened instinctively around the little boy in his arms. "Yes, I do. We do," he amended quickly. "I was wrong. You were afraid. You did what you thought was right. And I can't hold that against you."

Laura crossed her arms over her chest. She swiped at the moisture dampening her cheeks. "None of that matters. I just want to do what's right for Robby now."

"So do I." Nick took a step in her direction. "But I want us to do it together."

Hope flashed in Laura's surprised gaze. "You do?"

He smiled. "I thought I made that pretty obvious a couple of times while we were in Bay Break."

Laura pushed her hair back, her hand trembling visibly. "I was afraid that it hadn't meant as much to you as it did to me. I can't be sure if you feel the same way I do."

Nick reached out and touched one soft cheek. "It meant the world to me—*you* mean the world to me." His heart ached at the worry etched across her beautiful face. "It's been hell giving you the time and space you asked for. But this had to be your decision."

Her expression grew suddenly solemn. "I love you, Nick."

"Could you put up with me for the rest of your life?" he suggested softly.

"Are you asking me to marry you?" Her eyes widened with anticipation.

"Absolutely." Nick leaned down and kissed those sweet lips. Her arms flew around his neck and she kissed him back. "Is that a yes?" he murmured when he could bear to break from her sweet kiss.

"Yes," she whispered.

Robby added his two cents worth in baby talk. Nick and Laura laughed. Nick stroked her cheek with the pad of his thumb. His fingers curled around her neck and pulled her closer. "I love you so much, Laura," he told her softly. "I've loved you since the day I first laid eyes on you." Robby squirmed between them. "And I love our son."

Nick gazed lovingly at his son.

Laura's child.

His gaze moved back to the woman he loved with all his heart. A frown creased Nick's brow. "You weren't really going to leave Robby here and me with no clue as to how to take care of him, were you?"

She grinned. "Are you kidding? If you hadn't stopped me before I got out the door, I was going to turn around and demand that you marry me."

"I suppose it's only right that you make an honest man out of me."

"It'll be my pleasure," Laura murmured, before kissing Nick soundly on the lips.

Nick held his child and the woman he loved against his heart as he planned to do for the rest of his life.

Epilogue

Victoria looked up from her desk when a knock sounded at her door. She smiled. "Ian, come in."

Ian Michaels crossed the room and paused before her desk. "You wanted to see me, Victoria?"

"Yes, have a seat, please."

Ian settled his tall frame into one of the chairs in front of her desk. As always, the man looked impeccable. Dressed in an expensive black suit, he presented himself in a manner very becoming to the Agency. His job performance remained at a superior level no matter how tough the assignment. He displayed numerous characteristics that Victoria admired. "I wanted to compliment you on your work here," she said finally. "You've done an outstanding job, Ian. The Colby Agency is very fortunate to have you."

"Thank you," he replied noncommittally.

Victoria almost smiled. Ian wasn't one to discuss his attributes, and he had many. He and Nick shared that particular characteristic. With Nick most likely not coming back, she needed to fill his position. Victoria had never seen Nick happier, and she couldn't be happier for him. Laura and Robby were just what he needed…what he deserved. But his absence left Victoria with a dilemma that required immediate action.

Directing her attention back to the matter at hand, Victoria leveled her gaze on Ian's. "I'm sure you know that Nick has taken an indefinite leave of absence to be with his wife and child."

"Yes." That gray gaze remained steady on hers.

"That leaves me without a second in charge."

"There are several top investigators on staff. I'm sure you'll be able to find a proper temporary replacement."

Victoria did smile this time. "I already have."

"What can I do to assist in the transition?" he offered politely.

"You can direct Mildred to issue a memo announcing your promotion, effective immediately."

A hint of a smile touched Ian's lips. "Of course." He stood. "Is there anything else?"

"One more thing," Victoria said as she rose to match his stance. "I'd like you to personally handle this inquiry." She passed a thin red folder to Ian.

"Any specific instructions?" Ian glanced only briefly at the folder before meeting Victoria's gaze.

"The contact is Lucas Camp. He's a close personal friend. You have complete authority to handle whatever he needs."

"I'll keep you informed of my progress."

"That would have been my next request."

Ian smiled fully then, giving Victoria a tiny glimpse of just how much charm the man commanded. Without another word, he turned and walked to the door.

"Ian." Victoria halted his exit.

He turned back. "Yes."

"Don't let Lucas give you any flack. He can be a bit pushy at times."

Ian lifted one dark brow. "We'll get along fine."

"I'm sure you will."

Victoria watched with satisfaction as Ian Michaels walked away. She had made a wise choice.

PROTECTIVE CUSTODY

This book is dedicated to a very special lady,
Mary Bauer.
Thank you, Mary, for being a cherished friend
and an inspiration to us all.

Prologue

"Absolute trust is essential." Nicole Reed's solemn gaze settled heavily onto Victoria's. "Both our lives will depend on my being able to trust your investigator completely. I know Ian Michaels. I can trust him."

Victoria Colby considered that last statement for a time before she spoke. Not a single doubt existed in her mind that Ian would be the wisest choice. He was not only the Colby Agency's most experienced investigator, he was a man of his word. With Nick Foster's retirement, Ian had transitioned into the position of second-in-command. Victoria employed only the finest in their fields at the Colby Agency, and Ian had proven no exception during his three years of service.

"Miss Reed, I understand your need for a civilian investigator. Obviously, you can't trust anyone in your own organization."

"I can't trust anyone even remotely connected to the bureau or the Witness Security Program." Nicole sighed. "I wish that weren't the case, but it is. There have been two attempts on my life already. My director is dead, as well as another agent I've worked closely with in the past. Until I get to the bottom of what's going on, I need someone I can trust to watch my back. Your agency has an impeccable reputation, Mrs. Colby, and I *trust* Ian Michaels."

Victoria relaxed into the soft leather of her chair and studied the client seated across the wide expanse of her oak desk. The woman's features were striking. She looked as if she had just stepped off the pages of *Vogue*. A navy silk jacket and trousers lent an air of professionalism as well as elegance to her image. Blond hair fell around her shoulders. Wide, assessing blue eyes highlighted a face that could only be called beautiful. So, Victoria noted, this woman was the reason Ian Michaels had walked away from a promising career as a U.S. Marshal.

Victoria arched a speculative brow. "Your history with Ian may be a problem, Miss Reed."

Nicole frowned. "I don't understand."

Victoria almost smiled at the look of innocence Nicole Reed could adopt. "Before I employ anyone at this agency, I research their background thoroughly. I evaluate their strong points as well as their weak points, and I familiarize myself with their past mistakes. You worked with Ian Michaels on a high-profile case just over three years ago. The Solomon case, I believe."

Nicole's expression grew guarded. "That's right."

"I'm aware of your personal involvement with Ian, and the subsequent outcome of that involvement," Victoria added, leaving no question as to the point she intended.

"Raymond Solomon died, Mrs. Colby. We did our best to protect him, but he died anyway. End of story."

Between the suddenly blank look in the other woman's eyes and the emotionless tone of her voice, Victoria had her doubts as to whether the story had ended. But that wasn't the issue here. Nicole Reed needed help, and the Colby Agency had made its reputation by providing the kind of help she required. Victoria straightened, then pressed the intercom button. "Mildred, ask Ian if he's free. I'd like him to join this meeting."

Nicole blinked, then looked away. Asking for Ian's help couldn't be easy, Victoria imagined. After all, it was Nicole who had helped end his former career. And if Victoria had Ian pegged right, which she likely did, Miss Nicole Reed had probably broken his fiercely guarded heart as well.

"You need help," Victoria told her finally. "And I believe this agency can help you, Miss Reed." Nicole relaxed visibly. "However, I don't feel Ian is the proper choice considering your shared history." Their gazes locked, Victoria's firm, Nicole's hesitant. "But I will allow him to make the final decision."

Nicole lifted one shoulder in a semblance of a shrug. "Fair enough."

The moment Ian entered the room Nicole knew she had seriously overestimated the healing value of time. His stance stiffened and those silver eyes frosted with indifference when his gaze collided with hers. His expression was exactly the same as it had been the last time Nicole had seen him, filled with unmasked contempt. No matter, he was the one person she could trust. She might be a fool for even asking for his help, but it was worth a shot. Besides, that's the way their relationship had been from the beginning, overpowering attraction, yet bordering on enmity.

"Ian, I'm sure you remember Miss Reed," Victoria announced, breaking the awkward silence.

His icy gaze never left Nicole's. She didn't miss the slight hesitation before he spoke. "Yes. Of course."

Nicole steeled herself against the shiver generated by the

low, raspy sound of his voice. Deep, sexy as hell, and laced
with a hint of European flavor. Ian Michaels had the kind of
voice erotic dreams were made of. Tangled sheets and long,
hot nights immediately leapt to mind. From the moment they
had first met, the man's tone and speech pattern had tripped
some sort of desire trigger deep inside Nicole. He only had
to look into her eyes, speak, and she melted. Despite what had
happened between them and the passage of three years, his
effect on her remained unchanged. But she couldn't let him
get to her this time. This time she had to maintain strict control.

Nicole swallowed, then stood. She extended her hand and
produced a smile. "It's good to see you again, Ian."

Ian's gaze traced her body with painstaking slowness,
making Nicole too warm despite her determination not to
react. Then he stared, long and hard, at her hand before taking it in his own. Long, tanned fingers wrapped around hers
and she fought the added reaction his touch evoked. She
could not allow this. Too much depended on the next few
minutes and this one man to permit emotion to override reason.

Ian acknowledged her greeting with nothing more than a
ghost of a nod, then released her hand and turned to Victoria. "You wanted to see me."

"Yes. Please, have a seat." Victoria indicated the remaining chair in front of her desk.

Seemingly from some faraway place, Nicole listened as
Victoria recounted their earlier discussion, the words barely
registering. Nicole could not take her eyes off the man now
seated next to her. Still tall and amazingly handsome. Still a
commanding presence that stole her breath. He wore his hair
longer now, she noted with reluctant admiration, its dark

length curling at his nape. Nicole almost smiled as her greedy gaze swept over his body. Though the suit was more elegant now, probably Armani, the color was the same. Black. Ian always wore black. And he would certainly be as good at his job today as he had been three years ago. No fugitive ever eluded him for long. No witness ever failed to make it to court or to safety when Ian was assigned the case.

Ian Michaels never failed. That's why he had been assigned to the Solomon case three years ago.

And that's the reason Nicole had received her assignment as well. To see that Ian failed in his.

Now, with the memory of betrayal still screaming between them, she had come to ask Ian for help. There was no one else she could trust. Nicole held her breath as she waited for him to respond to the request that he handle her case personally.

"I'm sure you'll be pleased with the investigator Victoria assigns to your case," he said coolly, his icy gaze once more connecting with Nicole's. "But it won't be me."

"YOU'RE COMFORTABLE with your decision then?"

"Yes." Ian didn't turn around. He knew Victoria was disappointed in him, but right now he didn't care. All he wanted to do was watch Nicole storm across the parking lot four stories below. She had left Victoria's office as if his refusal to help her didn't matter, but he knew better. He had seen the uncertainty, then the defeat flicker in her blue eyes. Whatever her current situation, she considered Ian's refusal to help her a significant loss. Ian almost smiled. However, it didn't come close to evening the score.

"You're not concerned with her refusal to work with Alex?" Victoria again interrupted his moment of savoring victory with another dig at his already chafed conscience.

"Why should I be?" Ian clenched his jaw at the denial that crowded his throat. He no longer gave one damn about Nicole Reed. No matter that his traitorous body had reacted as if three years had not passed…as if Nicole had not already cost him dearly. Had she really despised him enough to purposely get in the way of his work? Had her own ambition meant more to her than a man's life? Ian would likely never know the answers to those questions. Did it even matter? No. He couldn't change the past. It was over, done with. Solomon was dead.

"Nicole can take care of herself," he said in answer to Victoria's question. His voice sounded harsh to his own ears. Reacting on emotion was not something Ian allowed, but he hadn't been able to help himself today.

The squeak of leather alerted Ian when Victoria stood. She had more to say on the issue, of that he felt certain. Three near-silent steps later and she was at his side watching Nicole's determined march toward whatever vehicle she had arrived in.

"I know very little about what happened between the two of you, but I do know a woman in trouble when I see one."

Ian kept his gaze glued to that mane of long blond hair fluttering in the September breeze behind Nicole. How could the mere sight of her still make him ache with need? Even knowing what he knew. Why in hell would Nicole come to him for help? She had to know he would refuse. She had to be desperate.

Victoria had made the decision his, and he had decided. Nicole's subsequent refusal to work with another investigator was not his problem, Ian reminded himself as that annoyingly restless sensation twisted inside him. The feeling was all too familiar, but he intended to ignore his instincts this time. Nicole was on her own.

"Perhaps she'll change her mind," Victoria suggested.

"She won't," he murmured. A thought spoken. Nicole had entirely too much pride. The fact that she had come to him at all spoke volumes about her proximity to the edge. But she definitely would not come crawling back for what she would consider second best, and begging had never been her style. Remorse trickled through him before he could stop it. He knew her too well.

"Well, then, I hope you're right." Victoria folded her arms over her chest. "I hope she *can* take care of herself."

"I stopped caring one way or another a long time ago," he affirmed aloud. Who was he trying to convince? he wondered with self-disgust. Victoria or himself?

As if to refute his words an earthshaking explosion rattled the glass in front of his face. Debris from what used to be an automobile flew in a dozen directions. Black smoke mushroomed skyward as flames licked the remaining, mutilated frame. Ian's heart lurched. He frantically scanned the parking lot. Panicked pedestrians rushed toward the building for cover. He clutched the edge of the windowsill as his heart stilled in his chest.

Nicole! Where was Nicole?

Chapter One

The ground trembled beneath Nicole's feet. An invisible wall slammed into her face, shoving her backwards until the pavement stopped her. Her head hurt. Badly.

Nicole struggled to open her eyes…to fight the vortex of thick, heavy darkness sucking her toward oblivion. She had to wake up. To run from the danger! But her body refused to cooperate. She couldn't move…couldn't scream.

Nicole heard herself groan, the sound giving her hope that she wasn't dead after all. Pain exploded inside her head. She clung to the pain. You had to be alive to feel pain. She felt herself move, a simple side-to-side motion of her head, which initiated another burst of fiery pain at the back of her skull. She groaned again. Louder this time.

"You're safe, Nicole."

She stilled. That voice…

Ian. Her lids fluttered open and her eyes labored with the effort to focus in the near darkness. The face that had invaded her dreams for more than three years finally came into focus.

"Ian?"

"It's okay," he said soothingly.

Nicole closed her eyes and savored the erotic sound of his voice. Memories flooded her mind. The explosion. Hitting the ground. And then Ian was there…taking care of her. A weary sigh eased past her lips, her body aching even with that tiny exertion. He had insisted on having her examined at the E.R., then he had taken her back to his place. She remembered falling into an exhausted sleep in his arms.

"My head hurts." She opened her eyes, and her gaze connected with his. Those emotionless gray eyes gave nothing away.

"I know." With gentle fingers, he brushed a wisp of hair from her face. "I'm sorry."

Ian's refusal to accept her case suddenly hit with the same impact as that invisible wall. "Why are you doing this?" Nicole sat straight up with the surge of adrenaline that accompanied that thought. Pain twisted inside her head. She rubbed at the tender spot on the back of her scalp.

"You were badly shaken. The doctor said you shouldn't be alone," he offered quietly.

Bracing her hands behind her to maintain her upright position, Nicole leveled her gaze on his. "The explosion?"

"Your rental car apparently." He searched her eyes. "I've taken care of things with the police. Why don't you tell me what's going on?"

This time had been too close. Nicole clenched her teeth and forced herself to breathe deeply and slowly. She needed to be calm—to think. She surveyed the darkened room. Ian's bedroom. His scent, so familiar, suddenly enveloped her. That clean, subtle musky scent that was his alone. That stirred her blood even under current circumstances.

His bed. She was in his bed—with him hovering over her. Why had she let him bring her here? He wasn't going to help her. He had made that point quite clear. Anger shot through her veins, sending her heart back into double time.

"I have to get out of here." Nicole scrambled from beneath the covers. She wasn't safe here. She wasn't safe anywhere. She had to run as fast as she could.

"We need to talk."

Instinctively Nicole rolled to the other side of the bed, out of his reach. She jumped to her feet and immediately regretted both moves. The insistent throb inside her skull erupted with a vengeance, threatening her unsteady legs. Not quite a concussion, the doctor had said; she would be fine. She had been very lucky to only be close enough for the force of the blast to knock her to the ground. Nicole squeezed her eyes shut and focused on blocking out the pain. There was too much to be done. No time to waste. She had to reschedule her flight. She had a witness to relocate and protect. And she couldn't trust the regular channels to handle it. Someone wanted her and her witness dead. How had the bastard tracked her to Chicago? She had been so careful. No mistakes! No one knew her location.

No, that wasn't true, Nicole realized grimly, because *he* had found her. And he would find her again. She needed her things. Did she dare go back to the hotel and get the few items she had brought with her? She would need a change of clothes.

Clothes.

Nicole stared down at herself. The shimmering glow of moonlight from a nearby window confirmed her sudden realization. Her clothes were gone. She wore nothing but her skimpy, lacy bra and matching blue panties.

"Where the hell are my clothes?" Nicole looked up to find Ian towering over her, his tall, dark frame almost lost in the shadows. Something, some emotion flitted across his features too quickly for Nicole to analyze, and then that mask of iron control fell back into place.

"I thought you would be more comfortable like this." His gaze moved slowly over her. "I sent your clothes to be cleaned," he added in that maddeningly calm way of his.

That tone. That controlling, no-arguments-tolerated tone. He had no intention of working with her, yet he had taken charge of the game strategy. She was no different than one of his fugitives. He would handle the situation until he could wash his hands of her. That was his way. Ian Michaels always did the right thing. He never deviated from the straight and narrow—never failed.

Except once.

And then he had turned his back on her as if nothing had happened between them. As if what they had shared hadn't mattered in the final scheme of things. He hadn't given her the benefit of the doubt. Hadn't waited around for her to explain. Ian had simply walked away. From her. From everything.

Because she had betrayed him. The fact that she had only been doing her job was of no consequence—even if she had been able to tell him the truth. Nothing she could have said or done would have altered his opinion of her. If the man were capable of emotion he might display some sort of reaction. Anger, pain, remorse, something. Nicole almost laughed out loud. But this was Ian Michaels. She glowered at him. He didn't allow himself to feel. Hadn't she learned that three years ago? Hadn't she learned anything at all?

"Where are my clothes?" she repeated with all the force she could marshal. She should have known better than to come to him. Why would he care if she lived or died? And how could she blame him?

"I've already answered that question."

"This was a mistake. I shouldn't have wasted my time." Nicole attempted to brush past him only to be halted by his half step to the right.

"You need to tell me what's going on, Nicole," he argued quietly.

"Get out of my way, Michaels." Nicole darted to his left. Ian moved more quickly, effectively blocking her once more.

His unreadable gaze locked on hers. A hint of a smile curled his irritatingly full lips. "You have no clothes, no transportation, no money. How do you propose to leave?"

He had her clothes and her bag. Another rush of anger flooded Nicole. She stood before him exposed, emotionally as well as physically. She glared into his handsome face, his perfectly controlled emotions angering her all the more. She manufactured a caustic smile of her own. "Don't sweat it, Michaels. I'm sure I can get a ride." Nicole ran the fingers of both hands through her hair, allowing the long strands to drift down over her shoulders. "In fact," she added tartly, ignoring the protest of her sore muscles, "if push comes to shove, I feel certain I can earn myself some fast cash." Not that she would ever resort to what she was suggesting, but he didn't have to know that, and if it hit the mark… "You don't need to worry about me at all. I can take care of myself."

Nicole knew she would not soon forget the collection of emotions that danced across his handsome face. But it was anger that ultimately took center stage and held his features captive. The uncharacteristic outward display fascinated her for about two seconds then trepidation kicked in. Before she could take a step back, he grabbed her by both arms.

"You will do exactly as I say, Nicole." Those long, tanned fingers tightened to the precise point just short of pain. That silvery gaze darkened as he pulled her closer to him. "The issue is not up for debate."

Nicole met his intense glare with lead in her own. "Then you'd better be prepared to stick to me like glue. To watch every move I make," she warned. "The first time you turn your back I'm out of here. I've had the same training as you, Michaels, and we both know I'm very good at my job."

Loaded silence followed that summation. A muscle flexed rhythmically in his chiseled jaw. Heat mushroomed between their almost-touching bodies. Nicole's heart pounded so hard she felt sure Ian could hear it threatening to burst from her chest. To her utter frustration, her gaze drifted to his lips. She licked her own, her mind immediately conjuring up his taste.

"Look at me," he demanded softly, the sound of his voice wreaking havoc with her senses.

Nicole's breath caught when her gaze connected with his once more. Desire, hot and fierce, burned in his eyes. She blinked. That one thing was all they had ever truly shared—overwhelming attraction, soul-shattering desire. The kind that diminished all else. "What do you want from me?" she demanded. Nicole searched his eyes for an answer beyond the heat and memory that connected them body and soul.

"When that car exploded and I couldn't see you, I thought…" He released her arms only to gently cup her face in his hands. His thumb glided across her cheek, sending shivers down her spine. The breath of his reluctant sigh whispered across her lips. "I thought I'd lost you."

Nicole steeled herself against what she wanted to feel. Just words. That's all they were. She couldn't trust Ian with her heart any more than she could trust her life to the bastard who was trying to kill her. She understood Ian's probable motivation—revenge. Would he take this opportunity to do to her what she had done to him three years ago? If he only knew…

Ruthlessly squashing the tiny spark of hope his words elicited, Nicole encircled his wrists with trembling fingers and attempted to remove his hands from her face.

Ian swallowed…hard, the play of muscle beneath tanned skin doing strange things to her stomach. "I can't lose you again," he murmured.

"You never had me," she assured him with forced contempt.

He laughed softly and raised one dark brow in mock speculation. "I can recall having you at least four times, Nicole." That eclectic accent he had gained from growing up in half a dozen European countries thickened as his voice lowered to a more seductive level. His fingers slid around her neck and urged her closer still, his thumbs working a sensuous kind of magic. "I remember every detail of every moment we spent together. Each time we made love proved more intense than the last. Don't try to tell me you've forgotten."

He pressed a silky kiss to her cheek, Nicole shivered as much from his words as from his kiss. "Stop," she whispered hoarsely.

He stopped but didn't pull away. His lips remained only a hairbreadth from her skin. "You want me to stop?"

"Yes," she lied. Nicole didn't have to look to know he smiled, she felt it. Electricity crackled between their heated bodies.

"And if I refuse?"

Nicole closed her eyes and released a shuddering breath. She shouldn't have come to him. Did she really expect to be able to spend five minutes with the man and not want him? Only a few hours ago she had eluded death for the third time

An Important Message from the Editors

Dear Reader,

Because you've chosen to read one of our fine romance novels, we'd like to say "thank you!" And, as a **special** way to thank you, we've selected <u>two more</u> of the books you love so well **plus** an exciting Mystery Gift to send you — absolutely <u>FREE</u>!

Please enjoy them with our compliments...

Pam Powers

Lift here

How to validate your Editor's
"Thank You"
FREE GIFT

1. Peel off gift seal from front cover. Place it in space provided at right. This automatically entitles you to receive 2 FREE BOOKS and a fabulous mystery gift.

2. Send back this card and you'll get 2 brand-new *Romance* novels. These books have a cover price of $5.99 or more each in the U.S. and $6.99 or more each in Canada, but they are yours to keep absolutely free.

3. There's no catch. You're under no obligation to buy anything. We charge nothing—ZERO—for your first shipment. And you don't have to make any minimum number of purchases—not even one!

4. The fact is, thousands of readers enjoy receiving their books by mail from The Reader Service. They enjoy the convenience of home delivery...they like getting the best new novels at discount prices BEFORE they're available in stores... and they love their Heart to Heart subscriber newsletter featuring author news, special book offers, book reviews and much more!

5. We hope that after receiving your free books you'll want to remain a subscriber. But the choice is yours— to continue or cancel, any time at all! So why not take us up on our invitation, with no risk of any kind. You'll be glad you did!

GET A *Free* MYSTERY GIFT...

SURPRISE MYSTERY GIFT COULD BE YOURS **FREE** AS A SPECIAL "THANK YOU" FROM THE EDITORS

The Editor's "Thank You" Free Gifts Include:

● *Two BRAND-NEW Romance novels!*
● *An exciting mystery gift!*

Yes! I have placed my
Editor's "Thank You" seal in the
space provided at right. Please
send me 2 free books and a
fabulous mystery gift. I
understand I am under no
obligation to purchase any
books, as explained on the
back and on the opposite page.

PLACE
FREE GIFT
SEAL
HERE

393 MDL D39C   193 MDL D39D

FIRST NAME   LAST NAME

ADDRESS

APT.#   CITY

STATE/PROV.   ZIP/POSTAL CODE

(ED2-SS-05)

Thank You!

The Reader Service — Here's How It Works:

Accepting your 2 free books and gift places you under no obligation to buy anything. You may keep the books and gift and return the shipping statement marked "cancel." If you do not cancel, about a month later we'll send you 3 additional books and bill you just $4.99 each in the U.S., or $5.49 each in Canada, plus 25¢ shipping & handling per book and applicable taxes if any.* That's the complete price and — compared to cover prices starting from $5.99 each in the U.S. and $6.99 each in Canada — it's quite a bargain! You may cancel at any time, but if you choose to continue, every month we'll send you 3 more books, which you may either purchase at the discount price or return to us and cancel your subscription.

*Terms and prices subject to change without notice. Sales tax applicable in N.Y. Canadian residents will be charged applicable provincial taxes and GST.

in less than two weeks. And right now all she could think about was how it would feel to make love with Ian again. To have him touch her in that slow, thorough manner of his. To have him whisper sweet things to her in that lightly accented voice. To make him believe that she hadn't meant to hurt him three years ago—that she had only been doing her job.

What if she had died today?

Nicole blinked. She would never have had the opportunity to make things right with Ian. She lifted her gaze to his, watched the renewed desire turn those silvery depths to a deeper, gunmetal gray. *One last night.* They could have one last night together and then she would disappear from his life forever. She would face whatever the future held for her…alone. If death awaited, Nicole decided she would just have her taste of heaven now.

She moistened her lips and smiled up at him. "Well," she said languorously as she began to slowly unbutton his shirt. "I suppose that leaves me with no choice." Nicole slid her hands inside and over his muscled chest, the feel of that sculpted terrain making her weak with want. How she had missed him. No man would ever be able to make her feel the way Ian had. Would this thing between them still be as it once was—even after what she had done to him? Nicole cleared her mind. She didn't want to think…she wanted to feel. To touch…to forget.

He remained absolutely still as she plunged her fingers into his long, dark hair and pulled his head down to hers. She nipped his lower lip with her teeth, then traced that sexy cleft in his chin with her tongue. He moved then. His hands slid over her shoulders and down her back, caressing, arousing her naked flesh. And then his mouth captured hers.

His kiss was slow, thorough, tantalizing, with a kind of

erotic finesse only Ian possessed. Her heart thudding with anticipation, Nicole watched the intent expression on his face as he deepened the kiss. Then her eyes closed with the ecstasy she could no longer deny. Desire burst inside her like shattering glass, sending tiny shards of heat throughout her. Her head no longer hurt, her muscles no longer complained of their bruising. All conscious thought vanished. Ian's masterful hands squeezed her bottom, then pulled her against his thick arousal. Nicole shuddered with the need now gripping every fiber of her being.

She wanted his bare skin against hers—now. Nicole jerked his shirt open, scattering the remaining buttons across the lush carpet. She reveled in the feel of his strong back as she slid the material down, then pressed her body to his. Smooth and hot. His skin singed hers as their bodies melded. Ian groaned his approval deep in his throat, the sound urging Nicole's own frenzied desire. She tugged his shirt from his slacks, then slowly peeled it off his body.

He lifted her against him and she instinctively wrapped her legs around his lean waist. His mouth continued to torture hers, his tongue delving inside, tasting, tempting, then retreating. That slow in-and-out pace foreshadowing what she knew would come. Her legs tightened around him, pressing the moist heat between her thighs more firmly into his hardened length. This was what she had fantasized about a thousand times in the last three years.

Ian carried her to the bed and lowered her gently onto the tangled sheets. His body aligned over hers, he looked down at her, those amazing gray eyes analyzing her too closely. Nicole struggled to read the emotions cluttering his face. Sadness, maybe, or pain…almost. Had he missed her half as much as she had missed him? Did he want her as she wanted him?

"You do have a choice," he said softly.

Nicole tried one last time to decipher that distant look in his eyes, but to no avail. "I know," she whispered, then smiled. "I choose this." She unbuttoned his fly, then lowered the zipper. His eyes closed on a tortured groan as she eased his slacks and briefs over his hips, then caressed him intimately. Her own need suddenly careened out of control. Instinctively her body arched against his, the resulting friction making her cry out with want. One solid yank was all it took for Ian to relieve her of the tiny, strappy panties.

And then he was inside her, filling her, turning her world upside down. Their movements turned frantic, out of control. His powerful thrusts propelled Nicole closer and closer to the climax that had begun the moment he touched her. Ian kissed her again, hard and fast. He murmured desperate words in a language she didn't understand. She gripped his broad shoulders, trying to hold on longer…to make it last. But she couldn't, one more thrust and she tumbled over the edge. Heat and light and pleasure cascaded over her, swirled inside her. Ian followed close behind, driving into her one last time.

His taut body relaxed, his forehead rested against hers, their ragged breathing the only sound in the room. "You should rest now." He brushed a soft kiss across her lips. "I'll keep you safe."

Nicole nodded, suddenly feeling totally exhausted all over again. "I trust you, Ian," she murmured, her gaze holding his. "I trust you with my life."

"Sleep, Nicole," he insisted gently. "I'll be right here when you wake up."

IAN PARTED the blinds and checked the parking area outside his town house once more. Still no sign of Martinez. He paused to listen for Nicole. The sound of water spraying in the shower continued. Good. He wanted her occupied until after Martinez arrived.

He had spent the entire night watching Nicole sleep, memorizing each delicate feature of her sweet face. She was as beautiful as ever. Her body slender and feminine, yet toned and amazingly strong. Ian swallowed back the emotions he knew he should not feel. Merely touching Nicole aroused him to the point of insanity. The sudden image of water sluicing over all that satiny skin made his groin tighten. He closed his eyes against the memory of her scent, her taste. Nicole did things to him...made him feel things he could not begin to describe. Ian sighed and shook his head slowly from side to side. This could not be.

He was a fool.

His foolishness had cost a life once before; he refused to risk a repeat of that mistake. Ian plowed his fingers through his hair and crossed the room once more, silently cursing his compunction every step of the way. He had paced this room for the past ten minutes.

Guilt gnawed at him for feigning sleep when Nicole had awakened this morning. She had kissed him tenderly on the cheek, then slipped quietly into the bathroom to shower. And what had he done? He had immediately called Martinez and hastily dressed. Nicole would not be happy when he informed her of his plan. But her displeasure was of no consequence in the matter. Ian understood what had to be done. He knew no more now regarding her case than he had known yesterday when she had left Victoria's office. But he did know with complete certainty that he could not stay objective where Nicole was concerned. And her survival depended on the kind of objectivity and focus he lost all sight of in her presence.

The moment he had set eyes on her in Victoria's office, Ian had experienced a sense of rage unparalleled by anything he had ever known before. She was the last person on the planet he would have helped do anything. Or so he'd thought. When that car had exploded, and he hadn't been sure if she were dead or alive, the truth had hit him like a bullet between the eyes. He still had deep feelings for Nicole. The past changed nothing. He couldn't bear the thought of losing her forever.

But, after last night, Ian realized that he could not determine the threat to her safety with her so close. It was true three years ago and it was still true today: when he was with Nicole, he could not maintain the necessary focus required to perform his mission. Taking that kind of risk was out of the question. She would simply have to go into hiding with Martinez while Ian did what had to be done.

The issue was closed in his opinion. Nicole would do exactly as he instructed. He set his jaw determinedly.

Or else.

The anticipated knock came just as Ian turned to retrace his path across the room. He repositioned the Glock tucked into his waistband at the small of his back, then made his way to the door. He breathed a sigh of relief when he checked the peephole and found Martinez on the other side. Finally. Ian opened the door only wide enough for Martinez to enter, and quickly closed it behind him.

"Thanks for coming on short notice."

"No problem, man." Martinez, the Colby Agency's newest investigator, scanned the room. "Nice place."

Ian nodded. He wasn't accustomed to having visitors in his home, but there was no getting around it this time. The spray of water in the other room stopped. Ian glanced in the direction of the bedroom door, Nicole would appear at any moment. He was out of time. Without preamble, he related the details of her case as he knew them to Martinez.

"Good morning."

At the sound of Nicole's voice Ian turned slowly to face her. He did not relish the next few minutes. "Good morning," he returned with a tight smile. An unfamiliar sensation squeezed his chest at how vulnerable she looked in an old pair of his sweats, her long blond hair still damp from her shower.

Her gaze darted from Ian to the other man, then narrowed with suspicion. "I didn't know you had company," she said stiffly.

Ian glanced at the man standing beside him. "This is Ric Martinez." Ian leveled his gaze on Nicole and steeled himself for her fury. "He will be keeping you company at one of our safe houses until the investigation is over."

Pain, then anger stole across her features. She gave a jerky nod. "I see."

Ian took the four steps that separated them. "It would be a conflict of interest for us to work together," he explained quietly.

Nicole lifted her defiant chin and glared at him. "Whose interest, yours or mine?"

Irritation flared. "It would be in both our best interests for you to cooperate with Martinez." He matched her insolent expression. "And that's what you're going to do."

She shoved a handful of hair behind her ear, the fight-or-flight urge already evident in her posture. "Last time I checked this was still a free country."

Ian snagged her arm when she would have pushed past him. "If the story you told Victoria is true, then walking away from our help would be a serious mistake. Someone has tried to kill you three times already, Nicole. You're not leaving alone."

She glowered first at his offending hand, then at him. "Just try and stop me, Michaels."

His grip tightened. "Don't be a fool, Nicole."

"Miss Reed, I think maybe you should listen to him," Martinez suggested soberly.

Her disdainful glare flicked to Martinez. "This isn't your fight."

He held up his hands stop-sign fashion and backed off. "Whatever you say, lady."

Ian pulled her closer to him, an unspoken demand for her full attention. "You know the rules of survival as well as I do," he ground out.

"Why don't you tell me about the rules, Michaels." She struggled against his hold, but he tightened his grip, angering her all the more. "What was last night all about, huh? Survival or retribution?"

One beat turned to five, the tension growing thicker with each. "You had a choice, you decided," he reminded coldly. "I have a choice this morning, and I have decided."

"Go to hell."

"I've been there, Nicole. Don't you remember?" Watching Solomon die and knowing he was responsible had been pure hell for Ian.

She blinked, but not before he got a glimpse of the regret in those wide blue eyes. Nicole sighed defeatedly. "Fine," she relented, then lifted a repentant gaze to his. "I suppose you know what you're doing, Ian. And I—" She shrugged half-heartedly. "I'm just totally confused."

Ian relaxed his brutal grip on her arm and exhaled his own burst of relief. "Good. Martinez will stick close to you and I'll work the investigation."

"And what will I be doing?"

"You'll lie low until we know exactly what's going on. That's standard operating procedure. You know the drill."

Nicole nodded. "Sounds as if you have everything covered."

Ian held her gaze, urging her to understand. "I will do whatever it takes to neutralize the threat to you, Nicole."

"Well." She smiled, her lips trembling with the effort. "I guess we should get going then." She glanced in Martinez's direction. "No point dragging this out."

"You'll be safe as long as you do exactly as I tell you," Ian assured her.

She paused and turned back to him. That crystal-blue gaze softened, grew misty. "No kiss goodbye?"

Ian's chest constricted with regret and something else he refused to acknowledge. Before he could stop himself, his hands went immediately to the face permanently etched in his memory. The feel of her skin ripped him apart inside. How could he let her out of his sight? But, how could he permit this thing between them to get in the way of what had to be done?

As if in slow motion, he lowered his head, his mouth yearning to mate with hers. His eyes closed at the first brush of their lips. Nicole's arms slid beneath his suit jacket, around his waist, caressing him as she had last night…as she had in his dreams so many times.

She had the weapon in her hand two endless seconds before his body accepted the command to react. Nicole backed away from him, her expert aim shifting quickly to Martinez. "Get your hands up where I can see them," she demanded sharply.

"Think, Nicole," Ian suggested calmly, while mentally cursing himself for the idiot he was. He never made mistakes like this. *Only with Nicole.* "You came to me for help. How can we help you if you won't let us?"

"Just yesterday you refused to help me. Now I've decided I don't need your brand of help, thank you very much." She moved cautiously toward the door, skillfully alternating her focus between him and Martinez. "Your keys," she said to Martinez when she reached the door.

He shrugged as if he didn't understand, his olive skin a good deal paler than when he arrived.

"Your car keys. Give me your car keys," she ground out impatiently.

"Okay, lady, just stay cool. My brother is going to kill me. That Explorer's brand new." Martinez reached for his pocket with his right hand.

"Wait! Hold your hands up high and turn all the way around," Nicole instructed curtly.

Martinez glanced uneasily at Ian. Ian nodded for him to do as she said. Martinez turned around slowly, his hands held high. The form-fitting muscle shirt, which he wore tucked into his jeans left no doubt that the man was unarmed. Ian swore silently. He should have warned Martinez to be fully prepared. Not that it would have done any good since Ian obviously had been ill-prepared himself.

"Now give me those keys—with your left hand," Nicole ordered.

Martinez complied without hesitation.

Nicole reached behind her and opened the door. "Nobody moves until I'm out of here. *Nobody.*" She allowed Ian one final look before she stepped across the threshold and slammed the door behind her.

Ian hissed a four-letter word. How in the hell had he fallen for that old trick?

"Hey man, are we going after her or what?" Martinez asked uncertainly.

"Go out the back. See if you can get around behind her to cut her off," Ian told him roughly as he stormed across the room. Dammit, the woman was going to get herself killed. She knew better. Nicole knew the code of survival and protection. So far she had done nothing but act like a frightened civilian, breaking every rule.

Ian cursed again when he stepped into the early-morning sun. Fortunately it was Saturday and his neighbors would likely still be in bed at this hour. He quickly scanned the seemingly deserted street. But his neighbors weren't the concern at the moment. He shook his head in disgust. Nicole was a damned open target standing there fumbling with Martinez's keys. His gut clenched.

"At this rate you won't make it very far, Nicole." Ian took the steps two at a time.

Nicole's head jerked up. Instantly, she focused a bead on him with her left hand, while continuing to try and manipulate the keys with her right. "Stop right there, Michaels."

"I suppose you're going to shoot me if I don't."

Her head came up again. Ian smiled when her resolve visibly faltered. "I didn't think so," he concluded aloud, his supreme annoyance making his voice sound more lethal than he had intended.

He walked right up to her, the muzzle of the Glock pressed into his chest. "Give me the weapon."

"No way. I don't need any help," she said tightly, her eyes suspiciously bright. "I decided last night that I wasn't going to involve anyone else in *my* problems."

"Was that before or after we made love?" Ian held her gaze. His entire being reacted to the uncharacteristic fear he saw in her eyes.

"It'll be better this way." She drew in a shaky breath, but

firmed her grip on the Glock. "Now get the hell away from me, Michaels. People are dropping like flies around me. First my director, then Daniels."

"No."

"Now who's being the fool?" Lowering her weapon, Nicole jerked the vehicle door open and slid behind the wheel. "Goodbye, Ian."

Without warning, glass shattered, the sound echoing in the otherwise quiet street. Fragments from the truck window sprayed in Ian's direction. Simultaneously, something propelled him back a step, the impact and burn clicking an instant recognition in his brain and sending him diving for cover. Thankfully Nicole was in the vehicle. He hoped like hell she stayed put. Ian hit the ground. A stab of pain knifed through his left shoulder and radiated down his arm.

The squeal of tires and the roar of an engine pierced the still morning air. Then the report of Ian's Glock, three shots in rapid succession, echoed. Nicole was returning fire. Ian swore savagely and pushed to his feet. Nicole whipped around and quickly surveyed him.

"Where are you hit?" Worry traced lines across her face, her gaze darted back to his left shoulder. "Damn," she breathed. Gingerly she pushed his jacket away to view the damage.

"It's nothing."

She gave him a look. "Yeah, right."

Ian gritted his teeth when she unbuttoned his shirt partway and pulled it from the wound. He winced inwardly. "I am now fully convinced that you're trying to get yourself killed, Nicole. Why didn't you stay in the truck?"

"Shut up, Michaels." She grimaced. "You need a doctor."

"I got a partial on the license plate," Martinez reported breathlessly as he skidded to a stop next to Nicole.

"We have to get Ian to a hospital." She tugged him toward the passenger-side door of Martinez's borrowed truck as she spoke.

Ian manacled her right wrist and halted her forward movement. "I'll take this." Before she could protest he relieved her of the Glock, then tucked it into his waistband beneath his jacket. "And don't even think about leaving my sight."

"Fine," she snapped, her eyes shooting daggers at him. "As long as you get in the damned vehicle."

Martinez quickly brushed the glass from the driver's seat and dropped behind the wheel. "My brother is definitely going to kill me," he muttered.

"Drive, Martinez," Nicole ordered as she slid in next to him, "or he won't get the chance."

Chapter Two

Blood...

Oh God.

Nauseated and feeling more than a little faint, Nicole stared down at her bloodstained hands. This was by no means her first time to exchange gunfire with a hostile, nor was it her first up close encounter with spilled blood.

But this was Ian's blood.

The hospital's medicinal smell didn't help. Nicole swiped her palms against the baggy gray sweatshirt she wore. She squeezed her hands into tight fists and dropped them to her sides. Moistening her dry lips and careful not to make eye contact, she slowly lifted her gaze to the man seated on the examining table. He sat on the very edge, poised, intent, as if anticipating the need to make a tactical move at any given moment. His torn and bloody shirt lay on the exam table behind him, the damaged suit jacket next to it. Nicole closed her eyes against the panic that still threatened to suffocate her each time she relived those few seconds between the sound of the gunshot and the moment she confirmed with her own eyes that Ian wasn't mortally wounded.

The sound of Ian's smoky voice as he answered some question the doctor asked dragged Nicole back to the here and now. Young and obviously nervous, the doctor pulled another suture through the nasty wound on Ian's shoulder. He kept muttering something about the injury looking like a gunshot wound to him. Poor guy, Nicole thought to herself, he had to be an intern. Otherwise Martinez would never have had him even half believing that idiotic story about Ian's falling into a window.

Ignoring the doctor's concerns, Ian did nothing to lessen the thick tension. His dark, brooding presence would unnerve a war-zone veteran. He had refused the offer of pain medication, and, in that arrogant, dangerous tone of his, had ordered the doctor to do what he had to do as quickly as possible. The wound wasn't so bad, Nicole told herself again. Just a nasty slash through skin and muscle. Had the angle been slightly different Ian might be in surgery now—or worse.

Shuddering with a chill that went bone deep, Nicole wrapped her arms around her middle. Ian could have been killed. And it was her fault. She should never have gotten him mixed up in this. How could she drag him into her problems with no regard for his safety? Had she been so absorbed in saving her own skin that she hadn't thought through the consequences of her actions? Nicole let go a heavy breath. She closed her eyes and willed the mixture of fear and frustration to retreat. Ian was going to be fine, she told herself again. He was safe.

And she was leaving.

She could do this alone. She was a highly trained federal agent. All she had to do was make sure she wasn't followed when she made live contact with her witness. She didn't need Ian. Denial rushed through her at that thought. She needed him all right, but not in the way she should.

Suddenly, more from some innate need than true courage, she met Ian's gaze for the first time since their arrival at the E.R. He hadn't taken his eyes off her since they'd entered the examining room. It wasn't necessary for her to look to confirm her suspicions; she could feel his gaze on her. Steady and relentless, those piercing gray eyes held hers even now, then reached past her defenses and touched her.

Nicole trembled with reaction. The only indication that Ian felt anything at all was the flexing of that muscle in his rigid jaw. He was probably just annoyed that her stupidity had got him shot. Whatever he was feeling, one thing was certain, Ian Michaels was planning his next move. Nicole knew his methods as well as she knew her own. No matter that he was surely in serious pain, Ian would develop a plan, and then a backup plan for that. Analyzing her current emotional state would be part of his strategy. He read her too easily. Nicole looked away. Why give him any more ammunition?

A cell phone chirped, startling Nicole. She took a slow, deep breath and ran a shaky hand through her hair. She was seriously rattled. Of course, dancing with death would do that, she reminded herself. Next to her, Martinez murmured responses to his caller.

"It's for you," he announced, offering Ian the compact phone. "It's Victoria."

Ian accepted the phone, then placed it on the examining table next to him. Nicole knew he was still watching her, so she kept her gaze purposely averted from his. He reached beneath his jacket lying on the table beside him and retrieved his weapon. He handed the Glock, butt first, to Martinez.

"Don't take your eyes off her," he warned. "If she makes a move for the door, use it."

The doctor made an odd, choking sound of disbelief. "Did

I see a badge? Are you gentlemen police officers? If this is a gunshot wound—"

Indignation exploded inside Nicole. "Screw you, Michaels," she hissed, cutting off the doctor. Those tender emotions she had felt only moments ago evaporated instantly.

Ian held her gaze for one long beat. "I believe you've already taken care of that."

"You bas—"

"Miss Reed," Martinez interrupted firmly. "I'd like you to have a seat. Please," he added quickly as he tucked the weapon into his waistband.

"I...I really need you to be still," the doctor said hesitantly, his gaze darting to the weapon at Martinez's waist, then back to Ian. "I can't do this properly unless—"

Ian waved him off. "In a moment." His formidable focus remained fixed on Nicole, watching, waiting for her reaction to Martinez's request.

One second lapsed to five before Nicole gave in and plopped onto the molded-plastic, institutional-orange chair. Knowing Ian, he would have sat there and bled to death before relenting. Still stinging from his remark, she mentally recited every vile word in her vocabulary and Ian's connection to each. Martinez stationed himself between her and the door. Did Ian really believe he could prevent her from leaving whenever she got good and ready to go? Nicole smiled to herself. She would just see about that.

Obviously satisfied that he had won, he picked up the cell phone and turned his attention to Victoria. "Yes." He paused, listening. "No, I'm fine. There's no need for you to rush back. I have everything under control." Another brief pause. "Yes, I'll do that." He flipped the mouthpiece closed and tossed the phone back to Martinez.

"I do have other patients, Mr. Michaels," the doctor said pointedly, obviously finally finding his courage. Or perhaps just anxious to rid himself of present company.

"Of course." Ian leveled one final warning glare on Nicole.

She produced an exaggerated smile, then, while he watched so intently, she silently mouthed a most descriptive adjective—one that fit Ian perfectly in her opinion. The promise of a smile tilted one side of his usually grim mouth, making her pulse react. Nicole released a weary sigh and for the first time today had the presence of mind to thank God that they were both safe.

But how long would either of them stay that way?

The door suddenly swung open and Ian's attention jerked toward the intruder.

"We've got another bleeder, Doctor," an efficient-looking nurse called from the doorway. Her gaze immediately flew to Martinez, and then the weapon at his waist before he could turn away. "A seventeen-year-old with a knife wound to the right forearm," she added slowly, her eyes widening with fear.

The doctor spared her a brief glance. "Prep him, I'll be right there. Almost finished here," he said distractedly. The nurse managed a smile in Ian's direction before she disappeared into the hall. The wide door closed soundlessly behind her.

Ian gave Martinez a discreet nod, then angled his head toward the door in silent instruction. No doubt, Ian reasoned, that nurse was at the desk calling the police at this very moment. When the police arrived, there would be confusion, distraction. Too much opportunity for Nicole to give them the slip. Not to mention he didn't want her position with the bureau brought to the attention of the locals.

"Let's take a walk, Miss Reed," Martinez suggested.

Nicole looked him up and down as if he'd just suggested something lewd. "I don't think so, Martinez."

"Do as he says, Nicole," Ian ordered quietly. She shot him a drop-dead look, then heaved an impatient sigh before pushing to her feet. Reluctantly she followed Martinez out the door.

"Hold still just a little longer, Mr. Michaels." The doctor paused, surveying Ian with a look of concern. "Now that we're alone, are you sure you don't want something for the pain? That local can't be doing much for you."

"I'm fine."

The doctor shrugged and returned to the business at hand. Ian needed his head clear. He would have to deal with the police, which wouldn't be that difficult. Victoria had a great many influential connections. Known for following the rules and cooperating, Colby Agency investigators rarely got any flack from the local authorities. Maybe this time Ian was stretching the rules, but that couldn't be helped. He set his jaw hard against a particularly fierce stab of pain.

Nicole was anything but simple. Dealing with her required Ian's full command of all his senses. His strategy was as straightforward as you could get. First he planned to get the truth out of her—one way or another. She knew a lot more about the threat to her life than she was telling, of that Ian felt certain. Secondly, he intended to stash her away someplace safe while he handled the situation.

Then, he would walk away and never look back. Ian refused to acknowledge the protest that twisted inside him. He couldn't deny what he felt for Nicole. The emotions were fierce, overpowering. But he couldn't trust her. She had betrayed him before, what was to prevent her from doing it again? Ian almost smiled at the memory of her reaction to his comment earlier. He closed his eyes and allowed Nicole's image to envelop him. All attitude and sass on the outside, but soft and vulnerable on the inside, Nicole was the one woman who could make him lose control. She held a power over him that defied all else. Ian blinked away the vision. But he wasn't a masochist at heart, nor was he without pride. He had allowed that mistake once.

Nicole cared only about her career. She was attracted to Ian he knew, but that was all. Her complete allegiance lay with the cloak-and-dagger stuff that epitomized shadow operations. Ian bit back a laugh at the thought of Nicole as someone's wife. But the rush of jealousy that surged through him was no laughing matter. Ian frowned and quickly reined in his wayward thoughts. No more, he determined. From this point forward his every connection with Nicole would be strictly business.

A quick rap on the door drew Ian's gaze in that direction. Two uniformed Chicago police officers entered the room. Both looked entirely too young to own a weapon, much less use it.

"Ian Michaels?"

"Yes," Ian replied.

The doctor looked up; a frown knitted his brow. "Sorry, guys, you're going to have to wait until I'm finished here," he warned as he placed a bandage over the newly sutured wound. "My patient's health comes first."

"No problem, sir," the taller of the two replied. "We've got all the time in the world." The look he shot Ian was arrogantly challenging.

Ian answered that bold gaze with bored amusement. This was going to be a piece of cake.

The door suddenly flew inward again. The two officers whirled toward it in a flash of dark blue. Martinez stumbled in holding his nose with both hands, blood gushing between his fingers and down his shirt front. Ian bounded off the exam table amid the doctor's protests.

"Where's Nicole?"

"She's gone." Martinez used one hand to swipe the blood from his mouth. "Hell, man, I think she broke my nose."

Ian's heart shifted into warp speed. "How much head start does she have?" he demanded curtly.

Martinez shook his head defeatedly. "Five minutes maybe."

Suddenly everyone was talking at once. The doctor shouting for a nurse. The policemen demanding to know what was going on. And Martinez trying to explain how a female he outweighed by nearly a hundred pounds and towered over by at least a half-dozen inches had managed to beat the hell out of him, leave him stunned on the floor and get away.

The voices and faces around Ian faded into insignificance as his mind raced forward. *Where would she go?* She was breaking every rule of survival in the book. In Ian's experience, when an agent broke code there was compelling motivation. Something worth the risk.

What was Nicole hiding?

"I'VE GOT IT," Martinez announced in a distinctly nasal voice as he rushed into Ian's office. The white tape stretched tautly across the bridge of his nose looked stark against his dark skin. "The car the shooter used was stolen. And Nicole had a room at the Sheraton downtown. She checked out just over an hour ago."

Ian glanced at his watch: one-fifteen. "Did she call for a cab?"

"The doorman said she got into a Ford Explorer parked on the opposite side of the street." Martinez swore. "My brother is going to *enjoy* killing me."

"It'll show up at the airport," Ian said distractedly. He needed to know where Nicole was headed and from which airport. And he needed to know now.

"I'm sorry I lost her, man," Martinez offered again.

Ian met the other man's concerned gaze. Though inexperienced, Martinez was a good investigator. In time he would be a force to be reckoned with, and there was no time like the present to gain valuable experience. Ian knew he could trust Martinez completely. Besides, Nicole was a formidable opponent. Ian didn't know anyone, not even himself, he mused, that she couldn't best if she put her mind to it. Martinez might as well learn the hard way.

"It's okay, Martinez. Nicole is not your typical vulnerable female client." At least not on the surface, Ian amended silently.

Martinez huffed. "You got that right."

"Mr. Michaels, I have that information you requested."

Ian motioned for Mildred, Victoria's secretary, to come in. He accepted the documents she offered.

"Miss Reed has a reservation on every flight on all airlines headed to D.C. and New York that are scheduled to leave O'Hare and Midway between three o'clock and eight o'clock today."

Ian scanned the list of flights. Eight different flights arriving at five different airports. He shook his head. Nicole had no intention of making this easy.

"And here's the report on Miss Reed's car. I asked Murray the at city's lab to put a rush on the preliminary and fax me a copy ASAP." Mildred smiled with satisfaction. "He came through, as usual."

Ian returned her smile. Mildred had been with the agency since the beginning, when Victoria's husband had been in charge. The vivacious middle-aged woman knew the Chicago PD like the back of her hand, and had something on anyone who was anybody employed there.

"Thank you, Mildred." A frown creased Ian's brow as he scanned the relatively brief preliminary report. No timer. No evidence of an internal detonation device. *Remote-detonated.* The bomb had been remote-detonated by someone watching Nicole's car, Ian concluded. But why had they not waited until she was in the car?

"Call Kruger," he instructed Mildred. "I need a ride to D.C."

"Yes sir." Mildred turned back at the door. "I'll ask him to be ready within the hour."

"Good," Ian agreed.

"You think she'd go back to D.C.?" Martinez gingerly fingered the tightly taped bridge of his nose.

"Yes, I do."

"I'll drop you at the airport," Martinez offered. "That is if you don't mind me driving your car, mine's still in the shop."

"That's fine." Ian estimated that Victoria's private jet could have him in D.C. a good half hour before the earliest commercial flight on Nicole's schedule. He stood, mentally ticking off the items he would need to take with him. He would need to stop by his place and pick up another weapon and a change of clothes. Nicole probably left his Glock in the Explorer, but there was nothing he could do about that right now. He glanced at Martinez. "Let's go. I'll confirm the itinerary with Kruger en route."

"After I drop you off, I'll look for the Explorer," Martinez grumbled as they headed toward the elevators. "I can't believe she stole my brother's truck." Martinez shook his head disgustedly. "And, man, I've never had my butt kicked so badly. By a female at that." He flashed Ian a look of dismay. "I hope you're not going to tell anybody about that."

Ian stabbed the elevator call button, then shot the man next to him an amused look. "Don't worry, Martinez, your secret is safe with me."

"Mr. Michaels, wait!"

Ian paused before getting onto the elevator. Amy Wells, the newest member of the agency's clerical staff, hurried toward him, those long, coppery curls bouncing around her shoulders.

"Miss Wells," he greeted patiently, though impatience pounded through his veins. He had to get to D.C. before Nicole did.

"Mildred needs your signature before you leave since Mrs. Colby won't be back for another week." Amy indicated the report she held and offered him a pen. She blushed, clearly intimidated at having to speak to him much less request anything of him.

Ian produced a smile. "No problem." He quickly penned his official signature.

"Gosh, Martinez, what happened to you?" Amy asked abruptly, all wide-eyed innocence.

Before Martinez could come up with a suitable explanation, Ian leaned toward her and whispered, "It's a secret." He touched his lips with one finger in a gesture of silence and stepped inside the elevator. The doors closed, leaving Miss Wells staring in dismay after them. Martinez wasn't going to live this down anytime soon.

NICOLE PARKED her car down the street from her apartment building. Darkness shrouded the old neighborhood she had called home for five years now. Only forty minutes from her office, the small Virginia community boasted quiet living with all the conveniences of the city. Nicole sighed, then closed her eyes for a long moment. She was tired. Her trip to Chicago had been a fiasco, and a colossal waste of precious time. Nicole glanced at the digital clock on her dash. Only two hours until her flight to Atlanta. She had to get a move on. She had wasted enough time stopping to purchase something to wear besides Ian's sweats.

"Suck it up, Reed," she scolded herself as she scanned the deserted street once more. Walking into that building and then her dark apartment was not something she looked forward to—especially since the only other tenant was probably out of town as usual. But what choice did she have? She needed clothes and cash, and new ID. She had left her purse at Ian's. No way would she have chanced going back to get it. Her next flight was reserved under an alias. She certainly couldn't go anywhere broke and without clean ID. It would take lots of hard cash to do what she had to do. Replanting a witness wasn't cheap. Or easy. Not to mention the fact that she was doing this on her own. She knew better than to risk anyone at the agency finding out. And she definitely couldn't hang around D.C. long. It wouldn't take the man—or woman, she amended—long to track her back here. Ian wouldn't be far behind her. And he would be royally ticked off. Nicole decided she had better be gone when he arrived.

Her gaze sweeping left to right, then back, Nicole emerged from the car. She adjusted the baseball cap she had crammed her hair into, then rolled her head to loosen up her neck. God she was tense. Her right hand slid instinctively to her weapon she had retrieved from an airport locker. She tucked it more firmly into the waistband of her jeans at the small of her back. The denim jacket she wore concealed it well. She could have taken it to Chicago with her, but hadn't wanted to go through the hassle with airport authorities. So she had left the weapon and her bureau ID in a locker. She had left Ian's Glock in the Explorer back at O'Hare. He wouldn't be happy, but he would get over it. Martinez would find it when he picked up his brother's vehicle. Losing a weapon wasn't conducive to sleeping at night.

Nicole breathed a sigh of relief when she entered the well-lit courtyard that flanked the right side of her building. Only three stories, each floor of the old building housed just two apartments. The place was definitely small compared to the others in this neighborhood, but it was clean and well kept. And quiet. How could it be anything else? she mused. In the five years since she'd moved in, more than half the other apartments had always been vacant. Like now.

The sound of a dog barking on the next block reminded Nicole that she was wasting time. She glanced up at her un-adorned, second-story balcony. On the first floor, the only other tenant's terrace contained an assortment of flowering and green plants. Nicole was never home long enough to care for plants or pets. She shrugged listlessly. People like her didn't have time for such distractions.

The pool shimmered like a tranquil lagoon in the full moonlight as she hurried past it and around to the front entrance. A slight breeze whispered through the leaves of the surrounding trees. This lovely courtyard had been the main selling point for the place in Nicole's opinion. With one more look to either side of her, she slid the key into the lock and entered the deserted stairwell.

Nicole paused to listen for sounds. The answering silence

soothed her frazzled nerves. *Okay,* she assured herself, *everything is going to be fine.* She had done this plenty of times before. But no matter how she fought it, the memory of her car exploding right before her eyes kept replaying in her head. The connection could no longer be denied, she realized as more images reeled through her tired mind. The director's telephone exploding while he sat at his desk. The death-dealing explosion at Agent Daniels's house. The letter bomb that had exploded in her mail carrier's bag just before he reached her apartment building's mail station. The single shot she knew deep in her gut had been meant for her in that shopping-mall parking lot. Then her rental car. Nicole shook off the lingering images before her next memory could take form. She had to focus. Even without the warning letter she had received from Daniels two days after his unsolved murder, things were all too clear now.

Someone knew their secret.

Slowly, silently, Nicole climbed the two flights of stairs that seemed to go on forever. The white walls and absolute quiet allowed other images and voices she didn't want to hear or see to creep into her thoughts. Ian's cold, hard look when he had come face-to-face with her in Victoria Colby's office. The soft, sensual whispering of his voice as he made love to her. Nicole forced away the vivid memories. Fear gripped her heart when her errant mind replayed the scene outside Ian's town house when he had been shot. She thanked God again that he hadn't been hurt worse.

What a fool she was for seeking him out and dragging him into this mess. She would do this alone. She had thought it through. She could do it. And Ian would be safe. Last night had opened her eyes to the truth she had wanted to deny for three years now. No matter what happened to her, Nicole could not bear to take a chance on Ian getting hurt again—physically or emotionally.

Distraction was a dangerous risk. One neither of them could afford to take. Nicole would do her job to the best of her ability…alone. And Ian could live his life the way he deserved without her interference. He had a posh job, a great house. And probably lots of women, a little voice added. Nicole clenched her teeth and refused to consider Ian's social life. She was an even bigger fool for not stopping to think that he might even be seriously involved with someone. He was, after all, incredibly good-looking, and that voice…

Just thinking about the sound of his voice made her insides quiver. Nicole paused as she reached the landing outside her apartment. *Get a grip, Reed,* she chastised silently. *That line of thinking is hazardous to your health.*

She listened outside her nondescript gray door for what felt like half an eternity before she inserted her key into the lock. The only sound was her heart thudding in her chest. Willing herself to be calm, she reached beneath her jacket for her weapon. Nicole pushed the door inward, spilling light into the dark foyer. She stepped inside, hit the switch for the overhead light and with one foot eased the door closed behind her.

She scanned the darkness beyond the foyer for any movement, while listening intently past the hush of the central unit. Nothing. Relieved, she reached behind her and locked the door, then stepped soundlessly toward the living room. Every nerve ending on alert, she eased quietly into the room. Holding her breath, she leaned down and turned on the table lamp. A soft, golden glow lit the center of the room. The far edges remained in shadow. Years of training not allowing her to relax her guard until she had checked every nook and cranny, Nicole moved cautiously around the perimeter of the room.

After giving her bedroom and bathroom the all clear, Nicole finally took a deep breath. She silently retraced her steps down the hall and slipped into the kitchen, caution still restraining her. The light from the hall glinted against the array of stainless-steel pots and pans hanging from the rack over the island bar. White cabinets and countertops reflected the minimal light reaching out to them.

Paranoia could be a good thing, she told that lingering sensation that made the hair on the back of her neck continue to stand on end. But enough was enough. There was no one here. The place was as quiet as a tomb.

"Poor choice in words, Reed," she muttered as she lowered her weapon. She was starved. Beyond starved. She frowned—she was so hungry she could actually smell food. Nicole closed her eyes and inhaled deeply of the scent her imagination had conjured. Chinese. Wouldn't it be nice if she could take time to drop by Won's on her way back to the airport? Her stomach rumbled in agreement.

"God, I'm starved," she said aloud then flipped on the overhead fluorescent.

"Eating is essential to survival, Nicole."

Nicole's pulse jumped, her heart rocketed into her throat. She whirled toward the sound of Ian's voice in the far corner of the kitchen, her weapon instinctively leveled on the target. She blinked twice to adjust to the bright light. Drinks and containers of Chinese takeout—Won's no less—sat in the middle of her kitchen table.

He'd remembered.

Nicole almost smiled as she lowered her weapon, and relaxed her fire-ready stance. Her attention shifted to Ian's left hand as he pushed one container forward, then to his right where he held a weapon trained expertly on her. *Uh-oh.*

Slowly, she lifted her reluctant gaze to his ever-unreadable one.

"I want answers, Nicole." He leaned back in his chair. "And I want them now."

Chapter Three

"Can't I eat first?" Nicole suggested, her gaze no longer riveted to the sleek silver barrel of Ian's weapon, but surveying the hard planes and angles of his handsome face. Her desire for food evaporated, replaced by a lingering desire of another sort that never seemed to go completely away in this man's presence.

"No."

Stalling, Nicole placed her weapon on the island, pulled off her cap and tossed it aside, then leaned casually against the counter. She was too tired to do this right now, and she sure didn't have any time to waste. But Ian would never let her off the hook this time. "Look, I—" she began.

He shook his head slowly from side to side, halting her attempted diversionary tactic. He placed his own weapon on the table's glass top, his fingers splayed on the grip. Ian wasn't going anywhere, she admitted reluctantly; he intended to wait her out. And time was the one thing she didn't have.

With a beleaguered sigh, Nicole crossed her arms over her middle and proceeded to give him the heavily varnished version. She kept her gaze carefully focused on the carryout box, even licked her lips for effect, but he ignored her not-so-subtle hints. "Three weeks ago my director stayed a little later than usual at the office. Everyone else was gone. Apparently his telephone rang and then exploded."

Nicole shrugged, then glanced beyond Ian's shoulder, giving the appearance of eye contact. "I'm sure you can fill in the resulting details." She had got the call from Daniels. Walked into that office and seen…

Nicole immediately suppressed the details she remembered far too vividly. Especially the image of Landon's devastated widow at the funeral. "A few days after that—"

"Look at me, Nicole."

She blinked, hesitated, then leveled her gaze on his. "Satisfied?"

He nodded, once.

She clenched her jaw to prevent the directions she wanted to give him on exactly where he could go. Why hadn't he just stayed in Chicago and let her do what had to be done? Why did he bother coming after her? Nicole plunged her fingers into her hair and massaged her aching skull. She would never understand the man. Blocking the emotion she knew would give her away, Nicole commanded her body to relax. She dropped her arms to her sides and continued. "Four days after Director Landon's death, Agent Daniels died in another explosion."

"What kind of explosion?"

"Gas leak. His house." Nicole struggled with the effort to keep her emotions at bay. Distance. She was a pro, she knew how to disengage emotionally. *Just do it,* she instructed silently. "There was hardly anything left to identify."

Nicole fell silent, unable to continue…unable to look away from Ian's penetrating, metallic gaze. Years of training weren't supposed to disintegrate like this. The realization that death was hot on her heels tugged at her composure. Ian's expression remained perfectly cool, unaffected. His damned black suit and shirt looked as if he'd just put them on. Nicole thought about her own disheveled appearance—unwashed jeans and T-shirt, her hair a mess. She almost laughed. But not Ian. Every perfect, dark hair was in place. The barest hint of five o'clock shadow darkened his rigid jaw, lending him an air of danger.

She had to get out of here. Nicole was out of time. The tangle of emotions she could no longer restrain gripped her with an intensity that shook her to the core. She drew in a harsh breath. How had things got so screwed up? Two people she knew personally, had worked with for years, were dead. She trembled inside, barely concealing the reaction. And now their killer intended to see that she stopped breathing too. This wasn't supposed to happen. They had taken every precaution.

"Go on," Ian instructed when she remained silent.

Nicole swallowed the tears of frustration that swelled into her throat and glared at him. "Two days after Daniels's murder, I received a letter from him, postmarked the day before he died." She paused. *Okay, girl, get a grip.* This would be the tricky part. Her attention focused inward, beyond the knot of feelings hovering way too close to the surface. She couldn't allow Ian to see the lie in her eyes. "Daniels said that he believed someone was trying to kill him. The same person who killed Director Landon. He warned me that if anything happened to him that I should consider myself next on the list."

Nicole gripped the counter, hard. "That's it," she finished, hoping like hell he would leave it at that.

Ian considered her last statement for a time. "Why?"

That tone. That damned irritatingly calm-in-the-face-of-disaster tone. "How should I know?" she snapped. Nicole resurrected the rage she had initially felt upon hearing of

Landon's, then Daniels's death. She used that anger as camouflage now. "It's not like we're the blooming Red Cross." She flung her arms upward in frustration. "You know how this business works. You make enemies. Lots of them."

"Why?" he repeated, so annoyingly calm that Nicole jerked with tension.

"I don't know," she ground out.

His assessment took about three seconds. "You're lying."

Nicole stared at the tiled floor and bit the inside of her cheek. This was pointless. Ian read her too well. She turned and looked him square in the eye. "That information is sensitive. Shared on a need-to-know basis only."

His long fingers curled around the nine-millimeter's grip. "Right now, Nicole, you *need* to tell me the truth more than you've ever *needed* to do anything in your life."

Nicole rubbed her tired eyes with the heels of her hands. God, she wished this nightmare were over. "I don't have time for this, Ian." She blew out a breath of frustration. "Someone is trying to kill me and I have to get out of here."

"Where are you going?"

She shot him another deadly glare. She wanted to scream—to force him to react. "That's none of your business."

Ian stood. Nicole's tension escalated to a new level. Maybe she would get that reaction after all. His gaze never leaving her, he reached beneath his jacket and tucked his weapon away. She frowned. Why did he do that? Then he walked right up to her, sending her heart into a violent staccato. Ian placed one hand on the counter on either side of her, and leaned in close.

"I'm making it my business." His accented tone was so soft, yet so clearly lethal.

Nicole steeled herself against his nearness. His scent invaded her senses, making her weak. Making her want to tell him anything he wanted to hear. "Just let me get my things together and I swear I'll tell you on the way to the airport," she hedged.

"You'll tell me now."

Nicole moistened her lips. "Please, Ian, I can't miss that flight."

"Now."

She closed her eyes and shook her head in defeat. This was a mistake. "Fine." Nicole opened her eyes and took a long look into Ian's cool, unsuspecting gaze. What would he do when she gave him that truth he wanted so badly? One thing was certain, helping her wouldn't be on his mind. Killing her, maybe. Despising her, definitely.

"All right. Three years ago, I was assigned the most sensitive, not to mention the most important, case of my career." She hesitated, dreading the metamorphosis she would see in those silver eyes. "Landon made the decision. He concluded that as long as the witness was alive, there was no way to ensure absolute safety."

Ian's gaze narrowed slightly. "There are never any guarantees. Witnesses know that going into the program."

Nicole cleared her throat, it didn't help. "This one was special."

"How special?" Ian asked cautiously.

"Special enough to warrant a blackout operation." She leveled her gaze on his, hard as that proved. "Total blackout," she added.

A trace of denial flickered in his now-wary gaze.

"My assignment was to make sure the world thought this one was dead." Nicole watched the confusion, then outrage slowly replace the denial. "It was the only way to keep him safe. If anyone had suspected that he'd survived, his life wouldn't have been worth squat." She swallowed convulsively. "It was the only way, Ian."

"The forensics report was conclusive," he countered, his voice as cold as ice.

"Daniels took care of the explosion and a John Doe body to keep forensics happy." Nicole reminded herself to breathe. She squeezed her eyes shut before meeting his relentless gaze once more. She would have given almost anything within her power not to have to answer the question she knew he would ask next.

"And what, precisely, were your instructions?" Icy, edged with steel, his words cut through her like a knife.

"It was my job to make sure you failed in yours."

He straightened. Nicole jerked in reaction to the abrupt move. His fists clenched at his sides, a muscle jumped in his jaw. "Why me?"

"You were the best," she admitted reluctantly, knowing she was only adding insult to injury. "Your reputation was widely known. The cartel would have expected us to use our best. We had to consider every contingency."

"You're telling me that Raymond Solomon is alive."

Nicole backed against the counter as far as she could to escape the arctic chill radiating from Ian. "Yes."

"You didn't request the assignment for the publicity of working a high-profile case as you told me? It had nothing to do with competition between the bureau and the marshal service? Nothing to do with getting yourself another promotion?"

Too sick with self-disgust to answer, Nicole slowly shook her head. What had seemed so right, so just at the time, now felt devious and twisted.

Something dark and forbidding surfaced in his eyes, the angles and lines of his handsome face turned to granite. "You played my backup—had *sex* with me—just to make sure I was properly distracted?"

This was the reaction she had expected, dreaded. Nothing she could say would make him believe that she hadn't meant things to go so far. That their lovemaking—

"Answer me," he demanded, that softly accented voice uncharacteristically harsh.

"I did my job." Nicole pleaded with him to understand with her eyes. "But I swear, Ian, sleeping with you wasn't part of it."

He smiled. It wasn't pleasant. "Just a little something extra thrown in for good measure, huh?"

Nicole trembled visibly, as much from the anger mounting inside her as the pain constricting her chest, making if difficult to breathe. "I did what I had to do to keep Raymond Solomon safe. The job I was sworn to do. What happened between the two of us was personal."

He glared at her with so much disgust that Nicole felt sick with the fallout. "You're damned right it was personal," he said bitterly. "You allowed me to believe for three years that my negligence had cost a man his life."

The air raced out of her lungs on a shudder. "Yes, I did," she admitted. Nicole dragged in a harsh breath. "And I'd do it again if it meant keeping that witness alive." She laughed then, a short, brittle sound. "The hell of it is, Michaels, you would have done the same thing, and you know it."

Three long beats passed, the tension thickening with each. Then he released a heavy breath. "Yes. I would have."

Weak with relief, Nicole watched his features slowly relax, his eyes return to that calm, translucent silver. He might not ever forgive her, but at least maybe he understood. That was something "So." Nicole straightened, then tucked her hands into her back pockets and went for a subject change. "Are you going to let me eat or what? I told you I'm on a tight schedule here."

To his surprise, as swiftly as it had risen, Ian's rage receded. He stepped back so Nicole could move. He watched her slip into a chair at the table, pulling one foot beneath her. She opened a container and quickly lifted a forkful of rice to her mouth. She closed her eyes and moaned her pleasure. Ian looked away. His emotions were far too raw now to even look at her.

Relief suddenly washed over him as the realization that Solomon was alive sank in. He had lived with the weight of guilt for so long that he felt light-headed without it. His instincts had been right all along. The cover story of why Nicole had been assigned to work with him on that case had never really fit, in his opinion. The whole thing had felt wrong from the beginning.

Nicole had betrayed him. Ian had fully expected a different reaction when he finally got the truth. He definitely hadn't anticipated this complete deflation of his darker emotions. But somehow he just couldn't manage the wounded warrior bit. The fact that she was following orders cast a slightly different light on things.

But betrayal was betrayal, he reminded himself. He frowned. Nothing. No incensed outrage, no roaring desire to retaliate. He shook his head. He, apparently, wasn't ready to exact his pound of flesh from Nicole. He glanced at the woman who had wreaked such havoc with his world. But it would take time for him to come to terms with the reality of what had taken place between them three years ago. Maybe he never would. Understanding was one thing, forgiveness entirely another.

But right now, he had a more pressing problem. Someone was running a game. And she seemed to think it had something to do with the Solomon case. Ian crossed the room and sat down at the table with Nicole. Though he might never forgive her for what she had done, he couldn't live with himself if he allowed anything to happen to her. Nicole Reed presented a facade that was tough as nails, but she had limits just like anyone else. And right now she was very close to exceeding those limits. She needed his help. He would give her the help she needed because he couldn't do otherwise, but then it would be over. He would walk away.

His decision made, Ian watched her devour the sesame chicken for a while before he interrupted. He smiled to himself when he recalled how frequently Nicole actually forgot to eat. But she always made up for any missed meals when she remembered.

"Who gave Landon the order to take charge?"

Nicole looked thoughtful for a moment. "I don't know. Daniels and I were given our orders and we didn't ask questions."

"You're certain the threat to your life has something to do with Solomon?" Ian pressed.

She nodded adamantly, then swallowed. "Daniels thought the same thing. He said so in his letter." She took a quick drink of cola. "There were three of us directly involved in the operation." Her eyes grew somber. "Two are dead." She stared at the food in front of her as if she had suddenly lost her appetite.

"All three of you knew Solomon's final location?" Ian took Nicole's fork and stabbed a nugget of spiced chicken, then popped it into his mouth.

"No. Daniels had nothing to do with that part." She frowned in thought. "In fact, I'm the only one who knew exactly where Solomon ended up."

Ian considered that statement. "What do you mean where he ended up?" He laid the fork aside.

"About six months after his highly publicized demise, Solomon contacted me." She made a disgusted sound in her throat. "After all we'd been through to plant him safely. I gave him considerable hell for taking such a risk."

Ian suppressed a grin. "I can imagine." Nicole smiled warmly, and something inside Ian softened. He immediately checked the reaction.

"Solomon was convinced that someone was on to him." She shrugged. "So I replanted him and told him I'd kick his—well, that he'd better not rear his ugly head again."

Nicole pulled one knee up and propped her elbow on it, then plowed her fingers through her long hair. Ian clenched his fingers into fists to prevent the almost involuntary reaction to reach out and touch those long, silky tresses.

"I've even considered that it might be Solomon himself trying to kill me," Nicole said doubtfully. "That way there would be no possibility of a future leak. But I really can't see that weasel engineering all this." She massaged her temples. "I guess there's always the possibility that he contacted someone from his former life."

"Whoever it is," Ian assured her, "he isn't trying to kill you."

Her startled gaze connected with Ian's. "Have you been listening at all? You saw my rental car explode. The ambush outside your place—"

"If he intended to kill you, you'd be dead now."

She searched his gaze, the wheels turning inside that pretty head with this new, unexpected information. "Your basis for that conclusion?"

"The explosive device in your car was remote-detonated." Ian leaned back in the chair and stretched his legs in front of him. Exhaustion clawed at him, but he ignored it. "He had to be watching. If he wanted you dead, he would have waited until you were in the car, or at least closer."

Realization dawned in those sky blue eyes. "You've seen the lab report already?"

"The preliminary," he clarified.

Nicole shook her head. "I don't get it."

"And any shooter worth his salt would have taken you out sometime during the ninety or so seconds you fiddled with Martinez's keys before you got into his vehicle." The memory still sent fear rushing through Ian's veins.

"Yeah," she agreed. She stabbed another piece of chicken, but paused before putting it into her mouth. "That was kind of a stupid thing to do." Those full lips dipped into a worried frown. "If he isn't trying to kill me, then what is going on?" She dropped the fork and untouched chicken back into the box.

"By the way." Ignoring her question, Ian cocked a brow and shot her a look. "Martinez is quite upset with you about his brother's truck."

Nicole scrubbed a hand over her face, her body language giving away the depth of her own exhaustion. "Sorry," she offered with feigned humility.

"I would avoid him in the near future."

Nicole's forehead creased with her deepening frown. "Just because I borrowed his truck?"

Ian sighed loudly. "Well, you did break his nose."

"What can I say?" She flared her palms. "The guy had a gun. Old habits are hard to break."

Ian settled a serious gaze on hers. "Just try and remember which ones are the good guys in the future."

Nicole sent him a mock salute. "Yes, sir."

"Now," Ian began, turning his attention back to business. "What's our plan?"

"*Our* plan?"

"That's right," he told her bluntly, his tone brooking no argument. "And this time there will be no secrets."

"You still want to help me?" The look of genuine surprise mixed with hopefulness in her eyes sucked at something deep inside him. "In spite of what I just told you?"

"Yes."

Nicole blew out a relieved breath. She was no fool. She knew she needed his help. "All right. I say we stash Solomon some place safe until we can get a handle on what's going on."

"Wrong."

Irritation stole across her delicate features, enhancing the lines of fatigue around her blue eyes. "What's wrong about that? Do you have a better idea?"

"No."

She rolled her eyes. "Then what's your point?"

"The point is that you would be doing exactly what they want you to do."

"Oh, really? And how might I be doing that?" she snapped.

Ian draped his arm over the empty chair next to him and studied her for a long moment. She was tired, she wasn't thinking clearly. "If you make live contact with Solomon, you'll be leading the shooter right to the mark. You said yourself that no one knows where he is but you."

She shook her head, sending that blond mane into action. "Daniels thought maybe someone was already on to Solomon's location. Besides, I know how to lose a tail."

"Some are more difficult to shake than others." Ian shrugged. "And if Solomon's location had already been compromised, why bother coming after you with all these elaborate death threats? Why waste the time or the effort? The shooter could just go straight to the mark."

"You're right." The reality of what she had almost done hit Nicole hard. "Why didn't I see that?"

Ian caught himself before he covered her hand with his own. The only way he could help Nicole was to keep his distance. Their relationship had to be maintained on a strictly professional level, for more reasons than one. "You've been through a lot in the past three weeks with no backup. Emotion and instinct have gotten all tangled up."

Nicole sat bolt upright. "I have to get word to Solomon to sit tight. If I don't show tonight without letting him know, he might get spooked."

"Don't worry. I'll have Martinez show up in your place to hold Solomon's hand."

"Good idea," Nicole murmured distractedly. "Solomon might do something lame." Nicole's questioning gaze landed on Ian's. "What do you think we should do next?"

It was Ian's turn to be surprised. Nicole usually preferred doing things her own way. "We sit tight and let the shooter come to us," he suggested.

"You think he'll do that considering I've hooked up with you now?"

Ian studied her concerned expression. Nicole was willing to risk her life by going it alone in order to protect Solomon. Ian wondered sometimes if the people they protected deserved such selfless sacrifice.

"If he wants Solomon, he won't have a choice," Ian assured her.

Glass shattered in the living room, followed by a thunderous whoosh. Ian shot to his feet, automatically reaching for his weapon. "Stay in here," he ordered curtly.

Before Nicole could protest, he moved cautiously into the hall. A distinct chemical odor filled his nostrils. A quick survey of the living room confirmed his suspicions. The east side of the room, including the front door, was already engulfed in flames. This was no simple Molotov cocktail. Ian gritted his teeth. He pivoted to find Nicole standing right behind him.

She swore. "We have to get out of here," she murmured distractedly as she considered the ravenous flames. The walls seemed to melt wherever the flames reached.

"The balcony," Ian agreed, grabbing her arm and ushering her in that direction.

Nicole shook her head, still staring at the mushrooming devastation. "Why is he doing this?"

"Hurry, Nicole," he ground out as he ushered her away from the threat.

Ian jerked the French doors open and dragged a hesitant Nicole out onto the balcony. He glanced over the balcony's railing at the pool below, then assessed the rapidly growing destruction behind them.

Nicole took one last glance at her home which was swiftly going up in smoke. "We have to get out of here," she repeated distractedly.

"You do swim, don't you?" Ian asked slowly.

She glared at him as if he'd lost complete control of his senses. "What? Yes!"

"Good, because we need to jump *now*."

Realization suddenly dawned in Nicole's eyes. "Have you lost your mind?"

"Probably," he agreed, his full attention on the inferno

edging ever closer to their location. He wondered briefly if there were any other tenants in the building. He would have to see that everyone got out. Ian took another look over the railing. "Ladies first," he suggested, trying to sound optimistic.

Nicole balked. "Who knows if we'll even hit the pool. There's no way I'm jumping off this balcony, Michaels. We'll just have to figure out an alternative."

"Is that your final decision?" His gaze darted back to the flames now licking their way up the curtains of the balcony's French doors.

"Damn straight," she retorted, still assessing the situation.

Ian tossed his weapon into a small Dumpster two stories below and to the right. Then, before Nicole fully comprehended his intent, he picked her up and pitched her over the side.

He followed—hoping like hell he hadn't underestimated the required trajectory for a splash landing.

Chapter Four

Gasping for breath, Nicole dragged herself out of the deep end of the pool. She shoved the wet hair from her face and glared at the man emerging from the chilly water next to her.

"We're lucky we didn't break our necks," she complained crossly. "You could have killed us both."

Looking dark, wet and insanely wicked, Ian smiled. "But I didn't. In fact—" he swiped the dark hair from his eyes "— I saved your life."

Nicole got to her feet. The wet cotton T-shirt lay plastered to her chest like a second skin. At least she still had on her denim jacket. "Do me a favor," she groused, then shivered as the cold seeped into her skin.

Ian got to his feet, water puddling around him. "What?"

"Next time you want to save my life, just shoot me."

"Don't tempt me." He flashed Nicole a look that could have meant any number of things, none of which she wanted to consider at the moment. "We need to make sure your neighbors got out safely," he suggested, turning his attention to the building they had so hastily exited in such an unorthodox manner.

Nicole inhaled sharply as the roar of flames and the distinctive crackle of destruction drew her attention back up to the balcony. Damn. They had got out just in time. She swallowed the lump of emotion rising in her throat. Agent Daniels hadn't been so lucky when his house went up in flames. How long would her luck hold out?

"We're okay," Ian assured her softly.

Nicole's gaze moved back to his. A frown tugged at her mouth. She must look pretty shaken if he was showing this much concern. Nicole watched, feeling oddly displaced, as Ian straightened his dripping wet jacket and strode to the nearby Dumpster. She scrubbed away the rivulets of water streaming down her face with the back of her hand. She wondered briefly how the man could look so good soaking wet and digging through a trash container. Nicole shivered again, whether from the cool night air or from simply looking at Ian, she couldn't be sure. She almost laughed out loud. What was wrong with her? Her apartment building was going up in flames and she was standing there ogling the only man she could trust to help her. And who, she reminded herself, had every reason to walk away without looking back.

When Ian found his gun, he tucked it into his waistband and turned in Nicole's direction. That silvery gaze connected with hers, and Nicole's knees went weak. She was losing it. That much was clear. Too much stress, not enough sleep…

"Stay behind me," he ordered.

Too tired and disgusted with herself to argue, Nicole obeyed. She stuck close behind Ian as he stole to the front corner of the building. Several tense seconds passed while he surveyed the street and sidewalk for any recognizable threat. No matter what she had done to him in the past, Ian would not walk away. He intended to protect her at all costs, and that bothered Nicole. But wasn't that what she wanted? She studied his intent features. She didn't want any of this to hurt Ian.

And she definitely didn't want to fall in love with him again. Her heart couldn't take that kind of abuse a second time.

But she needed him. There was no one else.

"Let's go," he instructed quietly.

Half running to keep up with his long strides, Nicole followed Ian to the front entrance of her building. A crowd from the neighboring apartment complexes was already gathering in the street. Their murmuring grew louder as she and Ian took the front steps two at a time into the burning building. Nicole hesitated long enough to glance up at her apartment one last time. Flames shot out of the living-room window and licked upward, charring everything in their path. Panic tightened her chest when she allowed herself to briefly consider that she had just lost all her worldly possessions. Anger rushed through her veins then, quickly replacing the lesser emotion. Pushing aside the sudden and almost overwhelming urge for revenge, Nicole hurried after Ian. A voice from the crowd shouted an unnecessary reminder that the building was on fire as she disappeared inside.

"Which apartments are occupied?" Ian demanded the moment she cleared the door. Smoke drifted and curled down the stairs like eerie black fog.

"That's the only one besides mine." Nicole pointed to the door of the first-floor apartment on Ian's right. "The guy lives alone and he's out of town most of the time." Nicole resisted the urge to hold her breath. She blinked rapidly to fight the burn in her eyes.

"Let's hope he's not home now." Ian moved closer to the door, checked to see if it was locked, then kicked it hard near the knob. One more solid kick and the door flew inward. Ian surveyed the now-useless lock as he entered the apartment. "He really should have a dead bolt installed. Anyone could just walk right in."

Nicole rolled her eyes at his macho display. "You couldn't just do the thing with the credit card?" she chastised as she followed Ian inside.

"There's no time." Ian paused a beat at the sound of distant sirens. "Check the kitchen, I'll get the bedroom and bathroom," he said, already halfway across the room.

Less than a minute later, they met in the living room once more. "All clear," Nicole reported. The screaming sirens sounded much closer now.

"Good. We should go." Ian snagged Nicole's hand and moved quickly out the apartment door and through the thickening smoke in the stairwell. Nicole covered her nose and mouth with her free arm until she emerged into the fresh night air. A police cruiser careened around the corner at the end of the block, followed by two fire trucks. Ian pulled Nicole in the opposite direction, using the crowd of spectators as cover. No one paid them any real heed now that the red and blue lights had captured their collective attention. Shattering glass echoed through the night as windows exploded from the intensifying heat.

Once on the other side of the street, Ian unlocked and opened the driver's side door of a black sedan. "Get in," he commanded brusquely.

Unable to prevent one last look back at her former home, Nicole trembled with aftereffects. When would this end? She hugged her arms around her cold, wet middle. And, more important, how would it end?

"Nicole," Ian urged softly.

Nicole turned away from the devastating sight, then blinked away the lingering images. She had no place to go now. She had no home. And she definitely couldn't go back to her office.

Nicole swallowed tightly.

Ian's hand pressed gently against the small of her back. "Get in the car, Nicole," he murmured close to her ear.

Ian. At least she still had Ian.

But once he'd had time to really think about all that she had told him, would he turn his back on her?

"WE NEED a room for one night," Ian stated with as much charm and a smile as persuasive as anything the current James Bond had ever managed on the silver screen.

The expression on the hotel receptionist's face was priceless. Nicole could just imagine what must be going through the woman's mind. Ian stood before her counter as handsome as sin, and looking for all the world as if he had just been baptized, Armani suit included.

"Of…of course, sir." The receptionist blinked, obviously having just realized that she was staring. Blush stained her cheeks. "Smoking or nonsmoking?"

Ian removed his wallet and placed a damp credit card on her counter. "Nonsmoking, downstairs and facing the parking lot, please," he answered with another smile that made the woman's eyes widen in appreciation.

"Certainly, sir," she purred. "Is there anything else I could help you with?"

Ian leaned over the counter a bit. "Would you happen to know an all-night dry cleaner, *Jean?*" he inquired smoothly, using the name emblazoned in gold letters across her name tag.

The receptionist's eyes sparkled with glee. "I'm sure I can arrange that."

Nicole resisted the urge to kick Ian. She supposed that he couldn't help it if charm literally oozed from his magnificent body. The sound of his voice alone was enough to make most women's hearts beat a little faster. Deep, velvety, lightly accented in that unusual European blend. And he was so devilishly handsome. Nicole released a heavy sigh. She was wet, tired, homeless, and at this point, even beyond being affected by Ian's many fascinating attributes. Watching him focus that mesmerizing charm on another woman was about as far from entertaining as could be, in Nicole's opinion.

When the paperwork was finished and the receptionist properly dazzled, Ian led the way to the ground-floor room. He unlocked the door and stepped aside for Nicole to enter. A bed had never looked better, Nicole thought with overwhelming relief. She peeled off her jacket and kicked off her shoes. She shuddered as the air-conditioned temperature of the room penetrated her wet clothing.

"Take a hot shower," Ian told her as he locked the door and checked the window. He turned then, and stared at her with too much concern. "Leave your clothes and a towel outside the door."

Nicole nodded. She pivoted and hurried into the bathroom. After locking the door behind her, she removed her FBI identification and placed it on the back of the toilet tank, then stripped off her wet clothes. She opened the door only as far as necessary and deposited a towel and her soggy attire, sans her panties and bra, on the floor. She quickly removed the remaining towels from the towel bar and hung her underwear there. They would dry in no time at all and she had no intention of allowing Ian to touch them. That would just make putting them back on that much more difficult. Before she could stop it, the memory of their lovemaking only twenty-four hours ago loomed large in her mind. Ian could use his hands, his mouth, in ways that made her breath catch even now, just thinking about him. How would they ever spend the night together in this tiny room without wanting each other?

Wanting each other wouldn't be the problem, Nicole decided as she stepped into the hot spray of water. Not taking what the other had to offer would be the real test of self-discipline. Nicole closed her eyes and allowed the hot, heavenly liquid to flow freely over her face and down her body.

She had to remember that their time together couldn't be about what had happened between them three years ago, and it couldn't be about the lust that still lingered.

It had to be about one thing and one thing only, staying alive long enough to catch a killer who had already murdered at least two federal agents.

IAN GENEROUSLY TIPPED the hotel employee who showed up at the door to take the laundry bag containing their wet clothes. The guy looked more like a night custodian than a bellboy, but that didn't matter to Ian. He was quite certain that this particular service was not usually provided by the hotel, and he appreciated the effort. The helpful employee had also located a first-aid kit. Ian rotated his injured shoulder. It hurt like hell, and he'd had to remove the wet bandage. The wound would require another dressing.

Ian stepped over to the bed and tossed the first-aid kit next to his bag. He removed the shirt he had packed. He'd brought along only one change of clothes, so he and Nicole would have to share. Ian would wear the black slacks, Nicole would get the black button-up shirt.

Ian moved to the bathroom door and hesitated a moment before knocking. The sound of spraying water abruptly ceased and Ian moistened his lips as he imagined Nicole emerging from the shower amid a billowing cloud of steam, water droplets trickling down her bare, satiny skin. He closed his eyes and savored the vision of her slowly drying first her long blond hair, then her toned, slender body.

"What am I supposed to wear?"

The muffled demand snapped Ian from his erotic fantasy. He rubbed a hand over his chin and swore hotly under his breath. What was wrong with him? He could not allow this consuming desire for what he should not want to take control again. Nicole had betrayed him once already he couldn't set himself up to allow it to happen again.

Ian hung the shirt on the knob. "It's on the door," he said tersely and turned away. He had a plan to lay out and arrangements to make. He didn't have time to lust after a woman, especially not Nicole.

Ian heard the door open then quickly close again. He gritted his teeth against the need welling inside him in spite of his renewed determination. Sharing quarters this close was going to be pure torture. Ian clenched his fists at his sides and mentally reviewed all that had happened in the past thirty hours.

After three years, Nicole had come to him for help. His refusal had been short-lived. The rental car exploding with Nicole entirely too close had put a kind of fear in his heart that Ian had never before experienced. He still cared too much. And that was not a good thing. He had to stay focused and keep his distance. For Nicole's sake, and for his own. He would not permit himself to fall for her again, but he would see that she stayed safe. And, one way or another, he would get the bastard threatening her life. Ian remained convinced that these were only attempts intended to send Nicole rushing to relocate Solomon. But each incident was proving more haphazard with the kind of high-risk variables that could easily get Nicole and anyone else who happened to be in the way killed.

Nicole seemed certain that this was the work of one man, someone who knew about Solomon. That conclusion didn't sit quite right with Ian. If their enemy was someone inside the bureau, then what did he hope to gain by killing Solomon? Would there be a payoff from the cartel? That sounded the most reasonable and probable to Ian. Whoever was behind this scheme had strong motivation. Ian frowned when he considered that a scumbag like Solomon had warranted a blackout operation. Sure, the man was a major witness in a high-profile federal case, but Ian had seen plenty of others in his time. Solomon was the first in Ian's experience to garner such special treatment. And there was that little detail—the bureau had personally handled his case rather than inducting Solomon into the program through regular channels. Ian wasn't naive, though. He knew that too often cases weren't handled by the book, especially those over which the FBI wanted to retain absolute control. Perhaps it was a mere coincidence that Landon worked this special operation, then wound up dead, along with one of the only two other agents involved, but Ian doubted it. Coincidences of this nature were rare.

With Landon and Daniels dead and Nicole on the run, that meant that someone privy to Landon's original decision was behind this little game of cat and mouse. Ian's frown deepened, setting off an ache in his temples. He didn't like the sound of that at all. The only office with the authority to give Landon the kind of leeway he had taken was the attorney general's. Ian knew personally, or at the very least by reputation, most of the people in that office. He found it difficult to believe that one of them would stoop to working for the cartel.

But it wasn't an impossibility, he admitted.

The bathroom door opened again and Ian stiffened. The scent of shampoo and soap quickly permeated every square inch of air in the suddenly too-small hotel room. Images flashed before Ian's eyes like scenes from a movie on fast-forward. Touching Nicole's skin. Kissing her full mouth. Licking, then suckling the dusky peaks of her breasts. Being inside her…

"Did you order any food?"

Ian grabbed back control and turned slowly to face her. She lingered near the bathroom door, keeping her distance. Her damp blond hair hung around her shoulders. The too-big shirt clung here and there to her warm, moist body where she had missed a spot or two with her towel. The black contrasted sharply with her porcelain skin. Ian swallowed hard as his gaze fell to those long, slender legs. She shifted under his perusal and his gaze shot up to meet her assessing blue eyes.

"Yes," he replied so calmly that he surprised himself. "Steak-Out. It should arrive soon." Ian turned back to the bed and picked up the small first-aid kit.

Before he realized she had moved, Nicole was right beside him, assessing the injury to his shoulder. Only Nicole could get this close to him undetected.

"Damn," she breathed. "I forgot about this." With warm, gentle fingers she touched his shoulder. She winced. "Let me see what's in that kit."

Nicole relieved Ian of the first-aid kit and ushered him to a chair. She placed the small plastic container on the nearby dresser and opened it. Lines of frustration creased Ian's brow as she picked through the limited options available. Nicole stood mere inches from him, her thigh against him. This close, he could see the outline of her breasts, the budded points of her nipples. His pulse reacted.

"I can take care of this myself," he protested, however belatedly.

"Don't be ridiculous, Ian," she argued while continuing to prowl through the kit.

Ian looked up at her, pinning her with his most intimidating glare. "I would prefer—"

"Be still," she ordered. Nicole edged even closer then as she turned her attention to his shoulder.

Ian tensed when those soft fingers touched his bare skin once more. First, she swabbed the wound with what he assumed to be an antibiotic cream or lotion. Ian gritted his teeth when pain speared through his arm. At least the pain drew his attention from those other thoughts. The ones he knew he shouldn't be thinking.

"I'm sorry," Nicole murmured, her face entirely too near to his. "I'm trying not to hurt you."

"I'm fine."

Nicole arranged then taped the gauze into place. Her delicate scent and the feel of her fingers on his skin tugged at Ian's senses. He wanted to turn toward her and pull her onto his lap. Onto the arousal already straining against his slacks. His hands tightened on the arms of his chair. Her thigh grazed his fingertips, fire shot through his veins, twisting the desire already knotted inside him.

"There," she announced as she stepped back to view her effort. "It's not my best work, but, considering what I had to work with, it'll do."

"It's fine." Ian stood and brushed past her.

"You're welcome," Nicole snapped.

Ian closed his bag and strode to the closet to store it. "Thank you," he allowed impatiently.

Nicole huffed a frustrated breath. "This isn't going to

work," she announced crossly. "We can't keep tiptoeing around each other like this."

Ian leaned against the wall next to the closet, using his good shoulder for support. "What do you propose we do?" he asked, sarcasm weighting his tone.

Her hands went to her hips and she advanced on him. "We can't work together if every time we look at each other or touch each other, we have flashbacks from the past."

"Agreed." Ian starred down into that irritated blue gaze. "We can go back to plan A."

"Plan A?" Nicole frowned.

"You holed up in a safe house with Martinez while I get to the bottom of what's going on."

Fury flashed in those baby blues. "No way."

"Then I would suggest that you keep your distance."

The anger in her eyes turned patronizing. "That's going to be a bit difficult considering there's only one bed, Mr. Charm-the-receptionist."

Ian stared at the bed. Why hadn't he thought of that? Every night he and Nicole had spent together had been spent in a shared bed. The notion of requesting two beds had not entered his mind. Ian swore silently. His gaze connected with her now-triumphant one. "It's a big bed, Nicole. I don't have a problem, do you?"

"Absolutely not." She smiled knowingly. "But then, how would you know if I did?" One brow arched in challenge. "And we both know *you* can't always hide what you're feeling."

Ian felt that muscle in his jaw begin to tic. "I'm beginning to agree with you, Nicole. Perhaps this isn't going to work."

She blinked, twice. Ian almost smiled. Now he had her attention.

"Do you want to hear plan B or not?" he inquired, satisfied that he had won that round.

Nicole dropped wearily onto the end of the bed. "You know I do," she said disgustedly.

"Good." Ian turned his back on her and strode to the chair he had been sitting in minutes before. He remained silent a full minute for good measure. Nicole squirmed visibly. He smiled then, just a little.

"Solomon is the most probable target," he began. "I would hazard a guess that the cartel is willing to pay a handsome sum for his termination."

"That's my theory." Nicole shoved a handful of hair behind her ear. "Since the only case of this caliber that Landon, Daniels and I have in common is Solomon's, I would say that's a safe assumption."

Ian thought for a moment, recalling the most prominent personnel in the AG's office. "Landon never once mentioned the name of the person who coordinated Solomon's case on the attorney-general's end?"

Nicole shook her head. "No." She shrugged. "And I didn't ask. You know the drill—need-to-know basis only."

Ian nodded. He knew the drill all right. But someone had to give that order. Ian would just have to tweak his old contacts and see what he could shake loose.

"There was one thing," Nicole said suddenly as if just remembering a significant piece of the puzzle.

"What's that?"

"Landon said that the order came from the highest level." Nicole chewed her lower lip. "Do you think that means what it sounds like it means?"

That would mean the attorney general himself, in Ian's opinion. Ian had known Blake Edwards half a lifetime. Blake had been something of a legend in the U.S. Marshal Service as far back as when Ian had first signed on. There had never once been even the vaguest of accusations against the man. He was squeaky clean. Always had been.

Ian scrubbed a hand over his face noting in some distant part of his consciousness that he needed a shave. "Anything is possible." He resisted the urge to protest. No one was immune to falling prey to the lure of money. And this was most certainly about money.

"If it goes that high, how do we get the guy's attention? He could be a G-man or he could be a hired gun."

"He's on the inside," Ian insisted. "He knows too much." Ian didn't buy the hired-gun theory at all. This guy was a pro, and he knew far too much about Nicole's every move to be working on the outside. "If we go with the scenario that it's all about Solomon and someone's desire to find him," Ian began. "Then all we have to do is set a trap and wait for the bait to be taken."

Nicole settled a determined gaze on Ian. "To make the trap work you have to have the right kind of bait."

Ian shook his head slowly from side to side. "We're not going there, Nicole. Don't even think about it." He knew exactly what she had in mind. No way would he allow her to be the bait. He would find another way.

Nicole stood, placed her hands on her hips again and glared at him with the kind of determination that Ian knew wouldn't be easily swayed. "Landon was my director and Daniels was my fellow agent. Solomon is *my* witness. I will do this."

"No." Ian allowed his eyes to convey his own determination.

Nicole cocked her head and pinned him with a look that spoke of having an ace up her sleeve. "Since I'm the only one who knows Solomon's location, then I don't see that you have a choice."

Ian's lips twitched with the need to smile, but he suppressed the gesture. Nicole was good…too good. "I suppose you have a point there."

"You're darn right I do." Nicole plopped back onto the end of the bed. "Now, let's talk about that trap."

"Remember I'm sending Martinez to keep Solomon company so he doesn't panic," Ian reminded her. "All I need is the location. Then we need some out-of-the-way place to hole up for a few days."

Nicole's expression brightened. "I know just the place," she said quickly. "My cousin has a cabin in the southern part of the state. It's secluded, but not too far from civilization."

"Then we leave first thing in the morning," Ian concluded.

"We'll leave a trail any fool could follow," Nicole added, the plan already taking shape in her head. "And with Labor Day weekend starting tomorrow, maybe our guy will think we took a little vacation."

Ian did smile then. "Or a lovers' tryst," he offered.

Nicole looked startled. "What are you suggesting?" she asked hesitantly, but Ian didn't miss the flicker of something like desire in her eyes.

Ian shrugged his one good shoulder. "If the guy knows our history, which he likely does, then falling back into each other's arms would be within the realm of predictability. If he thinks we're caught up in our lust, maybe he'll feel a little braver and make a bolder move out in the open."

Nicole's smile returned full wattage. "You're a genius, Michaels. Let's call Martinez now."

Now if only Ian could pretend his suggestion wasn't so close to the truth.

Chapter Five

Awareness came in slow, languid degrees for Ian. It was a creeping, swelling warmth that excited and weakened him at the same time. The next level of consciousness to filter through the cloak of sleep heightened his senses. The feel of smooth, satiny skin against his, the pleasant swell of firm breast in his palm, and the moist heat scorching his thigh. Ian inhaled deeply, savoring the subtle essence of Nicole before he released the breath. Slowly, very slowly, Ian opened his eyes. The exquisite detail of Nicole's perfect profile, the delicately carved bone structure, her full, lush mouth zoomed into focus. The fragile curve of her throat was so very near to his lips. He ached to touch her there with his mouth, to taste that elegant column with the tip of his tongue. The desire to move against her was a pleasure-pain in his loins.

While he lay there watching her, the blood thudding in his ears, Nicole's eyes drifted open. She blinked rapidly, her mind likely sorting and analyzing the flood of sensations washing over her senses as her own awareness kicked in. Nicole tensed, her responsive body no longer pliant beneath his. Ian was fully and painfully erect. With his arousal pressed against her belly, her sudden tension sent another stab of desire through him. Nicole's warning that Ian could not always hide what he felt echoed harshly inside his head. Instantly, irritation absorbed all else. Ian rolled away from her, sat up, then pushed to his feet without pause. He would not give her any additional satisfaction.

"Good morning," he tossed over his shoulder as he strode into the bathroom. Ian closed the door without waiting for her response. He swore hotly, repeatedly, something he rarely did. He plowed his fingers through his hair and forced himself to relax enough to take care of business. Maybe he couldn't always hide how he responded to Nicole. But one thing was certain, his condition this morning could just as easily be attributed to other biological urges. Except, Ian amended reluctantly, for the accelerated beating of his heart.

Long minutes passed before Ian regained complete control. No one but Nicole had ever wielded this much power over him. Somehow he had to find a way to numb himself to her presence.

Ian released a long, heavy breath. Remaining focused was the key. He had to keep his full attention on the matter at hand. Martinez was babysitting Solomon. Alexandra Preston, one of the Colby Agency's finest researchers, was pulling together updates on every member of the cartel Solomon's testimony had brought down or affected negatively. That left Ian and Nicole with the job of drawing out the hit man, hired gun or player, who seemed to have a penchant for blowing things up.

Ian stared at his reflection in the mirror. He needed a shower and a shave. And clothes. The hotel employee had assured him that their clothes would be ready first thing this morning. Maybe he should buzz the front desk and see if they were there waiting for delivery. Then, he and Nicole could be on their way. Composed now, Ian turned toward the door, but something in his peripheral vision brought him up short.

His gaze shot back to the towel bar near the tub. Scant, lacy pink panties, and the matching frilly bra captured his full attention just long enough to suck the air completely out of his lungs.

A full ten minutes passed before Ian came back into the room. Nicole averted her gaze immediately, feigning interest in the channels she continued to surf. But the image of his bare chest, broad shoulders and taut abdomen were forever emblazoned on her memory. The way his dark hair curled around his neck. She shivered.

Ian paused at the bedside table, which was covered with the now-dry contents of his wallet, and picked up the telephone's receiver. Nicole used that opportunity to escape into the bathroom. She closed the door and sagged against it. She squeezed her eyes shut and exhaled a shaky breath. Even now her body hummed with the slowly retreating desire. Waking up with the feel of Ian's lean, hard body crushing into hers, his palm and long fingers cradling her breast, and his firm lips so frustratingly close to her sensitized skin, Nicole had almost burst into flames. Her whole body had been steaming hot, ready to absorb him right through her skin.

Nicole straightened and glanced at herself in the mirror. The telltale flush of sensual heat lingered on her skin. The expression in her eyes was nothing short of wild and needy. Nicole closed her eyes again and concentrated on calming the wanton beast still roaring inside her. The sound of Ian's voice, all tone and no words, reached her, touched her through the useless barrier of the wall and brought her blood back to an instant simmer. Nicole pivoted abruptly and paced the tiny room, three steps one way, and three steps back. Again and again she retraced her two-yard path. *Calm.* Reach for the calm, she commanded herself. She would control her reactions to Ian. Somehow. She had to.

She was homeless. A target running for her life and Solomon's. She had to think, reason and take the necessary steps to ensure Solomon's safety, as well as her own. Her breath snagged in her throat at the abrupt memory of Ian's too-close encounter with a bullet. Nicole had to see that he stayed safe too. She had dragged him into this mess, and she would have to see that his insistence on helping her didn't get him killed. She shuddered at the thought, then quickly blocked it.

"Nicole."

She jumped, then turned to face the closed door. She had to pull herself together. "Yes," she managed as she threaded her fingers into her hair and massaged her tense scalp.

"I have your clothes. When you're finished in there I'd like to shower," he said, in that voice that melted her fledgling resolve not to be affected by him.

The unbidden image of Ian naked, with water sluicing over his powerful body rocked Nicole to the core. "Fine," she said curtly, then gritted her teeth so hard that her jaw ached. She knew too many techniques for maintaining control to allow this sort of distraction. It was past time she took charge. Whatever had once been between the two of them was no more. That fleeting connection had been under false pretenses in the first place, and Nicole's subsequent betrayal had severed the bond forever. All that remained was physical attraction, lust borne of familiarity. Nothing else. When this was over, assuming either of them survived, she and Ian would go their separate ways.

End of story.

Forcing away any further thought of Ian, Nicole turned her

attention to essential functions. She washed her hands and face, then rinsed her mouth with the complimentary small bottle of mouthwash. It wasn't quite the same as brushing her teeth, but it would have to do until she could purchase a few personal items. While she finger-combed her hair, Nicole made a mental list of items she would need to purchase for the weekend. Filing insurance claims, finding a new apartment and starting over from scratch would simply have to wait until later.

Much later.

Nicole frowned. She supposed that calling her office and checking in would be appropriate, though she was on approved leave. If any witnesses from last night's fire had described her to the police or the media, the guys at the office might get worried. Nicole would do that while Ian showered. Tamping down the images that thought immediately conjured, Nicole grabbed her dry lingerie and ID and tucked the items under her arm, then opened the door and breezed back into the room.

As Ian passed, his bag and freshly laundered suit in hand, he paused directly in front of Nicole. He offered the gun, butt-first, to her. "Don't open the door for anyone," he warned.

Nicole accepted the weapon without looking at him. As soon as he had closed the bathroom door behind him, Nicole laid the weapon aside and quickly stripped off Ian's shirt. She held the fabric close to her face and took a long deep breath. Ian's scent still lingered where his warm body had lain against her all night. Chastising herself, Nicole tossed the shirt aside and swiftly dressed. She felt a great deal less vulnerable wearing her own clothes. Wearing nothing but Ian's shirt had somehow made her more susceptible to him.

All she needed now was her own weapon and Nicole would be whole again.

THE COMMERCIAL FLIGHT into Charlottesville, Virginia, had proven decidedly uninteresting in Nicole's opinion. The hassle of obtaining approval to carry weapons on the flight had tried even the patience of the forever-unflappable Ian. Finally, all parties had agreed that, per the pilot's request, the weapons would be locked away in the cockpit until landing.

Taking the Colby Agency jet would have alleviated the entire situation, but the whole point was to leave a wide, easy path for their shadow to follow. If Nicole had ever been this careless with her travel plans, she had long since blocked the memory. First they had stopped by her office and picked up a weapon from her personal office safe. Her bureau ID was a little the worse for wear, but still usable. Nicole made sure all her co-workers knew that she planned to take a little weekend trip to her cousin's secluded mountain cabin. A few suggestive glances in Ian's direction and the whole office assumed she and Ian were lovers taking a little getaway.

After that, Nicole had led Ian on a whirlwind shopping trip in Georgetown. By lunchtime they had everything they would need for a long weekend in the wilderness, from the eyewear to the hiking boots. Their wardrobes looked straight off the pages of L.L. Bean. Ian always wore suits, his appearance nothing less than impeccable. That look was right for him; fit his personality to a T. Nicole blew out a disgusted breath and forced her attention to the passing fall landscape. Who would ever have suspected that he would look so hot in jeans and flannel? The man was six feet two inches of lean, hard muscle. Nicole blinked the image of his sculpted body from her mind. Don't go there, she warned that part of her that wanted so desperately to take whatever he would give during their short time together.

If that wasn't bad enough, Nicole had also got a glimpse of the kid in Ian when he'd selected the SUV at the rental agency. According to Ian it was exactly like the one he was currently considering purchasing. Black with tinted windows, four-wheel drive, fully loaded, the Range Rover was nice, Nicole had to agree. She stole a glance at its driver. But she could have gone the rest of her life without having to see his pleasure at how the vehicle handled, at how much he admired the interior. She didn't want to know the little things that pleased Ian. The more she knew about him, the more dangerous he was to her heart.

With only soft rock whispering from the speakers to break the silence, and two and one half hours of picture-perfect landscape behind them, the sign welcoming visitors to Town Creek was a truly welcome sight. Ian slowed to take in the view. Nestled between the gorgeous Appalachian Mountains, Town Creek and its Deep River proved a breathtaking sight no matter how many times Nicole saw it. Her cousin George, a psychiatrist in Richmond, was a diehard bass fisherman. In his opinion, there was no place on earth like the Deep River in Town Creek. He had been so impressed with the fishing as well as the friendly community that he had bought himself a vacation home here years ago. Nicole had visited a couple of times when George had had his thirtieth birthday or some milestone in his career he wanted to celebrate. The place was serenity exemplified. And George always left a key under the third rock from the front right corner of the cabin.

"Take the next right," Nicole said abruptly, almost forgetting that Ian didn't know the way. Her voice sounded strangely loud after the long drive without speaking.

Ian made the turn and began the winding journey that would take them high into the mountains and deep into the woods. Though the cabin was only ten or twelve miles from town, the narrow, winding road made the going slow. With the dense forest of soaring trees closing in around them, the dim light of dusk swiftly gave way to total darkness.

Thirty minutes later, Ian braked to a stop in front of the rustic one-story cabin. The place wasn't very large. There was a great room that served as a living room, dining room and bedroom. A small kitchen and an even smaller bathroom lay beyond that. There was no telephone or cable television, but there was electricity and running water compliments of a heavy-duty generator and a deep well. George always re-stocked before he left. There would be canned goods in the cabinets and a full tank of gas in the generator, with additional fuel stored in the small outbuilding.

"You have a key?" Ian asked as he shut off the headlights and then the engine.

"No, but I know where he keeps it." Nicole reached into the back seat and retrieved the flashlight Ian had purchased with the rest of the gear.

Nicole tried to ignore Ian's brooding presence directly behind her as she made her way to the corner of the cabin, but it was impossible. She could feel the masculine warmth emanating from him in seductive waves. His heat pulled at her senses, made her want to turn and face him and then move into his arms. Giving herself a mental shake, Nicole crouched down and collected the key from beneath the rock. She dusted the dirt from it and strode purposefully toward the porch. Ian followed, saying nothing. But when Nicole inserted the key into the lock, he placed his hand on her arm.

"Let me go in first," he said, more of a quiet command than a suggestion.

Nicole shrugged off his touch. "Whatever." She stepped

back out of his way. Let him play the big, tough protector. What did she care as long as the mission was accomplished?

Ian unlocked and opened the door. Nicole offered him the flashlight, knowing that would be his next request. At least if she handed it to him first, he wouldn't have to ask for it, and she wouldn't have to hear his voice unnecessarily. Nicole shook her head slowly in resignation. The situation was completely and utterly ridiculous.

The beam of the flashlight moved over the great room. Hewn and chinked log walls, four windows, three interior doors, wood floors embellished with braided rugs and cathedral ceilings with huge wood support beams. George's taste in decorating was "bare and essential," but his housekeeping was immaculate. Though the furnishings were sparse, Nicole knew them to be comfortable. A round wood table with four chairs, an overstuffed sofa with matching arm chairs flanking it, one chest of drawers, a bookcase and a huge king-size brass bed. The sight of the bed always caught Nicole off guard. Everything else in the place was wood, or plaid upholstery. But the bed—unfortunately singular—was shiny brass and covered with elegant linens.

"Lights?" The sound was hardly more than a whisper, but it glided along every nerve ending in Nicole's too-attentive body.

Nicole reached for a key on the hook by the front door. "We have to start up the generator," she said quickly. "It's around back. We can go through the kitchen and out the back door."

This time Ian led the way. He paused at the back door and surveyed the perimeter outside within the boundaries of the flashlight's beam. Satisfied that no one waited in the bushes, he descended the steps. Nicole followed.

The generator started a little sluggishly. Nicole supposed that it had been a while since her cousin's last visit. With him traveling around promoting his latest published work, she felt certain he was far too busy for fishing. But, knowing George, he would make up for it another time.

Nicole located the breaker box behind the kitchen door and flipped the breaker for the lights and the well pump. The cookstove and the hot-water heater were gas and only required that the pilot lights be lit. Ian insisted on lighting them, which suited Nicole just fine. She had been up close and personal with too much heat in the past couple of days as it was.

Once their gear was unpacked and stored away, Ian prowled the place like a caged animal. He adjusted the primitive country curtains to his liking, and examined the locks on the doors, twice. Bored with watching Ian's precise, methodical movements and trying to stay unaffected, Nicole pushed up from the comfortable sofa and strolled into the kitchen to do a little prowling of her own. She might as well inventory the supplies. They did have to eat for however long they would be here. That, at least, would occupy her restless mind.

One can of coffee, three cans of chili, six cans of beef stew, a twelve pack of canned sodas and several cans of juice. And wine. Nicole smiled. More than a dozen bottles of wine. Nicole searched through the remaining cabinets. Cleaning supplies, fire extinguisher, condoms. Nicole did a double take.

Condoms?

Under the sink?

She shook her head, closed the cabinet doors and stood. Now where would he hide the Godiva? George had a sweet tooth that only Godiva chocolate would assuage. Nicole shared in that little addiction. She rummaged through the cabinet drawers. It had to be here. George always kept a supply on hand.

"Hungry?"

Nicole snapped to attention and whirled around as if she had been caught with her hand in the cookie jar, her face flushed guiltily. "I was inventorying supplies," she said quickly. "We'll need a few provisions to carry us through the weekend," she added for good measure. Nicole moistened her lips and avoided that analyzing gray gaze. Ian probably didn't have even one bad habit. He was perfect.

Too perfect.

"If you'd like to rest, I'll take care of dinner," he offered in that smooth, liquid voice that made her quiver inside.

Nicole pushed away from the cabinet. "That's a good idea," she answered without looking at him. She paused long enough to take a look inside the fridge when she passed it. Nothing. The motor whined a bit, struggling to cool the warm interior now that electricity flowed again.

Standing in the middle of the great room, Nicole considered where George would hide his decadent treasure if not in the kitchen. *Dammit*. She wanted some chocolate, and she wanted it now. If she couldn't have Ian, at least she could have that.

Nicole resisted the urge to stamp her foot. What was wrong with her? Ian was off-limits. She glanced at the wide, inviting bed. And what were they going to do about that? Nicole released a big breath. Sure the bed was big, like the one at the hotel. But no matter how wide the bed, their bodies would draw each other like light to the dawn once sleep robbed them of conscious restraint.

Ian would just have to sleep on the couch.

With that decision behind her, Nicole resumed her search. She shuffled through the books and magazines in the bookcase. Her hands slowed as one title caught her eye. *Burn, Baby, Burn.* Nicole's expression twisted into one of distaste. When she leafed through the publication, her suspicions were confirmed. Numerous sexual positions were described in graphic detail, pictures included. Aphrodisiacs of all kinds were enumerated. Nicole slapped the cover closed and shoved the magazine back into its original position, but not before she checked the address label on the back cover.

When had George started ordering such sexually explicit material? Several other shocking titles speared her attention. Nicole shrugged off the curiosity. Maybe he was working on a new medical journal. Sex and its many various and associated problems were often the subject of medical journals. After all, George was a shrink. He most likely had patients who needed counseling in that area.

Nicole moved on to the chest of drawers. Socks, underwear, pajamas. More condoms. Nicole frowned again. What the hell was George expecting? An orgy?

No chocolate there either.

Pacing back and forth as Ian had earlier, Nicole worried her bottom lip. Maybe George had depleted his supply the last time and had simply forgotten to bring more. Or perhaps he intended to replenish his stock the next time he visited.

The bathroom.

Nicole knew it was a long shot, but it was the only place she hadn't looked already. Aspirins, antibiotic ointment, alcohol, peroxide, the medicine cabinet contained them all, but no Godiva. The linen cabinet contained towels, washcloths, soap, feminine products. Nicole did another double take. Since when did George need feminine hygiene prod-

ucts? Okay, so maybe he brought his girlfriends here sometimes. Maybe one of his lady friends had left the intimate
items. One brow lifted in skepticism when she eyed the array
of scented bubble bath. Nicole closed the cabinet door and
shuffled back into the great room. No chocolate. She looked
up to find Ian pouring wine into stemmed glasses.

And damn if he didn't look good enough to eat. The perfect combination of elegance and danger.

She swallowed, hard.

"Have a seat, it's ready," he told her when she made no
move to come closer. "Beef stew and a great red wine." He directed one of those rare ten-thousand-watt smiles in her direction.

Keeping her eyes on the hypnotic movements of his hands,
Nicole slowly walked to the table and sat down. Ian settled
into his own chair directly across from her and sipped his
wine.

"Your cousin has outstanding taste," Ian commented, then
licked the residue of wine from those full, firm lips.

Nicole blinked. What was Ian implying? Oh yeah, the
wine. She grabbed her own glass. "Thank you," she said
tightly. "I'll tell him you said so next time I see him." Nicole
all but gulped the rich, red liquid. She had to get ahold of herself. The case. She had to concentrate on the case.

"How long has he owned this place?"

Nicole's head came up. "What?"

That silvery gaze connected fully with hers then. "You
shouldn't worry so much, everything is going to be all right,
Nicole."

Nicole's relief was palpable. He thought she was upset
about the case. "I know," she replied quietly, then quickly
averted her gaze.

"You should eat and then get some rest. I'll take the first watch."

Why did he have to do that? Make her feel like she mattered more than anything else in the world to him? They were partners in solving this case. Nothing more.

That lie reverberated clear through to her bones.

Nicole took another big sip of her wine. Eat, Nicole, she ordered herself. The sooner you eat, the sooner you can leave the table. Three feet wasn't nearly enough space between them. Forcing herself to chew, then swallow, Nicole finished off her beef stew. She turned up her wineglass and emptied it as well.

"I'll take care of the next meal," she offered as she pushed back her chair and stood. "We can take turns." Nicole grabbed her plate and empty glass and headed to the kitchen without looking back. If Ian responded, she didn't hear him. Nicole rinsed her dishes and dried her hands. Now what? No TV. She supposed she could read. Several of the available titles flitted through her mind. Nope. That wouldn't do.

The chocolate. She had to find that chocolate. Nicole walked back into the great room and considered where else she could search. She had looked everywhere already. Hadn't she? Nicole frowned and scanned the big open space once more. Ian was busy clearing his dishes from the table. She ignored him.

A smile sent the corners of Nicole's mouth upward. The bed. She hadn't looked under the bed. Desperation driving her on, Nicole dashed across the room and dropped to her knees next to the bed. She lifted the spread and peered into the semidarkness beneath the big brass bed. A few dust bunnies skittered across the floor. Nicole's smile widened to a triumphant grin. She tugged two large plastic containers clear of the bed. Through the translucent sides she could see that the boxes contained a variety of items. Godiva chocolate had to be in there somewhere. Nicole just knew it.

Nicole opened the first container and elation surged through her veins. Two large gold boxes were perched atop the other contents. The shiny gold winked beneath the light as Nicole quickly opened one package. A moan of pleasure escaped as she placed a small chunk of the heavenly chocolate in her mouth and closed her eyes in pure ecstasy.

"What's all this?"

Nicole's eyes popped open. Ian crouched right next to her. She had been so engrossed in finding her treasure that she hadn't even realized he'd moved. Pleasure exploded on her tongue and another tiny groan seeped out.

"Chocolate," she murmured with delight. "The very finest chocolate on earth. I adore it. George is absolutely addicted to the stuff."

"No, I don't mean the chocolate," Ian explained quietly. "I mean this."

Nicole stared down at the container as Ian moved aside the boxes of chocolate. Her eyes bulged in disbelief.

"It looks as if chocolate isn't Cousin George's only addiction."

The array of sex toys was far too comprehensive and—Nicole stared, agog, as Ian lifted the lid from the other container—too state-of-the-art to be called anything less than a very serious hobby.

"I take it the man likes to play games." Ian picked up a set of handcuffs and dangled them.

Nicole fingered a bottle of expensive-looking body oil. George into S and M? That couldn't be. He was much too straitlaced for that. The memory of the magazine with his name and address on the back cover flashed through her mind, along with a half-dozen other titillating titles.

"Apparently," Nicole finally murmured. Images, sounds, erotic and forbidden, flickered through the private theater of her mind. She and Ian, touching, tasting, reaching...

Nicole blinked away the prohibited fantasies. She hurriedly placed the lids back on the containers and shoved them under the bed.

Out of sight, out of mind.

Right, Nicole thought with self-disgust. She pushed to her feet, chocolates in hand, strode back to the sofa and plopped down on it. She set the box of chocolate on the cushion beside her, then crossed her arms over her chest and stared at the far wall. What was she supposed to do for the next forty-eight hours in this secluded cabin with nothing to distract herself from disaster?

At precisely that moment, Ian settled himself at the other end of the couch. Nicole darted an uncharitable glance in his direction. *Burn, Baby, Burn* snagged her attention. Ian had the magazine, reading it...looking at it...whatever.

One dark brow lifted speculatively. "Interesting," he noted aloud.

Nicole groaned inwardly. How would she ever survive this weekend surrounded by sex toys and "how to" guides for the sexually depraved?

Ian made a small sound of disbelief, then a slow, rich laugh drew Nicole's reluctant gaze back to the lights and shadows of his angular face.

She was doomed.

Chapter Six

Ian came instantly awake.

He held perfectly still as he listened for the sound again. A board creaked, then the distinct sound of a footstep just outside the front door. Ian withdrew his gun from beneath his pillow, threw back the blanket and sat up on the couch. He listened again. The knob turned with a definitive click, once, twice. Ian stood and moved silently across the room. He was halfway to the door when the mattress shifting alerted him to Nicole's movement. His eyes already adjusted to the darkness, he saw her rise from the bed, weapon trained expertly on the threat. Ian waited until she moved closer to ensure that she understood when he indicated that she should move to the far side of the door. Soundlessly she glided into a position where the opening door would provide cover from immediate danger.

Anticipation pounding through his veins, Ian flattened against the wall at the same instant that the knob turned again and the door swung inward.

One quick sweep of Ian's right foot and the startled intruder lay facedown on the floor. In one fluid move, Ian had his knee pressed into the man's back, the barrel of his weapon nudged into the back of the man's skull.

"Don't move," Ian warned. He slipped the fingers of his free hand into the man's pocket to retrieve his wallet and check for identification.

The lights came on and Nicole crouched next to Ian as he pulled a driver's license from the wallet. "George?" she demanded in disbelief. "What the hell are you doing here?"

Ian glanced from the man pinned to the floor to the Virginia driver's license he held in his hand. *George Reed.* Ian scowled and shifted his weight from the man's back.

"I could ask you the same thing," George said, a bit shakily as he pushed to his knees.

Ian tucked his weapon into his waistband at the small of his back and offered his hand to assist George in getting up. George shot Ian a cross look, but accepted the assistance. So this was Dr. George Reed, Ian mused as he closed and locked the door. He looked to be several years older than Nicole. Same blond hair and blue eyes. Tall and lean. Ian suppressed a smile when he remembered the hidden treasure beneath the bed.

"Why didn't you tell me you were coming up?" George was asking as he dusted himself off. "I would have planned dinner with you or something," he added, casting another less-than-appreciative look in Ian's direction.

Ignoring George's dubious glances, Ian noticed for the first time since this little episode began what Nicole was wearing. A white T-shirt that hit mid-thigh. Ian swallowed hard as he imagined what color those lacy panties might be this time. Lavender? Red? His groin tightened. Red satin against Nicole's creamy skin. A slow, diffused excitement oozed forth and spread across his own skin. That same hot, tingly sensation exploded inside him, and Ian felt himself harden.

Ian gritted his teeth and forced away any thought of Nicole's body or her attire. "Were you followed up the mountain?"

"What?" Frowning, and still a bit unsteady, George pivoted to face Ian.

"We don't want anyone to know we're here," Nicole explained, drawing George's attention back to her.

"Why not?" he demanded to know. "Does this have something to do with your position at the bureau?"

Nicole said yes at the same time that Ian said no.

George looked from one to the other, his frown deepening. "Which is it, yes or no?"

Ian pinned Nicole with a warning look.

"Well," she began slowly. "Ian and I used to work together," she stammered. "So, it's sort of work related."

George's expression did a complete turnaround. "I see," he said knowingly. "A little *internal affair.*"

Ian wasn't amused. "Did anyone follow you?" he asked again.

George hooked a thumb in Ian's direction. "Who is this guy, Nicole? He's even more serious than you."

Nicole cleared her throat. "Sorry," she offered. "George, this is Ian Michaels." Nicole gestured hesitantly, then shrugged. "We're former colleagues and we've been comparing notes on an old case that's still unsolved." She gave the men her back and strode across the room to place her weapon on the dining table.

George snagged Ian's hand and pumped it once, firmly. "Any friend of Nicole's is a friend of mine."

Ian held on with an insistent pressure when George would have pulled his hand away. "Did anyone follow you up the mountain?" he asked slowly and for the third time. Ian pressed him with a gaze that he hoped conveyed the full significance of his request.

George's amused expression wilted instantly. "No," he said quickly, pulling his hand away even more swiftly. "No one followed me. There was no traffic at all, in fact."

"Good."

"Well," Nicole chimed in with too much enthusiasm. "Why don't we have a cup of coffee and catch up?" She looked from George to Ian and back, uncertainty shimmering in her wide blue eyes.

"Will you be staying?" Ian asked of George. Nicole narrowed her gaze at Ian. He supposed he deserved that—after all, the cabin did belong to the man.

George shook his head adamantly, and held up his hands stop-sign fashion. "I don't want to intrude."

Nicole shot Ian the evil eye. "Don't be ridiculous, George," she argued sincerely. "It's 2:00 a.m., you have to stay. If you don't want to have coffee now, we can go back to bed for a few hours and then have coffee *together* when the sun is up."

"No, no, I can't do that," George countered with a bark of choked laughter. "I have a very pretty, and very impatient lady warming up in town at the lodge."

"I'm sure you don't want to keep her waiting," Ian suggested.

Nicole flashed her palms upward and adopted a look of feigned dismay. "You should have brought her with you. We could have had a party!"

Ian was definitely going to wring Nicole's lovely neck when George left…if he ever did.

"Another appealing offer," George considered aloud. "But Stephanie hates the woods. She won't come up here at all." He shook his head slowly from side to side. "She maintains that it makes her feel like she has the lead in a *Friday the 13th* sequel." He rubbed his chin. "I'm delving into her childhood to see if I can find the root of the problem."

Nicole arched a speculative brow. "Stephanie is your patient?"

"Oh no," George rebutted quickly. One hand fluttered magnanimously. "I just can't help myself. I'm always evaluating my friends." George cocked his blond head in Nicole's direction. "And family," he added pointedly. "Unfortunately, it appears to be the nature of the beast."

Ian stared at the floor for a moment until the urge to laugh at Nicole's appalled expression subsided.

"I just dropped by to pick up a few things," George explained. "Stephanie absolutely adores chains," he added as he hurried to the bed.

Nicole's mouth dropped open. Ian chewed the inside of his cheek. He would never have guessed that Nicole would be so prudish when it came to sexual fantasy. Based on past experience, Ian found it difficult to fathom the result if Nicole abandoned all inhibitions and control. He responded instantly to the notion.

"I wanted to ask you about that, George," Nicole began as she moved slowly toward her cousin. George knelt and pulled the large plastic storage containers from beneath the bed. "You seem to have a new hobby."

"Just having some fun, cuz," he said while rummaging through one box. "You should try it. It's a real tension breaker. You and Ian feel free to use anything you'd like."

"Don't even think about taking the other box of Godiva," Nicole said abruptly. She snatched the remaining box from his hand. "I might be stuck here longer than I think."

George huffed an indignant breath. "Well, don't get all bent out of shape." He shoved the box, less the Godiva and chains, back under the sorely out-of-place brass bed. "I'm only too happy to share."

Nicole set her confiscated chocolate on the bed and dropped a quick kiss on George's cheek. "Thank you, George, you're a jewel among men." Nicole flicked a disdainful glare in Ian's direction.

Ian frowned. George, the sadomasochist, gets a kiss, and Ian gets a drop-dead look? Where was the justice in that?

Nicole walked George back to the door. "I wish we could meet for lunch or something," she was saying contritely.

George stole a final glance at Ian. "Your friend looks as if he plans to keep you all to himself."

Nicole sent Ian another glower. "Don't let his attitude fool you, George, Ian's nothing but a big teddy bear."

Ian felt one brow arch of its own accord. *Teddy Bear?* Ian didn't think so.

"Have a safe trip back into town, George," Ian offered politely.

"Love the accent," George remarked casually as he paused in the doorway. "It must thrill the ladies."

Ian's jaw tightened in an effort to refrain from comment.

"We may be in town tomorrow," Nicole told him as he pressed a farewell kiss to her cheek. "I'll call, maybe we can do lunch."

"Think about what I said. You need to relax!" George called over his shoulder as he trotted out to his Jeep Cherokee.

Ian watched until George was out of sight, then he closed and locked the door. He turned back to Nicole, and the sadness he saw in her eyes made something shift near his heart.

"Lunch isn't a good idea," he said quietly.

She folded her arms over her chest and sighed. "I know. I can't risk endangering George, or anyone else for that matter. Though I may be safe until this guy has Solomon's location, no one around me is." Nicole's worried gaze sought out Ian's. "That includes you, you know."

"I know how to take care of myself," Ian assured her. He wanted desperately to draw her into his arms and hold her until the sadness in her eyes went away.

"Daniels knew how to take care of himself, too," she returned, her voice lacking any inflection. "And he's dead anyway."

Ignoring the warnings his brain was already sending him, Ian took a step closer to her. "Daniels wasn't expecting the danger. I am. The element of surprise is everything. You know that as well as I do, Nicole."

She trembled visibly. Ian clenched his fists at his sides.

"Yeah, I know." She shook her head. Those big blue eyes looked suspiciously bright. "But dead is dead. Daniels was a highly trained and very skilled agent, and he's dead. Someone wants me dead as well." Her gaze connected fully with Ian's. "And you'll be dead if you get in his way."

Ian's resistance dissolved. He pulled Nicole into his arms and held her close. She smelled so good, like sweet, ripe peaches. She shuddered and his arms tightened around her. Ian closed his eyes then, and allowed himself to simply hold her. The case, their past, everything else ceased to matter. There was only Nicole and the way she needed him at the moment.

Beneath the thin cotton of her T-shirt, her nipples pebbled, creating an exquisite friction against his bare chest. The silk of her hair tantalized his hands. He wanted to thread his fingers into her hair and draw her head up for a long, steamy kiss.

But he didn't. Ian continued to hold her and nothing more.

"You should get some more sleep," he whispered against

her ear. His eyes closed with the exquisite torture of continuing to hold her this close.

Nicole pulled back a little, her gaze directed at the floor. "You're right. We should both get back to sleep." She glanced up at him then, and Ian saw the flicker of desire that burned briefly in her eyes. "Good night, Ian." She broke free of his embrace and padded to the enormous bed.

"Good night," he murmured. He closed his eyes and sighed. No matter how tough she wanted to appear, Nicole was vulnerable right now. Almost fragile. And she was wrong, he added with mounting determination. He *would* keep her safe.

No matter what the cost.

NICOLE AWOKE to the delicious scent of fresh-brewed coffee and the calming sound of running water. She stretched languidly. *Ian.* The memory of how he had held her last night, so tenderly, so chastely, warmed her even now. Nicole sighed. Just when she was convinced that their relationship was about nothing more than sex, just when she thought she had figured the man out, he went and did something like that. Holding her as if he really cared, as if nothing else mattered.

She smiled when she considered George's visit in the wee hours of the morning. And his little secret. George was a great deal more adventurous than Nicole would ever have guessed. How could she have known him her entire life and not have gotten even an inkling that the man was into kinky sex? The image of Ian, handcuffed to the wide brass headboard, suddenly took center stage in Nicole's mind. A tiny barb of pleasure twisted low in her belly, followed by a slow warmth that gradually consumed her. She could see herself in the fantasy, on her hands and knees, moving over Ian's helpless but unbearably aroused body. She would take her time tasting him, licking here and there, then drawing mercilessly on all the right spots. He would beg her to take him inside her, plead for release, but Nicole would linger, making the pleasure last until the desire reached a frantic pitch.

Nicole pushed up to a sitting position, wrapped her arms around her legs and rested her chin atop her knees. She blew out a disgusted breath. *Final warning, Reed. You've gone way beyond reason here,* she scolded harshly. Nicole closed her eyes and considered her predicament. Where was her willpower? Her self-discipline? Why couldn't she just look at Ian and pretend he was anybody else? A partner on a case? Someone she used to know in another life, when things were clearer and her job made much more sense? Someone *temporarily* back in her life?

Because it was impossible to describe Ian that simply. Everything about him and between them was complicated. Too complicated. And entirely too intense.

"Good morning."

Nicole opened her eyes to the subject of her worrisome reverie. Nicole blinked in surprise. He wore blue jeans that fit as if they were tailor-made for his long, lean body, and a gray cable-knit sweater that emphasized the breadth of his broad shoulders as well as the darker silver of his eyes. His dark hair was still slightly damp, and Nicole had the sudden almost overwhelming urge to run her fingers through it.

One side of his mouth lifted in a ghost of a smile. "Would you prefer your coffee in bed?"

No, she thought wickedly, *I'd prefer you in bed.* Nicole swallowed in an effort to halt the swell of need tightening her throat. "Good morning," she managed, her voice thick with sleep and the lust her fantasy had elicited. "I'll get my own coffee, thank you," she added with a tad more resolve.

"Fine." He turned and strode to the kitchen.

Nicole shivered. She could learn things about sensuality just by watching him walk across the room. He moved like a panther, slow, graceful, each step a fluid motion that encompassed his entire being. He appeared at once completely relaxed, yet poised for anything that might come his way. And his voice… Nicole hugged herself tighter. She tried to analyze the effect, tried to get used to it, but she was never fully prepared for the way it flowed over her, absorbed her in its essence.

A shower. She threw the covers back and bounded off the bed. After she'd showered and dressed they could drive into town for a few provisions. The trip would serve two purposes, a much-needed distraction and the opportunity to show themselves in public, to make sure the bait was taken. Nicole selected a pair of jeans and a red sweater. Red was always a definite eye-catcher. And today she needed something that stood out amid the earth-tone colors of autumn and the other diehard back-to-nature tourists. Nicole just hoped that their little excursion would garner the right attention. Dragging this weekend out any longer than necessary wouldn't be too smart.

Nicole hurried into the bathroom and quickly closed the door behind her. She needed distance. If she couldn't distance herself physically from Ian, which was impossible in the present scenario, she would simply have to distance herself emotionally from him. Her attempts had proven woefully inadequate thus far. But that was about to change. Nicole was finished playing around. It was time to get serious.

No one she cared about would be safe until this was over. Especially Ian.

TOURISTS, attempting to make the most of summer's last holiday, had descended upon the tiny village of Town Creek. Ian closely monitored the knots of shoppers bustling up and down the sidewalks. Of course, the hit man following Nicole could be waiting behind any one of the pairs of designer sunglasses adorning the many faces around them. The clink of cheap dinnerware and the steady hum of conversation vibrated in the small, filled-to-capacity café as they had lunch. Unscuffed hiking boots and brand-new outdoorsy clothing separated the tourists—Ian and Nicole included—from the locals.

Ian watched Nicole pick at her chef's salad. She looked preoccupied, which, in this business, was a dangerous state of mind. Remaining alert at all times was top priority.

"How's your salad?" he inquired casually.

Nicole's gaze shot up to his. "Perfect," she responded quickly, flatly.

Ian studied her blank expression for a time. "Then why aren't you eating it?"

Nicole laid her fork aside and pushed her plate away. She leaned back into the padded vinyl upholstery of the wide booth and gave him a sardonic look. "I'm not hungry."

Ian fingered his sweating water glass. "Why?" he asked eventually.

"I don't have to have a reason, Michaels," she returned, an impatient edge in her voice.

Michaels. Ian understood now. She was closing him out. Building a wall around herself so he couldn't touch her. Preparing mentally for whatever fate lay in store for her. He supposed that was wise, the right thing to do even. But he didn't like it.

He looked straight into her eyes, and, to her credit, she

didn't look away. "This may not turn out the way we've planned. He may not show at all," Ian suggested quietly.

"If he wants Solomon, he'll show." Steely insistence laced her tone, her gaze remained emotionless.

Ian dipped his head in acknowledgement. "*If* he wants Solomon," he agreed.

"He wants Solomon."

"You're certain of that?"

Nicole adopted a look that said she was bored with the subject. "We've been over this already."

Ian gestured for the passing waitress and then to his empty coffee cup. "Do you have a problem with going over it again?" He smiled his appreciation when the waitress filled his cup.

Nicole watched the woman walk away, then shifted her gaze back to Ian. "I'm bored with the subject."

"This could all be related to a different case," Ian suggested, choosing to ignore her comments.

"The only significant case Daniels and I had in common was Solomon's. Daniels thought the same thing, he said so in his note. That's proof enough for me." She sipped her lemonade and turned her attention to the pedestrians passing on the other side of the plateglass window.

She was right. Not a single doubt existed in Ian's mind about that. The cartel never forgot, and they damn sure never forgave. If Solomon was found, he would die, slowly and painfully. The man playing with all the explosives knew that Nicole was the key—the only one left who could lead him to Solomon. Ian was certain that if Nicole made no move to lead the shooter to Solomon, he would eventually come after her to get what he wanted. Ian's gut clenched. That thought scared the hell out of him, but he knew it was the only way.

They had put the ball in the other guy's court. He had the next move. Ian and Nicole only needed to wait for him to make that move. But waiting was proving nearly unbearable.

With Nicole still staring out the window, Ian took a moment to study her. She was beautiful. His chest constricted. And he wanted her again more than he had ever wanted anyone or anything in his life. But she was on the defensive now. She wanted this to be business, as it should be. Not allowing physical intimacy would make walking away easier. Ian had to remember that. Because he *would* walk away. He would not give Nicole the opportunity to hurt him again. He would protect her, but nothing more. Right now, Nicole was vulnerable and she needed him. When this was finished and she no longer needed his help, she would return to her life, and, just like before, she wouldn't look back. Not once.

This time Ian wouldn't be looking back either.

Ian swallowed hard. Somehow he would put aside all that drew him to Nicole. He had never met a woman like her. She was the *only* one who could hold her own with him…his match.

Let her erect her defensive barrier. She was only doing him a favor. Ian had a life to get back to as well. He enjoyed his work at the Colby Agency, and he liked living in Chicago. Nicole's home was in Washington. She lived for the bureau. When she'd had time to really consider all that had happened, she would only be more determined to remain loyal to her chosen profession.

"Are you ready?"

Nicole's sudden question jerked Ian back to the present. She was watching him, trying to discern his thoughts. "Yes," he answered. He placed the appropriate amount of cash on the table, then stood. Ian followed Nicole out the café door;

the bell jingled, announcing their departure. The warm golden sun reigned supreme over the soft blue dome of the sky. Ian carefully surveyed the street and the dozen or so meters between them and the rented SUV. The packages from their earlier stops were already stowed in the back of the vehicle. Milk, eggs and cheese were stored in a cooler Ian had found in George's small storage building.

Ian suddenly found himself wondering if George and his girlfriend were all tied up in the lodge down the street. A smile teased his lips. The image of Nicole in leather that fit exactly like skin abruptly filled his head. Every muscle in his body contracted at the vivid visual stimulation. Ian's gaze immediately darted to Nicole's softly swaying hips. Her long, shapely legs were nicely defined by her body-hugging jeans. And then there was that silky veil of long, blond hair swinging against that sexy red sweater. Ian moistened his lips. The memory of waking up, their bodies entangled, aroused him further.

Nicole whirled around unexpectedly. She stepped back at the intensity she met in his eyes. "What's wrong? Why are you looking at me that way?"

Because he wanted to take her right then and there. Ian advanced the step she had retreated. She faltered back another tiny step, but the SUV stopped her.

"I've been thinking," Ian began, the idea gaining momentum even as he spoke. He leaned in closer, and placed one hand against the vehicle on either side of her. He inhaled her gentle fragrance—sweet, succulent peaches. A rush of renewed need made his next breath a chore. "If we want this to work, we have to make sure our guy believes it's for real."

Uncertainty flickered in those pretty blue eyes that exactly matched the day's perfect sky. "Agreed," she said hesitantly.

Ian leaned closer still. "Then we have to appear distracted," he whispered discreetly. "Distracted with each other."

She swallowed, the effort visible along the slender column of her throat. His fingers burned to trace that delicate terrain.

"I suppose so." Her words were barely a whisper.

The walls she had erected only this morning crumbled around her. Ian saw it in her eyes as a distant flame of desire kindled, and he felt it in her posture as she leaned forward, ever so slightly, without even realizing it.

"Then you agree," he suggested, his lips almost brushing hers, his gaze devouring every perfect, up-close detail of her lovely face, "that I should kiss you right now, just to be certain this looks authentic."

The tiny hitch in her breathing undid Ian completely. His mouth claimed hers. He kissed her, softly at first, absorbing the essence of citrus scent and hot, sweet Nicole. Desire pounded him brutally, and his kiss grew equally savage. He thrust his tongue into her mouth, pressed his arousal into her soft body. Fire surged through his veins, urging him on, compounding his need. His fingers splayed on the sun-warmed glass of the rear passenger's window. His assault was relentless, until Nicole whimpered helplessly beneath his siege, then and only then did Ian pull back. His breath raged in and out of his lungs. Nicole's breathing was just as ragged. Her lips were pleasure-swollen, her eyes glazed with desire.

Enough, he ordered silently.

Ian opened the front passenger's side door. "Let's go," he ordered quietly, ignoring the look of disbelief swiftly claiming her features. He did another quick scan of the street as she climbed into the vehicle.

"You're a real bastard, do you know that, Michaels?" she hissed, daggers shooting from those piercing blue orbs.

Ian allowed her a half smile. "Yes."

He closed the door.

Chapter Seven

Nicole literally seethed. She donned her new sunglasses and glared out the tinted passenger's side window of the SUV as Ian slid behind the wheel. Damn him! All morning she had worked hard at distancing herself, setting boundaries. She knew what she had to do, and she had done it for the first time since laying eyes on the man. Forced herself to concentrate on anything but Ian and the heat that lingered between them. She snapped her seat belt into place with a little more force than was needed as the engine roared to life. What had he been trying to prove with that kiss?

...we have to make sure our guy believes it's for real.

But it wasn't for real. The emotions his every look, every touch evoked inside her weren't real. At least not for Ian. He was simply doing his job. Once he had decided to help her, that was a given. Ian Michaels never failed. He would do whatever it took to ensure her safety and catch the bad guy. If he personally enjoyed the kiss, that was just a perk. And why not? Nicole closed her eyes and shook her head grimly from side to side. She had done it to him, hadn't she? Ian would never forgive her for what had happened between them three years ago. What she had thought might be his lingering feelings for her were probably only his way of exacting his revenge. Well, she wasn't falling for it again. Ian Michaels had better keep his distance, because Nicole damn sure intended to maintain hers.

The chirping of Ian's cell phone jerked Nicole back to the present. Still in the parking slot, Ian shifted back into Park. She handed him the compact phone he'd asked her to carry in her purse.

"Yes," he answered, then listened for what seemed like an eternity.

Nicole studied his face carefully, looking for any subtle change in expression that might give the subject of the call away. But Ian was too good at masking his emotions. Nicole huffed a breath of exasperation. She hated being at anyone's mercy.

"Yes, that sounds like the next logical step," Ian told the caller. Another long pause. "Keep me posted." He flipped the mouthpiece closed and turned to Nicole. "That was Alex Preston." Ian waited for Nicole to recognize the name of the other agent Victoria had recommended. "So far nothing has turned up on any of the cartel members. No one seems even remotely involved in what's happening to you. But," he qualified, "Alex has only scratched the surface at this point."

"What about Solomon?" Nicole kept her gaze steady on his, feeling more confident behind the concealing glasses.

"Martinez checked in this morning. Solomon is fine, a little testy about his accommodations, but otherwise fine."

"Good." Nicole directed her attention straight ahead. Unless Ian had additional new information, there was nothing else to discuss. She was still enormously annoyed with him about the kiss.

"Alex has decided to call in an outside source to obtain a more detailed report on the cartel."

Nicole stiffened. She wasn't sure she wanted anyone else brought in on this case. The fewer people who knew, the safer Solomon would be. "Who?"

"His name is Sloan. He's good."

Nicole considered the name. If it should ring a bell, it didn't. "What makes her think that this Sloan can get any closer to the cartel than she did?"

"Because Sloan plays as dirty as they do. He's a mercenary of sorts."

That got Nicole's undivided attention. She gave Ian a long, sideways assessment. "Since when does a firm like the Colby Agency deal with mercenaries?" Nicole couldn't picture Victoria Colby with a character resembling early Sylvester Stallone work in her elegant office. "Is she certain he can be trusted?"

"I don't know him personally, but if Victoria trusts him…" Ian offered, allowing the rest of his statement to trail off. A hint of a shrug lifted one broad shoulder. "That's all I need to know."

Victoria obviously lived up to the reputation that preceded her. Ian didn't trust easily. "I'd like to borrow your phone." Nicole held out her hand. "I want to make sure George made it back to his girlfriend last night," she explained when Ian hesitated.

He placed the phone in her open palm. "Make it brief."

Nicole rolled her eyes and punched in the telephone number she had memorized from the menu jacket in the café. Several local business logos were displayed on the plastic cover, including the River Lodge.

"Hello." The greeting was a breathless rush of syllables.

Nicole smiled. "George, just wanted to make sure you didn't want to come have dinner with us this evening." Her brows furrowed as she listened intently in an effort to decipher the strange background noises accompanying George's heavy breathing. From the corner of her eye, Nicole saw Ian's fingers curl into a fist on his thigh. Two could play the game of pushing the other to the edge.

"Sorry, Nicole, but I'm a little busy at the moment." The pitch and intensity of the muffled sounds on the other end of the line increased. "How about we get together another time?" George suggested, his voice strained as if he were struggling.

"Okay. See you soon." Nicole closed the phone and offered it back to Ian. His glower was lethal.

"Don't play games with me, Nicole," he told her, in an equally lethal tone. "You know we have to do this alone."

Nicole shrugged innocently and dropped the phone she still held into her bag. "Who's playing games? I only wanted to make sure George was okay. I knew he wouldn't accept the offer." She faced forward again. "He was otherwise occupied."

"Look at me, Nicole."

The order was almost soft, but the skin on the back of her neck prickled with warning. Ian was deadly serious. Slowly, reluctantly, Nicole turned her head in his direction, her chin parallel with her shoulder. Resisting the urge to flinch, Nicole sat perfectly still as one long-fingered hand darted up to her face and plucked off her sunglasses. She blinked at the sudden brightness.

"Don't test my patience," he warned, pressing her with a gaze that reiterated his words.

Nicole sighed and faced forward again. "Whatever," she

said flippantly as she grabbed back her eyewear. Ian would not tolerate her indifference well she knew. That thought pleased Nicole inordinately.

Several tense seconds passed before he shifted into Reverse and, watching over his right shoulder, slowly backed from the parking slot. Nicole stared, not really seeing but looking through the tourists strolling past the quaint shops. She would never be, had never been like those people. Nicole had spent her entire adult life training or working for the bureau. The bureau was her life. Regret, abrupt and unbidden, trickled through her. She was twenty-nine years old. Wasn't there supposed to be something else? Ian's whispered words in that language she hadn't understood as he made love to her echoed through her mind.

She would never have that either.

Something familiar about someone in the crowd they passed grabbed her attention. Nicole frowned and spun around in her seat. "Wait!"

Ian braked to a stop in the middle of the street. "What's wrong?" A horn blasted behind them.

"Park," Nicole commanded as she unfastened her seat belt. By the time Ian had killed the engine in their new parking slot, Nicole was climbing out the door. "Over there." She pointed to the sporting goods shop on the corner across the street. "In the alley between the buildings."

Without question, Ian sprinted across the street, dodging traffic. Nicole followed, ignoring the irritated shouts and blaring horns. She concentrated hard on the image that had caught her eye. She had only seen the back of the man, but something about the way he moved seemed familiar. Instinct niggled at her even now. She knew him.

They reached the corner of the sporting goods shop. "He's

wearing a navy blue jacket. Medium height and build, dark hair," she said quickly. "I know him," she added thoughtfully. Ian paused briefly to assess the situation and Nicole focused inward on the slow, deliberate walk of the man she had seen.

"Stay behind me," Ian commanded as he started forward.

Halfway down the alley, Ian reached beneath his sweater to the small of his back and withdrew his gun. Nicole's heart pounded with the anticipation flowing swiftly through her veins. Her fingers curled around the butt of the Beretta cradled in the back of her waistband. She withdrew her weapon and kept it pointed toward the ground as she trailed Ian through the shadowy, deserted alley. She turned around slowly from time to time to ensure they weren't being followed. Fear for Ian welled in her chest, suffocating her with its intensity.

They reached the end of the alley, and Ian waited, listening. Slowly he moved around the corner of the building.

Nothing.

Nicole swore hotly.

She shook her head, fury replacing the fear she had felt only moments before. "I know what I saw."

Ian studied the architecture of the buildings on either side of the alley as he spoke, "I don't doubt you, Nicole."

Ian's supportive response did nothing to slow Nicole's growing agitation. He was here. She saw him. Every instinct told her he was the one. Nicole followed Ian's gaze as he traced the landscape that rose sharply behind the buildings. The overgrown grass appeared undisturbed. To their left the alley abruptly dead-ended.

Ian started moving again. "This way," he said quietly.

Nicole followed, her hopes rising again. A door on the far end of the building to the right had captured Ian's attention.

As they approached, Nicole could see that the door led into the sporting goods shop. Concealing his weapon once more beneath his sweater, Ian opened the door and entered the shop. Nicole did the same. The door led to what appeared to be the shipping and receiving section of the store. Another door, standing wide open and marked Employees Only, led into a short, narrow hallway that emptied into the large store.

"Stay right here," Ian instructed, before disappearing into the men's room.

Nicole leaned against the wall near the ladies' room door and watched the comings and goings at the end of the hall.

When Ian stepped back into the hall, he shook his head to indicate he had found nothing. "Check the ladies' room, just in case," he told her.

Nicole pushed the door inward and entered the bathroom. Two empty stalls, a sink and a short bench greeted her. No window, no other avenue of escape. She rejoined Ian in the hall and reported her findings.

Ian continued down the hall and drifted into the crowd of milling shoppers. Nicole scanned every face, every backside. He had to be in here. She stopped. A man with dark hair, wearing a navy blue jacket was rifling through a rack of golf shirts, his back turned to Nicole. Her heart rate kicked into overdrive. She blocked the steady murmur of conversation around her to focus solely on her target. Slowly, not taking her eyes off the man, Nicole approached him. Just when she would have reached out to him, a hand darted past her and grabbed the man by the shoulder. Ian whirled the guy around, his free hand already gripping his well-concealed weapon.

"What the—?" The man struggled to pull free of Ian's grip. He faltered back a step. "What's your problem?"

Nicole wilted. It wasn't him. Ian looked to her for confirmation. Nicole shook her head.

"Sorry," Ian offered. "I thought you were someone else."

The man muttered something under his breath and left the shop as fast as he could.

"You're sure?" Ian asked.

Nicole nodded. Though she hadn't actually seen the face of the man on the sidewalk, something in his manner spoke to her "The way this guy carried himself was wrong," she explained. Where could the man she had seen have gone?

Nicole followed Ian through the rest of the shop, but there was no one else with dark hair and wearing a solid-colored navy blue jacket. Doubt set in. Nicole began to wonder if she could have imagined the man. Maybe her eyes were playing tricks on her. Maybe she wanted this to be over so badly that she was conjuring up people who weren't there.

"If he was here, he's gone now," Ian said quietly. "We should be going."

If.

Nicole couldn't blame Ian for not believing her. She wasn't sure if she even believed herself anymore. As they walked back to the SUV, Nicole searched the pedestrians for any sign of a navy blue jacket. Ian appeared watchful as well. Still nothing. Nicole reached for the handle on the passenger-side door of their vehicle, but a paper fluttering beneath the windshield wiper caught her attention. A sales flyer. Henrietta's Florist and Gifts. Nicole frowned as she yanked the unwanted document free of the wiper. She tossed her bag and the flyer into the vehicle and climbed into her seat. Her temples pounded with frustration. He had to know they were here. She and Ian had left a trail a mile wide. He had to have followed.

Nicole stared out the window as Ian cruised down the

street. In less than five minutes they had left the town behind and were halfway up the mountain road leading to George's private getaway. Images flickered in front of Nicole's eyes. The destruction in Landon's office. His bereaved widow weeping over his closed coffin at the cemetery. The absolute devastation at Daniels's house. The mysterious note from Daniels after his death. Her rental car exploding...the bullet crashing through the truck window and hitting Ian...her apartment going up in flames.

Nicole closed her eyes and forced the painful memories away. She summoned the figure she had seen for those few short seconds. She replayed the way he had moved. Nicole released a disgusted breath. Nothing. It was his body language that spoke to her and her mind just couldn't play it back precisely enough at the moment to capture the quality that she had recognized.

"Stop thinking about it, Nicole."

Ian's silky voice penetrated the layers of frustration shrouding her. She looked at him for a full minute before she replied. Did he have any idea how deeply she responded to the mere sound of his voice? "It was him," she murmured.

Ian regarded her briefly, those assessing gray eyes analyzing far too much and far too deeply for Nicole's comfort. "He'll be back," he assured her.

Nicole propped her elbow on the door and massaged her aching forehead. Yeah, he would be back. He wanted Solomon. And the only way he could get to Solomon was through Nicole.

Something crinkled beneath Nicole's boot when she shifted in her seat. The forgotten flyer had fallen onto the floor. Annoyed, she glared at the offending document and kicked it aside. Bold, bloodred letters drew her gaze back when she would have looked away.

I'm waiting for you, Nicole.

Her hand trembled as she reached for the wrinkled paper. She read it again when she had it in her hand. On the backside of the florist's advertisement, large printed letters spelled out the words. Her heart froze in her chest. Straining for a calm she didn't feel, Nicole forced herself to analyze the evidence she held. Identifying the block-style printing would be impossible even if they had a clue as to where to begin a comparison. Since there was no way to know how many people had handled the flyer, fingerprints would prove useless.

I'm waiting for you, Nicole.

It was a warning, plain and simple. He wanted her, Nicole knew. But he was waiting. Until she was alone. The thought shook her. Nicole glanced at the driver. Her heart kicked back into that rapid staccato.

Just her. He was waiting for her to be alone. And then he would make a move. Not before.

"What's that?"

Nicole jerked to attention. Ian had already parked in the driveway in front of George's cabin. She swallowed. "A message." Nicole handed the paper to Ian. "It was on the windshield after we came out of the sports shop. I thought it was just a local advertisement."

Ian studied the document for a time, then lifted his gaze to her. "He was watching us."

Nicole nodded.

"Good." Ian laid the paper on the console. "Lock the doors. Don't get out until I tell you it's safe to come inside. If anyone approaches this vehicle, drive away." Ian opened his door and stepped out, then turned back to Nicole. "Move over here." He indicated the driver's seat, that silvery gaze intent and determined. "Drive away if you hear or see anything suspicious. Use the cell phone to call for help."

Nicole choked out a laugh. "Like hell."

"Do it, Nicole," he commanded harshly.

"All right," she relented, though there was no way she would ever drive away leaving Ian behind.

Ian pressed the lock button and closed the door. Nicole chewed on her lower lip as she watched him move cautiously around the cabin, his weapon readied. She held her breath until he appeared again from the other side. He studied the ground, and each window in the cabin as he passed it. He was looking for tracks or any other signs of entry, she knew. He crossed the porch and unlocked the door. Nicole's breath went still in her lungs as he disappeared once more, this time inside. Her gaze continuously swept the area around the cabin and the vehicle in which she sat, always moving back to the door, watching for Ian.

"This is nuts," Nicole muttered under her breath. She should be in there with Ian. Another minute ticked by. Making up her mind and steeling her resolve, Nicole withdrew her Beretta and opened the vehicle door. She was no untrained civilian. She knew the drill. Moving as swiftly and soundlessly as possible, Nicole stole across the yard. When she reached the porch steps, she relaxed a bit. Five seconds later she was at the door. Gripping the nine-millimeter with both hands she stepped across the threshold. She surveyed the room from left to right and back.

No Ian.

Adrenaline surged, stinging through her veins. Nicole stepped cautiously toward the kitchen, her gazed roved from side to side. She made a slow turn in the middle of the room to check the front door and the porch beyond it one more time.

"I told you to stay in the truck."

Nicole whipped toward the kitchen door. Ian loomed in the seemingly small opening, his expression fierce. Nicole relaxed her fire-ready stance. "I got lonely," she retorted as she tucked her weapon away.

After glaring at her a moment longer, Ian scanned the room. "I don't think anyone has been here."

"But he definitely knows we're here," Nicole countered. "He knows."

She pushed a handful of hair over her shoulder. "He wants me alone," she remarked more to herself than to Ian.

Ian shot her a pointed look. "That's not going to happen," he said, a warning, not a reassurance.

Nicole moistened her lips. "What if he won't show with you hanging around?"

Ian cocked his head in that arrogant manner of his. "Then he won't show."

"So the point of this entire exercise is?" she demanded, her temper flaring as rapidly as her impatience.

Ian gazed steadily at her. "To keep you and Solomon alive."

"Gosh, I guess I forgot about that." Nicole pivoted and stormed toward the door.

Ian snagged her arm before she took two steps. "Think, Nicole," he urged softly. "When he gets desperate enough, then he'll come, despite my presence. He'll rethink his approach and make a move."

Nicole tried to shrug his hand off. "We need to unload the supplies."

Several more seconds passed before Ian released her. Without another word, he followed Nicole to the SUV. He unlocked and lifted the rear hatch, then picked up the cooler while Nicole collected the two small bags from the back seat. Her mind raced with possibilities. She searched her memory for something, anything that would trigger that feeling of recognition again.

Nothing came.

Nicole stole a glance at Ian as they carried the supplies into the cabin. She closed and locked the door, then joined him in the kitchen. Ian was right, she supposed. The guy eventually would make a move. He had to if he wanted Solomon. The problem was, how long would he wait? And how long would she and Ian survive living under the same small roof without making another heart-damaging mistake?

As if to validate her point, Nicole found herself suddenly and unavoidably mesmerized by Ian's precise, graceful movements. He reached to put a can of soup in the cupboard, placing it exactly in line with the other canned goods, the label facing outward. His lean, muscled frame made her want to feel his weight against her. He reached into the next bag and, one by one, removed the apples and oranges Nicole had selected in the market. Those long, artist's fingers closed around each fresh piece of fruit in a near-caressing manner.

Ian paused abruptly, a shiny red apple still in his hand. Seemingly in slow motion, he turned to find Nicole watching him so intently. The look that passed between them said more than any words could have. He smiled then, and brought that succulent piece of fruit to his full, firm lips and took a bite, his eyes never leaving Nicole's. He chewed slowly, his lips moist with the luscious juice of the fresh fruit. And nothing would have pleased Nicole more than to lick that sweet stuff from those sensual lips.

Deep, deep inside Nicole, where nothing or no one else could touch her, something moved, and a kind of yearning she had never before experienced awoke and roared like a hungry beast. The need grew until her every sensory perception was focused inward to that one mushrooming sensation.

She would never survive another forty-eight hours alone with this man. He meant entirely too much to her.

Nicole needed a plan.

An *escape* plan.

Chapter Eight

By late afternoon on Sunday, Nicole felt ready to explode. Furious with herself as much as with Ian for feeling so helpless, she reached for the hand towel on the kitchen counter at the same time as he did. They glanced at each other briefly, but not briefly enough. Electricity zinged between them. Ian acquiesced with a barely perceptible nod, abandoning the towel to Nicole then turning his attention to the salad he was preparing. His long fingers poised on the tomato as he diced it with the skill of a master chef. Nicole dutifully dried the just-washed utensils, undeniably aware of Ian's every move. Disgusted, she tossed the towel aside and glanced at the battery-operated clock on the wall. Nicole quickly performed her second mental calculation of the day. Forty-three hours, twenty-seven minutes together, alone, in this growing-smaller-by-the-moment cabin. She bit back the urge to scream or break something.

The tension in the cubicle-sized kitchen was thick enough to cut with the knife Ian was currently using to chop the bell pepper. Taking a deep breath, Nicole decided to check on the pasta and sauce. Ian had insisted that, this being a holiday weekend, they should have some sort of celebratory meal. Nicole started toward the stove; Ian turned in the direction of the sink and she barreled smack into his mile-wide chest.

"Sorry," he murmured.

Nicole jumped back, holding her palms out to ward off any further apology or moves in her direction. "It's fine."

While he watched contritely, Nicole stepped around him, maintaining a safe distance between their bodies. She stirred the pasta, then the sauce, staring into the thick, red concoction as if it held the answers to all her problems.

"Almost done, don't you think?"

Startled, Nicole jerked away from the sound of Ian's silky voice. Standing entirely too close to her for comfort, he regarded her for a long moment. Nicole's heart flip-flopped hard beneath her sternum. He hadn't bothered to shave this morning, and the day's beard growth only intensified his sexy aura. He looked dark and dangerous and absolutely delicious.

"Why are you so jumpy, Nicole?"

Nicole set the wooden spoon aside and placed the lid on the sauce. Ian didn't move, he hovered over her as if she needed his full attention. She pushed her suddenly damp palms over her jean-clad hips and lifted her chin defiantly. She glared at Ian to produce the full effect.

"I'm not jumpy," she snapped. "I'm just tired of bumping into you that's all." She folded her arms over her middle and retreated a step. "You're crowding me, Ian. Every time I turn around you're there."

He shrugged vaguely, his gaze carefully controlled. "It's difficult to stay out of each other's way in such close quarters," he said so calmly, so reasonably she wanted to slap him to see if his expression would change.

Irritation, desperation and a dozen other emotions whirled inside her. She had to get out of here. No one was coming as long as Ian shadowed her every move like this. Nicole had to find a way to ditch him. She would never get Landon's and Daniels's killer otherwise. The note had been specific. He had been waiting for *her*. Sure, he might eventually show with Ian here, as Ian had suggested, but Nicole was out of time. She could not tolerate another hour alone with Ian. And even if she could, staying only put Ian at risk.

Decision made, she took another step back, edging toward the kitchen door. "I think I'll take a bath," she announced out of the blue.

Ian frowned. "What about dinner?"

"I'm not hungry." She gave him her back. "Don't wait for me," she added as she stalked toward the bathroom. Once inside, she closed the door and pressed her forehead against it. God, she needed her head examined. She knew her time with Ian was only temporary. She knew that he would only break her heart...just like last time. Though last time hadn't really been his fault. Duty bound or not, she had no one else to blame but herself for that one. But how could she still want him so very desperately? How could she long for him with such need that simply looking at him propelled her toward orgasm? Because she admired and respected everything about him, she admitted. Ian was the one man who drew her on every conscious level. Could she risk his being in any further danger?

Nicole had to find a way to slip away from him. She had tried leaving late last night while Ian was sleeping, but he had awakened instantly the moment she rose from the bed. Nicole had pretended she needed to use the bathroom. He had waited until she was safely back into bed before relaxing again. Ian was too smart to fool that easily, too fast to outrun and too damned good to trap.

Unless…

A wide smile suddenly spread across Nicole's face. Ian wasn't immune to the physical attraction between them. He felt it too. He wanted her as much as she wanted him. Nicole moistened her lips and tried to recall the array of items George had stashed under the bed. She made a mental list of the erotic and kinky toys available. The handcuffs and body oil would do very nicely, she decided with a little too much glee.

Acting quickly before she lost her nerve, Nicole knelt in front of the cabinet beneath the bathroom sink. She dug through the items stored there until she found what she was looking for, a half-dozen bath scents. Ian loved apples. She picked up the one called Enchanted Apple and closed the cabinet doors. Nicole adjusted the tap until the water flowing into the tub was to her liking, then she added the bubble bath. She closed her eyes and inhaled the steamy scent. Good enough to eat, she thought with a wicked grin.

Oh yes, this would do nicely.

In record time Nicole stripped off her clothes and dropped them onto the floor, ensuring that her panties and bra lay atop the pile. She pinned her hair up and reached for a towel. On second thought, she opted to forego the towel. That would be her excuse. Nicole stepped gingerly into the welcoming warmth of the softly scented water. She slowly sank beneath its surface with a moan of pure pleasure.

Relax, Nicole, she ordered. *For it will take every ounce of willpower and persuasion you have to do what has to be done.*

Ian would never know what hit him.

IAN GLANCED at the still-closed bathroom door and frowned. Why had Nicole been in there so long? The salad was in the fridge; the bread, pasta and sauce in the oven keeping warm; and the wine, open and ready to serve, stood on the table. The only holdup was Nicole. She had said not to wait, but Ian waited anyway. He massaged his unshaven chin and considered her behavior since their arrival here, especially the last twenty-four hours. Maybe the note had shaken her more deeply than he had first thought. She was certainly jumpy enough. Then, maybe it was simply a matter of cabin fever.

No. Ian released a heavy breath. It was none of those things. Nicole was suffering from the same ailment that plagued him, sexual frustration.

He wanted Nicole. He wanted her so badly that it was a bone-deep ache. The thought of touching her had been there all day, prowling in the deepest, darkest recesses of his mind, like an enemy preparing to close in. If something didn't happen soon, one or both of them would lose control. Today had been the most difficult. Absolute silence surrounded them. It was as if even the birds knew it was Sunday and they should rest from their twittering and chirping. The sky was a magnificent canvas of blue with the occasional fluffy white cloud here and there like the smudges of a careless painter's brush. A slight breeze whispered through the trees from time to time, momentarily disrupting the utter silence.

Inside, the mouthwatering aroma of garlic and tomato sauce filled the air. He should be hungry, but like Nicole, he wasn't. Ian's gaze flitted across the room. The big brass bed stood waiting, beckoning to him like a buoy in deep waters. Ian knew that if he didn't do something soon he would drown of suffocating need. A desire that never completely went away smoldered just beneath the surface of his own flimsy hold on control.

He needed a walk. A very long walk. And before he came

back inside he would have this fire under control once more. Ian stepped to the bathroom door and knocked once.

"Nicole, I'm going outside to check the generator," he said flatly, then turned to make good on his announcement, but her tentative voice stopped him.

"Ian?"

The sound of his name on her lips drew him back to the door, closer than he had been before, his face pressed against the smooth wooden surface. "Yes," he answered stiffly.

"I'm sorry to bother you," a pause accompanied by the splash of water, "but I failed to get a towel before I got into the tub. Now I can't get one without dripping all over the place. Would you," another agonizing pause, "come hand me a towel?"

The image of Nicole in that tub, surrounded by frothy water, bloomed before Ian's eyes. He could smell the clean, sweet fragrance of the scented water. Want speared through him, immediate and fierce. Ian braced his hands against the door frame and summoned his crumbling resolve. The taste of her lips, the smell of her skin, how it felt to hold her in his arms kept playing through his mind. If he hadn't kissed her yesterday, maybe the need wouldn't be quite so savage. But he *had* kissed her. And he wanted to kiss her again.

"Ian?"

Soft, sultry, her voice tugged at him, destroyed the last of his defenses. "Yes," he rasped. His hand moved to the knob, gripped hard, ready to turn it and remove the one tangible barrier between them.

"The water's getting a little cold."

Ian turned the knob and pushed the door open. The warm, moist air enveloped him with that irresistible fragrance he couldn't quite name as he stepped into the small room. His gaze riveted on Nicole reclining against the end of the tub in water just deep enough to conceal her breasts. Mounds of bubbles floated around her. She smiled lazily up at Ian, those blue eyes liquid with feminine heat. All that silky hair was haphazardly pinned on top of her head, several strands had fallen free and now clung to her damp neck.

Forcing his gaze away from temptation, Ian took a towel from the linen closet. He swallowed with major difficulty, his body growing harder with each passing second, and turned back to her. Something in his peripheral vision drew him up short, pulling his attention to the floor. Nicole's discarded clothing lay at the foot of the tub, a ruby-red bra with matching panties topped the pile like a ripe cherry. Instantly, the vision of Nicole wearing those wicked undergarments played before his eyes. Full, rock-hard arousal tightened his loins.

Nicole suddenly sat up and wrapped her arms around her bent knees, but not before Ian got a gut-wrenching view of her breasts, water and bubbles sliding over their fullness. His hardened length twitched with urgency. Nicole nodded toward the washcloth hanging on the side of the tub.

"Would you mind washing my back?" She laid her cheek against her knees and closed her eyes.

Ian's hungry gaze roved over every delicious rise and hollow. The firm curves of her legs; the swell of her breast where it was pressed against her thigh; the exquisite detail of her spine; the lovely length of her neck.

"Please," she urged when Ian didn't move fast enough.

Unable to dredge up a verbal response, he knelt next to the tub and picked up the damp washcloth with his left hand. He dipped it into the warm water and then slowly caressed the smooth skin of her back. His right hand fisted into the soft terry cloth of the towel.

"Hmmmmm," she moaned, "that feels nice."

Fire flashed through Ian's veins, heating him from the inside out. He couldn't take much more of this. Again and again he traced that soft, creamy terrain until he felt ready to explode. Nicole straightened and looked directly into his eyes. Ian saw the same need in those azure pools as was roaring through him. A muscle jerked in his tense jaw when his gaze traveled down to her nearly exposed breasts, then back. He wanted to kiss her...to touch her, but it would never stop there. Ian was well past holding back.

"Thank you," she murmured, her gaze examining his lips before moving back to his eyes.

"You're welcome," he said tightly.

"The towel?"

Ian lifted the towel he still clutched in his right hand toward her. Before he realized what she intended, Nicole took the towel from him and stood. Ian blinked, twice. He pushed to his feet, trying his level best to ignore her naked body as she smoothed the towel over her skin.

"Anything else?" he asked, his control a single frayed thread away from snapping.

"Actually, there is one thing." Nicole wrapped the towel around her, tucking the end between her breasts. She stepped out onto the polished wood floor directly in front of Ian.

Ian waited, his body pulsing with need.

She smiled sweetly. "Would you pour me a glass of wine? I'm suddenly very thirsty."

Ian looked away and licked his parched lips. "Sure."

Nicole closed her eyes until Ian had disappeared from her line of vision. She shivered with the need vibrating inside her. How would she ever be able to see this through? She gave herself a mental shake. She had to do it. One way or another, she had to get out from under Ian's watchful gaze. The bastard she wanted would never show with Ian so close. And if he did, Ian's life would be in serious jeopardy. Firming her resolve, Nicole dropped the towel to the floor and quickly pulled on her red undies. The realization of just how much she affected Ian made her giddy with excitement. But there was no time to dwell on that right now. She had to move swiftly. If Ian suspected her motives for one instant, the game would be over before it began. Nicole shouldered into one of Ian's flannel, button-up shirts. She left the top three buttons undone and squared her shoulders, then smiled. This would do just fine.

After checking her reflection in the mirror, Nicole padded into the great room. Ian filled the second of two glasses and placed the wine bottle on the table. He turned to greet her, glass of wine in hand. Nicole almost sighed out loud. She could spend the rest of her life just looking at him like this. His gaze so intent on her, a smoldering fire turning those silvery orbs to a darker gunmetal gray. The scene almost made her falter. Sharing a glass of wine after a long day at work. Making love until an exhausted sleep overtook them. A yearning so fierce rose in Nicole that her breath caught.

This, she reminded that silly part of her that wanted to dream, was all she and Ian would ever share. A few days alone before they took down the hit man stalking her, or, she admitted, before he took one or both of them down. Nothing with Ian was permanent. They had no future. Nicole blinked back the tears that burned behind her lids. She sucked in a harsh breath and forced her feet to take her all the way to his side.

"Thank you," she managed without her voice quaking. Nicole sipped the sweet wine, then emptied the glass. "Another, please."

Ian frowned a bit, but didn't argue. Those incredible hands merely set to the task, the long fingers of one hand cradling the bottle of wine, the other holding the slender stem of Nicole's glass. Her gaze made a path up his arm to his broad shoulders, then to the face that stole the breath she had only just regained. Ian Michaels was devastatingly handsome, completely honorable and totally selfless.

And Nicole would never, ever recover from the destruction to her heart.

She accepted the refilled glass and walked to the bed. She placed her drink on the night table and crouched down to pull one of the plastic containers from beneath the bed. She angled the chocolates on the table in front of her wine, then prowled through the container until she found what she was looking for. She hid the item she would need most behind the chocolates, then reached back into the container for the body oil. Strawberries and champagne. Nicole smiled when she considered that Ian was likely watching her every move. She pushed the box of wicked toys out of the way and climbed onto the bed. With painstaking slowness and thoroughness, Nicole massaged the scented oil into her skin. Her right leg was first, her foot included. Nicole stretched it this way and that until she had given full attention to every square inch. Then she gave the same treatment to the left.

When Nicole stole a glance in Ian's direction from beneath her lids, he was standing stock-still by the table, his empty glass still clutched in his hand. Time to turn up the heat, she decided. Nicole dropped her feet back onto the floor and stood, her back to Ian. She unbuttoned the shirt and shrugged it off, allowing it to drop to the floor. With the same ambition, she rubbed the oil on first one arm and then the other. The scent was fabulous. Nicole closed her eyes and inhaled deeply. She moaned her approval. How could anyone resist this tantalizing fragrance?

"What are you doing, Nicole?"

Nicole shivered. He was right behind her. Her eyes opened. She bit back a little smile of triumph. "I'm bored, Ian," she said languidly. She turned to face him. His eyes immediately moved over her body, heating her skin as if he were touching her. "There's nothing else to do but talk and I don't want to talk," she added nonchalantly. His analyzing gaze riveted to hers, Nicole took the opportunity to smooth her oil-covered hand over her chest, then the part of her breasts exposed above the red satin. His gaze traced her every move. Nicole inhaled deeply and released it on an exaggerated sigh of contentment. "This feels really nice. Would you like to try it?"

"Don't play games with me," Ian warned in a distinctly tight voice.

Nicole allowed him a teasing smile. "Games can be fun, Ian." She thrust the oil into his hand and climbed back onto the bed. "Here," she instructed from her prone position, "do my back." Several tense seconds clicked by while Ian's gaze traveled the length of her. From her vantage point, there was no way to miss just how she was affecting Ian. The thick bulge of his arousal made her feminine muscles tighten, sending a tingle through her.

Ian's gaze connected with hers and Nicole's heart thudded in her chest at the sheer heat she saw there. But she didn't miss the rhythmic flexing of the tiny muscle in his tense jaw. He was fighting rather than yielding to the desire so obviously burning inside him.

Nicole scrambled to her knees then and moved to the edge of the bed, within easy reach of him. She hadn't gone this far to give up without a fight of her own. She reached up and undid her hair, allowing it to slip down around her shoulders. Nicole pitched the pins in the general direction of the bedside table. She snagged Ian's hand in hers and tugged. He resisted at first, but then allowed her to pull him a step closer to the bed. Nicole moistened her lips in one long, languid stroke, then pressed a tiny kiss to his lips. "Don't make me beg, Ian," she murmured, her eyes searching his, urging him to react.

Surrender flared in those silvery depths, the oil dropped to the floor. Ian cupped her face in his hands and pulled her mouth up to his. His kiss was brutal, relentless and unmercifully hot. Too many feelings to name rushed through Nicole, all focusing on her center, making her wet and hot and needy. Her hands went to his chest and found their way under his sweater. The feel of his muscled body beneath her fingers almost undid her completely. Nicole drew back, but Ian stole another taste of her mouth before she escaped his reach. She tugged his sweater up and over his head, then tossed it to the floor. She couldn't prevent the smile of approval when she surveyed his tousled hair and amazing chest. He no longer wore the bandage on his shoulder. The wound was healing nicely. A reminder of how close she had come to losing him. She would make sure that didn't happen again. Nicole encircled his waist, removed his gun, and placed it in the container on the floor next to the bedside table.

Ian pulled her hard against him and lowered her to the bed. His weight covered her, making her weak with want. Not until he had trapped her fully between his powerful thighs did Ian lower his mouth to hers once more. His taste filled her, tempted her beyond all reason. Nicole fought to hold onto her sanity. Slowly, thoroughly, he kissed her as no one else ever had, and it went on forever. Taking a moment to catch his breath, he nibbled her lower lip. Nicole whimpered as he moved lower still, down the column of her throat. Each tender kiss took him closer and closer to the pebbled peaks begging for his attention. He exposed one taut nipple. Nicole's fingers fisted in the smooth sheets beneath her. Ian's wine-kissed breath rushed over her breast, sending another wave of intense desire to her core. He licked and taunted with the tip of his tongue, again and again, before he took that wanting peak into his mouth and sucked. Nicole writhed beneath him, the feel of denim against her skin only adding to the delicious friction.

She had to stop him, regain control before she lost it completely. Nicole placed the heels of her hands against his shoulders and forced his tempting mouth from her body. His breath ragged, his eyes fierce, he looked to Nicole for an explanation of why he had to stop. She summoned her most alluring smile. "I want to be on top," she whispered, then rubbed her knee along the inside of his thigh. Ian rolled over, pulling her onto his waist. Nicole pressed her heat against his arousal to show her approval. Ian groaned and closed his eyes with the same agony she felt.

Nicole blinked away the image of how he looked beneath her. Dark, dangerous and completely at her mercy. She had to get a grip on the situation. Ensuring that her body grazed his, she reached for the oil, then settled astride his lean hips. Nicole pulled his hands from her thighs and placed them above his head. She leaned down to nip at his lips, allowing that dark stubble to tease her skin. He tried to capture her mouth, but she was too fast for him.

"Hold on right here," she murmured as she guided his hands to the spindles of the brass headboard. When he obeyed her command, Nicole rewarded him with several long, undulating strokes of her heat along the length of his arousal. Each languid move propelled her closer and closer to release. She squeezed him with her thighs, making him groan savagely with pleasure. Nicole massaged the scented oil onto his chest, tasting every now and then, paying particular attention to the ruddy peaks of his male nipples. Ian lifted against her, and Nicole closed her eyes to fight the almost overwhelming need to take him inside her. Her feminine muscles clenched and throbbed. She was so wet, the thin panel of silk between her thighs was drenched with the evidence of her desire. She had to finish this now, or she would never be able to stop. Nicole planted a trail of slow, hot kisses to his navel. She hesitated there, laving that part of his body with special attention. Ian stiffened, then relaxed. He was on the verge. Any second now, he would be beyond stopping. He would simply roll Nicole over and bury himself inside her, and she would be too far gone to stop him. She wanted him…badly.

When Nicole unbuttoned his fly and flicked her tongue there, he jerked. She slowly slid his zipper down, then pushed her hands between the denim and smooth silk of his navy blue boxers. He made a strained sound and his hands tightened on the brass spindles. His muscles flexed, making Nicole's heart flutter beneath her sternum. She tamped down the urge to reach up and glide her hands over all that taunt muscle. She eased back, pushed his jeans off his hips as he obediently lifted them from the bed. Nicole removed his shoes and socks, tossed them aside, then tugged his jeans the rest of the way off. They landed on the floor atop his shoes.

He was very hard. The thick ridge of his arousal beneath the dark silk made Nicole ache with the need to be filled by him. She crawled on her hands and knees up the length of his body, pausing to torment his sensitive navel once more. She was pushing him ever closer to the edge, she knew, but she just couldn't stop herself. Ian's hands went around her arms and he pulled her up to him. Nicole's heart froze. Too late. His breath was hot on her lips. His eyes were frantic.

"This is your last chance to stop, Nicole," he rasped, that soft accent thick with his desire. "If you're having second thoughts…" His eyes searched hers as his words trailed off.

Nicole swallowed, then essayed a mischievous smile. "This is my show, Michaels." She pulled free of his grasp and pushed his hands back above his head. "We do this my way." Nicole closed her eyes in ecstasy as she ground the throbbing heat between her thighs into his arousal one more time for good measure. With nothing but the thin layers of silk between them, pleasure screamed through her. "I promise it will be like nothing you've ever experienced," she said tautly.

Ian's answering groan was all that Nicole needed to hear. She opened her eyes to find his closed tight. His hips moved restlessly beneath her. He was ready, she decided. Leaning down to suck hard on his right nipple, Nicole used the distraction to reach behind the chocolates and retrieve the item she had hidden there. She moved to the left nipple, nibbling with her teeth, then sucking hard. Before the movements of her hands penetrated Ian's haze of lust, Nicole had the handcuffs around his left wrist and one metal spindle about midway on the headboard, effectively shackling him to the bed. Frowning, Ian reached for her with his free hand. Nicole scrambled backwards out of his reach.

Fury flashed in his eyes, devouring all signs of desire. He jerked against his restraint. "Give me the key," he said in a tone just shy of lethal.

Nicole flipped her hair over her shoulders. "All right, all right. Don't get all bent out of shape, Ian, it was just a thought. I'll find the key." Nicole climbed off the bed. Her heart pounding so hard she felt certain he could hear it, she knelt by the box and dug for the key. When she had it in her hands, she shoved the container, Ian's gun still in it, beneath the bed. She stood quickly, and took two steps back.

Ian sat up straighter in the bed. He shook his head slowly from side to side. Nicole felt certain that she had never seen, nor would she ever again see, a look quite that dark, that intent. She swallowed. Ian just might not forgive her for this. Just one more thing for him to hold against her. But she had to do it.

She backed all the way to the dining table. "I'll leave the key right here," she told him with as much bravado as possible. "I'm doing the right thing, Ian," she said when he didn't respond. "It's the only way. Nicole jerked on a pair of jeans and the discarded shirt as swiftly as possible, her gaze darting back to Ian every few seconds. He said nothing, he simply stared at her with a kind of disappointment and disapproval that stabbed at her heart. She tugged on her socks and boots, and made quick work of tying them. Nicole tucked her Beretta into her waistband at the small of her back and shouldered into her denim jacket. She snatched up the keys to the Range Rover and turned back to Ian. He hadn't said a word.

"It'll be better if I do this alone," she told him. "He's not going to approach me as long as you're around." Nicole closed her eyes for a moment to dispel the image of him sprawled across the bed, almost naked, and completely at her mercy. Finally, she opened her eyes and faced the inevitable.

"I'm sorry," she stammered. "It's the only way." Nicole whirled and rushed toward the door.

"Nicole."

She turned around slowly, reluctantly. She winced inside when she met the arctic chill in his eyes. She lifted her chin and held that icy gaze. "Yeah?" she asked.

"It will take me approximately fifteen minutes to dismantle this bed, drag the headboard across the room and reach the key." His tone was stone-cold. "Five minutes after that I'll be out the door. I'll find you within twenty-four hours, and then," he paused, giving her time to absorb the impact of his words, "you will regret this."

Nicole grabbed her purse and rushed out the door without looking back. She had twenty minutes. She climbed behind the wheel of the SUV and started the engine. She had to get out of here.

Ian Michaels never made idle threats.

Chapter Nine

Removing the first rail from the headboard proved the most awkward. Once that was accomplished, the rest was easy. Ian pushed the mattress and box spring away from the headboard as far as he could with the other rail still in place. A couple of minutes later the headboard was completely disconnected from the rest of the bed. He didn't take time to analyze the fact that he had once again permitted Nicole to get the upper hand while he was lost in the lust he should never have allowed in the first place. He could kick himself for that later. Right now he had to catch up with Nicole. He clenched his jaw to hold back the string of curses poised on the tip of his tongue. That would do no good, he didn't have time to waste stewing over his mistake.

He had to find Nicole.

Before anyone else did.

Ian snatched the key to the handcuffs off the table and liberated his hand from the brass spindle. He tossed the key onto the table and shook his head at his own gullibility. He was a first-class fool. And now Nicole was in danger and she was too damned hardheaded to see her error. His fury growing with each step, Ian carried the headboard back to the bed and pitched it, rattling handcuff and all, onto the mattress. If

George dropped by unexpectedly this evening, he probably wouldn't be too pleased about the mess. Nicole could explain the circumstances to him...

If she didn't get herself killed first.

Ian jerked on his jeans, adjusted the throbbing arousal she'd left him with, then pulled on his sweater. Her scent lingered on his skin, making him ache for her all the more. Gritting his teeth against the desire still humming in his body, he fished his gun from beneath the crippled bed. He tugged on his hiking boots and quickly laced them. Combing the fingers of his right hand through his hair, he glanced at his watch. Fifteen minutes. A hint of a smile twitched his lips. Five minutes earlier than he had anticipated. Ian pulled on his jacket on his way out the door. It was nearing dusk now. The sky was clear and the moon was full, that was good. If he hurried and maintained a steady pace, he would reach town in an hour, an hour and fifteen minutes tops. He needed a telephone. His cell phone was in Nicole's bag. Another mistake. He never suffered those kinds of lapses in judgment.

Only with Nicole.

When he reached town, it would take only one call to Alex and Nicole wouldn't get far in the SUV. The state police would stop her before she got across the line. But, knowing Nicole, Ian thought ruefully as he jogged down the driveway and out onto the paved road, she would dump the SUV somewhere in town and rent—or *borrow*—another vehicle to make her escape clean.

The thought that she might not make it into town tightened the knot of dread growing in his gut. If they were being watched as Ian suspected, the predator would already be tailing his prey, moving in for the kill.

Unfortunately, that was exactly what Nicole wanted. She

intended to force the issue—force a confrontation. And to keep him out of it. Ian swore as he scanned the darkness falling swiftly around him, then the low-hung moon.

He hoped he wasn't too late already.

NICOLE DROVE as fast as she dared down the curvy mountain road. A plan had already formed in her mind. She would ditch the SUV near the sporting goods store and check into a room at the lodge where George was staying. Ian would think she had hitched a ride out of town. To increase the odds in her favor, maybe Nicole would give George a call and tell him that she had found a ride back to Charlottesville and that she intended to fly back to D.C. Ian would no doubt contact George the moment he made it into town. That little ploy would throw Ian offtrack and keep him busy for a few hours at least. In the meantime, Nicole would hang out in the local diner or the pub and see if she could attract herself a guy with a *dynamite* personality.

The vehicle suddenly jerked as if the engine might die. Nicole frowned and quickly checked the gauges. All registered normal—except the gas gauge.

Empty.

Nicole swore under her breath.

Another jerk, sputter, and the engine died completely. The steeply inclining road was all that kept the vehicle moving then. Nicole wrestled with the steering wheel until she had navigated the next curve and could pull the SUV off the road onto a stretch of narrow shoulder that looked the least treacherous.

"Damn," she muttered shakily. She needed to get a grip here. She forced the image of Ian and his final words out of her mind. Nicole tried the ignition again, just in case the gauge was wrong. It wouldn't start. She banged her fist against the steering wheel and surveyed the dense woods on either side of her. Several more miles of deserted road cut through the terrain before her, curving like a snake between the thick woods and flowing ever downward. This was a hell of a mess, she mused with a disgusted huff of resignation. Her fail-safe plan hadn't been so safe after all. Ian would laugh his head off when he found her stranded halfway down the mountain. Well, he might laugh after he had finished with her. Revenge would be his first order of business. Why hadn't she noticed the gauges when she started the damned vehicle in the first place? When had they got fuel last? Not since that first day, she remembered. Ian had filled the tank the day they arrived in Town Creek. But they hadn't gone anywhere, except into town that once. Surely they hadn't used an entire tank....

The tiny hairs on the back of Nicole's neck suddenly stood on end. They definitely had not used that much gas. No way. She surveyed her seemingly deserted surroundings once more.

He was here.

If not in the immediate vicinity, nearby. Anticipation mushroomed inside her, making her heart beat faster. She had to get out of the open. Nicole slammed the side of her fist hard against the dome light to break the bulb, then opened the car door. She emerged from the vehicle slowly, her gaze scanning constantly. She closed the door behind her with one hip. The burn of adrenaline heightened her senses, made her more alert. It was almost completely dark now, except for the brilliant moon that hung just over the treetops.

The way Nicole saw it, she had two options. She could head back toward the cabin and risk leading the bad guy right to Ian, not to mention she would likely meet Ian on his way down. Nicole shook her head at that thought. Ian was supremely annoyed. She definitely didn't want to see him again until he'd had some time to cool off—maybe not even in this century. On the other hand, she could head into town.

Town, she decided when the vivid mental picture of Ian's furious gaze flashed through her mind. Besides, she wanted the man in the navy blue jacket whose movements tripped some sort of vague memory for her. She wanted him badly. She wanted him to pay for what he had done.

Nicole adjusted the weapon at the small of her back and turned herself in the direction of town. What was five or six miles? she mused. For cover, Nicole decided to walk along the edge of the woods. No point in making herself an easy target. If Ian's theory was true, she would be safe until she gave up Solomon's location, but why take the risk?

She jumped across the narrow, sloping ditch and started for the woods, but a sound behind Nicole froze her in her tracks. She whirled around, instinctively going for her weapon, drawing it and assuming a fire-ready stance. Another burst of adrenaline shot through her. Nicole strained to make out the dark figure standing near the passenger's side of the SUV. In some recess of her brain she reminded herself she hadn't gained the woods just yet, leaving her almost as open a target as the guy standing on the side of the road.

Almost…

…but not quite. The outline of the trees still shadowed her presence.

"Take one more step and you're a dead man," Nicole warned in a loud, firm voice.

"You can't kill a man who's already dead, Agent Reed."

An eerie stillness fell over Nicole. *That voice.* Her heart froze in her chest, but somehow continued to beat, pushing pure ice through her veins. *It couldn't be.* Her mouth opened, worked, but the words she needed would not form on her tongue.

Daniels.

"A little slow on the uptake on this one, huh, Reed?" He moved closer, out of the concealing blackness of the SUV.

"Forensics was conclusive," she heard herself say in a tone so emotionless, so dead calm she barely recognized it as her own.

He laughed, a dry, humorless sound that grated along her nerve endings. "What's one more missing John Doe body? It won't be the first time we've borrowed something no one will ever miss, right, Agent Reed?"

The memory of the conversation she'd had with Ian on this very subject back in her D.C. apartment echoed through her stunned mind. Of course, forensics would be muddled in a case like Daniels's, there was hardly anything left to identify. Hadn't Daniels done the very same thing in Solomon's case? Landon had given the order; Nicole and Daniels had simply carried it out…to the letter.

"Sorry about your apartment," he offered contritely as he took another step down the steep bank. "But you didn't leave me much choice. I had to turn up the heat to prod you into action. But then you came here and holed up with lover boy. I need Solomon, Nicole."

His words snapped Nicole from her disturbing reverie. "What do you want with Solomon?" she demanded, easing back a step. She maintained a steady bead on Daniels. She had to keep reminding herself that this was real. Daniels was alive and the man was trying to get to Solomon—through her.

Another of those cynical laughs shattered the silence.

"Let's just say he has something I want. That's all you need to know."

Ire flowed through Nicole at the implication of his statement. "I can't believe you would stoop to working for the cartel, Daniels. Which one of the scumbags hired you?" she ground out. "Did they pay you extra for taking Landon out, or did you do that one just for the fun of blowing someone up?"

Another couple of feet of tall grass disappeared between them. "Who said anything about the cartel?" Daniels smiled, a sinister gesture that made Nicole shudder inside. "Oh, I see." He ran a hand over his balding head, then down to massage his chin as he studied her with those beady black eyes. "Don't worry, Nicole, you'll be pleased to know that this has nothing at all to do with the cartel."

That habitual movement—stroking his chin. That was part of the mannerism that had caught Nicole's attention in town the day before. Though he'd had his back turned, some small part of her had recognized his body language.

A new kind of calm settled over Nicole as all the pieces fell into place. Daniels knew everything—except the final location of Solomon. He had access to her every move, to Landon. He was one of the best explosives experts in the country. He knew all the tricks of the trade. Cloak-and-dagger games were his favorite kind, she remembered as he moved closer still.

"Stop right there, Daniels," she commanded, warning bells going off inside her head. He was too close. She needed to think. There was no way she was letting Daniels get away with this. No way. But could she shoot a fellow agent, rogue or not, without him drawing his weapon? She tightened her grip on the Beretta and leveled her gaze firmly on his. "I'm taking you in," she told him bluntly. The blood was pounding in her ears, urging the adrenaline through her veins.

Daniels reached behind him and drew his own weapon. The oxygen evaporated in Nicole's lungs. Her finger snugged against the trigger of her weapon. The desire to fire now was a palpable force pounding away at her consciousness. Nicole gritted her teeth against it, resisted the urge. If she killed Daniels now and Ian was right about there being someone else working with him, Nicole might never be completely safe again. Solomon sure as hell wouldn't be. And justice would never be served.

"All I want is Solomon, nothing else," Daniels assured her, holding his palms up in a magnanimous manner. His weapon hung loosely from the fingertips of his right hand in a non-threatening manner, as if he had no intention at all of using it.

Nicole licked her lips and retreated a few more inches. "What does Solomon have that you want?" Daniels wanted something big. Big enough to make him throw away his career at the bureau only five years from his pension, not to mention his complete identity since he was considered dead. She vaguely remembered someone commenting after his supposed death that he'd never been married, had no children. There had been no one left to ask questions, or even to grieve. He had nothing to lose, Nicole realized. Alarm slid down her spine. And everything to gain. Solomon had been the cartel's accountant, which meant he handled their money. He could have even stashed some away for his own future use. He had to know that WITSEC wouldn't support him forever. A little here, a little there, and pretty soon he would have accumulated himself a really nice nest egg. Unless or until he got caught, then he would end up dead.

Or under WITSEC's umbrella in the witness protection program.

Daniels smiled as if he knew Nicole had just realized his motivation. "Enough of the small talk," he announced impatiently. "Let's go, Nicole. My car is only a hundred or so yards back up the road."

Nicole laughed, a choked sound. "I'm not going anywhere with you, you bastard." She moved back another half step.

Daniels shrugged, his weapon still dangling from his fingertips. "Fine. I guess I'll just have to go back and get what I want out of lover boy."

Nicole tensed. Had Daniels gone into the cabin immediately after she had left to find Ian still helpless and unarmed? Before Nicole could shake off the horrifying possibility, Daniels charged at her. He knocked the Beretta from her hand, then slammed into Nicole with the full force of his heavy body. They rolled, Nicole kicked him hard in the shin while struggling to keep the barrel of his weapon away from her. His hot curses shattered the dark silence around them, his strong fingers went around her neck. Panic shot through Nicole but her instinct for survival was greater, she kneed Daniels hard in the groin, then pushed him off her. She scrambled, half crawling, half running in the direction of where her weapon had hit the ground. Daniels was still howling, trying to stagger to his feet. Nicole grabbed her weapon from the grass, rolled to her back and fired. If she killed the son of a bitch, so be it. Daniels hit the dirt low, crawling for cover of his own.

"Come back here, you bitch!" he screamed.

Nicole scrambled to her feet and lunged into the concealing woods before Daniels could get a good bead on her. A shot fired over her head. Damn. She moved faster, more deeply into the woods. She rushed up the steady grade of the mountain, tripping over exposed roots and fallen branches. Underbrush grabbed at her clothing and scratched at her face like gnarled, bony fingers. The steep incline fought her, but Nicole pressed on. She had to get as much distance as possible between the two of them. She forced the images of Landon's dead body, his grieving widow, from her mind. Daniels had done that. Nicole encouraged the anger, allowed it to diminish the lesser emotions clawing at her consciousness. She had to run fast. If Daniels caught her, she would be dead as soon as he extracted Solomon's location from her. Though she was prepared to die before giving up the information, there were ways to break even the toughest and most highly trained agent.

The covering of decay on the forest floor sank here and there beneath her scrambling feet, yanking her back precious inches instead of giving her purchase to propel herself forward. Fear and frustration swelled in her throat, choking her, but Nicole ignored it. Faster and faster she climbed, stumbling forward occasionally on the rugged, steep terrain. Nicole moved faster, the instinct for survival kicking into high gear. She was much younger than Daniels, more physically fit. Daniels called out to her twice before going silent. Her breath raging in and out of her lungs, Nicole dived behind a large boulder and flattened herself against its surface. She listened above the sound of her ragged breathing.

Daniels was good, she had to give him that, but she was better. When her respiration had slowed and she felt certain he was nowhere nearby, she slowly, quietly picked her way deeper into the woods. She couldn't let him catch her. She needed time to think what her next move should be.

If Daniels caught her now she would end up just as dead

as Landon. She had to stay alive to protect Solomon, and to bring Daniels and whoever might be working with him to justice.

And she had to draw the danger away from Ian. She had hurt Ian too badly already. Nicole could not bear the thought of him enduring any further pain because of her.

She loved him too much.

Nicole stilled. Loved him? Yes, she did. But he would never love her. The sad part was, she couldn't really blame him.

IAN SKIDDED to a halt at the sound of gunfire. One shot, then another a few seconds later. His heart hammered wildly in his chest. *Nicole.* Fear, cold and brutal surged through him. Ian pushed forward, running harder. He had to reach her before it was too late. Judging by the sound of the shots, he was close, very close.

He slowed only long enough to see that the dark, nondescript sedan on the side of the road was abandoned, then he ran even harder. A hundred yards later he rounded a sharp curve in the road and spotted the Range Rover.

Ian slowed to a walk when he approached the deserted SUV. He scanned the surrounding darkness, but noticed no movement, heard no sound. Nothing appeared amiss. He hesitated near the Range Rover to look for anything out of place. The driver's door was ajar, the interior light smashed. Nicole had known she was being followed or suspected danger was close. But why stop here? Some sort of malfunction would be the most likely reason. But the vehicle had been running perfectly yesterday. Someone could have tampered with it during the night, he supposed. Ian swallowed back the fear clawing at his throat. He surveyed the woods that seemed to go on forever around him. She had to be here somewhere, but he didn't dare call out to her. If his presence had not been detected as of yet, that was all the better.

The distant sound of a voice, male and gruff, drew Ian's gaze to the woods. The disembodied voice called out Nicole's name a second time. Ian moved slowly in that direction. Nicole was out there, and hot on her heels was the man who had been sent to find Solomon. Somehow Ian had to get between them. Head off the danger. He focused on slowing his breathing and calming his heart rate while blocking all else from his mind. He had to concentrate, focus on his goal. Sound was his enemy now. The ground was covered with fallen and decaying leaves, twigs and branches. The brush was thick, making the going difficult. Slowly, silently, Ian stole his way through nature's maze. He paused to listen frequently, assessing even the vaguest of noises, watching for movement in the shadows.

Nicole couldn't be far, nor her pursuer. That thought propelled Ian forward, pushing him faster, risking the possibility of making some attention-drawing sound. If he couldn't get between the two of them, his only option would be to draw the man's attention.

Anything to protect Nicole.

Chapter Ten

The minutes ticked by, each second punctuated by the beating of Ian's heart. The fear for Nicole's safety and the run from the cabin had caused Ian's fury with Nicole to abate. Later, when she was safely in his care once more, he would make good on his warning. For now, his every sensory perception was sharply focused on his surroundings. Each nocturnal sound was carefully analyzed and utilized either to avoid an area or to head in that direction. Ian moved steadily, discovering the occasional broken branch or disturbed cluster of leaves to indicate someone's passage shortly before him.

An hour crept by before Ian felt confident that Nicole had indeed outmaneuvered her pursuer. He smiled in spite of his irritation with her when he considered just how damned good Nicole was...in too many ways to list at the moment. And when he caught up with her, he was going to teach her a lesson she wouldn't forget. Ian blended into a stand of trees and paused to allow the sounds, however remote, to saturate his senses. With Nicole apparently safe, he intended to concentrate on overtaking her shadow. And when Ian got his hands on the bastard, he would regret every moment of anguish he had caused Nicole. Ian knew ways to inflict pain, physical as well as mental, that made even him cringe. He intended to use every single technique in his extensive repertoire.

A twig snapped, jerking Ian to full attention. Twenty-five or thirty yards to his right, he estimated. Slowly, making sure to keep himself camouflaged by the trees, Ian moved in that direction. He was close now. Very close. Anticipation flowed swiftly through him. Leaves rustled, slightly farther away. Nicole's shadow was moving back down the mountain. Had he given up so soon?

Ian frowned. Instinct warned that this was just another ploy of some sort. The man had been entirely too relentless, had taken too many extreme measures, to simply call it a night when he couldn't track Nicole down as quickly as he had hoped. No, Ian determined, the bastard was doubling back. Another smile tugged at Ian's mouth when realization dawned. The man knew Ian was here, and he had decided that he would take Ian if he couldn't have Nicole. Well, Ian mused, he would just see how good this guy was at cat and mouse.

Soundlessly, Ian moved in the direction of his pursuer. He waited and listened. The other guy moved more quickly now. Time to throw him off course. Ian picked up a piece of decaying wood about the size of a shoe and pitched it to his left as far as he could. It rustled a few leaves then plunked to the ground. Silence ruled for the next ten seconds. Then the brushing of a branch against nylon fabric, the crinkle of leaves beneath the weight of a footfall. He had taken the bait. Ian moved with great care and as much stealth as possible in that same direction. His pulse jerked into high speed. He could almost smell the confrontation.

Snap. Ian froze. A small twig hidden beneath the leaves had broken under his right foot. Another snap directly in front of him…only a few feet away. Ian raised his weapon into position. A glint of something shiny in the moonlight caught his eye a split second before he heard the distinct click of the safety being disengaged on a weapon. Nicole's Beretta was solid black, no chrome. His breath stilled in his chest and he remained absolutely still. Waiting for the next move.

Ian whipped to the right ten degrees and prepared to fire. The glittering chrome barrel of a nine-millimeter leveled a bead right between his eyes. The man stood no more than ten feet away. He was shorter and stockier than Ian. A swiftly receding hairline and dark eyes stared back at Ian from a pale complexion that looked even paler against the dark jacket he wore. He didn't look the least bit happy. And that fact gave Ian a great deal of pleasure. While Ian watched, the man moved two steps closer, into a small moonlit clearing. Ian moved into the clearing as well, his gaze never leaving the other man's.

"Well, well," the man said, irony in his tone, "looks like the night might not be a total loss after all."

Ian lifted a skeptical brow. "I don't know," he mused. "From where I'm standing, it looks as though you've lost out all the way around."

A sly grin slid across the man's pudgy features. "Oh, I think Nicole will be more than happy to do business with me now. She seems to have a soft spot when it comes to you. I'm sure she'll want you back in working order."

Ian tightened his grip on his weapon. "I'm relatively certain she doesn't have any tender feelings at all when it comes to you," he said offhandedly. "So you don't mind if we cut to the chase and I simply shoot you now, do you?"

Anger flashed in the man's wide gaze. The low-slung full moon provided ample light for Ian to watch the changing expressions on his indignant face. The man might be annoyed, but he understood the situation perfectly. Without Nicole, he would never find Solomon. Right now, Ian was the only bargaining chip he had. It was not likely that he would do anything foolish, such as shoot Ian where he stood.

"What's to keep me from killing you first?" he demanded heatedly. "You haven't got anything I need."

Ian cocked his head and eyed him speculatively. "Are you certain of that? Nicole and I have discussed a great many things in the past few days, including the Solomon case."

The man snickered. "Don't try to fool me, Marshal—or should I say ex-Marshal? Nicole wouldn't give you Solomon's location. She's only using you, Michaels, just like she did three years ago."

Ian's anger flared. He didn't need to be reminded of what Nicole had done. He knew all too well. He gritted his teeth against the almost overwhelming urge to kill the bastard where he stood. But he couldn't do that...not yet. "Perhaps," Ian allowed tightly. "But it was me she came to, and I haven't let her down yet."

Another disgusting chuckle. "But she gave you the slip, didn't she? Never let it be said that Nicole Reed is anything less than one fine piece of work. When I get the information I want from her, maybe I'll give her a go myself."

Ian suppressed the reaction that burned in his chest. He blinked to clear the desire to destroy from his eyes. The man was baiting him. But Ian would pick the time to retaliate and it wasn't now. "Your agenda is none of my concern," Ian said calmly. "I have my own plan."

Some of the cockiness drained from the man then. "What plan?" he snapped.

"I didn't get your name," Ian said, ignoring his question.

The man grinned widely. "Daniels," he offered as if the knowledge was a trophy. "Agent Daniels, formerly of the Federal Bureau of Investigation."

Daniels. So Ian had been right. It *was* an inside job. And Daniels had faked his own death to cover himself. "Bravo, Agent Daniels," Ian allowed without enthusiasm. "You're smarter than Nicole thought."

Daniels's grin died an instant death. "Too bad I can't say the same for you. You didn't have a clue that Nicole was working you like a puppet on a string."

Ian smiled. "Not a one," he agreed. "But who's working whom this time?" he suggested.

Daniels nodded as realization dawned. "Makes no difference to me what you two are up to, I just want Solomon."

"Take a number," Ian returned. "You're not the only one who wants Solomon."

Daniels shook his head slowly from side to side. "You don't know squat about Solomon, Mr. Fancy-pants-P.I."

"You think I don't know about the money?" Ian was fishing now, though he was certain it was about money. The only thing he didn't know for sure was whose money and how Solomon had managed to get his hands on it.

A pallor slid over Daniels's features. "You can't know about that. Nobody knew about the money Solomon stole from the cartel but Landon. Not even Nicole knew about that," he argued hotly. "I saved Solomon's sorry ass, gave him a new start, the least he can do is pay up."

"Nicole knows more than you suspect, Daniels," Ian assured him. "Why do you think she replanted Solomon in the first place? She wanted him all to herself. In her mind, she was just as instrumental in saving his life as you."

Daniels's face darkened, a sharp contrast to the previous

paleness. He was irate now. "That bitch had better keep her hands off my money. I didn't kill Landon and give up everything for nothing. We have plans for that money and nobody is going to take it away from us."

Ian gave himself a mental pat on the back for scoring right on the mark. Daniels did have a partner. Now it would only be a matter of finding out who. "I wouldn't be so sure about that, Nicole has a few plans of her own," Ian said evenly.

"Screw Nicole!" Daniels roared. "She gets nothing but a bullet between the eyes. If you're stupid enough to go along with her, you'll get the same thing."

"Do I shoot first, or do you?" Ian asked casually. He steadied his gaze down the length of his weapon's barrel. "Nicole will get it all if we kill each other right now."

Daniels glared at Ian from behind his own weapon for five long, tense seconds. "We could strike a mutually satisfying deal," he proposed hesitantly.

"I'm listening," Ian replied as if he didn't care one way or the other.

"You give me Solomon's location, and I'll give you a third of the money."

"Half," Ian countered.

His jaw clenched, Daniels shook with fury. "I told you I'm not in this alone," he growled. "Including you, there's three of us, we cut it three ways."

Ian shrugged. "I'll have to think about that."

"You have ten seconds, then I shoot," Daniels warned.

Ian smiled. "Why wait ten seconds?" He angled his head slightly as if taking aim.

"Wait!" Daniels bellowed. "All right, all right! Fifty-fifty then."

"Think about it," Ian interjected. "Without Solomon you get nothing. I can produce Solomon."

"What about Nicole?" Daniels ground out.

"What about her?"

"She knows too much," Daniels clarified. "She'll never go along with this, she's a straight shooter."

"I'll take care of Nicole," Ian said coolly.

Daniels smiled again. "I guess you deserve that. After what she did to you, I don't blame you. I just want the pleasure of watching." His face twisted with the implication. "If it wasn't for her, I'd already have that money. She's been nothing but trouble."

"I'll contact you," Ian told him in a dismissing tone. "Call my office and leave a number."

"Don't try to double-cross me, Michaels," Daniels warned. "I'm not a patient man. You mess with me and I'll kill you." He smirked as if he had just remembered some significant point. "Remember, I'm dead. I've got nothing to lose."

"I'm sure your partner would appreciate your staying alive until he has his cut of the money," Ian reminded.

Daniels backed up a step, his weapon still carefully aimed on Ian's forehead. "My partner isn't worried," he said cryptically. "Can you say the same about yours?"

Ian silently watched as Daniels cautiously backed into the enveloping darkness of the dense forest. The man was one sick bastard. Ian had every intention of seeing that he got his, and his partner as well. Ian would follow Daniels, just to make sure he left as he had said he would. Only a fool would trust a man like Daniels to stick to his word. Once he had ensured that Daniels was out of here, then the real task would loom before him.

Ian had to convince Nicole to go along with this plan. She

wouldn't like it. Nicole wanted Solomon, the scumbag, protected at all costs. But somehow Ian would convince her to ignore her instincts and trust him on this one.

But first he had to find her.

And when he did, this time he would have his revenge. Remembered desire stabbed at his groin, arousing him instantly to the point of pain. Ian backed into the shrouding darkness of the nearby trees, then slowly lowered his weapon and tucked it into his waistband at the small of his back.

Tonight Nicole would learn that for every action there was an equal reaction. For three years the need to settle this score had seethed inside him.

After tonight they would be even.

NICOLE RELEASED a long, slow breath. She closed her eyes and thanked God she had finally given Daniels the slip. It had been more than fifteen minutes since she had heard any sound behind her. He was obviously lost, or maybe he had given up. She pressed her forehead against the tree trunk next to her and forced away the too-vivid images of Landon and his office...of her rental car and her apartment building. She was tired and cold. For one long moment she wished she *had* killed Daniels, but her shot had been blind, an effort to divert attention from her mad dash into the woods. It had worked, just barely.

Ian.

She had no way of knowing if Ian was safe. Her stomach twisted into a thousand screaming knots of agony when she considered that if he were okay he would have been here by now. She had to make her way back down to the road, and then to the cabin. She had to know. He might need her help. Pain sliced clear through to her heart when she considered that he might be hurt or worse.

And it would be her fault.

She had left him totally defenseless. Stupid. Stupid. And for what? Sure, she knew who the bad guy was now—or at least who one of them was. But what price had she paid? Why hadn't she considered that she was putting Ian in danger with her stupid ploy? Why didn't she think? She had known that they were being watched. She should have been more careful.

Just like three years ago…she didn't think.

And look at the price she'd had to pay.

Ian would never forgive her.

The cold hard muzzle of a weapon suddenly nudged the back of her skull. Alarm surged through Nicole's body, she stiffened. Fear tightened around her neck like a noose. A hand closed around the grip of the weapon beneath her jacket, knuckles brushed her lower back as he withdrew the piece. Nicole shivered and cursed herself for being distracted. She should have heard his approach. She knew better than to let her guard down like this. There was no excuse. She blinked back the tears of frustration gathering in the corners of her eyes. She would not cry. Nicole set her jaw hard. Let the scumbag kill her. She would never give up Solomon's location. Whatever Solomon had that Daniels wanted, as far as Nicole was concerned, he would never get his hands on it. She heard her weapon hit the ground somewhere behind her and to her left.

The cold steel pressed harder into the base of her skull, igniting her fury. Reluctantly she raised her hands in surrender. Did he want her submissive?

"You can rot in hell, Daniels," she spat. "I'll never give up Solomon's location."

His continued silence rattled Nicole more than if he had

ranted at her. He urged her forward against the tree. The bark felt rough against her face. The tip of the muzzle bored into her skull. Her heart slammed mercilessly, urging full-fledged panic. Her mind raced, grasping at fragments, but unable to hold on to anything long enough to form a coherent thought. She had to do something…had to run. Where was Ian? Her chest rose and fell with the breath storming in and out of her lungs. What would Daniels do with her now? Was he going to tie her up? Force her to his car?

"I'm not going to make this easy," she warned. Nicole could hear the fear in her voice. Dammit. She was trained better than this. Fight, she commanded. Her body froze, refused to respond. She was dead. He was going to kill her. She would never see Ian again. Nicole swallowed against the cold hard lump in her throat. A single tear slid down her cheek. And for what? A piece of garbage like Solomon. Her job…

Strong fingers fisted in the collar of her denim jacket and yanked it down and off her shoulders. Nicole jerked her hands free, frightened of being restrained in any manner. She shuddered inwardly. He probably intended to tie her hands with the jacket. She gritted her teeth when another tear fell. She hated to cry. Especially at the hands of a creep like Daniels. He reached around her, grabbed her shirtfront and ripped it open and down her shoulders. Buttons pinged through the air. Hysteria blurred Nicole's vision, made her head spin. *No!* She struggled, but he only pushed the weapon more firmly against her, a lethal reminder of what she had to lose.

"Don't do this," she choked out, the tears clogging her throat.

He moved closer, not quite touching her. Nicole licked her lips and tried to control the tremors racking her body. Just let him try what he had in mind, she resolved. It would be the biggest mistake of his screwed-up life. All it would take was one moment of distraction and she would make a move he would not soon forget.

She could feel his breath on her skin. His face was so close to her hair. The gun still firmly against her. She closed her eyes tightly and tried to draw away from him, but the tree stopped her, its bark rough against her bare skin.

"I swear," she managed, absolute hatred in her tone, "I'll kill you if you do this." Fear pumped through her veins so fast her heart felt ready to burst.

"Payback's a bitch, don't you think, Nicole?" he murmured against her ear in a softly accented voice that hummed with simmering anger.

Ian. Relief shuddered through Nicole, making her legs go boneless beneath her. The pressure from the cold steel muzzle eased instantly. Thank God. It was Ian. He had come to rescue her. He was safe.

And he was madder than hell.

Nicole tensed. "It was Daniels," she offered in hopes of disarming his temper. "It was him all along."

"I know, but I don't want to talk right now," he said furiously, his words clipped, rich with that European blend of accents.

Nicole swiped the moisture from her cheek with one shaky hand. Her skin was slightly chafed from the encounter with the tree bark. She drew in a steadying breath. He was really angry. And she deserved it.

"I thought it was the right thing to do," she murmured contritely. He would never believe her. Why should he? She had never done anything on the up and up where he was concerned.

"Turn around," he ordered tightly.

Nicole moistened her lips and slowly turned to face him. Savage determination glittered in those silvery depths. Nicole felt her heart start pumping wildly again. But this time it was different. The fear, the excitement was different…

"Remove your shoes."

His fierce gaze never deviated from hers. Nicole lifted one knee to her chest and unlaced her hiking boot, tugged it off, then repeated the process on the other foot. She rolled each sock off and tossed it onto the discarded boots. She stood then, waiting for his next instruction. The sliver of moonlight that cut through the canopy of branches cast a surreal glow over his handsome face, leaving devastating angles and shadows. She shivered visibly, then caught herself. She would not give him the satisfaction of knowing how deeply he affected her.

Not yet.

"Now the jeans," he instructed with just the right touch of danger and sensuality.

Nicole's breasts tingled beneath the satin encasing them. She could feel her nipples budding, yearning for his touch. Moisture pooled between her thighs. Need shuddered through her so fiercely that she thought she might not be able to stand long enough to take her jeans off. She released the button, then slowly eased the zipper down. Ian watched her every move, his gaze carefully controlled, giving nothing away. Nicole pushed the denim over her hips slowly, very slowly. Down her thighs, off one foot and then the other. The jeans joined the socks and shoes. She straightened, wearing nothing but those red panties and the matching red satin bra.

Ian surveyed her body thoroughly. Nicole's skin heated wherever his gaze touched her. Warmth welled inside her when she saw that little muscle tic in his tense jaw.

Nicole waited until his gaze connected with hers again, then she licked her lips and asked, "What do you want me to do next?" Her voice was deeper than usual, sultry, sexy she hardly recognized it as her own.

Ian stepped closer then. He shrugged off one shoulder of his jacket, placed his gun in the other hand and shouldered the rest of the way out of the jacket. He pitched it to the ground and turned his attention back to her. Desire zipped through Nicole as she anticipated his naked body. But her hopes were not to be realized.

One more step disappeared between them, her pulse reacted. "Put your hands above your head," he said quietly as if he had done nothing more than relate the time of day.

Nicole obediently placed her hands above her head. Her heart was racing now, her body literally throbbing with anticipation. Ian placed his weapon on the ground beside the discarded clothes. He picked up her shirt—his shirt actually. The one she had been wearing when she seduced him. The memory sent another barb of desire stinging through her. Ian stepped directly in front of her then, his body mere centimeters from hers. He reached up and swung the shirt around the tree and then tied it securely, trapping her hands between the soft material and the tree trunk. Nicole's breath caught in her throat when he looked down at her, his lips only an inch or two from hers. He stared at her mouth for what seemed like forever, then backed away. Nicole almost groaned with disappointment. She wanted to taste him, to feel his lips on hers. To feel his body against hers.

"Close your eyes," he commanded, the words nothing more than a whisper.

"Ian, I—" Her breath caught, stealing the rest of her thought. Trepidation tangled with the want twisting inside her. She wanted him in the worst way, but feared the intensity shimmering beneath that controlled exterior.

"Close your eyes," he repeated. His fists clenched at his sides, the only outward display of his own tension.

Nicole closed her eyes, surrendering to his complete domination. She no longer cared what he did to her as long as he made this mounting ache inside her go away.

The tip of one long finger touched her lips. Nicole trembled. He traced her jaw, then the length of her throat and along the strap of her bra until he reached the swell of her breast. He tugged the satin cup down to expose her taut nipple to the cool night air. He circled that peak, rolled it between his thumb and finger. Nicole moaned his name. His hot mouth covered her breast then. She shuddered with the sensations exploding all over her body. He laved her nipple with his tongue, then sucked her hard. She squirmed against her bonds. She wanted to touch him, to hold him against her. He nibbled, licked and kissed his way to her other breast, then gave it the same attention as he had the first. Slowly, methodically, until her whole body writhed beneath his assault, he tortured her.

"Ian," she cried. The rough texture of the bark against her skin heightened her senses, contrasting with the pleasure.

He moved lower, dropping to his knees. His hands worked a magic of their own on her bare skin, touching her in places, behind her knees, the swell of her bottom, making her tingle, making her sweat. His fingers found their way inside the waistband of her panties. Slowly, so very slowly, the wisp of silk slid down her thighs, all the way to her ankles. She lifted first one foot, then the other as he removed them. Nicole imagined the red silk landing on the nearby pile of clothing, but she kept her eyes closed tightly just as he had instructed.

His lips pressed against her mound and a cry wrenched from her throat. Her heart thundered in her chest, she felt certain Ian could hear it. If he didn't finish this soon, she would surely die. But his mouth just kept on moving against her. He spread her legs so far apart that Nicole felt more exposed than she ever had before. His tongue flicked along her feminine channel, once, twice. She shuddered uncontrollably. Deeper, harder, he thrust his hot, wicked tongue into her most intimate place. Nicole tugged harder at her bonds. She had to touch him. She had to see him, but something, some inner force kept her eyes tightly closed. She couldn't look. She could only feel. And every touch of his tongue, every squeeze of her thighs by those skilled fingers was intensified by her inability to see, or to return the touch.

The tightening began so far away that Nicole was sure she would go out of her mind before completion reached her. Ian slipped one long finger inside her, urging her toward that end, his thumb doing something insanely marvelous of its own. Tighter and tighter her muscles clenched around that part of him. He licked her bare skin near her belly button. His free hand squeezed her bottom again and again as that one finger slid in and out of her until that coil of tension quivered, ready to explode.

He stopped then.

Nicole cried out. She opened her eyes, searching frantically for his. He towered over her now, staring into her eyes, his own glowing with fiery desire. She struggled to free herself again, to touch him, to pull him to her. Her body was on fire, throbbing relentlessly for him. She was wet with his touch, and with her own desire.

"Please," she whimpered.

He didn't speak, he just reached up and released her. Her

hands went immediately to his body. She pushed the sweater up, reveling in the feel of his muscled chest, but it wasn't enough. She needed him inside her. *Now.*

She wrenched open the button of his jeans. He stayed her frantic hands, choosing to lower the zipper himself over his hardened length. Nicole shoved his jeans and boxers just low enough to free him. He sprang forth, beautifully hard, deliciously male. Her body convulsed with need when she stroked him with her desperate fingers. He felt hot and alive. Ian's arms went around her and lifted her as if she weighed nothing at all. Nicole wrapped her legs around his waist and pressed into him. He groaned savagely as his arousal rubbed her tangle of damp curls. Somehow his mouth found hers and he kissed her brutally, sucking her tongue into his hungry mouth. He cradled her head with one hand and held her firmly against his mouth until he'd had his fill of tasting her, devouring her, taunting her with the flavor of her own heat.

Her body aching, Nicole rocked back and forth against him. His tip nudged her, then glided along her sensitized feminine channel. Nicole screamed her pleasure into his mouth. His kiss was relentless, drawing on her until she felt as if she were falling, becoming one with him. She lifted her bottom, and this time he guided that slick tip into her when she arched against him. One thick, hard inch at a time she took him. He stretched her, filled her completely. His fingers gripped her bottom and ushered her down to take that last inch or two. Climax crashed around her before she made another move. Wave after wave of pleasure, her feminine muscles clutched frantically around his hard shaft. Ian held her against his chest, crushing her tingling breasts against all that smooth muscle.

She knew he had moved, but the haze of lust was heavy,

she wasn't sure when he moved. Ian had braced himself against the tree. His thick organ throbbed inside her, propelling her toward release again when she had barely recovered from the first one. He started then, moving her up and down along his length. Slowly, patiently, as if they had all night. His lips brushed hers. She opened her eyes to look into his, but they were closed, his face was intent with the exquisite friction happening between their connected bodies. Nicole threw her head back and took control of the dance then. She bucked against him, bearing down on him to the hilt, then rising slowly, pulling up to the tip. Ian groaned. His fingers clamped hard around her thighs in silent approval. Nicole increased the pace. She wanted to see him lose control. She resisted the urge to close her eyes when the waves of ecstasy pounded her again, harder than the last time, drawing on the lingering pulses of pleasure still rocking her. She moved faster, squeezed him inside her until he roared like a wild beast with his own climax. She slid slowly down him one last time, and she felt his body sigh.

His eyes drifted open and Nicole knew she was lost. Her heart thumped in her chest. Her arms went around his neck and she pressed her forehead to his. "You scared the hell out of me, Michaels, do you know that?" she whispered, trying to pretend she wasn't so devastated by what they had just shared.

"Yes."

She watched his lips as they formed that single word. The sound of his voice made her want to cry with some emotion she couldn't fully define. She drew back and stared into his beautiful face in the glimmering moonlight. How would she ever live without him?

One hand came up and he gently pushed a tendril of hair

from her cheek. The look of tenderness on his face undid her all the more. "Don't ever take a chance like that again," he murmured. His gaze searched her face. "You're lucky he didn't kill you."

Nicole swallowed the emotion that rose in her throat. She had to know the answer to one question. "Why do you care whether I live or die?" Her voice quavered, and she gritted her teeth to hold back a sob.

"It's what you hired me to do, isn't it?"

Chapter Eleven

Ian led the way back down to the road and the useless SUV. Nicole had said that it ran out of gas. She was certain that Daniels had somehow tampered with it. Ian agreed. Whatever the case, he had no intention of trying to get it back in working order. He would simply send for a replacement. Nicole followed silently behind him as he moved around to the other side of the vehicle. She hadn't said a single word since he'd answered her question. His response obviously had not been what she wanted to hear. But Ian refused to give her the satisfaction of knowing how much he cared for her. He blew out a breath of self-disgust and admitted the truth he had hidden from himself for three years—he cared too much. That fact changed nothing however. Nicole had hired him to do a job. He would do that job and then he would walk away. But the memory of touching her, tasting her, making love to her would burn in his brain for the rest of his life. No other woman would ever complete him the way Nicole did.

He retrieved his cell phone from the purse Nicole had abandoned on the passenger's seat of the vehicle, then passed the purse to her. She slung the strap over her shoulder and folded her arms over her middle. The denim jacket was buttoned up from collar to hem. Beneath it she wore the ruined, buttonless flannel shirt. She looked like a recalcitrant child, pouting over her punishment. Ian swallowed the regret that rose instantly at the memory of how brutal he had been with her. He hadn't meant for it to be that way. His brows drew together in a frown. He hadn't planned on making love to her at all. He had simply intended to give her hell for what she had done. For the risk she had taken. And to clear the air once and for all. Instead he had only further muddied the waters. The moment his gaze had fallen upon her hovering in that cluster of small trees, a thousand emotions he had no control over whatsoever had flooded him, made him crazy. He wanted to frighten her, wanted to teach her a lesson…but, most of all, he wanted to tempt her until she melted into submission, then he wanted to take her for his own.

He had done that. He had crawled inside her skin, touched her in a way that changed him forever. Ian had no way of knowing if Nicole had been affected the same way, but he suspected she had—at least to some degree. Did it change anything? Ian didn't think so. Nicole was still bent on doing her job—at any cost. A renewed burst of anger swept through him when he considered that she had seduced him, shackled him to the bed, then left him to go do that job.

No. Nicole hadn't changed in three years. She might care about Ian, but her feelings were secondary to her loyalty to the bureau. He doubted she would ever change. Ian clenched his jaw and headed in the direction of the cabin. He couldn't change her mind, but he could protect her until they brought down Daniels and his partner.

And that was his job.

It was almost midnight before they reached the cabin. Neither had spoken. Tomorrow Ian would call the rental company to bring them a replacement vehicle. He unlocked the door, drew his weapon and entered the dimly lit cabin ahead of Nicole. When he was satisfied that all was as it should be, he tucked the gun back into his jeans.

Nicole groaned as she surveyed the partially dismantled bed. She pitched her purse onto the sofa and plowed her fingers through her hair. "George is going to kill me."

"At the rate you're going, he won't have to," Ian said flatly.

Her gaze snapped to his, those blue pools glittering with anger. "Oh, so we're back to that again," she said hotly. "I thought maybe I'd paid my penance for that one." The implication was scathing. "I'd almost forgotten your inability to let go of a grudge, Michaels."

Ian shouldered out of his jacket, then dropped it onto the back of the sofa. "What you did tonight," he began as he moved in her direction, "was very foolish, Nicole." He paused directly in front of her, leveling his unyielding gaze on hers. He was right, she was wrong. It was that simple. "Why can't you just admit that you always act before you think?"

Something, some emotion glimmered briefly in those crystal-blue eyes, but she blinked it away. "I accomplished what I set out to do," she said curtly. "I know what I'm up against now. It's always easier to do your job when you know your enemy."

Ian angled his head slightly and studied her. He winced inwardly when he considered her cheek where the tree bark had chafed it. That was his fault and he hated himself even more for it. "Sometimes your real enemy is yourself," he suggested quietly, pointedly.

"And you would know all about that, wouldn't you, Michaels?" she snapped. Nicole shook her head, her eyes suspiciously bright, and backed away from him, looking small and vulnerable in the big, buttoned-up jacket. "I need a bath," she added as she pivoted and headed in that direction.

Ian squeezed his eyes shut and forced away the need to soothe her hurt feelings. He had to focus. This game had just moved to a new level, and he had to keep his head on straight. Daniels was no fool. Pulling a fast one on him would not be an easy task. It would take both Ian and Nicole's full attention, and combined skill. Money was a powerful motivator. Daniels had nothing to lose and everything to gain. And he wanted Nicole dead. She knew too much. That's what he had said. Daniels wanted to erase any clue that Solomon had survived that car bombing three years ago.

Daniels didn't just want Solomon's money. He wanted Solomon just as dead as he wanted Nicole. Daniels would do whatever it took to achieve that goal. He had even faked his own death to ensure the perfect alibi and to protect himself while he pursued his treasure. Daniels might be desperate to get what he wanted, but he had every intention of protecting himself at all costs. He was the sort of man who didn't really care about anything or anyone, only himself and what he set out to obtain.

But Ian had one thing that Daniels didn't have…the courage to die for what he believed in, for what he cared about. And he cared deeply about Nicole.

NICOLE AWOKE to the whispered tones of Ian's sensual voice. For one long moment she was deep in the woods again, her hands bound above her head, Ian's hands and mouth working her body into a sensual frenzy. Climax screaming down on her, then him stopping, looking at her as if he could eat her alive, but not touching her. Nicole groaned and curled into a ball. The tremendous ache she had felt at needing him, wanting him, and him standing back, just watching her, reverberated even now. Then he had set her free and she had taken control, or lost control, depending upon the way you looked at it.

Daniels. The lowlife. He was the one. Nicole dragged in a long, deep breath. How could she have been fooled by him? How could she have worked with him for years and not suspected that he was off kilter? Daniels had killed Landon. The image of Landon's grieving widow flashed through Nicole's mind and she gritted her teeth. Daniels would pay. She would see to it. No matter what Ian said, Nicole would take Daniels down in her own way. And when this was over Ian would be out of her life…just as before, only this time it would be forever.

Nicole swallowed. She loved him. But there was no way she could tell him that. He would only consider it due punishment for the sins of her past. He would probably find it rather amusing. Nicole had ruined his career as a marshal, to a degree his life, actually, and in the process she had fallen hopelessly in love with him and was doomed to live alone and lonely for the rest of hers.

"You need to get dressed, we have to leave."

Nicole looked up to find Ian standing at the foot of the bed watching her. His silvery gaze was unreadable, as usual. His hands rested lightly against the brass footboard, his cell phone clasped in one. Who had he called? she wondered. Today he sported his preferred habit, black dress slacks, black shirt. And somewhere around here there would be a black suit jacket. Nicole sat up and shoved her tousled hair from her eyes.

"Where are we going?" she asked, her voice still rough with sleep, or perhaps the remembered events of last night. She kept her gaze on those long fingers, she didn't want him to read the emotions churning inside her even now. She wanted him to take her in his arms and tell her he felt the same way she did. She wanted him to kiss her the way he had kissed her last night. Then she wanted him to make love to her again, and then again after that. Her body warmed and softened in reaction to the mere thought of Ian's touch. The lingering discomfort of last night's hot, frantic sex did nothing to alleviate the need that surged so easily inside her this morning.

"We're going to Atlanta," he announced in that calm, controlled tone of his that irritated her beyond reason.

Nicole frowned. *Atlanta?* Solomon was in Atlanta. What was Ian plotting now? And without her input. She scrambled from the bed Ian had reassembled during her bath last night, and stalked over to where he stood watching her.

"What do you mean, we're going to Atlanta?" she demanded with as much challenge as she could garner, considering she was wearing nothing but a T-shirt and panties. She hugged her middle to shield her breasts. Her nipples were already hard from just looking at him.

His expression remained unchanged, he simply looked at her as if he felt nothing at all. "Alex is making the arrangements as we speak. The rental agency will have another car here within the hour."

Realization dawned with brutal clearness then. "You talked to Daniels last night."

"Yes."

Nicole swore. Things had happened so fast between them last night that she hadn't asked if he had run into Daniels. She had just assumed that Daniels had given up and retreated so that he could regroup. Fury, fierce and hot, rose in Nicole. She should have known better. There was no way Daniels would have gotten out of those woods without crossing Ian's path. *I know,* that's what Ian had said when she blurted Daniels's name. Ian had known even before she told him. Because he had talked to Daniels, reached some sort of compromise that didn't include Nicole.

She lifted her chin and glared at him defiantly. "Why are we going to Atlanta?" Nicole's pulse pounded in her ears. He intended to keep her in the dark. Well, she seethed, it wouldn't work.

Ian turned to face her more fully. Nicole resisted the urge to back up a step. That icy gray gaze connected with hers and Nicole knew that this was the old Ian, the one who had greeted her in Victoria Colby's office. Something that felt very much like regret filtered through her.

"I struck a deal with Daniels," Ian informed her. "I give him Solomon and he gives me half the money Solomon stole from the cartel three years ago."

Nicole shook her head slowly from side to side. "Daniels is too smart to believe that you would really cut him a deal," she countered, her emotions barely in check. She knew Ian too well—trusted him too completely—to believe for one second he was on the up-and-up about any such deal.

"Apparently Daniels believes that revenge is a strong motivation in this instance."

"I see." Nicole arched one brow knowingly. "Payback for what I did to you three years ago," she suggested. Tension radiated up her spine. This conversation was making her seriously uncomfortable. Ian's attitude wasn't helping.

"I can see where that would appear justified."

Nicole's jaws ached from clenching them so tightly. His perfectly controlled tone was driving her mad. "So you simply played along with his sadistic conclusions?"

"Something like that."

Rage boiled up in Nicole. She glared at Ian. "I won't take chances with Solomon's life," she warned, her voice barely maintained at a normal decibel. "And neither will you."

Their gazes were locked in a fierce battle of wills. "You will never be safe unless we get Daniels *and* his partner. I will do whatever it takes, Nicole," he countered darkly. "And so will you."

"Daniels has no idea where Solomon is," she argued evenly, despite the anger twisting in her chest, making her want to shudder. "Any place will do. We don't need to go to Atlanta. We don't need to be that close."

"Think, Nicole," Ian scolded, "Daniels knows you too well. He knows every alias you've ever used. Don't think he wasn't fully aware you were booked on a flight to Atlanta that last night in D.C. when your apartment went up in flames."

Nicole trembled at the memory and at the realization that she was losing this battle. "You can't be sure of that." Her argument was weaker this time. Ian had a point she couldn't really deny. And he knew it.

"No. I can't be certain, but I don't intend to risk tipping my hand either. We need him to lead us to his partner. If we screw up this opportunity, he won't make the same mistake twice. Alex has already instructed Daniels to go to Atlanta and wait at the Plaza Hotel for further instructions."

He was right. As much as she loathed to admit it. "And where do I fit into all this?"

Ian looked away. "I'm to contact him with Solomon's location," he said vaguely.

Nicole thought about that for a minute, and the answer hit her like a truck. "He doesn't know you know. He thinks you intend to seduce the information out of me," she said with a kind of choked laugh.

"That would be my guess." He still didn't look at her.

"And you allowed him to believe that," she fumed.

"Yes." He looked at her then, his gaze cool and distant. "I did."

Red swam before her eyes. She wanted to hit him. To demand some sort of retraction of his words. "What makes you think I'll go along with your little plan?" she said instead, bitterness dripping from her tone.

He stared down at her with that carefully constructed mask of control for two heart-stopping beats. "Because Martinez is with Solomon and I have your weapon, Nicole. From this moment, you can consider yourself in protective custody."

NICOLE CONTINUED her silent treatment the rest of the morning. Ian struggled with the need to make things right with her. But this was for the best. As long as this wall of anger remained between them, she would keep her distance. There was no room for error now. They would both need their full attention focused on the game as it played out, and the events to come as they unfolded. There was no room for anything else.

Ian stole a glance at Nicole's unyielding profile as the plane taxied to the airport gate in Atlanta. She didn't like being left out of the loop and Ian could understand that, but there was nothing to be done about it. This game had to be played by the rules Daniels set. Nicole knew that as well as Ian did. He had hoped she would come to see how well his plan would work, but that hadn't happened. Instead, she ignored him, continued to stew in silence.

The flight attendant gave the final instructions for disembarkation. Nicole released her lap restraint, keeping her gaze straight ahead. Ian pushed out of his seat and stepped to one side for Nicole to proceed him. He placed a hand against her arm, stopping her when she would have started down the aisle. Reluctantly, her gaze moved up to meet his.

"We'll have lunch here before we pick up our luggage," he told her. "Then we'll go to the hotel."

She shrugged off his hand. "Whatever." Nicole slung her purse over one shoulder and sauntered down the aisle.

Ian clenched his jaw against the irritation her indifference engendered in him. He followed her, working hard to ignore the way her hips, encased in some sort of dark blue knit that fit like a second skin, swayed so provocatively. The matching fuzzy sweater snuggled against her breasts and her slim rib cage. The effect was startlingly feminine, and undeniably sexy. Ian felt certain she had intended just that. But he wasn't buying in to her seductive ploy. This was one round she would simply have to play alone.

Ian signed for his weapon at the cockpit and tucked it beneath his jacket in the shoulder harness. He didn't like to wear the holster, but when traveling via commercial means and carrying a weapon, he usually did.

The airport was crowded. Ian stayed right behind Nicole, ensuring that she never got out of arm's reach, as they wove their way through the knots of people. He had a decidedly uneasy feeling about her attitude. Nicole Reed could be unpredictable, if not completely unmanageable when properly motivated by a situation.

"Will this place do?" she asked, stopping abruptly in front of a bar and grill. She appeared completely disinterested in his decision one way or another.

Ian surveyed the surrounding area. Gift shop, restaurant,

restrooms. No sign of Daniels. Ian fully expected the man to be waiting and watching at the airport. He would probably follow them when they left. Daniels would not wait for Ian's call. The man had every intention of setting the pace of this game, Ian was sure. If for some reason Daniels wasn't here, it was only because he hadn't managed an early enough flight.

"This place is fine," he replied, watching her reaction closely. He needed Nicole to work with him on this.

Nicole sighed dramatically and headed toward a table in that slow, graceful manner that looked more feline than human. She was purposely baiting him. What the hell did she expect to gain? Nothing she could do or say would change Ian's mind about how to proceed in this case.

She selected a relatively secluded table in the back corner, away from the passersby. A waiter appeared and offered menus as Ian sat down. Nicole thanked the guy with a wide smile, and an appreciative survey of his lean body. The waiter responded with an idiotic-looking grin. Ian tightened his jaw.

"May I get your drinks now?" the young man asked.

Another of those sultry smiles slid across Nicole's lips. "I'd like white wine, please," she said seductively.

Jealousy speared through Ian's chest. He almost flinched.

The waiter swallowed with obvious difficulty, then dragged his reluctant gaze to Ian. "And you, sir?"

Ian directed a lethal look at the waiter. "I'll have the same as my wife," he said quietly.

The color drained from the young man's eager face. His stupid grin drooped. "I'll get those right away, sir." He pivoted sharply and hurried away as if the hounds of hell were on his heels.

"You're such a comedian," Nicole said sarcastically, then

rolled her eyes. "I can just see you with a wife." She gave her head a little shake and laughed softly.

"You find that hard to imagine?" he asked in a voice heavy with implication.

That stopped Nicole cold. Her eyes widened slightly, and her pretty mouth dropped open two full seconds before she spoke. "Let's just say it would take some stretching."

Ian lifted one shoulder in the barest of shrugs. "Not really."

Nicole gave another of those sultry, utterly feminine chuckles. "Next you'll be telling me you're even considering children."

Ian just looked at her then. Did she really believe him that cold and untouchable? So heartless that no woman would love him, would want to bear his children? That thought cut to the bone.

"Here you go," the waiter announced as he cautiously approached the table. He deposited their drinks in front of them and stepped back slightly as if he feared Ian might take off his head…or worse. "Are you ready to order now?" he asked humbly.

Nicole was the first to recover. "Ham and cheese on wheat," she said vacantly. She picked up her glass and took a sip, feigning preoccupation with evaluating the wine.

"The same," Ian answered without taking his gaze off Nicole.

The waiter took their menus, made some vague comment and scurried away.

"There are a great many things I want, Nicole," Ian said, something hard that he didn't quite understand in his tone. "You have no idea."

"You're right," she said tightly. "I could say the same, you know." She glared at him defiantly. "You have no idea what I want out of life, either."

"To replace your director," Ian said with unexpected malice. He blinked at the harshness of his own voice. The remark hit home. Nicole's surly attitude faltered. Hurt flickered in her eyes.

"You would think that," she muttered without looking at him.

He was out of line. Jealousy had driven him. Ian cursed himself for hurting her. He was supposed to be helping Nicole, not fighting with her over things that would never be.

Ian would never marry.

Never have children.

If he couldn't have Nicole—and he couldn't—he didn't want anyone else.

They ate in silence. The waiter whizzed by a couple of times, offering refills, which Ian declined. Nicole had a second glass of wine. She refused to look at Ian and that bothered him a great deal more than it should. He shouldn't care. He should simply concentrate on the risky business that lay ahead of them.

But he couldn't.

Ian dropped a few bills on the table and stood. "We should go," he announced.

Nicole drained her glass and hurried to her feet before he could do the gentlemanly thing and pull her chair back. He followed her back into the crowded corridor.

"Luggage pickup," he reminded.

Nicole glanced at the signs overhead and started in the direction indicated. They passed a bank of phones, which reminded Ian that he should check in with Alex before they left the airport.

"Wait," he called after Nicole.

She turned around and walked back to where he waited. "What?" she demanded impatiently.

"I'm going to check in with Alex to see if Martinez has called before we go any farther."

Nicole folded her arms over her chest and gave him her back. "Whatever," she mumbled.

God, he hated that word. He turned his back to the passing travelers, pulled out his cell phone and punched in the number. It wasn't really the word, he amended, it was the way she said it. It made him crazy. He wanted to shake her. Or kiss her…or something.

Ian swore.

As he waited for Alex to pick up her line, Ian shifted to his right to make sure Nicole hadn't wandered too far.

She was gone.

He whipped around, adrenaline charging through his veins, his gaze scanning the crowd. There she was. A sigh of relief hissed past his lips. He frowned. She was talking to a man in uniform. Airport security. What the hell? he wondered briefly.

"Ian, are you there?"

"I'll call you back," he said distractedly and closed the phone, then dropped it into his pocket. Never taking his eyes off Nicole, Ian started walking in her direction.

Nicole's gaze connected with his. Ian frowned. She had a sort of deer-caught-in-the-headlights expression. Ian ignored the glares he got from the people he cut in front of, and the shoulders that banged into him. He moved faster. She was up to something.

The security guard's head came up. He leveled his gaze on Ian. Nicole said something to him, her expression frantic now. The big, burly guard ushered her away. Nicole took one last look at Ian before darting for the escalator. Ian started after her.

"Stop right there, sir!"

Ian would have kept going, but he knew the guard was armed. So he stopped, held up his arms in classic surrender fashion and waited for the man to approach him. Nicole waved mischievously as she disappeared from view. Ian barely contained the mixture of anger, frustration and fear that boiled up inside him.

"Turn around real slow, friend," the guard ordered nervously.

Ian obeyed. He was surprised to find the guard's weapon drawn and aimed directly at his chest. What the hell had Nicole told him?

"The lady said you'd been harassing her," the guard said pointedly, his eyes studying Ian closely. Sweat beaded on his mahogany skin. "Trying to pick her up, she claimed."

Ian smiled as if he had been caught with his hand in the cookie jar. "I'm sorry—" he looked at the name tag pinned on the man's massive chest "—Mr. Winslow, I wasn't aware that there was anything illegal about hitting on a pretty lady."

Winslow didn't smile. "There isn't. But there is a law against carrying a concealed weapon in an airport." He nodded toward Ian's jacket. "The lady said you have a gun."

"May I?" Ian inquired, barely banking his fury.

"I'll do it," Winslow said. He moved closer, then lifted Ian's jacket with his free hand. He removed the weapon in Ian's holster. "I surely do hope you have a license for this, sir."

"Trust me, I do."

Winslow did smile then. "Oh, I think we'd better go on down to the security office and straighten this out, Mr…"

"Michaels," Ian told him. "Ian Michaels. And the lady you just assisted in flight was in my protective custody."

Winslow looked a little startled by that news. "Well, if that's the case, Mr. Michaels, I surely do apologize. But unless you can produce a badge, we still have to go to the office."

Ian waved his arms in defeat. "Fine." He started in the direction Winslow indicated, then hesitated. "You don't mind if I make a call on the way."

Winslow had put his own weapon away, but still held Ian's. He quickly patted Ian's pockets with his free hand, identifying the cell phone. "No problem, sir, be my guest."

Ian pulled out the phone and depressed the speed dial button for Alex. Two rings later she answered. The muscle in Ian's jaw was jumping in time with the pounding in his chest as he followed the guard toward the security office. "Call Martinez," Ian ordered curtly. "Tell him to move Solomon to the alternate location *now*. Nicole is probably on her way there." Ian ended the call and dropped the phone back into his pocket.

Nicole better have a hell of a good reason for her actions.

Chapter Twelve

The taxi driver made the trip across town in record time. For that, Ian tipped him generously. Ian was out of the car before it stopped rocking at the curb. He paused on the walk and surveyed the quiet neighborhood in one sweep. Before long, the yards would fill with children returning home from school, then their parents returning home from work. Solomon lived in a three-bedroom, red-brick, ranch-style house in a middle-class neighborhood that defined the word *average*. A dog barked from behind the fenced backyard at the house next door.

Solomon, with his cover as a retired NASA engineer, would never set foot in this quiet, average home again. When this was over, Nicole would have to replant him.

And that would be the end of this mission.

The end of their time together.

That was definitely for the best.

And all that depended upon whether Nicole, not Daniels, had got here before Ian. Dread pooled in Ian's stomach. He had to find her first. If for no other reason than to wring her lovely neck.

Daniels could have been waiting for them at the airport. He could have followed Nicole here.

The blinds were drawn, Ian noted, directing his attention

back to what he had come here for. Nicole had had a twenty-minute head start on him, but the cabbie had regained some of that lost time. Ian moved cautiously up the walk and to the front entrance. Pristine white, the painted wooden door stood ajar. He glanced through the narrow opening and saw nothing but beige wall. No sound, no particular smells. Nothing.

Ian banished the thought that blood had a very distinct odor. He wouldn't think about that. Moving to a higher state of alert, he deadened his senses to all other distraction. She had to be here—or, at least, had to have been here. Nicole had not been privy to the alternate location Ian had arranged with Martinez. Nor did she know about the preliminary measures Ian had insisted that Solomon take once he was in Martinez's care. Nicole had no place else but here to look for Solomon. Ian reached beneath his jacket and withdrew his weapon. He flattened one palm against the smooth painted surface of the door and pushed it inward. The hinges groaned loudly, the sound echoing across the deserted entry hall. Ian stepped onto the polished oak floor, the leather soles of his shoes silent as he moved toward the first door to his left. The living room. An aging collection of value-priced furniture and a couple of cheap paintings made up the decor of the dimly lit space. He turned and started in the direction of the next door, this one on his right. The dining room probably.

Table, four chairs, sideboard along the far wall. A bowl of wax fruit as a centerpiece. Another painting.

No Nicole.

Anticipation rising steadily, Ian eased to the far end of the hall. Silence hung around him like a dark cloud, dragging down his hopes, nudging at his emotions. She was unarmed, defenseless. Anger and fear twisted inside Ian. Where could she be? She had really crossed the line this time. And this time, if she managed to come out of this unscathed, Ian intended to make sure she followed orders. Stashing her with Martinez would be the first order he initiated. She wouldn't like it, but that was too damned bad.

To Ian's left was a corridor that led to the bedrooms, he assumed, on the right another doorway. He readied his grip on his weapon and prepared to enter the kitchen.

The front door slammed shut.

Ian whirled toward it, his weapon leveled.

"You're losing your touch, Michaels." Nicole leaned casually against the closed door, pointed her finger at him as if it were a pistol and mouthed the word *pow.* "If I'd had a weapon, you'd be dead now."

A feeling Ian had never before experienced washed over him, something like rage, but stronger. Like relief, but more profound. The desire to lash out, strike something, was a pulsating need mushrooming in his chest.

"Is the house clean?" he asked calmly, despite the nuclear explosion of sensations erupting inside him.

"As a whistle," she said, angling her head a little to the side. "Martinez did a good job. I couldn't find one single piece of evidence that Solomon had ever even been here."

Ian essayed a ghost of a smile as he lowered his weapon, then placed it into the shoulder harness. "We're good at what we do at the Colby Agency," he returned, a tightness in his voice now.

Nicole straightened. The delicate features of her face hardened like stone. She walked slowly toward Ian. "This didn't happen in half an hour, Ian. Where is Solomon?" she demanded, uttering the words as if each were a separate statement from the other. She stopped right in front of Ian, glaring up at him, those blue eyes piercing points of smoky light.

"Martinez and I had anticipated this possibility. Solomon is safe." Ian leveled his gaze on hers. "Which is more than I can say about you, Nicole." He leaned his head a bit to one side and looked long and hard into her furious expression. "You're simply lucky, otherwise *you* would be dead now."

Her chin lifted in a graceful but defiant manner. "I'm not interested in a spitting contest, Michaels. I want to know where my witness is, and I want to know now."

Ian looked past her, at the door she had hidden behind. Only Nicole would think of such an obvious place. "We don't always get what we want, Nicole."

"You're interfering with the protection of a federal witness, that's a felony," she stated in a lethal tone. "Now, where is Solomon?"

Ian felt himself losing control. He clenched his jaw to hold back the irrational words he wanted to hurl at her. He curled his fingers into fists to prevent himself from grabbing her and shaking her. Nothing took precedence over her desire to prove she was the best the feds had to offer. Nothing else, not even her own life, mattered that much to her.

Ian's cell phone sounded, breaking the awkward, deafening silence.

His gaze still locked with hers, Ian pulled the phone from his pocket. "Yes." It was probably Alex confirming Martinez and Solomon's arrival at the alternative location.

"I've been waiting for your call."

Daniels.

Ian blinked, then averted his gaze from Nicole. His emotions immediately switched gears. "I'll call you when I'm ready."

"Thought maybe you'd run into a snag," Daniels suggested sarcastically. "Nicole's not giving you trouble, is she?" he asked knowingly.

"I have your number," Ian said flatly. "I'll contact you." He pressed the End button and pocketed the phone. Like hell Daniels had been waiting for a call. He had been waiting all right, waiting at the airport. Ian knew it as surely as he knew his own name. No doubt Nicole would confirm it.

"That was Daniels, wasn't it?" Nicole demanded, fury radiating from every inch of her.

With a reluctance that sapped his strength, Ian's gaze roved all the way down to her leather boots, then back to those fiery blue eyes. He wanted desperately to shake her, then to hold her. To prove to her that her career didn't have to be everything, that there was more to life than risking everything for scum like Solomon. But he couldn't risk opening himself up to that kind of rejection.

"It was, wasn't it?" she repeated.

"Yes," he admitted.

She shook her head determinedly. "This won't work, Ian. Daniels is too smart. He's playing you, just like he played me." Emotion glistened in her eyes then, ripping at Ian's already tattered defenses.

"And I'm playing him," Ian clarified. "The difference is that I'm not desperate. Daniels is. He wants that money."

Nicole flung her arms upward in frustration. "How can he be certain there is any money? Solomon could have blown it all by now!"

"That's not likely," Ian countered with complete confidence.

"Why not?" Her hands went to those luscious hips, and he struggled with the impulse to allow his gaze to linger there. "It's been three years," she added.

"He wouldn't take the risk of spending too much too fast. Big spenders draw attention. Solomon would be very, very careful with his finances." Ian's brow quirked. "After all, he was an accountant. He would know all about making his money work for him without anyone ever knowing he had any."

Nicole swore as if an epiphany had just this minute dawned on her. "No wonder he was in such a big hurry to testify against his boss. He was probably close to being caught for embezzling. Solomon knew he was dead either way. Witness protection was his only hope."

"And somehow Daniels found out about the money and decided to blackmail Solomon," Ian added.

"But how could he know unless someone from the cartel leaked the information?"

"So far, Sloan agrees with Alex," Ian told her, recalling his conversation with Alex that morning. "He doesn't believe the cartel is involved." Ian shrugged halfheartedly. "Daniels outright denied any connection to the cartel."

Nicole settled her gaze on Ian's. "Enough stalling. You're not leaving me in the dark like this, Ian. Where is Solomon?" she asked again, her impatience as evident as her anger.

Ian held that infuriated gaze for a couple of beats before he answered. "The only way I'll give you that information is if you agree to stay out of sight with Martinez until this is over." She opened her mouth to rant at him, and Ian stopped her with a withering look. "But first, you will explain to me why you pulled that little stunt at the airport. Then I'll have your word that you will do exactly as I say from this moment on."

"Hell no," she growled in a raw, animal-like tone.

"Well, then," Ian said slowly. "We have a real problem, because I won't budge on the issue."

Nicole hesitated, her fiery resolve wavering beneath his

unyielding glower. "You're not going to like it," she admitted cautiously.

"I already don't like it," Ian assured her in a low, lethal tone.

Nicole licked her lips, then shrugged. "Daniels was there. I saw him when you first stopped to make your call."

Ian swore hotly, his gaze boring relentlessly into hers. "You left the airport—unarmed—knowing that Daniels would follow you!" It wasn't really a question, Ian already knew the answer.

Nicole thought about his statement for a few seconds, then nodded. "Yeah, that's exactly what I did."

Ian rubbed at his forehead and the pounding, which abruptly started there. "You do realize how that sounds?" he returned, still not certain he believed her flippancy himself.

"I know Daniels," Nicole argued. "There was no way he was going to buy into the concept that I would give you Solomon's location without a fight. I had to make him believe that I was resisting the idea of giving up Solomon. Besides—" she shrugged nonchalantly "—one of us had to lose him."

Ian moved closer. "No more theatrics, Nicole," he ordered darkly. "I don't want you taking a risk like that again. In fact, I don't want you taking any risks at all."

Nicole squeezed her eyes shut and let go a ragged breath. "This is my responsibility, Ian," she countered. Vulnerability stared back at him when her eyes opened once more.

Ian encircled her arm with one hand and pulled her nearer. "We're in this together, Nicole. We're a team." His voice was taut with emotion now. "But I won't chance your safety."

Nicole turned her face into his throat and sagged against his chest. She sighed wearily and something shifted deep inside Ian. His arms went automatically around her, then tightened.

"I just want this to be over," she murmured.

"Soon," Ian promised. "For now Solomon is safe. And I will do whatever it takes to keep you safe." Her hair smelled like heaven and Ian wanted to hold her closer, make her believe that this would all magically work out. His body responded to hers much more than merely physically, it was as if their souls were somehow connected.

"Daniels and I worked the scene in Landon's office together," she said haltingly, her lips brushing his skin, making him ache for her. "How could I have worked with him, gone over and over the evidence and never suspected for one second that I was working side by side with the killer?" She trembled.

Ian tilted her face up and brushed the hair back from her cheeks. Tears glittered in her blue eyes. "You had no reason to suspect him. You can't blame yourself. This is not your fault, Nicole. You did the best job you could do."

She closed her eyes and sucked in a harsh breath. "I should have paid better attention. Things should never have got this far." She shook her head. "I bought Daniels's setup hook, line and sinker. I believed he was dead. I missed all the signs that are so clear now."

"Hindsight is twenty-twenty, Nicole," Ian pointed out, hoping to assuage her distress. "Things are always clearer when you're looking back."

Those wide, watery blue eyes searched his. "Daniels has gone over the edge. He's crazy. He'll kill you if he suspects for one second that you're setting a trap for him. I can't let you take that chance. This is between Daniels and me."

Ian stroked her soft cheek with his thumb, his fingers curled around her nape. He smiled, trying his best to soothe that fearful gaze. "You took this great risk because you were afraid for my life?"

She chewed her lower lip to prevent the smile that was already shining in her eyes. "Partly," she relented. "And partly because I was madder than hell at you for leaving me in the dark about your plans. But mainly because I knew that it was what Daniels would expect." She smiled, though a bit weakly. And Ian's heart felt oddly full.

"If anyone around here has a right to be angry, it's me," he corrected gently. "It took me fifteen minutes to persuade that security guard that I wasn't some pervert stalking beautiful, unsuspecting young women."

Nicole laughed, a soft, feminine sound that skittered along his nerve endings, making them tingle. "I thought that bit of improvisation was rather ingenious myself," she enthused. Her brows drew into a questioning V then. "You think I'm beautiful?" she asked almost shyly.

He sobered. "Yes."

"You rushed here to protect me?" she murmured, those wide blue eyes studying him too closely.

"You know I did." Ian's mood turned dark again. "You acted foolishly," he scolded softly. "What if Daniels had caught up with you?"

She frowned crossly, as if he should know better than that. "I didn't just wake up in this business yesterday, you know."

"No more, Nicole," he told her, his tone brooking no argument. "We do this my way or you're out of the game. No more taking off on your own. No more arguments."

She looked far too hesitant for Ian's satisfaction.

"You said you trust me. You told Victoria there was no one else you could trust," he reminded. "Have you changed your mind so soon?"

Nicole sighed impatiently, then shook her head slowly from side to side.

"If you want to get Daniels," he began, "you'll do exactly as I say." He looked directly into her eyes, urging her to pay close attention. "Solomon is safe, that won't change. And I will bring down Daniels and his partner."

"You won't keep anything else from me?" she insisted.

Ian shook his head. "No."

"We're in this together. At no time will you try to leave me behind or in the dark?" she prodded.

It was Ian's turn to hesitate. He wasn't sure he could promise her that. Her safety was foremost in his mind. He couldn't risk her getting hurt in the final showdown. Ian wanted her nowhere around when he and Daniels met face-to-face again.

"Promise me, Ian," she demanded. "If you want me to co-operate with you, then you have to keep me in the loop. I won't do it any other way."

"All right," he finally agreed, against his better judgment. "On one condition."

She straightened. "What would that be?"

"That you do exactly as I say, no exceptions."

She sighed wearily. "Agreed."

NICOLE HUGGED herself more tightly beneath the scratchy blanket. Only two of Solomon's bedrooms had furniture, the one she was in and the one across the hall that Ian occupied. Nicole blew out a breath of frustration. Ian had not returned Daniels's call. Ian wanted to make him wait, to heighten the man's anxiety. Nicole agreed. Once that strategy was decided, Ian had suggested that it would be simpler for them to stay the night here and Nicole hadn't argued. What did it matter if they were in Solomon's house or a hotel? They were alone, and without any luggage. Ian had kindly offered his shirt for her to sleep in. Nicole was thankful. She had no desire to sleep in anything that belonged to Solomon.

When her gaze had connected with Daniels's today at the airport, Nicole had lost it completely. Fear that he would kill Ian had nearly paralyzed her. Without thought of her own safety or anything else, she had made use of the only tactic available to readily lose Ian. Then she had taken Daniels on a hell of a speedy chase. She had tipped the cab driver generously. Daniels didn't stand a chance against a guy who knew the city the way a good cabbie did. Nicole blew out a breath. Admittedly, she had been lucky. But her diversion had served its purpose. By the time Daniels could have made it back to the airport to try and latch on to Ian, Ian was long gone.

She had accomplished her mission of maintaining the integrity of Solomon's location while keeping Ian away from harm.

Ian.

Nicole flopped over onto her side and tried not to allow her thoughts to drift to the night before. It was no use. The scene in the woods kept right on playing through her mind. Ian loving her so intimately. The intensity in his eyes. How would she ever survive the rest of her life without him?

Enough, Reed, she chastised.

But what would happen tomorrow? There were so many variables that would be out of her control. What if she or Ian lost their lives tomorrow as this game played out? She would have so many regrets. Not telling him how she really felt. Not making love with him one last time before…

Nicole stilled. It was true. She couldn't predict what would happen tomorrow. She clamped down hard on her lower lip to hold back the tears that instantly sprang to her eyes. Her whole life was out of control. She had realized that this afternoon. Ian must have thought she had gone off the deep end when she ditched him at the airport. But when he found her, rather than blow a gasket as she had fully expected, he had scolded her gently and then held her and assured her in that deep, sensual voice until she was thinking straight again. Nothing was right with her anymore. Her ability to do her job had obviously gone to hell. A killer had lurked right under her nose and she hadn't noticed. She had lost everything she owned when her apartment burned. When this was over, Ian would walk out of her life again.

This time forever.

What a mess.

She closed her eyes and banished the thoughts. She couldn't think about any of that right now, especially the part about Ian. It hurt too much. The conversation in the airport restaurant slammed into her heart with twisting force. Ian could see himself with a wife and children. He wanted those things.

Just not with her.

He didn't think of her as wife-and-mother material. She had never even thought of herself that way. But Ian made her want those things too.

Why was she torturing herself this way? Nicole threw off the covers and bounced out of the bed. She paced back and forth in the small room. She had known this day would come from the moment she'd walked into Victoria Colby's office and asked for Ian's help. Their time together would only be temporary. Why was she getting all weepy about it now?

Because she loved him.

Damn fate's twisted sense of irony, she mused.

That day in the Colby office she hadn't realized that significant fact just yet.

But now she knew.

And it didn't change a thing.

Ian would still leave her, just like before.

But what about tonight?

Could she make him feel the way he had made her feel last night? He had ripped the heart right from her chest. Left her mentally weak and physically satisfied. But was his motivation purely revenge? She had, after all, teased him ruthlessly before handcuffing him to the bed. But a part of her had wanted to make it real. Could she do that again? This time with the intent to follow through with what she started?

Her body warmed with anticipation.

Yes, she could.

Nicole walked to the door.

No, she couldn't do it. She pivoted and stalked back to the other side of the room.

The memory of his hands moving so expertly over her body sent an ache straight to her core. His mouth had tugged at her breasts. His fingers had played her like a finely tuned cello. Then he had possessed her so completely that her body shuddered toward release even now just recalling the mind-blowing moments.

She looked at the door once more. Just a few feet. That's all that separated them. They could make long, slow love tonight, then sleep the sleep of satiation in each other's arms.

Let tomorrow bring what it would.

Nicole retraced her steps, wrapped her fingers around the knob and turned. She opened the door and stepped into the dark hall. She could do this. They would have this one last night together. She shivered as chill bumps rushed over her bare skin. She would not live the rest of her life, however long or short it proved to be, regretting not having taken this one last moment with Ian.

Nicole paused at Ian's open door and whispered his name.

"What's wrong?" He sat up in bed.

Nicole could see his dark, tousled hair in the shaft of moonlight slipping in around the closed blinds. She moved closer to his bed…to him.

"I can't sleep," she whispered back.

Ian patted the covers beside him. "Sit down, we can talk until you're sleepy again."

Nicole crawled onto the bed beside him. Her arms went around his neck. "I don't want to talk," she whispered between the little kisses she planted along his throat.

Ian tensed. He encircled her arms with his long fingers. "Don't even think about it, Nicole," he warned.

Nicole realized her mistake then. She had said those same words to him before shackling him to the bed. She smiled against his jaw, his stubble sent currents of desire racing through her. "No," she clarified, then nipped his chin with her teeth. "I mean, I *really* don't want to talk."

Ian sat perfectly still for several moments, then he moved, pulling her down and rolling over so that she was beneath him. "You're sure about this?" he asked hoarsely.

Nicole didn't answer. Instead, she reached between them and unfastened his slacks. When she cupped him with her hands, he was exquisitely hard already, pulsing actually. Nicole made a low sound of approval in her throat. She stroked his length, glorying in the feel of him, the smooth satiny texture of his male skin. He shuddered.

"Kiss me," he ordered tightly.

Nicole obeyed. She lifted her parted lips to his, thrusting her tongue into his welcoming mouth. She stroked his arousal again, sucked his tongue into her mouth, then lifted her hips against his. Need ripped through her, sending electrical bursts all along her too-hot skin. She was wet and throbbing already.

His hand found its way to her panties and two fingers dipped inside her, stretching, stroking. She gasped into his hungry mouth. He pulled back from the kiss and moved down to her breasts, taking each hard peak into his mouth through the thin material of the shirt. He sucked hard, then nibbled, torturing her endlessly. The shirt buttons opened beneath his efficient touch. He pushed the fabric off her arms, tugged it from under her, then tossed it to the floor. Sensation after sensation flooded her senses in anticipation of his next move. She writhed beneath him when he began again, his mouth loving one breast, his hand the other. Silently, her body speaking for her, she begged him to take her completely. He murmured soothing sounds while he continued his relentless, sensual assault. His weight on her was a delicious feeling of rightness; she tightened her arms around his lean waist and pulled him more firmly to her.

His own control ready to snap, Ian slid her panties down and off. He loomed over her again, then buried himself fully with one long stroke. Nicole cried out his name. He held very still then, their ragged breathing loud in the consuming silence. Slowly at first, his movements began. He drove harder, faster with each rhythmic thrust. She held on to his strong back, trying to make it last, but she couldn't. When he exploded inside her, filling her with his hot release, Nicole's body contracted around him, plunging her into that heartstopping moment of pure physical pleasure.

For long minutes afterwards, they lay still, his forehead pressed to hers, neither speaking. Then he brushed his lips across hers and whispered something in that language she didn't understand, the sound exotic. Ian rolled to his side and pulled her against his chest, wrapped his strong arms around her.

"Sleep, Nicole," he whispered. "Tomorrow will be here too soon."

Something in his voice made the faintest flicker of uneasiness steal through Nicole. Ian knew their time together was drawing to an end the same as she did. Was he feeling the same urgency she was? Nicole snuggled closer to him, buried her face in the crook of his neck. Inhaled his unique masculine essence. Held him tighter than she ever had before…

…for the last time.

Chapter Thirteen

As darkness grayed into dawn Ian sat on the floor next to the bed and watched Nicole sleep. With the blinds partially opened, alternating slats of early-morning light and shadow fell across her prone form. His gaze traveled over the swell of her sheet-covered bottom, then up the smooth, bare skin of her back. Her arms were curled around the pillow, her right cheek snuggled against it. All that blond hair lay fanned across the pale blue sheets. She looked like an angel, all soft and vulnerable. Ian closed his eyes and summoned the vivid images that haunted him. The feel of her fingers on his skin, the taste of her lips. The tight, exquisitely hot feel of her body as he sank deeply into her. Those memories would have to last him a lifetime, because there would never be any more than this one moment between them.

He forced his eyes open and drank in the beauty of her one last time. Ian had been certain that he would never feel this way again. He had survived the devastation wreaked upon his heart once, but he would never get over her this time. She was the one and only woman for him…

…and the very one he couldn't have.

Ian blinked, then looked away. He did not possess the power to make Nicole happy. There was nothing he could offer her that would change the way this would all end. She would go back to D.C., back to the bureau. And Ian would go back to Chicago. He and Nicole shared just one thing—a kind of physical attraction that most people only dreamed about. Need welled inside at the mere thought of the intensity that drew them together. The kind that dwarfed all else. The fact that Ian loved her made no difference in the equation. The admission of his feelings to himself shook him a little. The realization that he couldn't have her shook him even harder.

But he could protect her.

Clearing his mind of the things he couldn't change, Ian dragged his gaze back to Nicole's sweet face. She was awake now, watching him, those wide blue eyes full of the same desire Ian could no longer conceal. She smiled, and something near his heart shifted.

"Good morning," she said sleepily. She glanced at the digital clock on the bedside table and frowned. "It's early." Her questioning gaze moved back to Ian as she raised up onto her elbows, the sheet now clutched to her bare breasts. "You're dressed." She studied him for a moment. "You weren't planning to cut out on me, were you?"

"No." Ian stood before she saw the truth in his eyes. Her statement had hit very close to the mark. He would very much like to leave her where she would be safe. "I'll get your clothes." He crossed to the door without looking back. He couldn't look at her one second longer without her seeing what he needed to hide, and without him wanting to take her again. That couldn't happen. He had to focus on the meeting with Daniels.

Nothing else.

"Do I have time for a shower?" she called after him.

"Sure," he returned offhandedly. Ian suppressed the images that accompanied the thought of Nicole in the shower, but not before they made an impact. The water gliding over her soft skin. Her breasts jutting forward for his attention. He blew out a breath of frustration and forced the mental pictures away. He moved quickly about the other bedroom gathering Nicole's carelessly discarded clothes. The shirt he wore was slightly wrinkled this morning. Nicole's scent lingered on the fabric, distracting him, making his body harden. His jaw clenched when Nicole met him at the door wrapped in the pale blue sheet from the bed they had shared.

"Thanks," she offered as she accepted the wad of clothing. "I'll only be a few minutes."

"Take your time." Ian stepped around her, ensuring that their bodies didn't touch, and headed to the kitchen. There had to be coffee around here somewhere.

The glimpse of vulnerability Ian had seen in Nicole yesterday tugged at him sharply. No matter how tough Nicole wanted to seem, she was still a bit fragile deep inside. Ian dumped the grounds into the basket and poured the water into the reservoir. The past few weeks—especially finding out that Daniels was the killer—had been hard on Nicole. Daniels would pay for that too. Ian intended to see that the bastard paid for every moment of discomfort he had caused Nicole. The smell of fresh brewed coffee drifted from the machine, but it did nothing to lighten Ian's mood. He had to find a way to convince Nicole to stay out of the line of fire today.

Instinct told him that he would have more luck trying to convince Daniels to forget about the money.

Ian's cell phone chirped. He withdrew it from his pocket and accepted the call. "Yes." It was Alex.

"We're ready to proceed," he told her. "I'm going to call

Daniels in ten minutes." Alex briefed him on the current status of Solomon and Martinez. The two were safely ensconced in a quiet suburb on the other side of the city. Ethan Delaney had arrived at the airport forty minutes ago in the agency's jet. He would arrive at Ian's location within fifteen minutes. Ian thanked Alex for the update and assured her that he would check in every couple of hours. She suggested again that he work a secondary backup plan with the local police, but Ian declined.

If this was going to work, it had to go down without a glitch. The more people involved, the greater the possibility of a breakdown in communications. And that meant a greater risk of someone getting trigger-happy.

"Smells good."

Ian turned to find Nicole, her hair still slightly damp, standing in the doorway. The blue slacks and sweater looked as good on her slender body today as they had yesterday.

"Have a cup," he offered, then smiled.

Nicole returned the smile with a bright one of her own. "Thanks."

The phone sounded again. This time it would be Daniels, Ian felt relatively certain. He took his time answering, his gaze on Nicole's every move as she poured the steaming coffee.

"Yes," he said finally.

"If this is your idea of a joke, Michaels, it's only going to blow up in your face," Daniels growled. "I've waited long enough for your call."

"I was just about to call you," Ian assured him.

Nicole's gaze met Ian's. He told her with his eyes that it was Daniels.

"When am I going to get Solomon?" he demanded.

"As soon as I meet your partner," Ian said bluntly.

"That wasn't part of the deal," Daniels screeched. "This is between you and me. You got your fifty percent, what else do you want?"

"I just want to make sure your partner understands our agreement," Ian explained. "We meet, face-to-face, lay all our cards on the table, decide how we'll access the money, and then we pick up Solomon."

"I think you've forgotten just one thing," Daniels said in a cold, menacing tone. "I'm running this show, and I decide how this is going to go down."

"When you're feeling more cooperative, you know how to reach me." Ian ended the call and dropped the phone back into his pocket. Daniels would be calling back shortly. Patience was definitely not one of the man's virtues.

"What did he say?" Nicole asked, then sipped her coffee. She held the warm mug with both hands.

Ian reached for his cup. "He wasn't happy." He took a swallow of the hot liquid. "But he'll call back," he added at Nicole's distressed look.

Nicole nodded. "Okay." Her gaze locked on Ian's. "Daniels is on the edge, don't push him too far. He might do something crazy. We don't need crazy."

Ian set his cup back down. He readied himself for Nicole's blast of fury. "That's precisely why I want you to stay here today," Ian said slowly. Nicole's expression changed from relaxed to irate before he got the last word out.

Nicole slammed her cup down on the counter, coffee sloshing over the rim. "No way," she shot back. "You promised you wouldn't do this, Ian." Disappointment and hurt claimed her features. "I won't let you leave me out. We've been over and over this, until I'm sick of it. I'm not going to change my mind. Just forget it."

"I promised you that I wouldn't leave you out of the loop," Ian said evenly. "I didn't say you would be going with me to meet Daniels."

Nicole shook her head adamantly. "Don't even think about it," she warned.

Ian closed the distance between them with slow, determined steps designed to intimidate. "You do realize that Daniels intends to kill you? You know too much, and you're still connected to the bureau. He won't allow you to walk away from this, Nicole."

She squared her shoulders. "I'll take my chances the same as you."

The doorbell sounded. She whirled toward the sound. She glared at Ian then, as if she knew full well who was at the door. Ian summoned the resolve it would take to do what had to be done. He strode to the front door, Nicole right behind him. This wasn't going to be easy. He had known it wouldn't be. After checking the peephole, Ian opened the door.

"Morning, Ian." Ethan sauntered into the entry hall and kicked the door closed behind him. He placed two rectangular cases on the floor. "Is that coffee I smell?"

Ethan looked nothing like the typical Colby Agency investigator. Ian doubted Victoria would tolerate the look from anyone else. His long brown hair was tied back with a thong. His jeans and shirt were worn, his boots scuffed.

But Ethan Delaney was one of a kind, and very, very good at surveillance. And there wasn't a better marksman alive.

Ian nodded his greeting. "Ethan Delaney, this is Nicole Reed."

An appreciative smile slid across Ethan's face as he offered Nicole his hand. "It's a pleasure to meet you, Miss Reed. A real pleasure."

Nicole glared first at Ethan's hand, then at Ian. "Tell him to leave," she ground out, her eyes shooting enough sparks to burn the place down.

"You're prepared to die today, then?" Ian asked tersely. Irritation churned inside him. Why the hell wouldn't she listen to reason? "Because if you go with me today, that's what might very well happen."

"And I'm the only one?" she demanded. "You think Daniels is really going to give up half of what he's worked so hard for? That he'll follow through with this so-called deal? You can take the chance, but not me?"

"I'm willing to risk my life." Ian felt that muscle in his jaw begin to flex rhythmically. "But I'm not willing to risk yours."

Nicole huffed a breath of frustration and shook her head. "How heroic of you, Ian." She planted her hands firmly at her waist. "But this is my case and it's my decision. You're not going without me." She glanced at Ethan. "And don't think your friend here is going to stop me."

Ethan held up both hands, palms out. "Hey, lady, I heard all about what you did to Martinez." He grinned. "Believe me, I'm on your side."

Ian had known this was the way it would play out. Nicole was too damned stubborn for her own good. But he had to try. "All right," he relented. "But don't make one move—don't even breathe—unless I tell you to."

"I'll need a weapon," was her only reply.

Ian turned his attention to Ethan. "You have what we need?"

"Absolutely." Ethan picked up the two cases and looked to Ian for direction.

"This way," Ian told him, then led the way to the dining room.

Ethan set the cases on the dining table but opened only

one. "Your weapon of choice, I believe," he said as he offered Nicole a Beretta nine-millimeter.

She tested the weapon's weight, then checked the clip. "Thank you, Mr. Delaney. I always feel naked when I'm unarmed."

Ethan made a sound of approval in his throat. "I can definitely imagine that."

Ian shot him a warning look.

"You knew I wouldn't agree to staying behind," Nicole said, drawing Ian's attention back to her. "That's why you had him bring me a weapon."

"The thought did cross my mind."

Ethan slapped two fresh clips in Ian's hand. "You're a lucky man, Michaels."

"You think so?" Ian countered. He put a fresh clip into his weapon and pocketed the other. "She's determined to get herself killed, and maybe me as well, and you call that lucky?"

"Well now, that's why I'm here, isn't it?" Ethan pointed out good-naturedly. "The best plan is the one with good backup." He opened the second case, which held a disassembled high-powered rifle and related accessories.

"Well said," Ian agreed. If he couldn't keep Nicole out of the picture, at least he could make sure she was well covered from the best possible angles.

"I don't know about this," she said uncertainly. "If Daniels gets wind of a third party—"

Ian leveled his gaze on hers. "Daniels will never know Ethan is there."

NICOLE STUDIED Ian's handsome profile as they drove to the rendezvous point. She wanted to commit each detail to memory, so she could call upon it during all those long, lonely nights that lay ahead of her. She would remember every moment they had shared. And she would love him for the rest of her life. She prayed that she would somehow be able to protect Ian as this sting played out. If Daniels hurt him...

Nicole couldn't bear that thought. She had to do whatever it took to keep him safe. The agreed-upon meeting place was at an old rock quarry with nothing but trees around it. That would provide plenty of cover for Ethan. Daniels had been outraged when Ian would not allow him to pick the rendezvous location. But when Ian refused to budge on the point, Daniels caved. Another indication of his proximity to the edge. Nicole hoped like hell that Ethan was as good a shot as Ian implied. Both their lives might depend on it.

Ian turned right onto the gravel road that would lead down to the quarry. Nicole's heart pounded hard in her chest. Fear gripped her throat in a serious choke hold. What if Daniels showed up with half a dozen cohorts? His partner might be a whole damned committee. What if—

Stop it, Reed, she scolded. *Keep your focus. Put everything else out of your mind.* Nicole took a deep bolstering breath and rolled her shoulders one at a time. No way would she allow Ian to die in the next few minutes. She would protect him, she reaffirmed. She had dragged him into this mess and she would see that he made it safely out of it.

"Stash your weapon there." Ian gestured to the small storage compartment in the car door. Ethan had given them his rental, and he had driven the car parked in Solomon's garage.

Nicole frowned. "Why?"

"He'll pat you down and take your weapon," Ian explained. "Daniels considers you hostile."

"He'd better," Nicole said hotly.

"Do it, Nicole," Ian insisted as he braked the car to a stop near the abandoned quarry.

"This is not a good idea," she complained.

"When this is over," Ian said, his words staying her move to obey his order, "we need to talk."

Hope flickered in Nicole's heart, but the reality of the differences between them quickly dashed it. "Sure," she murmured. "We'll talk."

Turning away from him, Nicole placed her Beretta, butt up, in the compartment that was most likely designed for maps or tissues. She would not dwell on Ian's unexpected statement. Was it a promise or a threat? she wondered briefly, then put it out of her mind. Before Ian turned the engine off, she powered the window down for ready access to her weapon.

Daniels was here already. A dark sedan was parked some ten yards away from where Ian had stopped. The driver's side door opened and Daniels emerged. Nicole suppressed the strong desire to destroy that rose immediately in her chest.

Ian placed a hand on her arm when she started to get out. "Slow and easy, Nicole," he warned.

Nicole nodded, then opened her door. She closed the door and leaned against it. Ian skirted the trunk, careful not to turn his back to the man sauntering toward them.

"Well, well, I didn't expect to see you again so soon," Daniels said disdainfully, his gaze traveling the length of Nicole, then back to her face.

"I guess I'm just lucky, that's all," Nicole spat.

"Maybe not," Daniels growled as he moved closer. He patted Nicole down, a little too thoroughly, too roughly.

"She's not carrying," Ian said pointedly.

Daniels turned and reached toward him.

Ian had the weapon in his hand and the muzzle pressed between Daniels's eyes before he knew Ian had moved. "You don't want to do that," Ian suggested in a dangerous voice that made even Nicole retreat farther against the car.

"Keep your weapon then," Daniels said quickly. "Just keep it holstered."

Ian took his time lowering his weapon, then putting it away. "Where's your partner?" he inquired, cutting to the chase. "I didn't come here today to see the sights. No partner, no Solomon."

"My partner is a little shy around strangers," Daniels said in an oily tone. "How about you and I take a little walk over to my car? We don't need Reed for this. She might make my partner nervous."

Nicole started to argue, but Ian stopped her with a look. She sagged against the car and crossed her arms in irritation. Daniels and Ian walked over to the other car. Nicole strained to listen to whatever was said. She wasn't about to miss a single word. She watched every move Daniels made. She felt fairly confident that Ian was safe as long as Daniels didn't have Solomon's location. But what about the partner? He was an unknown variable. He might go off half cocked and do something stupid. Nicole swallowed the metallic taste of fear rising in her throat. She cleared her mind and directed her full attention to the conversation taking place between the two men.

"You told me that she was being taken care of!" a female voice ranted angrily.

Nicole frowned. She didn't recognize the voice. Was Daniels's partner a woman? The passenger's side door of Daniels's car flung open and a petite redhead emerged.

Ice formed in Nicole's stomach. She shook her head in denial. It couldn't be…

Leonna Landon.

Director Landon's wife?

"I want her taken care of," Mrs. Landon demanded of Daniels. "She wasn't supposed to be here."

"All in good time," Daniels assured her. "All in good time."

"I was expecting a man," Ian said coolly, obviously to infuriate Leonna further.

Leonna laughed at him, her oversized purse swinging around her hips. "Get over it, Michaels, I am *the* man."

Ian turned to Daniels. "I'm not doing business with a middle *man*," he said curtly.

Before Daniels could respond, Leonna pushed between them, her hands on her thin hips. "I told you, I'm the one in charge here," she hissed.

"Convince me," Ian said evenly.

Leonna's rebuff involved a sexually explicit four-letter word and Ian.

"I don't think so." Ian gave them his back and strode deliberately in Nicole's direction.

The air evaporated in Nicole's lungs. He turned his back! He was an open target.

"Wait!" Daniels shouted.

Ian stopped. One side of his mouth lifted in a hint of a smile, for Nicole's eyes only. Then he slowly turned around.

Nicole dragged in a much-needed breath. The man was going to give her heart failure.

"Landon cut Solomon a deal," Daniels explained as Ian approached him once more. "That's why we operated outside the normal channels. Solomon bought himself special treatment. A total blackout operation. And the AG's office was none the wiser."

That chunk of ice in Nicole's stomach shattered with the

tension whipping through her body. Landon on the take? She wouldn't believe that. "You're lying," she charged angrily.

Ian cut her a warning glare.

Leonna appeared to get a cheap thrill from Nicole's distress. "Oh, yeah, Agent Reed, everybody's got their price." Leonna's red-red lips spread into a grin. "A cool million with more to come later was my dearly departed husband's. For one million dollars he gave the order for Solomon's special treatment. Then, when the time was right, there would be more money. A lot more."

"Can we get down to business?" Ian said impatiently.

"Back off," Leonna snapped. "I want little Miss Goody-Two-shoes to know how it was."

Nicole glared at the woman from across the short distance that separated them. Director Landon couldn't have been on the take. Nicole had respected him. She knew him. Defeat sucked at Nicole's composure. Landon had been… Oh, God, how could she have been so naive? Both Daniels and Landon had fooled her. Was she that gullible?

"Dear old Bobby was smart enough to take advantage of the prime opportunity Solomon offered," Leonna continued. "He just wasn't bright enough to keep me happy." She sniffed. "Stupid bastard thought he would keep the money hidden until he retired and moved away to some foreign country where no one would ever suspect where the money had come from. He was convinced he would get caught if he spent any of it."

At least Landon had been right about that, Nicole mused. If he had suddenly begun to live above his means, suspicion would certainly have come his way.

Leonna patted her salon-styled hair. "I wasn't about to wait until I was too old to enjoy the money to spend it."

"That's where I come into the picture," Daniels interjected. "Leonna and I go back a long way," he said smugly. "When Leonna confided in me what Landon had done, well, I decided we had to do something about it."

"You're sick," Nicole said with disgust.

Another of those warning looks from Ian arrowed in her direction.

"If Landon already had the money, then why are we here?" Ian demanded.

Daniels smiled a sinister smile. "Because there's way more than just one million. The word the cartel put out after Solomon's highly publicized demise was twenty million."

"Why settle for one when you can have more?" Ian suggested. "And what about Solomon's cut?"

Daniels laughed. "Solomon isn't going to get squat. I plan to take the full twenty million."

"Ten," Ian reminded.

"As you put it so eloquently a few minutes ago," Daniels retorted, "I don't think so." The barrel of his weapon was in Ian's face before the last word stopped echoing around them. "Now," Daniels said in a self-satisfied tone, "where is Solomon?"

"Go to hell," Ian said, enunciating each word carefully so that there was no misunderstanding.

Nicole glanced at the woods between their position and the highway. Ethan was out there, but with Ian standing between Daniels and the woods Ethan would never get a clear shot. Nicole swallowed convulsively. She placed her hand on the car door. Slowly, one inch at a time, she reached toward her weapon.

"The deal is off," Ian said flatly.

Daniels's face contorted with rage; his knuckles whitened around the grip of his weapon. "And you're dead."

The bottom fell out of Nicole's stomach.

"We have to have Solomon," Leonna cried, staying Daniels's next move. "Without him we can't get the money! The money is in a joint foreign account. You have to have a special PIN to access it. Solomon supplied half the number, my husband the other half. It was a built-in safety net to make sure neither one tried to take the money without the other's knowledge."

"Landon is dead," Ian reminded.

"But I'm his widow," Leonna shot back. "What was his is mine. I have his half of the code." She turned to Daniels. "We have to have Solomon."

"Okay, Michaels," Daniels ground out. "Either tell me where he is or I'll kill you both."

"Then no one gets the money," Ian rationalized.

"I said tell me where Solomon is!" Daniels screamed.

One second turned to five. Nicole glanced at the woods again. Where the hell was Ethan? Her heart hammered in her chest. He probably still couldn't get a clean shot. Her fingers were almost to her weapon, but she couldn't make any sudden moves. Couldn't risk Daniels pulling that trigger.

"Fine," Daniels relented when Ian remained silent. He reached beneath Ian's jacket and took his weapon. "Then Reed dies."

Nicole stiffened. She saw Ian do the same. Her fingers tightened around the butt of her weapon. Could she draw it quickly enough and take out Daniels before he fired his weapon?

She didn't think so.

"I'll give you the choice." Daniels shifted his bead to Nicole. "Either you do it, or I will."

"No."

The single word, fierce and at the same time desperate, came from Ian.

Daniels turned his head, meeting Ian's gaze, without taking his expert aim off Nicole.

"I'll do it," Ian said quietly.

"Now that's more like it." Daniels thrust Ian's weapon at him at the same time that he focused his own weapon back on Ian. "Remember, if you miss, I won't. In fact, I'll enjoy killing her."

Ian turned to Nicole. That intense silvery gaze settled fully onto hers. Nicole's heart rushed up into her throat.

"If you can't do it, Michaels, I will," Daniels reminded.

"I'll do it," Ian repeated as he raised his weapon and took aim at Nicole.

Chapter Fourteen

Ian gazed down the barrel of his gun and into Nicole's eyes. *Trust me, Nicole,* he tried to relay with his own eyes. She stood there staring at him with one of those expressions of uncertainty and disbelief that is beyond describing with mere words. The urge for fight or flight stiffened her posture.

"Do it!" Daniels demanded harshly.

The blood roaring in his ears, Ian steadied his arm and fired just over Nicole's left shoulder. As if she had read Ian's mind and knew what to do, she dropped as if she had been hit. Ian pivoted and fired at Daniels, sending him diving for some kind of cover. Somewhere behind Ian the crack of a high-powered rifle sounded, and then the blast of a handgun from Leonna's direction. Leonna crumpled to the ground next to the dark sedan, a look of surprised dismay on her face. Ian kicked out of reach the thirty-two-caliber pistol Leonna had dropped onto the ground.

"I've been shot," Leonna wailed in disbelief.

One shot whizzed past Ian's head, then another. He dropped to the ground and rolled to cover near the car Daniels had driven. He crouched there and listened. Where was Nicole? He couldn't see her on the passenger's side of their rental anymore. Where the hell was Ethan? He had taken care of Leonna and kept Daniels scrambling for cover, but where was he now?

Ethan's rifle sounded again, several shots, one right after the other. The crunch of gravel, then return fire, three shots, sounded next. Daniels again, or maybe Nicole. Definitely nine-millimeter. Ian moved around a groaning Leonna and to the front bumper of the sedan just in time to see Daniels duck for safety behind Ian's rental.

Ian's blood turned ice cold. His heart seemed to still in his chest. Daniels was going after Nicole. Keeping low just in case Daniels made any unexpected moves, Ian followed the same path he had taken. Ian waited, crouched at the front bumper of the car, until he had quieted his breathing.

Ian stole a quick look around the corner of the car. Daniels disappeared around the far end, near the trunk. Ian clenched his jaw, then eased in that direction, placing each step carefully so as not to disturb the gravel.

Voices then, but Ian didn't stop to listen. He kept moving cautiously in the direction Daniels had vanished.

"Tell me where Solomon is *now,*" Daniels threatened.

"Go to hell," Nicole rasped.

Her voice sounded strange, thin. Fear knotted in Ian's gut. Had Nicole been hit? Ian swallowed tightly, but controlled the urge to run to her. He couldn't risk alerting Daniels to his presence.

"Don't push me, Nicole, I swear I'll kill you," Daniels retorted, the desperation rising in his tone. "I want that money and I'm out of time."

"What good will the money do you, Daniels?" Nicole asked with blatant amusement, however faint. "You're dead, *you* just don't understand that yet."

Ian rounded the corner of the rear bumper just in time to see Daniels press the muzzle of his weapon to Nicole's forehead. "Last chance," he snarled. "I'm going to pull this trigger in three seconds."

Every muscle in Ian's body tensed. Nicole lay against the bumper, her face extremely pale. Ian eased a step closer and put his gun to the back of Daniels's head. "That would be a costly mistake for you."

Daniels stiffened. Nicole's glassy-eyed gaze connected with Ian's. She smiled weakly. Fear exploded in Ian's chest. She *was* hit.

Daniels's weapon bored a little harder into Nicole's forehead, she blinked as if the movement took tremendous effort. "Go ahead, Michaels, shoot me. She'll die too."

"If that's your final word on the matter." Ian pressed his weapon harder into Daniels's skull. "Then we have nothing else to discuss."

"Shoot him," Nicole whispered.

Ian's heart thundered in his chest. She was getting weaker by the second.

"All I want is the money," Daniels said in an almost pleading tone.

"We all want something," Ian replied, his voice strangely calm. "The only question is how badly do you want the money? Are you willing to die for it? I assure you that if you don't lower your weapon *now,* you are going to die."

Daniels's hand shook. Everything inside Ian stilled as he waited for Daniels to concede defeat. Nicole appeared to have lost consciousness. But Ian couldn't take his eyes off Daniels long enough to see where she was hit.

Daniels blew out a ragged breath, then lowered his weapon. "You win, Michaels," he muttered.

Daniels pushed to his feet; Ian moved simultaneously. "Toss your weapon to your right."

"I hope she was worth it," Daniels said flippantly, still glaring down at Nicole.

"Toss the weapon," Ian repeated firmly.

Daniels abruptly spun around and his weapon leveled on Ian's chest. Ian shot him before he could squeeze off a round. The deadly hit echoed deafeningly around them for what felt like forever.

"We got a live one over here!" Ethan called from where Leonna had gone down. "I've called for help."

Ian knelt next to Nicole. His worst fears were realized when he found the wound leaking blood from her side. She roused a bit when he sat down beside her and pulled her onto his lap.

"Dammit, Michaels," Nicole fussed, her voice thready. "I know I told you that the next time you wanted to save my life you should just shoot me, but I didn't expect you to actually take a shot at me."

"You did well, you didn't move," he murmured, trying to smile for her benefit.

"I trust you. I knew you wouldn't shoot me." She frowned. "But then Daniels was about to come around behind you after Leonna went down. I couldn't let him shoot you either." She groaned. "It hurts like hell."

Ian pressed his hand harder over the wound to slow the bleeding. God, she had lost a lot of blood. "I'm sorry," he murmured. Ian was supposed to keep her safe. This wasn't supposed to happen. She had been trying to protect him. Nicole leaned heavily against him then, and he knew she had lost consciousness again. Ian stared down at her, then at the blood oozing between his fingers. He couldn't lose her. He shook his head. He wouldn't let her go. Tears stung his eyes.

There were things he needed to say to her.

He wouldn't let her go.

NICOLE WOKE gradually. Her mouth was painfully dry. Where was she? she wondered as focus slowly came to her. The room was white. Her head felt heavy, her brain like cotton. Something beeped near her head. She turned, the motion more a gradual falling to one side to look. Agony speared through her. Nicole groaned at the fierce stab of pain that seemed to come from all over her body at once. A collage of monitors and an IV bag hung near the bed. Two long clear tubes from two separate IV bags extended down to the bed and were taped to her arm.

She had been shot.

Nicole moaned with sensory overload as the images came flooding back to her. Was it over? Was Daniels dead? Leonna? She frowned. Nicole didn't want to think about Leonna and Director Landon. She had respected him, worked under his strong leadership for years, and never once suspected that he could be bought at any price. Nicole tightened her jaw, and blinked back the tears. She hoped like hell Daniels was dead. He deserved to die.

But all that really mattered to her was that Ian was safe.

Ian.

Nicole cautiously moved her head to her left. He sat in a chair beside her bed, asleep. Nicole moistened her dry lips and smiled at how wonderful he looked. His jaw was covered in dark stubble, his suit was rumpled. But he looked like heaven on earth to Nicole. Had he been with her all this time? She frowned. She had no idea how long she had been in the hospital. She didn't even know what day it was. But Ian was here, and that made it all right.

"You're awake," that softly accented voice whispered.

Nicole's gaze connected with his as he stood and moved to her side. "How long have I been here?" she asked hoarsely. Her throat felt raw with thirst. "Could I have a drink, please?"

Ian quickly poured water into a small plastic cup and inserted a straw. He held it to her lips and Nicole drank long and deep.

"Not too much," he warned, then set the drink aside. "We came together in the ambulance yesterday just before noon. They took you to surgery immediately. You've been awake a few times since they moved you from recovery to this room but you may not remember."

"What time is it now?"

"Four-thirty in the morning."

"Have you been here all night?" Exhaustion was tugging at her ability to hold her eyes open. The bullet had hit her in the left side. She remembered lots of blood, savage pain.

"I'm fine," he told her in a tone that said he had no intention of leaving.

"Did they take anything out I might miss?" Nicole asked, her voice a bit wobbly. She went for a smile, but her lips wouldn't cooperate. Pain meds, she realized belatedly. She was fighting to stay awake, and they were working to drag her back into healing sleep.

Ian took her fingers in his and stroked her hand with his thumb. He kept his gaze carefully focused there when he answered. "The bullet snagged your intestines and grazed a kidney," he said quietly. His unreadable gaze moved back to hers then. "They repaired all that." He swallowed hard, the muscles along the tanned column of his throat struggled with the effort. "You'll be fine."

"Then why do you look so worried?" she whispered huskily.

He looked away then. "I swore I'd keep you safe. I failed," he murmured. "And I almost lost you."

Nicole's heart squeezed in her chest. "It wasn't your fault. I was trying to distract Daniels." Her eyelids felt so heavy she could barely hold them open. "Is he dead?"

"Yes," Ian answered quietly. "And this time he won't be resurrecting himself."

"Good," she said on a sigh.

"You should rest now, Nicole." She felt Ian's lips brush her forehead.

"You'll be here when I wake up?" she heard herself ask as if from someplace very far away.

"Yes."

The deep, rich sound of his voice followed her into unconsciousness.

WHEN NICOLE woke up again it was almost noon. Warm sunlight filtered in from the window on the far side of the room. The television flashed images across the screen, but the sound was muted. The clock on the wall showed two minutes before twelve. Nicole turned her head toward the chair Ian had occupied earlier. It was empty. Alarm fluttered through her.

Why had he left her?

Snatches of memories flitted across her still-groggy mind. Ian holding her hand, caressing her cheek, pressing a soothing, damp cloth to her face, murmuring soft words. He had been here all night and most of the day. Maybe he had taken a break to have lunch.

Nicole abruptly remembered his warning before the showdown with Daniels. *When this is over, we need to talk.* What did he mean by that? He probably wanted to say goodbye.

Nicole closed her eyes and willed the tears to retreat. She didn't want to cry. She just wanted to go back to sleep and pretend it all away.

She had not told him that she loved him.

She had not thanked him for helping her bring down Daniels.

She had made a mistake.

And it was probably too late now to make it right.

Nicole loved Ian with all her heart, but there was no way that he would ever love her. He felt something for her, that was clear. But it wasn't enough. It wasn't the kind of love she felt for him. She had known from the beginning this day would come.

Nicole forced herself to relax. Sleep was what she needed right now.

She didn't need Ian.

She just wanted him more than she wanted anything else in the world, but she had to let him go. She was no good for him.

Later, when Nicole woke again, a huge bouquet of lush red roses stood on the table across the room. There had to be two dozen or more. It was the most beautiful floral arrangement she had ever seen.

A small white business card lay on the table beside her bed. She reached for it and grunted with the pain her movement generated. She read the name there. It was an agent from the local bureau office. Nicole's gaze moved back to the flowers. Could the flowers be from the bureau? Disappointment shuddered through her. She wanted them to be from Ian. They were too beautiful to be from her office.

The door suddenly swung inward and two nurses entered carrying two more large floral arrangements, but nothing as lovely as the roses. One from Nicole's office, and the other from Victoria Colby, one of the nurses explained.

"May I see the card from the bouquet of roses?" she asked before the two could get out of her room. The nurse closest to the table dug around in the flowers for several moments.

"There's no card with this one," she announced, frowning. "Anything else you need, Miss Reed?"

"No." Nicole felt downhearted. "Thank you," she managed. Where was Ian? Why had he left without even saying goodbye? She hurt like hell, and she was miserable.

The next time Nicole woke up, a nurse was there telling her she needed to try and eat something that looked terribly unappealing. Disgusted, sore and downright depressed, Nicole just looked at the tray before her. "Yuck," she muttered, when the nurse had scurried away.

"If you expect to get well, you have to eat, Nicole." Ian was sitting in the chair by her bed, watching her. He had showered and changed. The stubble no longer darkened his jaw.

Nicole couldn't prevent the relieved smiled that spread across her face. "Where did you go?"

"I had some loose ends to tie up," he said cryptically. "Leonna Landon is in a room down the hall under close watch. She's stable, and in a hell of a lot of trouble. The local police wanted a statement and I had to deal with your friends from the bureau. I didn't want them to disturb you."

"There's a card here from an Agent Turner," Nicole mentioned, and gestured to the table.

"A persistent fellow," Ian said crossly.

"Thank you." Nicole wasn't sure whether she was thanking him for taking care of the authorities, or for coming back. Both maybe. Nicole closed her eyes and silently thanked

God Ian had returned. For whatever reason. She didn't want to be separated from him ever again. Her eyes popped open. But he would be leaving. Next time for Chicago. And then, he wouldn't be coming back. A stab of pain that had nothing to do with her injury or the resulting surgery pierced her heart.

"Would you like me to help you? You should eat something." Ian was standing next to her bed now.

"The roses are beautiful," she commented, her gaze shifting to the huge bouquet. She didn't want Ian to see the emotion shining in her eyes. He had to go. She had to let him. "I wish I knew who sent them."

"I sent them," he said quietly.

Nicole's heart leaped; she smiled up at him. "Thank you, Ian, they're beautiful."

Ian looked away from her as if she had slapped him rather than thanked him. Long minutes of silence passed with him just standing there looking away, and Nicole thought she would scream if he didn't say something…anything.

Suddenly, he took her left hand in his. "We have to talk," he said finally, his gaze settling on hers.

This was it. Nicole felt her heart quiver in her chest. He was going to tell her he had to leave. That he wouldn't be back. That she should never come to him again for help or anything else.

And how could she blame him?

Every time Nicole showed up in Ian's life bad things happened. First he lost his career as a U.S. Marshal, then he risked his life to save hers. She must have been out of her mind to think he could feel about her the way she felt about him. This was for the best.

"All right, we'll talk," Nicole said in as firm a voice as she could manage. Might as well get it over with. Maybe she should just let him off the hook, make it easier on both of them. "I suppose you want to go first," she suggested, hoping he would do the gentlemanly thing and let her go first.

Ian smiled, or at least hinted at one. "Yes."

Nicole stared at the far wall then. She blew out a big breath. So much for ladies first. "Look, Ian," she blurted impatiently, "you don't have to say anything. I know it's over. I don't want you to apologize for anything that happened. Just because we were...together doesn't mean I expect some sort of commitment from you. I wanted what happened as much as you did." Nicole pulled her hand from his and fiddled with the sheet to distract herself. "Maybe more."

"Do you mind if I have my say before you push me out the door?"

"Goodbyes are hard enough without dragging them out," she argued, still not looking at him. "I never had any expectations about the future and us." Nicole swallowed the bitter taste that went with that lie. "We had a job to do, nothing else. So why don't you just say the words and let it go at that?"

"You think I want to leave?"

Nicole looked at him then. It was impossible to know exactly what he was thinking. "I can't blame you, you know," she murmured. "I betrayed you three years ago." She closed her eyes and shook her head. When she opened them again he was still watching her, waiting for her to continue. "And I've put you through hell this time. I can't think of a single reason you would want to stay." Her voice shook with the emotion clogging her throat. The pain of her injury was nothing compared with this. Her heart would never heal from the hurt of losing Ian.

"I can think of at least one," Ian countered in that soft, seductive tone that widened the crack in Nicole's heart.

"Sex doesn't count, Ian," she chided.

"Does being in love with you count?"

Nicole's gaze shot to his; she searched his face. Could he possibly mean that? "That would definitely count."

"There you have it then, the single reason," Ian concluded.

She had to hear him say the words…to her. "You're saying that…?" Nicole waited for him to finish the sentence.

"I'm in love with you and I can't imagine living the rest of my life without you." He took her hand in his once more. "There, I've said it."

Nicole couldn't speak for one long moment. She could only stare into those silvery eyes and rejoice in the knowledge that Ian loved her.

"Did you have anything you wanted to say to me?" he asked, a barely masked uncertainty in his voice.

Nicole swiped at a tear that slipped from the corner of her eye, threatening her flimsy hold on composure. "But we never see eye to eye on anything. You hate my ambition. Your cool-in-the-face-of-disaster drives me crazy. It will never work. So if you're just saying this to make me feel better because I was shot, then—"

Ian silenced her with his lips. He kissed her until she couldn't think straight. The feel of his firm lips against hers, the heat of his tongue as he invaded her mouth, melted Nicole's resolve. He squeezed her hand in his, then broke the kiss, tasting her one last time before drawing away.

"I never say anything I don't mean," he said matter-of-factly. "I love you. I've loved you for three years. And whatever our differences, we'll find a way to work them out."

Nicole's heart was pumping madly, the machine next to her bed tracked the speedy staccato. She smiled, her face a contradiction of emotions as the tears slid down her cheeks.

Any minute now the nurses would come running. "Am I supposed to agree to your terms?" she asked teasingly. "Just because I'm in love with you too doesn't mean I'll cut you any slack."

"I wouldn't expect you to make it too easy for me," he returned in that tone that was equal parts elegance and danger. "That's half the attraction."

"So," Nicole lifted her chin in challenge. "What's the plan?"

"You get well, and when they release you I'll take you to my place in Chicago."

"Why your place?" she retorted.

Ian lifted one dark brow and gave her a look that said she should understand without his having to explain. "Well the last time I was at your place it was a bit hot for my liking."

Nicole frowned. "Oh, yeah, I'd forgotten that little detail."

"There's something else," Ian said solemnly, his gaze suddenly somber. "I was going to tell you earlier, but the doctor thought it would be better if I waited until you were—" he shrugged "—out of the woods."

A bone-deep chill settled over Nicole. She wasn't sure she could handle any more excitement—good or bad. She scrunched her toes and shifted her feet just to be sure. Everything seemed to be in working order. "You said I was going to be fine," she reminded him. Worry flickered in those silvery depths watching her so very intently. "It's not that simple, is it?"

"No." Ian brushed her cheek with his fingers. "There's more."

He paused, to give her time to brace herself, she supposed, but she would rather he get it over with. If she was never going to walk again, or if she had lost something she couldn't function properly without, she would just as soon know it now.

"When you arrived at the E.R. you had lost a great deal of blood. There was no time to waste. You were rushed into surgery, and numerous routine tests were run on the blood samples they took." His fingers tightened around hers. "Apparently, that first time we were together—" he glanced down at their joined hands, then back to her face "—you conceived. The trauma from the gunshot and the necessary surgery—"

"You're saying I'm pregnant?" Nicole interrupted, her thoughts whirling inside her head. Everything he said after *conceived* was lost to her. Surprise, then wonder claimed her. She felt cold, then hot, then frightened. A baby? Ian's baby?

"Yes, that's what I'm saying."

Nicole studied the pained expression on his face. What was he thinking? Was this why he had confessed his love for her? "Are they sure?" How could they know? It had only been a week. *Trauma.* The words echoed through her, but before she could say anything Ian spoke again.

"The blood test is conclusive within a few days of conception," he explained.

"Trauma," Nicole interjected before he could say anything else. "You said something about trauma."

"The trauma you sustained has put the pregnancy at risk." He inhaled a harsh breath. "There's a possibility that you'll lose the baby."

Nicole felt more vulnerable than she had ever felt in her entire life. A new kind of pain welled inside her. Her hand went instinctively, protectively to her belly. She closed her eyes against the mixture of joy and pain fighting for her attention. She was pregnant with Ian's baby, but the baby might not survive. A dozen emotions washed over her, intensifying with each wave. How could something she hadn't even known that she wanted feel suddenly as if it were all that mattered? The conversation in the airport restaurant abruptly flitted through her mind. Ian wanted children. He had said as much.

She opened her eyes and leveled her gaze on Ian's. "Is this why you've suddenly decided you're in love with me?"

Ian looked surprised by her question. "I love you, Nicole, and I'll love our baby, this one and however many others we choose to have." He pressed a tender kiss to her forehead, and whispered his next words close to her ear. "And if we lose this child and never have another, I'll still love you."

Nicole blinked back the renewed rush of tears. "Okay," she said, her voice a little shaky. "Which one of us is going to stay home with *her?*" she demanded, hoping to lighten the somber mood.

Ian smiled one of those genuinely charming smiles that stole her breath. "We'll take turns staying with *him.*"

"We'll need a bigger house," Nicole suggested.

"I know just the neighborhood," Ian agreed.

"A minivan and a nanny," she added for good measure.

Ian shrugged nonchalantly. "I can live with the minivan as long as I get to select the nanny," he offered generously.

"Forget it, Michaels," Nicole informed him. "You're going to be entirely too busy keeping me happy to concern yourself with a nanny." She grabbed his shirtfront and pulled him down for a kiss.

Ian brushed her lips with his own. "I look forward to the challenge." He sealed his words with a long, hot kiss.

Epilogue

"Do we have an update on the Richland case?" Victoria Colby asked as she scanned the report in her hand.

"Not yet," Ric Martinez told her as he shuffled through his stack of notes. "You know how Alex is, she calls in when she thinks about it, which isn't often. I don't have Ian's report either. He and Nicole went for their first ultrasound this morning," he added. "The baby is terrific, and they're ninety percent sure it's a girl."

"Excellent," Victoria said with a smile. "Those two deserve the best." Victoria removed her reading glasses and studied Ric. He was still a little rough around the edges, but she was pleased with his progress. Ian had taught him well. "I'm sure Ian appreciates your handling this status meeting for him. With a new wife and a baby on the way, he's more than a little preoccupied these days."

Ric shot her one of those killer smiles that had every secretary in the building swooning. His Latin good looks only made the gesture more appealing.

"Yeah, well, Ian's a lucky man. That Nicole is a real heartbreaker." Ric rubbed the bridge of his nose. "When she's not breaking other things."

Victoria set the report and her glasses aside, and leaned back in her chair. "I'm hoping to convince her to come to work for me if she decides not to go back to the bureau after her maternity leave."

"Nicole would be a definite asset," Ric agreed. He frowned then. "Speaking of assets, what's the deal with this Sloan guy?"

"Sloan?" Victoria couldn't hide the surprise in her voice. "Why do you ask?"

"Alex used him to gather some hard-to-come-by intel when Ian and Nicole were working the Solomon case. You were on vacation. Alex mentioned that Sloan once worked here. She called him some sort of legend."

Victoria almost smiled. It had been a very long time since she had thought of Sloan. She was surprised that he had agreed to help Alex. Maybe his circumstances had changed of late. Victoria would have to make it a point to give him a call. "He was with my husband from the agency's inception," she replied. "Sloan helped James to build the Colby Agency. And then he helped me keep it going after James's death."

"So he was second in command, like Ian," Ric suggested.

"Yes," Victoria told him, though that didn't begin to adequately describe Sloan. She wasn't sure she could properly relate in words the kind of man Sloan had been.

Ric shrugged one shoulder. "What was it that made him so special that Alex would refer to him as a legend?"

Victoria thought about that for a while before she answered. Sloan wasn't the kind of man who could be summed up in few words. "Sloan was the best tracker in the business. If you wanted to find someone no one else could, you called Sloan. He had this uncanny ability to read people even before he laid eyes on them. He studied their past, what they left behind, and he instinctively knew where to look to find them."

"Sounds like a handy guy to have around in this business," Ric commented.

"He was the best," Victoria admitted, too many memories flashing across the private theater of her mind. "The very best."

"Why did he leave the agency?"

Victoria pulled her attention from the past and back to Ric. "Things happened, he changed," she explained without really explaining at all. "Sloan isn't the same man who worked for the Colby Agency all those years ago."

"But the legend lives on," Ric offered.

"Yes," Victoria allowed. "I suppose it does."

Everything you love about romance...
and more!

Please turn the page for Signature Select™
Bonus Features.

Bonus Features:

BONUS FEATURES

FILES FROM THE
COLBY AGENCY

Day in the life...Debra Webb

Ever wonder how authors spend their days? Here's your chance to peek inside the life of author Debra Webb, who shared her description of a typical day.

4

HMMM...THIS MIGHT BE PRETTY BORING, but I'll give it a shot. My alarm clock (my husband) wakes me up around seven. The first thing I do is check to see if my daughter needs help with her hair or with any preparations for school. She's a teenager now and doesn't really like that I still do this, but that doesn't stop me.

At seven-thirty my husband drives our daughter to school. When he returns we have breakfast. I tell myself around this time of the morning that I should go take that walk I swear I'll take every day... Sometimes it actually works. We live on a quiet street where it's safe to walk the block. The neighborhood is well treed and the landscaping of my neighbors' yards is inviting. It's a truly soothing atmosphere. If I'm really feeling spunky I take my dogs, Trixie (a Maltese) and Toto (a cross between a cocker spaniel and a Scottie) along, as well. Toto loves it but Trixie prefers to be carried.

Refreshed after my walk (or watching *Good Morning America* and *Live with Regis and Kelly*) and shower, I take a look at what I wrote the day before and then plunge into the next chapter. I don't talk to anyone or even think when I write. I just write. The characters take me where we need to go usually. (Sometimes they wake me up in the middle of the night and I have to jot down a note or two about what they want to do tomorrow.) I stop around noon and have lunch.

Lunch can be interesting around my house. My husband is usually working on a project around the house that includes "stuff" being moved around or "wet" paint. He is the chief cook and bottle washer around here so I'm at his mercy when it comes to lunch (unless I call for delivery). I watch the news during lunch. It's a part of my new weight-loss strategy (big grin).

After lunch is generally up for grabs. I might watch the Home and Garden channel (which gives me the ideas that keeps my husband on those little projects I mentioned earlier) or I might have a meeting with my best writing friend, Rhonda Nelson. We keep each other on track. Usually I'm telling her that she really does have to write today and she's usually telling me that I can't let a character do something he or she just did (usually involves a gun or having sex in a ventilation duct). Sometimes I have to do copy edits or galleys on books that have already been written. This is no fun, trust me. The copy editor has usually pointed out places where I changed my mind about something but failed to change it earlier (like someone's age or eye color). If I'm really lucky my afternoon might involve a book signing where I get to actually meet people who read my books. Now this is fun!

At around three-thirty my husband returns from picking up my daughter from school (which saves me a tremendous amount of stress—school traffic is the worst). We talk about what we did that day. I always ask her what she had for lunch and whom she chatted with. She even tells me occasionally. Then I remind her of homework and she reminds me of how she doesn't have anything to wear for school or some dance that's coming up. Sound familiar?

By the time darkness falls (doesn't that sound cool?) we toss around what we might like to have for dinner, then my husband tells us what he intends to cook. My daughter and I whine about it but that doesn't generally change the menu. "The only way to change the menu," my husband informs us, "is to do the grocery shopping." I remind him that I must conserve my decision-making and analyzing skills for writing. I don't tell him that I hate the parking lot at the supermarket. It's always packed, and no matter where you park someone will park too close and then you can't open the door to escape.

Sometimes we cook dinner together. This usually means we shopped together because I couldn't stand it any longer. Now this is fun time. We would both be gourmet chefs if we didn't have a mortgage to pay. We love trying new things and attempting to create something we ate at some restaurant that we really loved.

After dinner I touch base with friends and family. There's my oldest daughter (who lives nearby but with whom I must speak every day to be sure she hasn't moved again—she was a gypsy in a former life); my niece (who is like my third daughter and who is moving close by very soon); and my younger brother (who survived many adventures with me as a child and to whom I probably owe a great debt since he was far too often a guinea pig for things I wanted to attempt but knew better—like jumping out of trees and floating down rivers using unapproved floatation devices). Then I must call my best nonpublishing friend, Donna Boyd. We generally spend our time gossiping or talking about stuff we like (men, clothes, sex, you name it).

Let's see.... What's next? Well, I suppose that depends upon what night of the week it is. On certain nights there is must-see TV, like the television show *24* or *Alias* or reruns of *Sex and the City* (even though I've seen them all, I still cry after certain episodes—this drives my teenage daughter crazy) or a History/Discovery channel special about serial killers or unsolved homicide cases. If it's not a must-see TV night, I might watch a movie. My favorite kinds are action/thrillers, but I also love plain old mysteries or romances. But if it's going to make me cry I have to be in the mood for it. I can watch an action or thriller movie anytime, anyplace, anywhere. Give me a man like Kiefer Sutherland (24); John Travolta and Hugh Jackman (*Swordfish*); Keanu Reeves (*Speed*); Samuel L. Jackson (*The Long Kiss Goodnight*), and I could just look at him and make up stories all day long.

I spend a lot of time on my laptop surfing the Web. I look for breaking news or new and bizarre medical accomplishments that might give me ideas for new stories. I listen to music whenever I'm driving and sometimes when I'm working. Music inspires me.

Eventually I go to bed and dream about the next book I'll write. Believe me, I have some truly twisted dreams.

Good night!

Colby Agency Trivia

How much do you know about the Colby Agency series? Test your knowledge by answering the following questions. Have fun, and good luck!

1. In the first Colby Agency story, *Safe by His Side*, the heroine suffered from a health problem. Can you name the ailment?

2. Lucas Camp walks with a slight limp. Do you know what brought about this condition?

3. In *The Bodyguard's Baby* Laura Proctor was running from a man who wanted to take something from her. Who was the man and what he was after?

4. *Protective Custody* featured a hero who is still Victoria's right hand today. Do you remember his name and the color he preferred in clothing?

5. Gabriel DiCassi was an assassin in one particular Colby Agency story. Can you name the story? What name was DiCassi known for in the business of murder?

6. Piper Ryan played a feisty investigative reporter in *Personal Protector*. Can you name the location where this story was set? Who was the man who ultimately betrayed her? How was she related to Lucas Camp?

7. *Physical Evidence* featured a secondary character from the Colby Agency who went on to have his own story entitled *The Marriage Prescription* in the Harlequin American Romance line. Can you name this character and his position at the Colby Agency?

8. Ethan Delaney had to chase down a runaway bride in what Colby Agency story?

9. What Colby Agency spin-off series features Lucas Camp?

10. In *Her Secret Alibi* the heroine had a best friend in whom she confided all her worst fears. What was the name of her friend?

11. Also in *Her Secret Alibi* we meet Simon Ruhl who goes on to become another of Victoria's right-hand men. What was

Simon's occupation before coming on
board at the Colby Agency?

12. *Keeping Baby Safe* starts out in chapter
    one in what dangerous setting?

13. *Guarding the Heiress* was the second Colby
    Agency story to appear in the Harlequin
    American Romance line. What were the
    names of the heroine's meddling friends?

14. In *Cries in the Night* what was the heroine
    caught doing at the cemetery?

15. The Harlequin promotional title *Striking
    Distance* reunited what two major
    characters of the Colby Agency?

16. *Romancing the Tycoon* was the last
    installment of the Colby Agency to appear
    in the Harlequin American Romance line.
    The heroine, Amy Wells, had been
    employed at the Colby Agency as a
    receptionist for quite some time. What
    were Amy's career aspirations? And do
    you remember the name of the book in
    which she first appeared?

17. In *Agent Cowboy* the hero was brought
    back home to Texas for an assignment.
    Do you remember what he once did for a
    living in Texas? Can you recall what
    unique piece of furniture proved to be the

perfect place for the hero and heroine to
make love?

18. Do you know the name of the Colby
Agency's archnemesis? In which story did
he finally get what was coming to him?

19. *Situation Out of Control* started the
internal affairs investigation into what
problem at the Colby Agency?

20. What incident from his past drove the
hero in *Full Exposure* to finish off the rest
of Leberman's evil legacy?

21. What was the name of Victoria Colby's
first husband? What happened to him?

22. Who has worked at the Colby Agency, side
by side with Victoria, longer than anyone
else?

23. What happened inside the Colby Agency
once that caused Victoria to have to
conduct a briefing in the ladies' room?

24. The Colby Agency is located in a large
office building not far from the
Magnificent Mile in Chicago. On which
floor is the agency located?

25. Who helped Leberman kidnap Victoria's
son when he was a small child?

1. Mitral valve prolapse

2. As prisoners of war, Lucas Camp and
James Colby shared a cell that was more
like a cage. Lucas threw himself in front of
a bullet to save James's life. The bullet
lodged in his leg and his captors refused to
allow medical treatment. James did all he
could to help Lucas but by the time they
were freed it was far too late to save his
friend's leg due to infection.

3. Her brother. He wanted her inheritance.

4. Ian Michaels has always preferred to wear
black.

5. *Solitary Soldier.* This assassin was also
known as the angel of death or simply
Angel.

6. Piper's father ultimately betrayed her. The story was set in Atlanta and Lucas was her uncle on her mother's side.

7. Zach Ashton was an attorney for the Colby Agency.

8. *Contract Bride*.

9. The Specialists.

10. Erica (also my oldest daughter's name).

11. Simon was an agent with the FBI.

12. The jungles of South America.

13. The friends' names were: Ella Brown, Irene Marlowe, Minnie and Mattie Caruthers.

14. Attempting to dig up her buried child.

15. Victoria Colby and her son James Colby, Jr. (aka Seth).

16. Amy wanted to be a full-fledged Colby Agency Investigator. She first appeared in *Protective Custody*.

17. Trent was once a bounty hunter. The two made love on a saddle mounted to a pedestal in the heroine's bedroom.

18. Errol Leberman finally got what was coming to him, in *Striking Distance*.

19. Someone leaking information about Victoria and the Colby Agency.

20. The murder of his brother and his brother's family.

21. James Colby was murdered by Leberman.

22. Her personal secretary, Mildred.

23. In *Keeping Baby Safe* the sprinkler system had gone haywire and the entire floor was flooded.

24. The fourth floor.

25. Howard Stephens.

Here's a sneak peek...

COLBY CONSPIRACY
by
Debra Webb

The murder of a Chicago police detective with ties to Victoria Colby-Camp and her family will shake the Colby Agency to its very foundation. There's only one man tough and objective enough to clear Victoria's name and the agency's reputation. But as the truth begins to emerge, it becomes clear that a ruthless Colby enemy wants certain secrets to stay buried...

SNEAK PEEK BONUS FEATURE

CHAPTER 1

THE RAIN had stopped. Victoria Colby-Camp stood near the massive window, staring out at the shimmering downtown city lights reflected in the inky black of the Chicago River. This wasn't really the best time for her to be distracted. There were more hands that needed to be shaken, more affirmations of gratitude that should be made. Only an hour ago, she had received her second prestigious award as Chicago's Woman of the Year, but she couldn't help being drawn away from the glitz and the glamour and toward the unknown and the darkness shrouding the city she loved.

No matter that she stood in the mammoth marble lobby of the R. R. Donnelley Building, with its ancient Greek and Roman architecture, or that hundreds of silk- and sequined-clad guests mingled around her. She could feel the subtle shift...the ever-so-slight change in the very atmosphere of her happy but fragile world.

She had every right to be ecstatic. After half a lifetime of hoping and praying, she finally had her son back, alive and growing stronger every day. Jim scarcely reflected even a hint of the Seth persona that had ravaged his life from the age of seven until just one year ago. Great strides had been made with therapy and the love of the woman who had somehow managed to touch his battered heart.

Tears welled in Victoria's eyes when she thought of all that Tasha had done to save Jim, to bring back the man, as well as the boy, who had barely managed to survive behind the ugly mask of a killer named Seth. Victoria smiled and blinked the tears away. Jim and Tasha had set a date for their wedding. All that Victoria had hoped for was finally coming to fruition.

"My dear, this is no place for the guest of honor to be hiding out."

Victoria turned at the sound of the familiar male voice belonging to the man she loved. He was the other long-awaited wish come true in her hard-won battle for happiness. The man she had loved and admired from afar for so very long was now her husband. Emotion tightened her throat. Though a part of her would always love James Colby, the father of her son, her heart now belonged fully to this man…to Lucas Camp.

She smiled, gloried in simply admiring his handsome, however rugged, face for a few seconds before she answered. "I just needed a moment to myself."

The heart-stopping smile that he reserved just for her spread across her husband's face. "This is your night, Victoria. You deserve this honor and more. Come." He folded her arm around his. "Let's have another toast to the Woman of the Year." He leaned down and pressed a gentle kiss to her cheek. "To my lovely wife."

Victoria allowed Lucas to lead her back into the midst of the festivities. She smiled, offered the expected gestures and comments with all the grace required of a woman in her position, but part of her could not let go of the nagging instinct that everything was about to change.

CHAPTER 2

THOUGH DANIEL MARKS had had no aspirations about going out tonight, he was glad the rain had stopped. He watched the flow of pedestrians as they ventured from the shops and restaurants on the Magnificent Mile from his vantage point in a luxurious suite on one of the uppermost floors of the historic Allerton Crowne Plaza. He'd never been big on hotels, but he had to admit that even he was impressed by the stately European decor of this one. But what he found most appealing was the location. Close to everything that was anything in the city of Chicago, and one place in particular—the Colby Agency.

Daniel had made this journey to the Gold Coast district of the Windy City by special invitation. After leaving his military career six months ago, he had taken some time to consider what he wanted to do with the rest of his life. Then he'd floated résumés to a few agencies of interest to see what sort of offers he might attract. Victoria Colby-Camp, the esteemed

22

head of the Colby Agency, had invited him to come to her fair city and spend a week or two getting to know the area—at her expense, no less.

He was scheduled to meet with her on Friday. It was Monday night, and he'd been here two days already. Time enough to get the general lay of the land, and, with one of the city's top real estate agents at his beck and call, to consider possible areas where he might want to live if he accepted a coveted position with the Colby Agency.

Daniel scrubbed a hand over his jaw and laughed at himself. He hadn't been made an offer yet. Maybe he was assuming too much. He'd only been invited to meet with the venerable head of the agency. But he understood from her come-get-to-know-us offer that she was more than a little interested. He didn't find that part surprising, since the Federal Bureau of Investigation and Homeland Security had been interested as well.

Hell, he wasn't oblivious to what he had to offer. He'd spent ten years in the Army as a military strategist and left with the rank of major, knowing he could have been promoted to lieutenant colonel immediately if he'd opted to continue in service. Like most everything else in his life, he'd been on the fast track from the day he'd entered Officer's Candidate School.

But he had grown weary of the bureaucracy. Of

the political head games that only the military could play with such precision and impact. Not that he'd left the Army with a bad taste in his mouth, not at all. Daniel, without question, maintained the deepest respect and admiration for those serving their country in any and all capacities. He simply felt as if he'd done all he could in that world. His momentum had hit a ceiling, and he was going nowhere fast, with more frustration than he cared to tolerate. A mere promotion in rank wasn't enough. He needed more… something where he could reach his fullest potential without all the political runarounds.

That was the reason he was here in Chicago, rather than in D.C. talking to bigwigs at the Bureau or Homeland Security. With any government agency, he was bound to run into the same thing that had prompted him to move beyond the military. He felt certain that the only way to escape all the bureaucratic crap was to go into the private sector.

So here he was, lounging in a swanky hotel and pondering what the future might hold for a thirty-two-year-old man who'd spent every day of his life since college proudly wearing the prestigious uniform representing the American Armed Forces.

He ran his fingers through his regulation short hair. He couldn't see that changing. It was force of habit. Every other week, he got a haircut. Nor were the physical rigors of his former career going to be left by the wayside. He intended to keep up the physical training for his general well-being, as well as to make him a better investigator—wherever he went to work. Keeping in shape served a dual purpose.

He turned away from the window and strode across to the minibar. The only thing he'd had any trouble getting used to was wearing civvies, civilian clothes. Twisting off the cap of a bottle of beer, he peered down at his stonewashed jeans and cotton cargo shirt. It wasn't any hardship, really; it just took a little more planning. He'd worn the same assortment of uniforms for ten years; he'd never had to worry if anything matched or looked right together. Army regulation had dictated his wardrobe, from the cap on his head to the shoes on his feet.

After a long draw from his beer, he dropped onto the foot of the bed and clicked on the local news. Might as well learn the bad with the good. If offered a position with the Colby Agency, he anticipated no reason why he would not be readily accepting. So far, he liked the city. Couldn't see any problems with fitting in.

A frown nudged its way across his brow and he wondered if he stayed here, would he finally move on to the next logical level of his life. His military career had proved too unpredictable for putting down any sort of permanent roots. He'd been involved in several short-term relationships, but nothing even remotely permanent or serious. His savings were quite adequate—he could afford to buy a home and finally put down those kinds of roots. Not that he'd actually known that sort of lifestyle even before joining the military. He was the quintessential military brat, moving from post to post his entire life, with the exception of the four years he'd spent at Columbia studying political science with an emphasis on prelaw. Rather than going on to law school, he'd opted for the military, just like his father. He'd felt the need to do his duty. He did not regret that decision now.

His own parents had retired to Florida five years ago. Needless to say, his father was not happy about Daniel's decision to return to civilian life, but he was man enough to restrain himself on the issue. Daniel's mother simply wanted her one and only son—only offspring, for that matter—to be happy. She wanted grandchildren.

Daniel didn't know if he was ready to do the whole wife-and-kids thing just yet, but he couldn't say he didn't feel the need to find something more stable, more long-standing, in a relationship.

He turned up his beer once more and downed a deep, satisfying swallow. Maybe he just needed to get laid. He'd steered clear of physical entanglements since officially exiting the military, more to ensure that a sexual relationship didn't influence his objec-

26

tivity about his future than anything else. He wanted to do this right. This was a big step for him.

The Colby Agency was where he wanted to be.

He'd researched a number of prominent private agencies and not a one could hold a candle to the Colby Agency's sterling reputation. Victoria Colby-Camp selected only the cream of the crop as members of her staff. Daniel liked the idea that he would be working with the best of the best from all walks of life. Some were former military, like him, but others came from the Bureau, from the ranks of various smaller law enforcement agencies or from everyday walks of life.

He eased back onto the mound of pillows and scanned the television channels, studying the faces that represented local media. Faces with which he would become very familiar, since the Colby Agency was a very high-profile part of this city. Whether Victoria knew it or not, he had already made up his mind. This was where he wanted to be.

And whatever it took, he intended to make it happen.

CHAPTER 3

CHICAGO BOASTED the largest Chinatown in the Midwest. Densely populated with more than 10,000 residents, mostly Chinese, the area south of Cermak Road was chock-full of Asian grocery and herbal shops, bakeries and restaurants. Traditional Chinese architecture filled the colorful streetscape, welcoming new visitors and longtime residents alike.

Amid the terra-cotta ornaments and mosaic murals, bold, sculpted lions guarded street-level doorways. But nothing in this eclectic culture could protect against the events playing out beyond the commercialized places where tourists wandered. Here, in this less-than-desirable section, there was no glamour or glitz, certainly no goodness. There was only fear waiting around every corner, and survival of the most ruthless was the single prevailing law.

The alley was long and narrow, dark and damp from the rain that had fallen earlier that evening.

Homicide Detective Carter Hastings was barely

three months from retirement. He'd turned fifty-five a few weeks ago. Most might not consider that milestone old, but it was damned ancient for a cop. He had decided that he would spend the rest of his life making up for all he'd missed or failed to accomplish these past thirty-odd years. In particular, he wanted to rectify his relationship with his only child, his daughter. He'd let the job rule his life for far too long. He wanted to know his daughter the way a father should.

But that wasn't going to happen now.

He stared into the cruel eyes of certain death towering over him. "I won't tell anyone," he pleaded. "I swear I won't." Carter had never considered himself a coward, but tonight, knowing what he knew, he begged for mercy. He needed just one more day to set to rights all he'd failed to follow through on…to say the things he hadn't said to the daughter he loved.

But this kind of evil knew no mercy. He should have realized years ago that this secret would come back to haunt him, that he could never trust a person who clearly had no soul to stand by any sort of promise. He had no one to blame but himself.

He prayed he would be the only one to pay for his error in judgment.

"Stand up and take it like a man, Hastings."

The words hissed out at him as if they'd risen straight from the hottest flames of hell. Funny, Carter mused, in a way they had. Even the grave's unyielding grip couldn't restrain this kind of evil.

"I kept that secret," he urged, a growl of anger roaring up into his throat, sealing his fate once and for all. He would die tonight. Nothing outside an act of God could save him, and with him would go the whole truth. "You don't have to do this. What purpose would it serve? It's over. Do you hear me! It's been over for nearly twenty years. No one has to know it was you."

Diabolical laughter echoed off the cold, damp walls of the dilapidated buildings crowding in on the place and time that now represented the rest of his life.

"You always were a softy," his killer taunted. "I knew that when you fell for the wife of the victim. All that stopped you from being just like me was your so-called principles." Another of those cruel sounds that couldn't really be called a laugh split the eerie quiet. "You brought this on yourself, Hastings. You should have stayed out of it. I will not tolerate your interference. Don't expect me to believe you're finally willing to set aside those fine principles."

Carter closed his eyes and said a final goodbye to the daughter he'd been less than a decent father to. Sent a quick prayer heavenward for the other woman whose life his long-ago actions would forever change. Now he would never have the chance to make up for his past sins.

The sound of the bullet exploded around him an instant before he felt hot metal sear his brain.

Carter watched his killer walk away without a single backward glance. Then his eyes closed for the last time.

...NOT THE END...

Look for the continuation of this story in
Colby Conspiracy *by Debra Webb, available in*
October 2005 from Signature Select.

SAGA

National bestselling author

Debra Webb

A decades-old secret threatens to bring
down Chicago's elite Colby Agency in
this brand-new, longer-length novel.

COLBY
CONSPIRACY

While working to uncover the truth behind
a murder linked to the agency, Daniel Marks
and Emily Hastings find themselves trapped
by the dangers of desire—knowing every
move they make could be their last....

Available in October,
wherever books
are sold.

Silhouette®
Where love comes alive™

COLLECTION

Somewhere between good and evil...there's love.

Beyond the Dark

Three brand-new stories of otherworldly romance by...

Linda Winstead Jones

Evelyn Vaughn

Karen Whiddon

Evil looms but love conquers all in three gripping stories by award-winning authors.

Plus, exclusive bonus features inside!

On sale October

Where love comes alive™

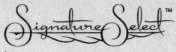

SPOTLIGHT

"Delightful and delicious…Cindi Myers always satisfies!"
—*USA TODAY bestselling author Julie Ortolon*

National bestselling author

Cindi Myers

She's got more than it takes for
the six o'clock news…

Learning Curves

Tired of battling the image problems that her
size-twelve curves cause with her network news
job, Shelly Piper takes a position as co-anchor on
public television with Jack Halloran. But as they
work together on down-and-dirty hard-news
stories, all Shelly can think of is Jack!

Plus, exclusive bonus features inside!

On sale in October.

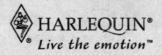
HARLEQUIN®
Live the emotion™

Signature Select™

COMING NEXT MONTH

Signature Select Collection
BEYOND THE DARK by Linda Winstead Jones, Evelyn Vaughn and Karen Whiddon
Evil looms but love conquers the darkness in this collection of three new stories of otherworldly romance.

Signature Select Saga
COLBY CONSPIRACY by Debra Webb
While working to uncover the truth behind a murder linked to The Colby Agency, Daniel Marks and Emily Hastings find themselves trapped by the dangers of desire—knowing every move they make could be their last....

Signature Select Miniseries
WINDOW TO YESTERDAY by Debra Salonen
In this compelling volume containing two full-length novels, old regrets and buried secrets come back to haunt Ren Bishop and Claudie St. James, leaving them unprepared for the journey that lies before them.

Signature Select Spotlight
LEARNING CURVES by Cindi Myers
In the cutthroat business of network news, thin is in, and Shelly Piper's size-twelve curves are causing viewers to demand a thinner coanchor. But Shelly has come too far to lose her job—or a dress size.

Signature Select Showcase
THE STUD by Barbara Delinsky
Jenna McCue wants a baby and she wants Spencer Smith to be the father...or rather the donor. Spencer agrees, but on one condition: he "donates" the old-fashioned way. But getting pregnant will mean she'll never see him again. That's part of the deal. Or is it?

The Fortunes of Texas: Reunion
THE GOOD DOCTOR by Karen Rose Smith
Peter Clark would never describe himself as a jaw-dropping catch. So why is beautiful New York neurologist Violet Fortune looking at him as if she would like to show him her bedside manner?